MISTY MORNINGS AT THE POTTING SHED

ALSO BY JENNY KANE

THE POTTING SHED SERIES
1. *Frost Falls at The Potting Shed*
2. *Bluebell Season at The Potting Shed*
3. *Misty Mornings at The Potting Shed*

THE MILL GRANGE SERIES
Midsummer Dreams at Mill Grange
Autumn Leaves at Mill Grange
Spring Blossoms at Mill Grange
Winter Fires at Mill Grange

MISTY MORNINGS AT THE POTTING SHED

Jenny Kane

An Aria Book

First published in UK in 2023 by Head of Zeus,
part of Bloomsbury Publishing Plc

9 7 5 3 1 2 4 6 8

A catalogue record for this book is available from the British Library.

ISBN (PB): 9781804549483
ISBN (E): 9781804549490

Cover design: Head of Zeus;
illustration Lindsey Spinks

Typeset by Siliconchips Services Ltd UK

Printed and bound in Great Britain by
CPI Group (UK) Ltd, Croydon CR0 4YY

Head of Zeus
First Floor East
5–8 Hardwick Street
London EC1R 4RG

WWW.HEADOFZEUS.COM

To my amazing children, Lucy and Isaac.

Not only are they brave, kind and clever – they also
love garden centre cafés as much as I do.
(As long as scones are on offer!)

SEPTEMBER

I

Flicking a switch, Maddie flooded the garden centre's shop with light.

'Sometimes I forget that this used to be the downstairs of my home. Other days I walk in and immediately picture Dad and me sitting on the sofa, right where the houseplant table is.'

Ed smiled at his girlfriend. 'He'd love it that so many of the locals visit The Potting Shed these days.'

'He really would.' A warming glow of satisfaction filled Maddie as she nodded towards the till. 'Are you okay sorting the shop float if I go and make sure Jo has enough change in the café?'

'No problem.' Ed took a pile of five-pound notes from Maddie and flicked them through his fingers.

'Great. Once we're open, I'll man this till until Sabi has finished walking Florrie, then I'll go and help Jo in the café.'

'Do you want me to be on carry-to-the-car duty in between watering the polytunnels this morning?'

'Please.'

'After that, if it's quiet, I thought I'd give the bluebell garden a bit of a tidy. It's not messy as such but...' Ed pulled a face.

'It's gone a bit straggly.'

'The lack of bluebells doesn't help either.'

'Drawback of it being September.' Maddie plucked a dead

leaf off a nearby cyclamen. 'I considered adding in a few shrubs, but somehow…'

'You ran out of time?'

'Don't I always.'

'There's just so much to do.' Ed grinned. 'Maybe you should advertise for another member of staff? Sara's proving a fabulous addition to The Potting Shed, but she only works part-time.'

'In truth, I could do with that, *and* another full-time person.' Maddie dropped the dead leaf into the nearest waste bin. 'But we aren't yet that comfortable budget wise.'

'Sabi still insisting you pay one loan off at a time before you take on another big expense?'

'Yes, and I'm grateful to her for it. It's so much less fraught knowing my sister has a grip on the finances. Means I can get on with the gardening and people stuff, without waking up in the middle of the night stressing about bank managers and spreadsheets.'

'Good job you have me working for free at the weekends then, isn't it.'

Maddie slipped an arm around Ed's waist. 'You can just rest you know; you've had a hectic week lawyering. I love that you help here, but I don't take it for granted. You might want to go walking on Exmoor, or simply put your feet up.'

'Don't be silly.' Ed shook his head. 'I love it. And it's a welcome balm after a week in a cut-throat office.'

'Cut-throat?' Maddie saw the briefest flash of unease in Ed's eyes. 'You've never described your new job that way before.'

Ed brushed the comment aside. 'Maybe cut-throat is a bit much, but the company I work for in Bristol is a very different type of legal business to Ronald's laid-back old-fashioned solicitors' office in Exeter. He was very much customer first.'

'Thank goodness!' Maddie thought of Ed's former boss. 'He was so kind when Dad's will got complicated.' She leant forward and kissed Ed's cheek. 'As were you!'

'Why, thank you.' Ed tucked an arm around Maddie as he opened the till. 'I do still like being a solicitor, but I'm not sure I'm a money-first, people-second sort of person.'

Gnawing her bottom lip, Maddie asked, 'Is it really like that?'

'I make it sound heartless. It's not. My new colleagues do care about their clients but, somehow the human touch is missing.'

'The human touch?'

'You know, like you have here.' Ed waved his free arm forwards, gesturing across the rows of houseplants, seeds, and baskets of fresh vegetables. 'The Potting Shed might have tripled in size over the last year, but it hasn't lost its heart. It feels as friendly and family-like as it did when it was just you and your dad in a small shed and a few polytunnels.'

Maddie smiled as she narrowed her eyes. 'And how do you know that Mr Tate? You didn't know me until after Dad died.'

'Mrs Johnson came in for coffee and cake with her pals. I overheard them discussing how proud your father would be of you, and how friendly you've kept the place; and I quote: "That Maddie's a credit to her father. Tony'd be that proud of how friendly it is here even now it's all big."'

A tear pricked at the corner of Maddie's eye as she chuckled. 'That sounds like Mrs Johnson alright.'

'Then one of her friends asked her about cress sandwiches. I stopped being a shameless eavesdropper at that point.'

Maddie laughed. 'Before Christmas, Mrs Johnson ordered cress seed from us for her grandchildren to grow. She got an extra packet for herself, as she didn't want to be left out of the fun. She enjoyed it so much she's been buying herself a packet every few months ever since.'

'Hence the cress sandwiches.'

'Sounds like they are becoming her signature dish!'

'Talking of signature dishes, do we have time to sneak a sausage sandwich from Jo before we open to the Saturday hoards?'

'Not a hope!' Maddie poked Ed's stomach. 'But as soon as Sabi arrives I'll get you a sausage sarnie and a takeout coffee. Good enough?'

'Perfect.'

Jemima unlocked the cake cupboard and gingerly extracted a large square box. 'Apple cake today?'

'If that's the one with the next use-by date, then bring it on.' Jo kept his eyes on the coffee machine as Maddie's twelve-year-old niece placed the box on the counter behind him.

'There's a few slices of Victoria sponge left from yesterday too.'

'Let's have those as well then, Jem. And there's some chocolate brownies in the fridge.'

Jemima opened the new cake box. 'Whoa, that is one huge apple cake. I don't think I'd better lift it out. If I dropped it, Mum would never let me help you again.'

Having given his hands a wash, Jo turned to help her. 'It is a bit of a brute. Could you lay out the brownies instead? There's a rectangular plate in the far cupboard under the counter.'

'Sure.' Jemima gave Jo a sideways look. 'I'm going to miss helping out in here so much.'

'I'm going to miss you too, once the new school year starts next week.' Easing the cake from its tight-fitting container, Jo added, 'You've been amazing.'

Jemima wrinkled her nose. 'I'd rather stay here with you, Mum, and Aunt Maddie.'

'No, you wouldn't.' Jo lowered the cake onto a large round board. 'You love school, and you must be missing people of your own age.'

'Okay, yes, maybe, but I love being at The Potting Shed with you oldies too.'

'Cheek!'

Jemima laughed. 'I'll still come in on Sundays if I don't have too much homework to do – and if that's okay with Maddie and Mum, of course.'

'I'm sure it will be. I know your aunt's thrilled that you like it here so much.'

'Ummm.' Jemima took the cling film off the remaining Victoria sponge cake.

'That was a loaded *um*.'

'I'm not sure Mum's so thrilled.' Jemima shrugged. 'She likes me working here as long as I don't get under anyone's feet, but despite all she's said in the past about me being able to make my own decisions, I'm not sure she'd like it if I told her I don't want to go to university, as I'd rather work here.'

Putting down the knife he'd been about to use to slice the apple cake, Jo gave her a hug. 'Come on, you haven't even done your GCSEs yet. Why not leave the rest of your life worries for a bit?' He returned to the cake slicing. 'You may have a change of heart in a few years and decide you'd like to be a doctor or botanist or chef, or anything at all. Or you might not. Either way, it doesn't matter. Options should always be left open. The Potting Shed will be your inheritance whatever happens.'

Jemima smiled. 'You're quite clever, for an oldie.'

'Why, thank you, my child.' Jo chuckled. 'Talking of clever, get your head working on this dilemma: when I last visited my mother's care home, I discovered that they haven't got enough money or staff to have inhouse activities anymore. At the same time, all of the residents are in desperate need of stimulus. What can we do to help?'

'Oh, that's easy.'

'It is?'

'Sure.' Jem unpopped the lid of a plastic tub. 'You bring them here.'

'You know your niece is a genius, don't you?'

Maddie hadn't taken more than a single step into the café when Jo announced Jemima's brilliance across the room.

'Of course she is.' Maddie's eyes twinkled. 'Her parents are very clever, and her aunt, well…'

A giggling Jemima waved from the other side of the counter. 'Thanks, *Aunt* Maddie!'

'What particular act of genius has Jem dreamt up this morning?'

Jo paused in the act of collecting up stray cake crumbs with a damp cloth. 'I was chatting to Michael, mum's carer at Charlton Lodge. They're desperate for activities at Mum's care home. Jem suggested we hold a dementia café here once a fortnight or monthly. Although, obviously, if you hate the idea, then…'

'I don't hate the idea.' Maddie looked thoughtful. 'How do

they work exactly? I'm guessing a small group of residents come here, we provide coffee, cake et cetera – maybe an activity of some sort? Or would it just be a change of scene and conversation over a drink?'

'I'd have to talk to Michael about that – and find out if they are even interested in the first place. But in theory, do you like the idea?'

'Very much.' Maddie beamed. 'Great idea, Jem.'

Jemima threw her ponytail over her shoulder. 'It's obvious really. This place is called the Forget-Me-Not Café. Where better to have a dementia group visit? You could get them talking about the old days and the memories would flow.'

Maddie headed to the café's till. 'Have a word with the home then, Jo.'

'I will, thanks.' Jo's smile became tight as an unsettling potential consequence of such a café group began to niggle at the back of his mind.

Memories… what if Mum has one of her forgetful moments? What if she…?

Jemima laid a hand on her friend's baggy jumper sleeve. 'You okay? You've gone pale.'

'I'm fine.' Giving himself a mental shake, Jo waved towards the wall clock. 'Just noticed the time, that's all. In ten minutes, those doors will be open, and we haven't got the bacon and sausages started for the sarnies yet.'

2

'Before we kick off this week's meeting,' Maddie addressed her staff as she stirred her coffee, 'I'd like to raise a toast to the Forget-Me-Not Café – a month old today!'

'Cheers!'

As Ivan, Jo, Maddie, Sabi and Jemima raised their drinks in a toast, Ed added, 'And a special well done to you, Jo. Your café has been the talk of The Potting Shed.'

Maddie chinked her mug against Jo's. 'Café manager supreme.'

'Hardly!' Jo laughed. 'I can't believe we've done four weeks already. I've loved every minute. Having my blends endorsed by Davina Ditz – the queen of gardening herself – has helped no end.'

'People still talk about the question-and-answer session she did in the spring,' Sabi chipped in. 'We were so lucky to have a celebrity gardener come here.'

'I'll second that.' Jo gestured to a large box of "Gardener's Coffee" blends, all bagged up in individual brown paper bags, with *Ditzy's Favourite* written down one side. 'I wondered if I'd miss the freedom of serving coffee from my camper van, but it has been fun. Not to mention that it's rather nice being undercover when it rains.'

Sabi, her tablet open in front of her, joined in the

congratulations. 'Profitable fun.' She tapped the tablet's screen. 'Basically, everything we purchased to either eat or drink this week has paid for itself. The profits can pay Jo's wages and go towards new stock.'

Maddie made a note. 'But it's going to be a while before we're earning enough to completely pay off the loan for the conversion of the café.'

'It is, but we've budgeted for that.' Sabi tapped on the screen again. 'This was opening month, so lots of folk came in out of curiosity. The challenge now will be to keep them coming back and spreading the word, so new customers come and try Jo's gorgeous coffee.'

'Which brings us nicely to the main item on the agenda,' said Maddie. 'Interviewing someone to help Jo, so I can go back to my plants.'

Jo looked over at Sabi. 'Thanks for holding the garden centre fort while I've kidnapped Maddie for so much of the last few weeks.'

'Not at all.' Sabi smiled. 'Actually, it's been quite nice. Several customers have asked about my new interior design sideline since we had those business cards printed to leave by the till.'

'You should put some by my cheese counter,' Ivan offered. 'At the risk of stereotyping, the type of folk who buy specialist cheeses are often the sort who'd employ an interior designer.'

'Good point.' Sabi rummaged in her handbag and passed a box of cards to Ivan. 'How are the cheese sales going? This is your third month inside the main body of the garden centre instead of in the former shop.'

'It is, and it's grand, lass. Custom's increasing, and while the post-three-o'clock trade is a touch meagre, the middle of the day makes up for it.'

'Excellent,' Maddie scribbled a note on her pad, 'and Florrie is certainly enjoying Sheba being around more.'

Ivan grinned at the thought of his black Labrador. 'Your Florrie is definitely better behaved when Sheba is around.'

Ed rolled his eyes. 'That's the truth.'

'Are you casting aspersions on my Border collie's behaviour?'

'Yes. She's a furry jumping cracker.'

Everyone laughed as Maddie stuck her tongue out. 'Be careful, Ed, or I'll send her to Bristol with you on Monday.'

'Talking of Monday,' Sabi said firmly, 'back to the interviews. We have a short list of three people for the café assistant job: Belle Shephard, Davy Parker, and Derek Symons.'

'I was thinking,' Maddie said, eyes down, 'why don't I give each candidate a tour of The Potting Shed, then Sabi and Jo can do the actual interviews.'

'But it's your business. You ought to do the interviews.' Guessing Maddie was feeling anxious about it, Ed added, 'It won't be as daunting as you imagine.'

'I've never interviewed anyone before. Everyone who has worked here in the past was a friend first.'

'I haven't either,' Jo admitted.

'Nor have I, if it comes to it.' Sabi pulled a face. 'But it's just a matter of finding out if you like the feel of a person – if you think you could work with them.'

'Come off it, Sabi, it's *much* more than that. It's being able to interact with customers, and work the machines and work to health and safety guidelines and...

'Fair enough. But as I'm not going to be working in the café, then...'

'Yes, I know. It's got to me be who does the interviews. Okay.' Maddie sighed. 'Some parts of being a manager I do not like!'

'At least The Potting Shed is closed on a Monday, so you won't have customers to look after as well.' Ed gave her a reassuring smile. 'Just relax and go with your gut instincts when it comes to choosing who gets the post.'

Not saying that she wished Ed would be there to support her, knowing it would only make him feel more guilty than he already did for taking a job in Bristol and so wasn't in Devon from Monday to Friday, Maddie said, 'I'm sure it'll be fine. Now, before you all go, I've been thinking about something else.'

'Go on.' Sabi closed her tablet.

'I'd like us – well, The Potting Shed – to show the local community how much we appreciate their support. We all know how easily this business could have failed, with such a large garden centre chain as Big In Gardens operating nearby – but the locals have rallied, and so we're still here.'

'And growing bigger and better all the time,' Ed added. 'BIG will be worrying about The Potting Shed soon, rather than the other way around.'

'I'm not sure I'd go that far.'

'So, what's your thinking, Maddie? You after ideas for community projects that can run from here?' Ivan rolled his mug between his large palms. 'I mean beyond the children's gardening group you already run?'

'Yes. Something other than the Little Acorns, which will bring people to The Potting Shed and give something beneficial to the community that helped us.'

Sabi looked thoughtful. 'That's a great idea. The marketing potential is huge.'

'I was thinking more about doing a good deed, but yes, I suppose it would help the PR.' Maddie turned to her niece. 'In fact, Jem had an idea about holding a dementia café here, which could work.'

Jo blew across the top of his mug. 'Like I said, if you're keen I can ask Michael about it at the care home when... Oh...' he picked up his mobile as it burst into life '...I could have sworn I'd turned the sound off.' Jo flicked a finger across the screen. 'That's Michael now. Excuse me a moment.'

As Jo moved away from the table, Ivan said, 'A dementia café is a great idea. I'll ask Elspeth if she's got other ideas as well. She's been something of a local community stalwart for years.'

Sabi tapped a finger against her tablet. 'Could you ask her if she has more stock? We've sold nearly all of her hand cream again. I'm amazed Elspeth can keep up with demand as she makes it all from scratch herself.'

'No problem.' Ivan smiled. 'That's why she gave up doing the selling herself. She's so grateful to be able to sell from here.'

'Our pleasure,' said Maddie. 'It's good to have a few non-gardeny things for sale.'

'I wondered about expanding on that side,' Sabi responded. 'Not beauty products – we'll leave that to Elspeth – but maybe hats, gloves, scarves – things that make good Christmas gifts as winter approaches.'

'Good idea.' Maddie scribbled another note. 'I'll be ordering the Christmas cards, paper, and decs soon, to arrive at the end of October, so I few extra items won't hurt.'

Jemima paused in the act of sipping her smoothie. 'Don't forget Halloween and Bonfire Night; they come first. It's only September!'

'Fear not, Jem, I've already got orders in for pumpkins, kindling for autumn fires and bottles of warming hot chocolate to have on bonfire night, as well as...'

Her sentence was cut short by the sight of Jo rushing back to their table. 'I have to go. Mum's had a fall.'

3

After parking his bright orange camper van in Charlton Lodge's driveaway, Jo dashed inside.

Michael was uttering reassurances before Jo had reached reception. 'She's okay.'

'You're sure?' Jo spoke automatically, before adding, 'Sorry, I didn't mean to sound as if I didn't believe you.'

Dismissing the notion, Michael came out from behind his desk. 'You're worried – it's natural to doubt things when something like this happens. Come on, the doctor's finished his examination and Iris is comfortable and back in bed.'

'How did it happen?' Jo followed Michael along a wide hallway, passing several closed bedroom doors as they went.

'Your mum doesn't remember. As I said on the phone, we found Iris on the floor at the foot of her bed. We suspect she tripped on something – possibly over her own feet – and didn't have time to break her fall with her arms.'

'Or forgot to?'

'It's possible, but instinct does tend to kick in, even with dementia patients.' Michael paused as they reached the door to bedroom number ten. 'She is rather bruised, but it looks worse than it is.'

'Right.'

'Why don't you go on in, and I'll fetch you both a cuppa. Tea for Iris and coffee for you, I assume?'

'Please.' Jo took a steadying breath before pushing open the shiny white door.

'Hey, Mum.' Jo sat next to the bed, hoping his eyes didn't give away how concerned he was. 'Michael tells me you've been inspecting the floor.'

Reaching a shaky hand out to her son, Iris chuckled. 'Needed to see if they'd been dusting under the bed.'

Relieved his mum was having a lucid moment and seemed to have kept her sense of humour too, Jo grinned. 'And had they?'

'Can't bloody remember.' Taking hold of her son's hand as he sat down, she squeezed it hard.

'Ouch, Mum! Still got a grip of steel then.'

Iris chuckled again as she let go. 'So they tell me.'

She's going to tell me about when I was born now.

'I fair bruised the midwife when you came along, you know.'

'Did you, Mum?'

'They thought I'd broken her wrist I held on to her so hard.' Iris tutted at the feebleness of youth. 'No stamina these young things.'

'Weren't you quite a young thing yourself then, Mum?'

Iris frowned, her eyes faded to concern as she turned her head to the left, searching the room. 'What? Have there been young people here?'

'No, Mum, only me. We were just being silly while we talked.'

'Oh.'

As Iris sank back onto her pillow, Jo held in a sigh. It was all he could do not to cry. His incredible mother, the woman who'd raised him single-handed, who had stood by him when so many had walked away, who had fought his corner again and again, appeared utterly defeated. Her forehead was a pattern of purple and black bruises and her eyes had abruptly lost their light.

Age is so damned cruel.

Jo was about to attempt some small talk, when Michael arrived with their hot drinks. 'How are we doing then?'

'Mum was telling me about how she bruised the midwife when I was born.'

'Was she now. What a brute.' Michael gave his patient a wide smile. 'I'm leaving Jo in charge of your drink, Iris. There's a straw to help you if it's too awkward to sip from the cup just yet.'

She gave him a blank look but nodded anyway. Jo was sure she had no idea what she was agreeing to.

'Come on, Mum, you need to get your strength back, so you can have a singsong with your friends next time you're all in the day room together.'

When Iris didn't respond, Michael turned to Jo. 'Carol and I – I think you've met Carol; she helps with your mum's partner in crime, Billy – we've been trying to persuade the managers that it would be a good idea to invite volunteers to come in and read, sing and so on.'

'But?'

'They like the idea in principle, but there's so much red tape involved. Frankly, if it isn't paid help, they are opening themselves up to being sued if something goes wrong and...'

'If that happened the whole place would have to close because there'd be no money left at all?'

'That's very much a worst-case scenario, but yes.'

Jo rested a hand on his mother's arm. It felt like a cotton-covered twig. 'Mum loved the painting and singing.'

'I know. And the singing group. Although we do try to have some singing time between the guests and staff when we can. No one hits the high notes of "Long Way to Tipperary" like your mum.'

'There aren't any high notes – are there?'

'There are when you sing it, aren't there, Iris?' Michael winked, as he turned to his charge. 'What was it you told me, if you want to sing high, then you sing high.'

'That's my mum!' Jo stroked a loose grey hair from her shoulder. 'You used to sing "Tipperary" to me when I was a kid. Do you remember, Mum?'

Michael smiled. 'If you're okay, I'll go and check on Billy.'

'How is the old Casanova?'

'Same as ever. Life and soul one minute, "away with the fairies" the next – to quote Billy himself. He's a contented chap though, and he adores your mum.'

'She's pretty fond of him too.' Jo's eyes returned to the now quiet old lady on the bed. 'They make each other laugh. There's an impish sense of humour under that bruised face.'

'Don't we know it!'

Jo had been sitting holding his mum's hand for almost an hour, when she abruptly burst back into life.

'How's your wife?'

'I don't have a wife, Mum.'

'Oh. Was it a husband?'

'No, Mum.' Jo's lips curved upwards. *Never one to avoid*

the realities of modern living, Mum. Thank you. 'I share a house with Sara. You remember Sara? She inherited that big house near Exmouth after her father died. Hawthorn Park.'

'Oh, so she did. Poor wee thing.' Iris paused and put a hand over Jo's. 'I like her – don't I?'

'Yes, Mum, you are very fond of Sara, and she's fond of you.'

'Jolly good.'

Iris rubbed a gnarled hand over her bruised forehead and winced. 'You were at school with Sara. She was one of the girls in your group.'

'No, Mum, I met Sara long after school.'

'Oh. Jolly good.'

'Sara would have come with me to see you, but she didn't work at The Potting Shed today. She's at Hawthorn Park looking after her Airbnb guests.' Not sure what to else say, Jo lifted up his mum's teacup and placed a straw in it. 'Fancy some tea, Mum?'

'Heavens no, it's like dishwater. Anyway, it'll be cold by now.'

Jo burst out laughing, partly because all the hot drinks at Charlton Lodge tasted as if they were warmed-up water in various states of disguise, and partly with relief at his mother saying something as if she was the real her, and not the old woman who'd been cruelly awarded Alzheimer's after a lifetime of being kind.

'Do you remember Michel bringing it in, Mum?'

'Course I do – sometimes I just choose not to remember things, my boy.' She flashed him a sly grin. 'I'm in control, and don't you forget it.'

'As if I could.' Jo's heart ached as he grappled for something to say that would keep her with him. 'It really is awful – the tea I mean. The coffee is appalling too. I'd be shot if I sold it in the café.'

'Café? What café's that then?'

4

Belle swept a swathe of deep purple curls from her face and glared into the mirror that hung in the hallway of her little home.

Smudging some concealer under her eyes, she re-examined her complexion.

'I don't know why you're trying to hide those spots, Mum.' Niall bounded down the stairs, his long thin legs, out of proportion to his short body, as if only half of him was having a growth spurt at once. 'They'll go on their own soon – that's what you tell me about mine.'

'That's because you're a teenager. You're supposed to have spots. I'm thirty-five! Spots just make me feel old.'

Niall stood next to his mum and stared into the mirror. 'Your skin's so dark, they're hardly visible. Now, if you were white, it'd look like mini satellite dishes had landed on your face.'

'Thank you for that vote of confidence – not!' Belle couldn't help but chuckle at her eldest son's teasing expression.

'I was being nice!'

'By telling me that the spots on my chin, which I saw as annoying, but small, are actually huge.'

'Why are you trying to hide them anyway?'

'I've got an interview on Monday. I was practising looking nice.' Belle wrinkled her nose. 'I'm not sure anyone will hire me to work with food if I have three volcanos on my face!'

Niall gave his mum a hug. 'You'll ace it. Every café needs a woman with bright purple hair.'

'Do you think I should wash out the dye?' Belle tugged at her mass of curls. 'Or I could dye it black, or…'

'Mum! I was joking. It suits you. Just put on your best tie-dye dungarees and you'll be perfect.'

'I'll be wearing a pair of trousers and a shirt and jacket.'

'Boring.'

'Sensible.' Belle left out a pent-up breath. 'I'm panicking aren't I.'

'Just a bit.' Niall sat on the stairs and glanced up at his mum through a mess of black curls. 'Are you okay? I mean, do you need this job or just want it?'

'Both.' Belle smiled, hoping her eldest child wouldn't notice the worry that was always in her eyes these days.

'If you get the job and have to be at work while we're at home, me and Milo will be okay.'

'Budge up.' Belle perched onto the stair next to Niall. 'It's obvious that that's what's bothering me, huh?'

'That you're worried about Milo – or about not being there for him – yeah.'

'I worry about you too.' Belle put an arm around Niall's shoulder.

'I know.'

Always conscious of inadvertently laying more responsibility on her older child than she meant to, Belle thought of Milo. He'd always been more of a handful than his brother and had taken the defection of their father three years ago hard, whereas Niall had seen it as a sad inevitability.

'If I get the job, I won't be home until almost five every day.'

'I know.'

'But what if...'

Niall got up and looked down at his mum. 'I'll make sure Milo gets home from school and does his homework.'

'But you shouldn't have to. You have your own...'

'I don't mind, Mum. Honestly.'

As Jo walked into Hawthorn Park's kitchen he was confronted with a cloud of dust.

'What on earth...'

'The bag exploded.' Sara coughed. 'Could you grab me some water?'

'Are you sure that's a good idea?' Jo tried and failed to stifle a laugh at the sight of her covered in flour. 'I could accidentally turn you into living pastry.'

'Oh, very funny.' Sara tried to be cross, but the ridiculousness of her situation got the better of her, and she began to laugh. 'I bet I look like a cross between Casper the Friendly Ghost and Miss Havisham!'

'More like a lost snowman!' Jo took the bag of flour from Sara's hands and led her outside. 'Come on, brush yourself off. I'll go and grab a broom and start on the kitchen floor.'

'Thanks, Jo.' Rubbing her hands together, Sara created an extra cloud of flour dust that made her sneeze as she called through the open doorway. 'I was going to make up some mix for American pancakes. There was so much air trapped in the bag of flour and I must have opened it too quickly, so...'

'It shot up in the air and turned you into Casper?'

'Yup.' She brushed down her arms, before deciding it would be easier to give up, remove her jumper and give it a good shake. 'How was your mum?'

'Not too bad all things considered.' Jo joined Sara as she stepped into the hallway that connected the outside world and the kitchen. 'Bruised and a bit shaken, but otherwise the same as usual. With me one minute, horribly absent the next.'

'Good – well, you know what I mean.' Sara drew a hand through her hair as she rejoined Jo, letting a waft of white dust sprinkle across the floor. 'I'm going to have to sweep out here now. I'm not firing on all cylinders today.'

'Like Mum.'

'Sorry, Jo, I didn't mean…'

'I know.' Jo frowned. 'Now that the activities at Charlton Lodge have stopped, they don't have anything except the telly and the occasional singsong with the staff. Nothing to keep their fading cognitive functions going.'

'That's awful.'

'I was going to tell Michael about an idea Jem had for a dementia café, but with Mum and everything, I didn't get round to it.'

'Is that what the staff meeting was about? I would have come in for it, but it clashed with guest arrival time.' Stepping back inside the kitchen, Sara groaned at the mess. 'So much for me getting ahead of the game for tomorrow's breakfast.'

'At least there's only two guests here.'

'And they are wonderfully quiet and self-contained.' Sara's eyes flicked to the kitchen door, as if half expecting Mr and Mrs Carter to walk through it. 'I've hardly seen them since their arrival.'

'Did you offer them pancakes for tomorrow?'

'I did.'

'Come on then. I'll sort out the mix while you clear up, and then we can have supper. I'm famished.'

Sara laughed. 'Says the man who works in a café all day.'

'Oddly, I don't feel hungry there. Seeing people eat all day is a sure-fire way to curb the appetite.'

Grabbing a cloth, Sara wiped the kitchen table. 'There, less like a disaster zone, more like a B&B's working kitchen.'

'Apart from the cook.'

'Pardon?'

'Why don't you go and wash your hair. I have nothing against women with grey hair, but the flour has made you prematurely white by at least thirty years.'

Sara ran a hand back through her hair, cursing as more flour sprinkled over her clean sink. 'I was going to warm up some casserole.'

'I can do that. Go on.'

Sara grinned. 'What would I do without you?'

Milo pushed his dinner around his plate. He loved his mum's jerk chicken and wraps, but today he wasn't going to eat it. He wasn't going to give her the satisfaction.

How dare she get a job that would stop her being able to pick me up after school!

'I'll eat yours if you don't want it.' Niall held out a hand for Milo's plate.

'No way. It's mine!'

'Eat it then.' Belle regarded her younger son. 'I made this because it's your favourite.'

'Because you feel guilty about abandoning me, you mean!'

'But...'

'You wouldn't have let Niall walk home from school on his own at thirteen – but with me, it doesn't matter!'

Belle blanched. 'Milo, sweetheart, you know that I walked with Niall because we lived much further away at the time.' She paused, steadying her breath, not wanting to dwell on their lives before the end of her marriage. 'I haven't even got the job yet. I might be a total dead loss.'

'And we need the money!' Niall levelled his dark brown eyes on his brother. 'How are you going to have new clothes and the latest Xbox and all that, if Mum isn't working?'

'We managed when *you* were thirteen.'

'Dad paid Mum maintenance when I was thirteen.'

Milo's fork stopped in the act of stirring his dinner. 'Dad's stopped paying you money to keep us, Mum?'

Laying down her cutlery, Belle spoke quietly. 'I didn't know you knew that, Niall. I was going to talk to you both, but I wanted to get the job first – or any job come to that.'

'Dad promised he'd pay until I was eighteen. He *promised.*'

Belle reached out a hand to Milo, but he didn't take it. 'I'm only doing this because we have no choice. I'd fight your dad in the courts for the money, but in all honesty, we're better off not having to rely on him. I wish it wasn't the case, but it is. And I'm so sorry I won't be there for you straight after school if I get this job, but Niall's promised to walk home with you.'

'But...' Milo bit his lip '...what about, you know – homework? I'm slow. I need time and if I don't finish my homework I'll get into trouble.'

'Oh, sweetheart.' Guilt rose in Belle's chest. 'Is that what's bothering you, that you won't get your homework done?'

'Maybe...'

'You'll be okay, little bro.' Niall took a handful of nacho chips from an open bag on the table. 'We'll get a routine sorted.'

Grateful for Niall's understanding of his brother's need for a strict routine, Belle smiled. 'We'll soon adjust. I just wish I wasn't so nervous! What if I fluff the interview?'

'We'll help, Mum.' Niall grinned. 'Come on, Milo, let's pretend to interview Mum.'

'Alright then.' Milo's solemn features softened.

'Although, if there's a hot man on the interview panel who you fancy, you could flirt your way in, Mum.'

'Niall!' Belle burst out laughing as Milo went pink.

'Do you good to have a bloke, Mum.'

'No, it wouldn't!' Milo glared at his brother.

Niall laughed. 'No need to be so horrified. Mum's entitled to a life! You just don't like the idea of someone else being around to tell you off!'

5

'Oh my God, it *is* you!'
Brushing his hands together, Ed blinked into the mid-morning September sunshine as he tried to place the person addressing him, dressed in expensive taupe chinos and a crisp white linen shirt. 'Tristan?'

'The very same!'

'Why the devil are you here?' Ed wasn't sure if he was pleased to see the man or not.

'Holiday.'

'Really?' Ed tilted his head to one side. 'Forgive me, but the Tristan Harvey I knew at university holidayed in the Bahamas and would not be seen dead in a garden centre on a Sunday morning – or at any time come to that.'

'Says the lawyer covered in compost!' Tristan gave the lopsided smile that Ed remembered had broken so many hearts when they were students. 'Things change. For a start, you've clearly got yourself a house with a garden.'

'You could say that.' Ed gestured around him. 'If you can call The Potting Shed a house and consider this a garden.'

'What?' Tristan's blonde fringe swished as he shook his head. 'This is yours? You aren't just shopping?'

'It's my partner's place. I help at the weekends.'

'Is that so?' Tristan's eyes sparkled with mischief. 'But

manual labour, Ed – it's not done for a lawyer to have unmanicured hands you know.'

Having heard a similar disparaging comment from one of his colleagues in Bristol, Ed chose not to respond, asking instead, 'Where are you staying?'

'Thatched cottage in Appleby. For a month.'

'A month! Very nice.' Ed returned to straightening the sacks of compost. 'Good pub over there if I remember rightly. Nice village.'

'True. Decent pint, despite being in the sticks.'

Feeling defensive on behalf of the West Country, Ed said, 'Exmoor Brewery stuff – it's excellent. Has a good reputation. I believe you can get a decent Wadsworth brew or something from the St Austell brewery should you prefer a pint from other parts of the south-west.'

'Alright, mate! Keep your hair on.' Tristan tutted. 'When did you go all rural?'

'I was always rural. I just took time out to study.' Ed lowered his voice as a pair of customers walked past. 'You still in London?'

'Of course.'

'Of course.' Ed was grateful to see an elderly gentleman walking his way, waving a receipt in his direction. Hoping it meant he'd purchased something heavy and needed it carrying to the car, Ed made his excuses. 'I'm sorry, Tris, but duty calls. Was nice to see you.'

'Hang on...' Tristan laid a hand on Ed's shoulder '...you don't actually *work* here do you? Aren't you just helping your girlfriend?'

Ed opened his mouth to respond, but closed it again, as the customer arrived at his side. 'How can I help you, sir?

★

Florrie settled herself at Ed's feet as he cut back a handful of wild grasses that had strayed into the bluebell garden from the field behind the garden centre's border.

'I trust you behaved yourself for Sabi.'

'I always behave, you know that, Ed.'

Surprised to hear a male voice, Ed swung around to see Tristan bearing down on him. 'Oh, hello. I thought you'd be long gone.'

Ignoring the comment, Tristan asked, 'Who were you talking to?'

'Florrie.' Ed dipped his head towards the Border collie–spaniel cross, who jumped up on hearing her name.

'A dog?' Tristan's eyes widened, as if the ownership of a pet was proof that Ed had stepped another mile from the path of high-flying lawyer.

'She belongs to Maddie.'

'And Maddie's your partner? Maddie Willand?'

Ed lowered his secateurs. 'How did you know her surname was Willand?'

'No need to sound so suspicious, mate. I was in the café just now, saw the Davina Ditzy coffee endorsement. Asked a local. They were *very* keen to show this place off. Proud old dear she was – if a bit batty.'

Keen to defend their customer but suspecting Tristan would take no notice if he did, Ed simply said, 'Jo – the guy who runs the café – he designs and makes up the coffee blends. Ditzy was kind enough to endorse them when she did a gig here in the spring.'

Tristan's eyebrows rose so high they were hidden by his

blonde fringe. 'You've been holding out on me. If Ditzy likes it here, then The Potting Shed must have more going for it than first appears.'

Glad neither Maddie, Sabi nor Jemima were within earshot, Ed snapped, 'This place has a good reputation and lots going for it.'

'Yeah, alright – I wasn't having a go.' Tristan paused. 'Davina Ditz though, mate. She's special.'

Ed didn't hide his surprise. 'When did a hotshot barrister like you come across Davina Ditz?'

'Are you kidding me? The woman's a national icon. Damn sexy too.' Tristan peered around him. 'You don't fancy a pint, or something do you?' Not at all sure he did, Ed was about to mutter an excuse, when Tristan added, 'To be honest, I find myself at a bit of a loose end, and it'd be great to catch up. Can't believe how lucky I was to come across you.'

'Oh right. Yes, sure, why not.' Ed found himself agreeing, before quickly adding, 'I can't leave the site for a while though. I need to be here in case someone wants something heavy carrying to their car, and I'm back in Bristol this evening.'

'Bristol?'

'I work there Monday to Friday.'

'Oh, thank goodness – for one terrible moment, I thought you'd gone totally "old man" and had settled for a village law firm or something.'

'Okay, enough of the rural-life bashing.' Annoyed by Tristan's causal dismissal of the life he loved, Ed was glad when Florrie came to his side, clearly realising he required moral support. 'I like it here. I have a happy life with an amazing woman. It might not be your cup of tea, but it's definitely mine.'

Holding up his hands as a peace offering, Tristan gave a

placating smile. 'You know me, always had a flippant side. I didn't mean any offence. Like I said, I'm just surprised that's all. You're Ed Tate, top ranker of our uni year. If anyone was going to be head of the bar at the Old Bailey, it was you.'

'I never wanted that.'

'You always said not, but I didn't believe you. I guess I was jealous of you back then.'

Ed's eyebrows rose in surprise. 'Whatever for?'

'Because you had all it took to be everything my father wanted me to be – but wasn't – without seeming to try. Whereas I…'

'Is that why you were always so…'

'Seemingly overconfident?'

'Well, yes.'

'My father had very set ideas about how my life was going to pan out from birth. He taught me that I'd never achieve my goals if I didn't believe in them one hundred per cent.' Tristan ran a hand through his fringe. 'I suppose that's why I could never believe you didn't want to go higher up the ladder than…'

A surprised Ed interrupted. 'I became an everyday solicitor, just like I always planned. It's not for me, the courtroom stuff. You took to it because – whether it's completely genuine or not – you have the confidence it needs. I don't. Just because I was capable, didn't mean I had to do it.'

'Understood.' Tristan watched customers browsing around the nearest polytunnel. 'You were very lucky, you know. My family left me with no doubt that if I didn't go all the way to the top, then I'd have failed them.'

'I had no idea you had that pressure hanging over you.' Ed wasn't sure what else to say.

'That's because I never told anyone.' Tristan slapped Ed on the back. 'How about a coffee then? Now? A peace offering from me to you'.

Finding himself wondering if he'd misjudged his former fellow student, Ed pulled his mobile from his pocket. 'Fair enough, I could do with a coffee. I'll just text Maddie.'

'Oh my God! You're not asking for permission, are you?'

'I'm simply letting Maddie know where I am. She may need me for something.' Lowering his phone, Ed felt his momentarily improved opinion of Tristan dissolve only seconds after he'd made it, as Florrie let out a short sharp bark of solidarity. 'If you can't respect the fact that I care enough about my girlfriend to want to save her rushing around looking for me if she needs me, then you can have coffee alone.'

Taking a step back from Florrie, who was eyeing him with pure distrust, Tristan gave an abrupt bark of laughter. 'Good for you, Ed, mate. You've not lost the famous Tate backbone after all. Excellent. Come on then, coffee time.'

'Wow! Busy.' Sara joined the queue for a cup of coffee, watching Jo and Maddie as they moved with methodical economy behind the counter.

Feeling the growl in her stomach steering her towards a slice of apple cake, but knowing she ought to have toast, as it would keep her going for longer, Sara remained undecided until she reached at the head of the queue.

'It's no good Jo, I'm going to have to have both.'

'Both of what?' Jo knew Sara liked everything on the café's menu as she'd spent ages with him deliberating what to include in it.

'I ought to have toast, but...'

Maddie passed her friend a large hot chocolate. 'Let me guess, you are, once again, stuck between something you'd like and something you think you ought to have.'

'Maybe. It's so tricky.'

'No, it isn't.' Maddie chuckled. 'You are young, you are fit and healthy, and any calories you eat will be burnt off as you work your way around the garden centre.'

'If only that were true!'

Maddie grinned. 'Either way, you're doing me a favour by working on your day off, so have whatever you want, woman.'

'Apple cake with white toast and marmalade please.' Sara laughed, as she turned back to the lady next to her. 'Who am I to argue with my boss?'

Jo chuckled. 'Are we going to have you wavering between cake and toast every day from here on?'

'Probably.' Sara handed over some money as Jo rang the staff discounted price through the till.

Rolling his eyes, Jo smiled. 'Just so we know.'

Tristan had been talking for some time about his job and how high his career was flying. Aware he'd tuned out, and that if he was going to maintain polite conversation, Ed seized his chance to break Tristan's monologue when he saw Sara crossing the café with her tray. 'Would you like to come and join us?'

Sara acknowledged Tristan. 'Hello there.'

'Hello, yourself.' Tristan gave a confident smirk.

Ed gave an internal groan. *Of course, he* would *flirt with her.* 'Tristan, this is Sara. Sara, meet Tristan Harvey. We were at university together.'

Pausing, Sara smiled as she rested her tray on the edge of the table. 'Pleased to meet you.'

'And you.'

Sara gave Ed an apologetic shrug. 'Forgive me though, I can't join you. I have a few emails I must reply to over lunch.'

'The Airbnb?'

'Bookings are going up all the time. I usually do the admin at home on a Sunday, but Maddie was short-handed today, so...'

'I totally understand.' Ed smiled.

'You're a woman of property? A businesswoman?' Tristan's smile widened.

'Um, yes. A property anyway.' Sara found herself the focus of the newcomer's sapphire blue eyes as she lifted her tray back up. 'It was nice to meet you.'

'Likewise. Enjoy your – goodness – toast *and* cake.'

'Yes. Umm... bye then.'

As Sara retreated to a corner of the café Ed whispered, 'Why did you have to say it like that? She's hardly overeating!'

'Well – you know... if women start getting used to big lunches when they're young, in no time at all they're ordering size fourteen clothes and...'

Wondering if his companion had somehow teleported them both back to the 1950s, Ed was about to object, but Tristan hadn't finished talking. 'That's sort of why I'm in Devon. My girlfriend and I are here having a trial period to see if I can live with her. She wants me to sell my flat, but I'm not so sure – a bolthole is always a good idea, don't you think? I'm sure you must have a place of your own in Bristol you can go to if the heat gets to you.'

'What?' Noting that Tristan had made no reference to whether his girlfriend might have trouble adjusting to living with him during their month together, Ed tried to remember if his former colleague had always been such a caveman.

'My girlfriend, Gemma, she's got a bit of a sweet tooth. I've had to be careful to keep an eye on things. Got to have her looking her best. I'm...'

'Stop right there.' Ed's patience suddenly ran out.

'Well, sorry, mate, but in my experience...'

'All women are stick-thin.' Ed stood up. 'I should get back to work.'

'But you aren't at work. This is just a hobby to help out the...'

'The *owner*...' Ed lowered his voice and did his best not to appear confrontational in front of the customers '...who, as I've already told you, is my partner. The woman I love. Who, if it is any concern of yours, is beautiful, clever, fun and happy – and a size fourteen! Oh, and by the way, you aren't now, nor ever were, my mate.'

6

Awoken by the gentle-ish pat of a paw on her head, Maddie mumbled, 'Morning, Florrie,' and immediately rolled over to hug Ed. As her arm met thin air, she remembered it was Monday morning, and he was in Bristol getting ready for a day in his open-plan office.

Sitting up, Maddie put her arms around her dog. 'As Ed's not here, you'll just have to put up with a morning cuddle instead.'

Yapping her acquiescence, Florrie wagged her tail, peering at her owner with expectant brown eyes. 'Yes, I know, you want to go for a walk.' Maddie threw back the duvet. 'Give me a minute to wash and dress then.'

It wasn't until she was halfway around the wood that backed onto The Potting Shed's land, that Maddie realised she'd had a good night's sleep, even though Ed hadn't been there. Watching Florrie investigate a tangle of oak tree roots, Maddie thought back to when she'd said goodbye to Ed the night before. There'd been a reluctance about him to leave that felt like it was about more than just knowing he'd miss her.

'Ed's really not warming to life in Bristol, Flo.'

Florrie bounded up to Maddie's side and nudged a cold nose against her jeans pocket until she extracted the tennis ball she kept there and threw it into the distance.

Maddie watched as Florrie darted after it. 'You know, Flo, I think you and I are adjusting to Ed not being here so often far more easily than he's adjusting to being away all week.'

A sigh escaped her lips. They had tried living together at The Potting Shed, with Ed commuting to Bristol via train each day, but it hadn't worked. Ed was constantly tired out and, as his hours could be long, sometimes he'd only be back in Devon for a quick meal and to sleep. A month later, he'd found a bedsit to rent near his office and had become a weekend visitor.

A frown settled itself across Maddie's face. 'I hope he's okay, Flo. I ought to have asked him more about...'

The buzz of her mobile announcing the arrival of a text from Jo stopped Maddie's words in their tracks.

First candidate ALREADY here! I'll make them a coffee while we wait for you to walk Florrie.

'Hell!' Maddie tapped out a quick affirming reply and called to her dog. 'Come on, Flo! We're needed.'

Walking as quickly as she could, conscious she had intended to change into some more interview-appropriate clothing before the first candidate arrived, the nerves Maddie'd expected to keep her awake all night arrived in a sudden rush.

'It'll be alright won't it, Florrie?' Maddie swallowed. 'These people want to impress us. It is them who should be nervous, not me.'

Knowing her self-reassurance was utterly pointless, Maddie noted the time on her phone. 'It's nine o'clock. They're an hour early!'

*

Sara was heading in Maddie's direction as she emerged from the woods. 'Jo sent me to intercept you. Shall I take Florrie?'

'Thanks, Sara. I can't believe they're here already!'

'Derek Symons.' Sara pulled a face. 'Seems okay – happy to be left to his own devices with a newspaper and a coffee. Apparently, he was offered a lift, and accepted so he didn't have to worry about the bus not arriving and potentially being late.'

'Makes sense.' Maddie could imagine doing the same – although she knew she'd have lingered somewhere away from the garden centre, not brave enough to be seen until it was time for the interview.

'Jo says you're to carry on with whatever you planned to do. He's happy pottering in the café and will look after our visitor until you're ready.'

'That's great. Thanks, although...' Maddie examined her clothing '...you know, these are my work clothes. If he is going to join the team, then this is how he'll see me. Perhaps I'll go and say hello and take him on the tour of the place that I'd planned to do after the interview.'

'Seems sensible. Do you want Florrie with you for the tour, or shall I still take her?'

'Best you have her. An interview is one thing; an interview and an overfriendly collie is something else.'

As soon as their second candidate had left the café, Sabi put her notepad down with an exaggerated groan. 'This is hopeless!'

'On paper, he was the best of the three we shortlisted.' Maddie felt equally defeated.

'Perhaps the next one…' Jo referred to his notes '…Belle Shephard, will be better.'

Sabi scribbled a note on her pad. 'I hope so, otherwise it'll be us carrying on as we have been, readvertising, or taking on Derek.'

'We can't!' Maddie looked aghast at her sister. 'You don't have to be here every day, but we do. You can't leave us – well Jo mostly – with someone who has opinions about meat eaters that he isn't inclined to keep to himself. We'd have no customers left within a week!'

'At least he was punctual.' Jo couldn't help but grin.

Sabi tutted. 'Can't argue with that.'

Maddie flicked her notes over to the where Belle Shephard's application sat open. 'Mrs Shephard has no café experience.'

'Neither did the blokes.' Jo stood up. 'It's time. I'll go and see if she's here.'

Sabi picked up her copy of Belle's application. 'What do you think, Mads, third time lucky?'

'Oh God.' Sabi turned her head and mumbled so only her sister could hear. 'She's got purple hair!'

'So what?'

'But… it's *bright* purple!'

'Sabi!' Maddie hissed. 'She looks fabulous – stop it.'

Not giving her sister's inner snob a chance to fully surface, Maddie stood up and held out her hand as a woman with the biggest smile she'd ever seen walked towards them.

'I still think she looks a bit hippy-dippy. Is that the image we want?' Sabi scribbled a circle on her pad.

'And you look like you've just swallowed a lemon, but I'm not expecting you to make tarts, so stop with the surface assessment. She's great.' Maddie calmed her tone. 'Come on, Sabs, I thought you'd stopped being the judgement queen from hell you used to be.'

'I'm not judgemental – I just...' Sabi let out a puff of air. 'Okay, I am a bit. Do you really think she'd do a good job? I grant she's friendly, but she hasn't worked in a café before.'

'Nor had we, but once Jo showed us the ropes, we got the idea.'

'You did,' Sabi muttered. 'I made a drink that wouldn't even have passed as pigswill.'

Maddie patted her sister's hand. 'We all have our strengths, Sabs. Look at the notes I made – she loves to cook...'

'But isn't qualified to cook – no hygiene certificates or anything...'

'We didn't ask for any. We're going to do the training, remember?'

'It would have been handy if we didn't have to.'

'True, but the chaps we interviewed didn't have certificates either.' Maddie got up. 'Come on, Jo should have finished doing the café kitchen bit of the tour. Let's show Belle our kingdom.'

Belle stood in the doorway of The Potting Shed's main sales area. She took in the lovingly arranged displays on each table, the eclectic mix of pots, houseplants and fresh produce. Her eyes rested on a rack near the till, full of home-made seed packets and accompanying recipe cards, clearly marked *Jem's Smoothies*.

'It's so different here when you're closed. As a customer you can see the care that goes into the place, but when there are no people around, I don't know – somehow you can feel its heartbeat.'

Suspecting her sister was thinking that her hippy theory had been correct, Maddie jumped in before Sabi could speak. 'That's a lovely thing to say. Thank you. I hadn't realised you were a customer.'

'We don't get to come as often as we'd like, but we were here for your fabulous market last Christmas, and again for some cheese at Easter.'

'You and your husband?'

'I'm divorced, so it's just me and my boys. I've got two: Niall and Milo.'

'Did they visit the Christmas grotto?' As she asked the question, Maddie imagined what was going through her sister's head. *A hippy who's divorced...*

'They're a bit old for that. Milo is thirteen and Niall is fifteen – almost sixteen.'

'How would working here, should you be offered the job, fit with school?'

'We have that sorted. Don't worry. I wouldn't have applied if I couldn't do the hours.'

Feeling guilty for asking the question, Maddie apologised. 'Sorry, of course.'

'Not at all. You need to know these things.' Belle pushed her mass of purple ringlets from her face. 'My boys have been very supportive. They were firing practice interview questions at me on and off all weekend.'

Sabi suddenly smiled. 'My daughter, Jemima, she was firing potential questions to ask at me and Henry – that's my husband – over dinner last night.'

'That's so lovely. Supportive kids is all we can ask for – well, kind and supportive.' Belle reached out to one of the purple-ribbon-swathed pillars that held up the ceiling. 'These ribbons are incredible. I've never seen them used as decoration like this outside of a wedding. Genius way to hide ceiling supports. Fabulous colour too.'

Maddie had to stifle a giggle of relief as her sister's face broke into a huge grin.

'That was me. I'm an interior designer when I'm not here.'

'Now that's a job! I am all over the place with colour...' Belle chuckled, as she brushed down her clothing '...as you can probably tell. But I do admire someone with a true eye.'

'Thank you.' Momentarily taken aback, Sabi rallied. 'You said in the interview that you used to be a teaching assistant. Lots of scope for using colour in that job.'

'Big time. Although, I must confess to drawing on my Buddhist roots to keep calm amongst the kids on many occasions.'

'You're a Buddhist?' Sabi's head tilted to one side.

'I try – I lapse often!' Belle continued to survey her surroundings with obvious pleasure. 'I helped with the tiny tots when I was working at school. Lots of poster paint all over the place.'

Maddie smiled. 'So you could certainly be said to have patience then.'

'Just a bit, sweetheart.' Belle's hand flew to her mouth. 'Sorry, Miss Willand! Habit.'

'Not at all, you can call me Maddie anyway. And this is Sabi.'

'Short for Sabrina.' Sabi pointed to the doorway. 'Would you like to see the polytunnels, Belle?'

'I'd like to see everything!'

Having gone full circle around The Potting Shed, basking in Belle's delight at all she saw, Maddie and Sabi escorted her back to the kitchen, where Jo was waiting. Maddie glanced in his direction while Belle sat back down with Sabi. His subtle nod told her all she needed to know.

'So, Belle, are there any questions you'd like to ask us before we let you head home?'

'Not really. You've already answered all the questions I thought of as we went around. You've done wonders with the place. I remember when I brought Niall here in his pushchair. There was just one man and a big shed. He was lovely – chatted to Niall for ages while I dilly-dallied over which veg I wanted to grow in the garden.'

The sisters exchanged looks, before Maddie said, 'That was our dad. He wanted to expand the place into a garden-centre one day, so…'

'So, you did it for him.' Belle tucked a stray curl back into her scrunchy. 'He was a kind man. I've never forgotten him.'

'Thank you.' Maddie swallowed. 'Now the aim is to open the place up to the community a bit more. I'd love to do something for the people who supported us against BIG, when they tried to take over our land.'

'Big in Gardens?' Belle's nose wrinkled. 'They're okay for a plastic-tasting coffee and some instant sponge but there's no positivity – their only aura is money.'

Not commenting, even though she agreed, Maddie went on. 'I already run a children's gardening group every other Saturday, but as we are low on staff, I can't increase the number of children who come along – there's already a waiting list. We're considering a dementia café as well.'

'How about doing school visits and school trips? I bet you'd be a whizz with the younger children.'

Maddie bit her lip. 'Oh. I'm not sure.'

Sabi regarded Belle with increasing respect. 'Brilliant idea.'

Maddie's eyebrows rose. 'It is if you aren't the one having to go in and stand in front of all those children!'

'It's still a fabulous idea.' Sabi turned to their visitor. 'Belle, you're marvellous.'

7

Jo gave the coffee machine a wipe, stacked the few mugs they'd used into the dishwasher, and checked he had enough milk in the fridge. He was taking off his apron when Maddie came back into the café. 'Would I be right in assuming Belle has got the job?'

'She has as far as I'm concerned, but the last word must come from you. It's you she'd be working with. What do you think?'

'That she's a breath of fresh air! Her positive outlook could be a godsend.' Jo paused. 'What about Sabi though?'

Maddie laughed. 'My sister's initial judgement, based on Belle's flamboyant hair colour, was swiftly knocked into shape when they got talking. Belle, it seems, is full of good ideas for this place in general. She is also keen to learn. Sabi is, right now, driving Belle home so she doesn't need to wait for a bus.'

Jo's mouth dropped open. 'Sabi is?'

'Yup.'

'Goodness.'

'Quite.' Maddie took her phone from her pocket. 'Should I text Sabi now, tell her to offer Belle the job?'

'Do it!' Jo hung his apron up on the nearest peg. 'To start as soon as possible.'

Texting fast, Maddie said, 'I'll say she can choose when she starts, latest possible date being two weeks from today. I know that would mean us coping without enough staff for another fourteen days, but she does have kids to consider.'

'Fair enough.' Jo took his grey beanie from his jacket pocket and dragged it over his head. 'We're good to go in here for tomorrow, Maddie. You okay if I head off? I want to pop in on Mum.'

'Absolutely. I hope she's feeling a bit more herself today. Thanks for coming in on your day off.'

'No problem. I'll be back in a couple of hours to collect Sara anyway. I'll talk to Michael about Jem's café group idea while I'm there, and report back.'

Jo was surprised to find his mum sitting in the garden with Billy. Side by side, they were propped on a large garden bench, surrounded by cushions, their legs covered in a fleecy throw.

On seeing him approach, Michael called out, 'Jo, good to see you. We thought we'd make the most of the late summer sunshine before autumn truly hits.'

'Fabulous idea, Michael. Mum loves being outside. We'd be out in the garden at home in all weathers.' Jo was delighted to see a calm serenity on his mum's face.

'Billy's been telling us about the chickens he used to keep.'

'Cool.' Jo sat on the nearest bench to his mum. 'I had no idea you had chickens, Billy.'

'Clucked like all hell they did, boy.'

'I bet.' Jo smiled. 'My friend Sara considered keeping chickens to provide eggs for her B & B.'

The old man looked up, his eyes sharp as he blurted, 'Tell her not to wash the eggs. Just wipe them.'

'Really? Why's that?'

'Eggs is porous. Any muck on the outside will wash inside if you put them underwater. Best to wipe 'em.'

'Well, I never knew that.' Michael's eyebrows rose. 'Did you keep chickens for long, Billy?'

'After the war. Mum had been a land girl. She liked them. Kept me awake squawking they did.'

Jo watched his mum as she beamed at Billy. He wasn't sure if she was taking in what was being said or not. 'You like a nice fresh egg, don't you, Mum?'

'Eggs?' Iris turned to face her son. 'Oh, Jo… hello. Not seen you for ages.'

After they'd got Billy and Iris safely back inside, Michael signalled that Jo should join him in the small office he shared with his fellow carers. 'Her tumble seems to have set your mum back a bit. I've called the doctor to come and take another look at her today. I'm hoping it's just shock after the fall, but she's been making more mistakes with her speech, and the dementia appears a little more pronounced.'

'She only fell on Saturday – surely she's just shaken up?'

'She's never forgotten that you've been when your last visit was so recent before. Sure, she'll forget if it's been a week – but overnight – that's new.'

Jo exhaled slowly. 'This would have happened anyway though, wouldn't it?'

'In time.' Michael opened Iris's medical notes. 'The lack of stimulation from outside sources hasn't helped. And now she's fallen her confidence has been knocked. She'll be less comfortable moving around on her own. I want to keep her on her feet as much as I can, but there's only me and Carol between four people, as well as the guests the other members of staff care for, and...'

Raising a palm to show he understood, Jo said, 'And that's a lot of them compared to two of you.' He sighed. 'You will let me know what the doctor says.'

'Of course.'

Jo hesitated, no longer sure if he wanted to act on the idea for the memory café, but knowing that if he didn't at least attempt to do something to improve the contact for the patients of Charlton Lodge he'd never forgive himself. 'I had an idea about some stimulus for the residents here.'

'Go on.'

'Actually, it was my friend Jem's idea. As you know I run the new café at The Potting Shed and we wondered – if you think it's feasible – whether an occasional trip to the garden centre, for a cuppa and a change of scene, might be a good idea for your residents?'

Michael beamed. 'It's an excellent idea. Do you mean for a memory café or just a trip out?'

'I think a memory café, although I need to research what that actually means a bit more.'

'The easiest way to think of it, is a set time to meet in a café, where the guests can relax, and – if the mood is right – a theme is discussed that might prompt memories – shoes, pets, flowers and what have you. It's always the most everyday objects that trigger thoughts of the past.'

'I see.' Jo played the thin grey wool of his beanie through his hands. 'Do you think Mum would be up to such trips?'

'Oh yes! And Billy would love it.'

'I was thinking about six at once – or is that too many staff wise your end?'

'I think maybe just three or four. I'll talk to Carol.'

Jo hesitated. 'Mum, she sometimes says odd things – out of nowhere. Do you think... I mean, is there a danger she might...'

Michael patted Jo on the shoulder. 'I can't promise she won't accidentally out you, but your friends are aware, are they not? And if anyone has a problem with it, then they have the problem not you – yes?'

'Thanks, Michael. I know it's silly to worry – but it's so jarring when I hear my former name. It sort of throws me off-kilter. I don't think about the time before I became me if I can help it. I was never *really* her, you see.'

'I can only imagine.' The carer smiled. 'Anyway, I'm the one who should be thanking you. A memory café so nearby would be rather fabulous.'

'Oh, hello.' Sara had been half listening out for a delivery van, due to bring in the cakes and top up juices for the next few days, when she'd heard the sound of tyres crossing the car park's gravel. Dropping what she was doing, she headed off to greet the courier, only to spot the good-looking man she had seen Ed with the day before, climbing out of his black Porsche.

'I'm afraid we're closed on Mondays, and Ed's not here if you're hoping to see him.'

'But you're here, so it's not all bad.' Tristan brushed his fringe from his eyes. 'Sara, wasn't it?'

'Um, yes.'

'I was hoping for a cup of Ditzy's amazing coffee.'

An unaccustomed blush burnished Sara's cheeks as The Potting Shed's visitor regarded her; his eyes focused on her face as if fascinated by what he saw. 'It's Jo's coffee – Ditzy just endorses it.'

Taken aback, Tristan's eyebrows rose. 'The guy behind the counter in the café?'

Not caring for the note of disbelief in Tristan's tone, Sara felt her cheeks get even warmer. 'As I said, we're closed. I'm afraid I'm going to have to ask you to leave – the gate is only open to let a delivery van in.'

Tristan slid nonchalantly back into his car. 'No problem. I'll see you soon, Sara. At least, I hope I will.'

Belle critically examined the salted caramel cake she'd made as a treat for the boys.

While delighted to get the job, she couldn't help feeling nervous about telling her children the news. It was one thing to say they were okay with her going back to work, but quite another to cope with it in practice.

She checked the time. There were two hours until she had to go and collect Milo. Belle gave a ragged groan and sat down rather heavily at the kitchen table. There was no doubt her joy at having got the job was tainted by concern for her younger son.

Milo had always been a little challenging. While generally quiet, kind and loving, it never took much to knock his confidence, his mood or his emotions. Milo was on the autistic spectrum. Belle helped him all she could. Kept his daily routine tight – collected him from school to avoid the hazards of him walking home alone from high school. His first few days at secondary school, back when Milo was eleven, had been full of less than kind comments from other children, who relished making fun of her son for being slower than them at completing any given task.

At primary school it had been much easier. Not only had Belle been a teaching assistant in the same place, but Milo had only had one teacher all day. She'd understood that Milo was perfectly capable of doing all the work he was given, he just needed another hour to do it compared to everyone else. Secondary school was a very different beast. It had taken almost the entire first school year for Milo to adjust to having a different teacher every hour, and by the time he had, it was the summer holiday, and he'd had to go back and adjust to another new set of different teachers. His second year had been no better.

She was grateful that the school was at least in agreement with her, that Milo was perfectly capable of doing the work required of him – and that he could have the extra time required in class providing he caught up in his own time. And that was the problem. There was always so much to catch up on, and he relied on her to be there to help him.

And now I'm not going to be there for the walk home or the first couple of hours of homework time.

Belle looked again at the cake she'd made. Milo's favourite. She already knew the gesture wouldn't be enough.

8

Ed raised his bottle of lager at the Zoom screen as if to salute the appointment of Maddie's latest recruit. 'That is fabulous news. Belle sounds great.'

'She is. Full of life.' Maddie chuckled. 'And anyone who can make Sabi do an about-turn of her opinions that fast has to have something special about them.'

'To be fair, your sister is far less snobby than she used to be.'

'Mostly.' Maddie smiled. 'I'm not sure I'm brave enough to stand up in a school and talk though.'

'You could do it – but I know what you mean. I wonder if it would be better for you to invite the local primary schools to have a trip to The Potting Shed instead. Maybe on a Monday, so there are no customers. You could do something like you do for the Little Acorns.'

'Maybe.'

'You'd feel more confident on home territory. Why not make a few enquiries and see what happens?'

'I'll add it to the list.' Maddie couldn't help sighing. 'I know Sabi doesn't want us to pay out for any other staff yet, but if we don't have more help soon, we're going to grind to a halt.'

Ed smiled and said, 'I had an idea about that. You know I'm no longer paying as much rent as I was in Exeter…'

Guessing what he was about to say before he'd said it,

Maddie was already shaking her head. 'No, Ed, you're not giving me the excess rent money so I can employ more staff. You might need that money for a better place in Bristol. I can't imagine you wanting to stay in a flatlet forever.'

'It's not so bad. I have a bedroom, lounge kitchen and a little bathroom – and I'm hardly there.' Ed raked a hand through his hair. 'The whole point of me taking this job was so we'd be better off, and you could invest in your business.'

Maddie sat back from the screen. 'But, Ed, I told you, you should only take the job because you wanted it – not for any other reason. You promised – you said...'

'I know what I said.' Ed took a swift glug of lager. 'And I meant it when I promised, but well, as I started saying the other day, this job – it's not really me. It would be much better if I knew that my being here was helping The Potting Shed – and therefore you – in some way.'

'Oh... Ed.'

'I miss you.' Ed's faded smile returned as Florrie popped up from where she'd been lying on the carpet. 'And you, Florrie – how could I not miss you too?'

Ruffling her dog's head, Maddie's heart contracted to see Ed so fed up. 'I hadn't realised you were finding the adjustment so tough.'

'Why would you? You're busy and happy. I didn't want to burden you – I still don't. I'll be fine. This is just a stepping stone on the way up, after all.' He quickly went on so that Maddie didn't feel the need to apologise further for something she wasn't responsible for. 'But, if I felt I was contributing to our future, it would make this bit feel more worthwhile.'

'You are wonderful – and I do miss you. Loads.' She put an arm around Florrie's neck. 'We both do, don't we, mutt?'

★

Maddie gave up on sleep as the early dawn light peeped through her bedroom curtains. Ed's slightly lost expression as he'd told her he missed her had worked itself into her dream during the fragments of sleep she'd managed to grab.

Hugging her duvet around herself as she sat up, Maddie spoke to the room at large. 'I'd love Ed to live here full-time again, but how can I ask that of him? The daily commute is exhausting. He tried it for a month, and it left him tired and grumpy.'

Dismissing the thought as selfish, Maddie swung her legs out of bed and tiptoed to the shower, hoping Florrie wouldn't wake up until she was dressed, mumbling to herself, 'He worked so hard to become a lawyer, I'm not going to stop him fulfilling his dreams. Anyway, as he said, the current situation is only while he climbs the ladder.'

And then what? A lifetime of him being in Bristol and me here?

Feeling increasingly dismal, Maddie flicked on the shower, determined to focus on positives as the water hit her shoulders. *At least Dark Skies begins again in October. That's only a month away. Ed will be home for an extra midweek stop every fortnight to go stargazing on Exmoor. I can't wait for that.*

Maddie had no sooner got back from taking Florrie for her first walk of the day when her mobile burst into life; Sabi's number flashed across the screen.

'Mads, I know the timing is awful, but I've a huge favour to ask.'

With her phone to her ear, Maddie unhooked Florrie's lead and hung it over her neck before retrieving the keys to the shop from her pocket. 'If I can, I will. So, what's the favour?'

'The thing is, Henry has been offered the chance to have a cruise – a business client of his owns a liner. Can you believe that!?'

'I suppose someone has to own them.' A furrow creased Maddie's forehead. 'And this is bad timing for us because?'

'Because…' Sabi paused, and Maddie realised her sister was having trouble getting the words out '…because I can go too. But the offer is instant – I mean, we'd have to go tomorrow.'

'Tomorrow!'

Immediately defensive, Sabi huffed, 'No need to sound so cross.'

Maddie unlocked the shop door and sat down on the nearest seat. 'I'm not cross, I'm in shock. Where is the cruise going?'

'Caribbean – and then the Med. I think.'

'Wow.' Maddie wasn't sure she wanted to ask the next question, but she did anyway. 'How long for?'

'Ah, well, that's the thing you see. It is something of a chance in a lifetime.'

'Sabs! Spit it out.'

'From tomorrow until mid-October – give or take a day or two.'

Maddie's reply came out as a squeak. 'That's almost two months.'

'Six to seven weeks, depending on connecting flights.' Sabi spoke more quickly. 'Jemima is fine with it, although – well, I did wonder if you'd collect her at the weekends – maybe let her stay at yours and…'

'Sabi! That's two huge favours! Running this place without you *and* niece sitting. I adore Jem, but when am I supposed to find time to collect her, sort her washing, help her with homework and all that?'

'Ed will help. I'm sure he'd do the school pick-up on Saturday and then taking her back on...'

'If you're about to say Monday morning – don't forget Ed goes back to Bristol on Sunday night.'

'I was going to say you could take her on Monday morning. The Potting Shed is closed on Mondays so...'

Maddie scrubbed a hand over her face, torn between not wanting to stop her sister having fun and wondering how she'd run the place with a set of hands down – even though those hands remained purely mud-free. 'But the weekend's the only time Ed is here. Our only alone time, Sabs.'

Maddie heard her sister tut down the line. 'Honestly, you've been together almost a year. Surely, you're past all that "need time alone together" stuff.'

'No, we aren't! How sad that you think there's a time limit on that!' Maddie sighed, knowing there was no way she'd be able to say no to her sister. 'You must go – as you say, it's the chance of a lifetime.'

Audibly relieved, Sabi regrouped, her tone less hectoring. 'Look, I know it's a pain – and bad timing when we're short-staffed – but...'

'Hang on, what about you? You've only just started your new business. You don't have your first client yet.'

'Oh, that'll be okay. What better place than a cruise ship full of wealthy people to tout for trade!'

Maddie sucked in her bottom lip. 'You must go. Call Jem's school. Let her and the staff know that either Ed, Jo or I will fetch her every Saturday lunchtime until your return. I want them to know who is coming, so they don't see her getting into a car with a stranger. Oh, also tell them that there may be the odd weekend we can't make – so you may have to pay for occasional extra nights' boarding. Deal?'

'Deal. You're the best sister ever.'

Maddie laughed. 'Just go and have a good time, make sure Henry packs enough socks – Ed never does.'

'You've only been away with Ed once – and that was only for one night.'

'Yup, and that one time he forgot his socks.'

Sabi laughed. 'Got it. Check Henry's sock situation.' She paused. 'I'll miss you.'

'You too. Now get going! You must have loads to do – oh, what about the house? Your plants will need watering.'

'It's okay, the chap next door is thick as thieves with Henry. He's going to keep an eye on the place for us.'

'Sabs, your nearest next-door neighbour is half a mile away.'

'He enjoys the walk.'

'Handy.' Maddie laughed again. 'Go on, get packing. Let me know when you're safely on the ship.'

'Will do – oh and Mads.'

'Yes?'

'Thank you.'

9

Sara spotted Tristan sitting in the corner of the room as soon as she walked through the Forget-Me-Not's doorway. Lounging back in the part-wicker, part-wooden seat, he was holding his mug of coffee in one hand and a mobile in the other.

'Toast and which cake today?' Jo slipped Sara's travel cup under the coffee machine's nozzle.

'Just the coffee, please.'

Jo's eyebrows arched in surprise. 'You sure? Not hungry?'

'No, I'm good.' Sara ignored the rumble in her stomach. As she examined the row of cakes longingly, the comments she'd overheard from Tristan about women and sugar two days before ran through her head. 'I just need coffee.'

'Fair enough.'

As Jo made her coffee, Sara asked, 'Have you discussed the dementia café idea more with Maddie yet?'

'Not since I spoke to Michael. I thought I'd let her get over Sabi's bombshell before I hit her with another time-consuming idea.'

'Fancy having a six-week holiday! Can you imagine?'

'Only in my wildest dreams.' Jo passed Sara her mid-morning drink. 'Even a sit-down during the working day is beyond my imagination.'

'You're not too busy in here yet.'

'Hopefully it'll stay that way. I'd like to be able to catch up on my stock orders at some point today, but it will depend on how hectic it gets.' Sara cast a quick glance over her shoulder to survey the café goers, only to be disconcerted by the realisation that she was actively seeking Tristan out.

Do I find him attractive, or am I just morbidly fascinated by his offhand manner?

Following Sara's eyeline, Jo asked, 'Do you know that guy? He was in with Ed on Sunday.'

'Not as such. Ed introduced him to me on Sunday. He's called Tristan – a university friend of Ed's. He came yesterday too. I had to turn him away.'

'He seems very…' Jo lowered his voice as he sought for the right word. There was something about the way Tristan was looking at Sara that made him uncomfortable.

'Relaxed?'

'Louche.'

Sara could feel Tristan's eyes on the back of her neck. 'You could well be right. I'm not sure Ed is that keen on him – although I could have read the situation wrong. Anyway, I'd best be getting on. Shout if you need help and Maddie can't get here.'

Sara didn't look back as she left the café. *Louche*. It wasn't often that Jo cast aspersions on someone he didn't know. *Why do I care anyway? Tristan's clearly a dinosaur.*

She took a sip of her coffee as she headed towards the herb greenhouse to restock the mint plants.

But an attractive dinosaur, nonetheless.

Surprised at herself, Sara pushed the greenhouse door open.

You only care because he's the first man ever to look at you as if you were attractive.

★

Maddie answered the phone without looking at the caller ID. 'The Potting Shed, how can I help you?'

'Mads?'

Immediately putting down the handful of ten-pence pieces she'd been counting, Maddie was surprised to hear from her sister. 'Sabi? Aren't you supposed to be on your way to the airport?'

'We are.'

Maddie thought she could hear a sniff. 'Sabs, are you alright? Sounds like you're crying.'

'Maybe – a bit.'

'What is it? Is the cruise off?'

'No it's – well, I know we're lucky that Jemima boards all week, but I've never left her this long and well... The Potting Shed. Will you cope? I was so excited I didn't stop to think – not *really* think. I've seriously dumped on you.'

'Oh, Sabs, we'll be okay, and I promise I'll take care of Jem. It's not like you're going forever.'

'But we can't even tell you when we're coming back. Information about the length of the trip is vague to say the least.'

'I'm sure you can leave at any port you like and head to the nearest airport when you've had enough and want to come home.'

The sound of a nose being blown came down the line before Sabi replied, 'Thanks, Maddie. Henry says I'm being silly, and that we can call every day to make sure you and Jemima are okay, but...'

'Henry's right.' Maddie tried not to think about how

much work Sabi not being there was already creating. 'Have fun, make the most of every day, and call whenever you like.'

'Thanks, sis. I'll make it up to you.'

'Just bring back a heap of duty-free and all will be forgiven!'

Belle hooked her rainbow-striped bag higher up her shoulder. Wandering into The Potting Shed's shop, she took her time to linger around each table of goods.

Niall had been delighted for her. He'd hugged her tight, wished her luck in her new job, and promised he'd keep an eye on his brother.

On the other hand, Milo had been tight-lipped. He'd glared at the cake she'd made for him for what had felt like an eternity, before issuing an abrupt statement. 'Bribing me with cake doesn't make abandoning me any better.'

As she stared at a collection of patterned flowerpots, tears threatened to gather at the corners of her eyes.

I knew he would be like that, so why did I bother?

Belle ran a single finger around the rim of a large blue pot. The echoing sound it made tingled through her touch.

We need the money – but if I'm going to spend my whole time stressed about Milo... Belle puffed out a sigh. *Buddha says we have to accept things and see how to turn what is happening into positivity.*

Belle headed towards the houseplants, muttering, 'Buddha didn't have a child with autism.'

The sound of activity from the café pulled Belle from her introspection. The double doors that separated it from the body of the shop were propped open. Chatter, a chink of cups

63

into saucers and a general happy hubbub met her ears as she listened, blind to the customers browsing around her.

I could work in there. I could be with those people all day. Belle hugged her handbag to her chest. *Milo must learn to adjust – if not now, when?*

'Are you alright, lass?'

Belle started as a man stepped in front of her.

'Sorry I didn't mean to make you jump.' He gave her a gentle smile. 'You looked a bit lost. Can I help you with anything?'

'Oh, umm. No, I...' Belle gave her head a little shake, sending her purple ringlets flying. She wondered where she'd seen him before. She was sure he hadn't been at The Potting Shed during her interview. 'It's okay. I was miles away.'

'Fabulous hair.' The words had barely left his mouth before he blurted out an apology. 'I'm so sorry, I didn't mean any offence.'

'Why on earth would I be offended by a nice compliment?' Belle patted her hair back in place.

'You never know whether saying something nice to a woman is allowed or not these days.' The older man gave a gentle grimace. 'It was a lot easier in my day – at least, I remember it being easier. Maybe I'm remembering it all wrong!'

'It still is your day!' Belle chuckled. 'I suspect it was easier a few years back, but you aren't that much older than me.'

'You flatter me.' He gestured towards the till. 'Forgive me, but I ought to get back to the counter in case a customer needs me.'

'Of course.' Belle tugged at a purple ringlet.

'I'm Ivan by the way. Pleased to meet you.'

'Belle.' She pushed her hair back over her shoulders. 'I don't suppose you've seen Miss Willand?'

'Maddie? Sure.' He pointed towards the café. 'She's helping Jo serve lunches. We are a bit short-staffed, hence me being here and not selling my cheese.' Ivan waved a hand towards the cooler and small till area beyond the café's doors. 'My friend Elspeth is helping me over there, so I can help here.'

'You're the cheese man!'

Ivan laughed. 'Sure am.'

'That's what my son calls you. I knew I'd seen you before but couldn't place you. The Exmoor Drifters' market that was here at Christmas.'

'Guilty as charged. I manage the market bookings, but I've given up my stall. I sell from here these days.'

'Your cheese is amazing.'

'Thank you.'

Belle felt rather awkward. 'I need to talk to Maddie – Miss Willand – but I don't want to interrupt if she's busy.'

'Would you like me to give her a message?'

'Yes... no. I ought to tell her in person. She's been so kind.' Seeing the puzzled expression on Ivan's face Belle elaborated. 'I was offered the job of café assistant yesterday, but sadly, I find I can't accept after all.'

'That's a real shame. You'd have been very welcome – and much needed. Talking of which, I'll have to leave you a moment.'

As Ivan walked towards the till to serve a young woman approaching the counter, Belle noticed he had a slight limp in his left leg – a problem with his knee, she guessed.

Not sure what to do, but knowing she couldn't simply loiter, Belle headed to the café. *I'll have a coffee, and then, when it's quieter, I'll break the bad news.*

'Oh, there is a God!'

Maddie looked so pleased to see her, that for a briefest second, Belle thought she was going to run around the counter and hug her.

'Jo, look, it's Belle.'

Peering up from where he was making a cappuccino, to see his new waitress among the queue of eagerly waiting diners, Jo – a sheen of perspiration at his temples – seemed as relieved to see her as Maddie did.

'At the risk of appearing unprofessional, and desperate, I don't suppose you'd be a total star, come and grab an apron, and clear some tables for us in exchange for a free coffee?'

Completely wrong-footed, Belle opened her mouth to say she'd help now, but wouldn't be coming back, when the woman in the queue before her said, 'Oh, do you work here now? How lovely? Bless, them, they're rushed off their feet!'

A quick scan of the few empty tables told their own story. Cups, saucers, teapots, and plates sat waiting to be cleared. When she'd walked from the bus stop to the car park, Belle had wondered where all the vehicles' occupants were, for not that many folks were wandering the garden centre. The answer was now starkly obvious: they were in here, and most of them were hungry.

Belle's handbag was already off her shoulder as she rushed to where Jo had shown her the clean aprons were kept.

Tying one on, she threw her bountiful hair back into a loose knot with the scrunchy she wore on her wrist like a bracelet and doused her hands with a hefty dose of sanitiser. Then, telling herself it would be easier to let Maddie and Jo down after she'd helped them – hoping they'd see that she wasn't someone who messed people around on purpose – Belle picked up a tray and began to stack dirty crockery.

Two minutes later, she was feeling her way around the unfamiliar kitchen, hoping like hell she could remember the instructions Jo had given her when it came to turning on the dishwasher, which was already full to exploding point. Relieved to hear the sound of water rushing into the machine, Belle dashed back into the fray, armed with a spray bottle of cleaner and a cloth.

It was only after she had cleaned three tables and cleared a fourth of the debris that could only have been left by a young child investigating how to eat a croissant for the first time, that Belle realised she was smiling. A further ten minutes later, having exchanged polite hellos with several complete strangers, each of which either congratulated her on her job or welcomed her to The Potting Shed family, Belle was more conflicted than ever.

If she took the job Milo might not ever forgive her, but if she didn't, then she'd be letting everyone here down, and she'd never be able to set foot in The Potting Shed again.

10

Sure that Tristan would come and find her as soon as he'd finished his cup of coffee, Sara was mildly put out that his blonde head had not poked around the greenhouse or the polytunnel she'd been working in.

Realising she only wanted him to find her to see if he'd pay her a compliment, Sara told herself off for being so shallow, and turned her attention back to the winter veg. But as she added a top-up of soil to the first in a long row of potato sacks, her mind strayed back to Tristan.

I'm only thinking about him because, even though I'm twenty-two, I've never had a boyfriend or the kind of attention that brings. She mumbled to herself as she plucked a stone from the nearest sack. 'The first handsome man who looks at me and I'm an attention junkie.'

Sara stood still for a second.

Do I really think he's handsome?

'It doesn't matter if he is or not, he said some awful things about women. He isn't worth the time of day.'

As her trowel scooped up another pile of compost a voice at the back of Sara's head whispered, *I bet he's fun though.*

'We can't thank you enough! Talk about in at the deep end!'

Jo took Belle's apron from her as he made her a coffee. 'You have really earned this.'

'Well, I...' Belle faltered, before her ingrained principles took over. 'Always happy to help someone in trouble.'

Maddie picked up an empty cake plate and moved it out of the counter's display case. 'You certainly did that. I thought it was busy in here last week, but this is something else.'

'Word is spreading.' Belle gestured to the coffee in her hand. 'Jo's fab coffee and the lovely attitude that surrounds The Potting Shed – it's a winning combination.'

'And now you!' Maddie admired the clean tables before her. 'Everyone took to you.'

'How can you know that?'

'Most of the people who had lunch her today are garden centre regulars. I've known many of them since I was a child. They'd have told me without a flicker of guilt if you weren't cut out for The Potting Shed.'

Belle felt the sand shifting beneath her feet. 'That's very kind of you, but...'

'But nothing!' Jo shook his head as Belle tried to pay for her coffee. 'I don't suppose you could do a few hours over lunchtime tomorrow? I know we said we'd spend time training you up once you officially started, but maybe it'll be more like training on the job now... if that's okay with you?'

'Ummm... I...' Belle swallowed. 'Tomorrow, yes – why not. Only over lunchtime though, as I haven't got things set up at home just yet.' She paused before adding, 'I wasn't expecting to get the job, let alone start so soon.'

Maddie gave her a reassuring smile. 'I'm so sorry, we really have dumped on you. You can still begin next Tuesday. It's totally fine.'

Belle was about to say that might be best, when she remembered she'd come to the Forget-Me-Not in the first place to say she wouldn't be working here after all. Confronted with Maddie and Jo's glowing faces, both red with happy exertion, she found she couldn't let them down.

'I could manage from ten until one tomorrow, if that would help.'

'Belle – you're wonderful!'

This time Maddie did give her a hug.

'So, this is where you've been hiding.'

Sara swung around, startled by the unexpected voice as she piled up tools in the only polytunnel closed to the public.

'Tristan! You can't come in here.'

'Why not?'

'Didn't you read the staff-only sign?'

'Yes, but I saw a friend in here, so I came in anyway.'

'A friend?'

'Sure. You?'

'You don't even know me!' Sara felt exasperated and flattered all at once; it was a strange, but not unpleasant sensation.

'You know my name and that I'm Ed's friend from university, so that's the next best thing.'

'Hardly!' Sara continued to stack her tools away.

'Tell me about yourself then. That'll make you my friend and the staff-only sign can be ignored forever onwards.' Tristan sat on a wobbly wooden stool, his elbows on the potting bench before him. 'I'm agog with interest.'

'I don't believe that for a minute.'

He winked as he said, 'What sort of barrister would I be if I lied?'

'Barrister? Not a solicitor like Ed?' Sara could feel her heart beating faster as she kept her back to Tristan, her hands wiping mud from her shovel.

'Ed could have been a High Court judge by now. He was the best at uni – no doubt about that – but the boy's gone all mud and wellies.'

Propping her shovel up against the other tools, Sara spoke firmly as her pulse returned to a more normal pace. 'Ed's a great lawyer. He helped Maddie save this place. We wouldn't be here talking if it wasn't for Ed.'

'Then I owe Ed a great deal.'

'Oh.' Feeling an intense blush spread over her face, Sara realised she'd intended to defend Ed's decision to work outside of London, but somehow Tristan had used what she'd said to make a complimentary remark about her.

'Would you like to go out for a drink?'

'What?'

'A drink. That stuff they put in glasses in pubs and customers guzzle by the pint or litre.'

What is it about this man? One minute I'm flattered, the next he is annoying as hell. 'I'm perfectly aware of what a drink is thank you. And I don't like being teased.'

Holding his hands up in surrender, Tristan nodded solemnly. 'Point taken. I apologise. So, a drink – in a pub – this evening?'

'You're serious, aren't you?'

'Always.'

Sara couldn't help smiling. 'And now you've lied to me – despite being a barrister.'

'Guilty as charged. I'm often frivolous rather than serious.'
Tristan jumped off his stool. 'So, how about I make it up to
you later? Drink and dinner? Appleby Inn? Eight o'clock?'

'I don't think so.'

'Whyever not?'

'For one, I have work to do.'

'And for two?'

'Jo and I always take a walk in the evenings.'

Tristan didn't bother to hide his surprise. 'The odd bloke in
the café?'

'He's not in the least bit odd!'

'But you're not *with* him – are you? You can't be!'

Sara's smile dissolved. 'I think I'd like you to leave now.'

Backtracking, Tristan spoke fast. 'Sorry, Sara. I'm always
doing that – my mouth fires off without thinking. Ask Ed,
he'll tell you I'm a horror for it. My mother says it's a defence
mechanism thing. Not that that's any excuse.' He took a short
breath. 'I'm sure Jo is a lovely guy. I didn't intend… I was just
surprised because you're so gorgeous, and he's…'

'My best friend!' Sara pointed to the door. 'I have work to
do here and then work to do at home, so if you wouldn't mind
leaving me to get on with it?'

'Best friend – not boyfriend?' he persisted.

'None of your business.'

'I only…' Brushing a hand through his hair, Tristan stood
up.

'Goodbye, Tristan.'

As he lifted the flap of the polytunnel, ready to leave, he
turned. 'I didn't mean any offence.'

'So you said.'

'Come on, come out with me tonight. It'll not take you a minute to drive over to Appleby from here.'

'And what makes you think I live around here?' Sara went back to work. 'If you'll excuse me, I must get on.'

It wasn't until Tristan's footsteps had faded away that Sara's shoulders started to shake. *I can't believe I stood up for myself.*

Two deep breaths later and her mind unhelpfully added a contrary thought. *But if you'd gone with him, at least you'd have discovered what it's like to go on a date.*

Zipping her fleece up to her chin, Maddie inhaled a lungful of crisp evening air. While summer hadn't yet given up on Devon, she was sure she could detect the taste of autumn in the air. Sitting at a picnic bench in the bluebell garden, she watched Florrie and Sheba, Ivan's dog, exploring the interesting scents to be found along the fence that divided the Willands' land from the neighbouring farm.

While the older dog took her time, Florrie dashed around her like a whirlwind. Relentlessly patient as ever, Sheba gave her canine friend a polite sniff, and a placated Florrie dashed off, before the whole cycle began again.

Spotting Ivan, Elspeth and Jo heading in her direction, Maddie couldn't help noting that Ivan, despite only being in his mid-fifties, walked rather slower than he used to; the arthritis in his knees was always stiffer by the end of the day. Elspeth, meanwhile, a woman who had an air of perennial youth about her, despite being in her eighties, tapped easily along beside him, her walking stick a resented companion.

Maddie felt a rush of affection for Jo, who neither hurried nor coaxed his friends forward, keeping pace with them both.

'Beautiful evening, Maddie.' Elspeth seated herself at the picnic table, her back regally straight. 'And a fun day. I hadn't realised how much I missed talking to the great British public.'

'I'm so grateful you could take over the cheese for me today.' Ivan sat himself down next to her. 'And judging from the empty state of my fridge, you sold well for me.'

'Nothing to do with me. I just sat there, and the customers came.'

Jo smiled. 'Talking of customers, the café did well today. In fact, now that Sabi has trusted me with the scary financial app she uses to keep track of things in the café, I can tell you that we've increased trade every single day since we opened. If we go on like this, then we are going to need more than one extra waitress by Christmas.'

Glad that Jo had agreed to keep an eye on the café's money side of things while Sabi was away, Maddie said, 'I was sure there was a market for tea and coffee at a garden centre – well, you proved that Jo, with your fabulous coffee van – but I hadn't imagined things would take off so fast.'

'The position of The Potting Shed is good. We're so near the M5, Taunton, Exeter and the link road to Barnstaple – not to mention the route to Cornwall.' Ivan waved a hand in the direction of the road beyond the shop. 'That's an advantage even before we factor in the actual food and coffee.'

'Thank you.' Maddie looked around at her friends. 'And to all of you for staying on after work. Don't worry, I won't keep you long. I know Sara needs your help back at Hawthorn, Jo.'

'Don't worry, there's only one couple staying in the B & B bit the moment, and they're very self-sufficient. Sara messaged me when she got home after her shift – they'd left a note saying they'll be out until late.'

'Well please thank Sara again for me anyway. It was very kind of her to come in yesterday and Sunday, even though they aren't official working days for her.' Maddie opened the pad she had with her. 'This is just a quick meeting to work out how we will run the place without Sabi here to do her part-time shop hours.'

Elspeth raised a hand. 'Ivan and I were talking as we closed up. I'm happy to come in and help a few times a week. I can't come full-time I'm afraid – too much of my own work to do. Not to mention I'm as old as Methuselah and conk out earlier and earlier every day.'

Maddie smiled. 'A few hours, as and when you can, would be wonderful. But you must not overdo it, nor must you let us interfere with the production of your home-made beauty products. Your *Bee Lucky* range is very popular here.'

'Let's say I'll pop by every other lunchtime for a couple of hours.'

'Fabulous.' Ivan too raised a hand. 'Talking of popping by, did I see Belle helping in the café at lunchtime?'

'I hadn't realised you'd met Belle yet.' Jo grinned. 'She was fabulous. We'd have never got through without her today.'

Surprised to find himself feeling hot as he spoke, Ivan mumbled, 'We met in the shop when she was looking for you, Maddie. She had a message.'

'Message?' Maddie frowned. 'She never gave me a message. Did she say anything to you, Jo?'

'No. I just assumed she was coming in for a coffee to see how the place ran before starting work – and got more than she bargained for.'

Maddie chewed the end of her pencil. 'I'll ask her about it tomorrow.'

'Tomorrow?' Ivan sat up a little straighter.

'Officially she isn't in until Tuesday, but we're so busy Belle's coming to help and do a little TTT training tomorrow lunchtime.'

'TTT?' Elspeth asked.

'Tables, till and toilets.'

'Oh, fun.'

'It's got to be done.' Maddie laughed. 'Now, Jo – could you ask Sara if she'd mind occasionally doing the main till if we get really busy? I meant to ask her before she headed home at four, but life overtook me. I have no problem if she doesn't want to – I can always catch up on the gardening after hours, but the till has to be manned nine to five.'

'I'm sure she'd be fine with that, but yes, I'll ask her tonight.' Jo looked around at his friends. 'I spoke to Michael at the care home. Would you like to hear about that now, or later?'

'Good a time as any.' Maddie readied her pen over her notepad.

'Well, it would take some logistical thinking through, but he's up for a dementia café.'

Maddie was about to say she thought it was a wonderful idea, but Elspeth got in first.

'That is a brilliant idea. Back in the day – long before you two were born – I was a care worker.'

'Seriously?' Jo's eyebrows rose.

'Oh yes.' Ivan nodded. 'Elspeth was fabulous. Her charges loved her.'

Patting her friend's hand, Elspeth gave a regal dip of her head. 'I gave up as I could no longer stand the poor treatment of staff and patients alike that my employer was happy to live with. As long as the money came in, he cared not two hoots. It broke my heart to leave if I'm honest. It was soon after that that I set up *Bee Lucky*.'

Maddie looked at her friend with renewed respect. 'If we did this, would you be willing to help out as an extra pair of hands and someone for our guests to talk to?'

'Of course – but think this through properly. This isn't as simple as inviting a group of pensioners for coffee and cake. These are human beings who've slowly had their identity robbed from them – from the inside out.'

'Understood.' Maddie twisted round to face Jo. 'Perhaps a meeting with your mother's carer would be a good idea first; but in principle, I'm game.'

'I'll sort that,' Jo said, adding, 'Let's not forget it was Jem's idea.'

Ivan smiled. 'Good kid that.'

'Oh, she is,' Maddie responded with a smile of her own. 'That brings me on to another thing. I need to collect her every Saturday lunchtime from school while Sabi and Henry are away. I'm rather hoping Ed will do that, but while she's here, she'll need looking after. She's too young to officially work here, but...'

Jo brushed the worry away with a wave of his hand. 'Fear not, we'll all keep an eye on her.'

11

The aromatic sizzle of bacon cooking told Sara that Jo had beaten her to the kitchen. She knew he'd already have prepped the food for her guests, having studied the breakfast request form they'd left on the kitchen table the night before.

He's a good kind person and not in the least bit odd.

Tristan's words had invaded her sleep. As had his request to take her out.

Should I have gone? I might never have another chance to go on a proper date.

Opening the front door of the house, Sara propped it ajar to let some air into the tiled hallway, before heading along a short corridor to the kitchen.

Walking with Jo was nice last night. I got to hear all about Maddie's plans and how his mum's doing, and about the dementia café idea. I'd have missed all that if I'd gone out with Tristan. Sara peered up at the ceiling as the sound of her B & B guests moving around upstairs got louder. *Our routine here is nice. Why would I want any more than that? Should I want something more, something... else? But Tristan would expect sex – I don't do sex, so, what's the point?*

Walking into her kitchen, Sara smiled as Jo waved the spatula he'd been using to turn the bacon in her direction.

'Sandwich to fuel the day?'

'Why not.' Checking that the guests hadn't made it down to the breakfast room yet, Sara grabbed a freshly baked loaf of bread. 'Thanks, Jo.'

Jo is a wonderful caring person, and I love him dearly. But is he just my best friend – or could he ever be something more? It certainly looked that way to Tristan, didn't it, so maybe…?

The number of emails in her inbox took Maddie by surprise, until she realised that four of the eight were from local schools. Having followed Belle's suggestion of inviting small groups of primary school children to visit, Maddie had quickly forgotten all about it in the face of the demands of her daily life.

Tempted to ignore them, Maddie told herself not to be so rude, and opened one email after the other, convinced they'd all say thanks, but no thanks.

They'd all said yes.

'Oh my God. If I'd known Sabi was about to take off, I'd never have emailed them all, Dad, and…' She broke off and looked around her kitchen, which had once been a bedroom. Everywhere she went within her home, and around the garden centre, she could picture her father.

Maddie addressed the fern on the windowsill, her long-time guru. 'He would be proud of what we are doing – I think.'

Very proud. Tony wanted this to be a place that welcomed the whole community.

Maddie brushed some dust from the fern's leaves, wishing Ed was there to talk to. He'd looked so tired when they'd spoken via Zoom last night, that she hadn't wanted to ruin their limited conversation time with her moans and groans.

'I'm offering the chance for the local schools to visit not to make me feel good, or even for Dad, really. This is payback to a community that helped The Potting Shed keep going – still helps it keep going.' Maddie spoke sternly to both herself and the fern as she focused on her laptop screen.

'I'll say that each school is welcome to attend, but due to staff shortages, it won't be until the next school term.'

Working quickly, Maddie was glad she hadn't been forced to say no to any of the schools, having been the one to offer the service in the first place.

Nibbling the edge of her breakfast toast, she turned her attention to a pile of Little Acorns paperwork.

'What do you think, Florrie, should we make the next session the one where we pick the blueberries and spinach they planted in the spring, ready to make Jem's blueberry and spinach smoothies – or does the spinach need another week in the ground?'

Taking Florrie's tail wagging as confirmation, Maddie scribbled down *Buy ingredients for smoothies* before dropping her pen with a clatter. 'Oh hell – I've just thought, Flo – how can Ed and I disappear to run the kids' club and leave just Jo and Belle to run the café on a Saturday afternoon?! All the parents are bound to go into the Forget-Me-Not – on top of our regulars. If custom keeps increasing like Jo said it has been...'

Closing her eyes, Maddie found herself wishing all over again that Ed were there. Opening her eyes, she checked the time. 'Seven-thirty. I could call him I suppose. He'd be up – probably in the shower.'

Florrie nudged Maddie's knee. 'Okay, so you're ready for a walk, and I suppose I ought to leave Ed to get ready for the day in peace. He'll only worry about me if I bother him, and he has enough work to do. I shouldn't be bothering about having too many customers anyway! There's no such thing as too many!' Getting up, Maddie grabbed her toast with one hand, and the lead with the other. 'Come on then, hound, let's see what interesting smells await you today.'

Ivan knew he was watching out for Belle. He wasn't ready to dwell on why. An in-depth conversation with Sheba the previous evening hadn't helped in the way his one-sided chats with his faithful companion normally did. She had been particularly unhelpful in discerning why Belle's visit to The Potting Shed had remained at the forefront of his mind for the past twenty-four hours. Or rather, her smile had – and her amazing purple hair…

Glad of a customer to distract him, Ivan was explaining the best way to keep the truckle of vintage Cheddar from drying out once the wax was removed, when he spotted Belle come in through the door.

She's beautiful.

The thought threw him so much that for a split second he forgot he was about to wrap some cheese for a customer. Forcing himself to concentrate, Ivan was aware he was flicking his eyes in Belle's direction at embarrassingly regular intervals.

Once the customer had gone on his way, Ivan cleaned the serving counter, making himself keep his eyes on the job.

You like her because she's a friendly person. You are always drawn to friendly people.

'Hello, Ivan.'

Ivan's head shot up far too fast. 'Oh, Belle. I didn't see you there.'

Idiot – she's bound to have seen you looking at her. 'I hear you were the hero of the hour yesterday.'

'Hardly.'

She looks tired. 'Well, hero of the lunch hour then. Back for more?'

'Yes.' Belle hooked her handbag up on her shoulder even though it didn't need adjusting.

'Are you alright, lass? Forgive me, but that radiant smile seems a bit low wattage this morning.' *What did I say that for?*

Surprised by Ivan's words, Belle answered quickly, 'Just new job nerves.'

'From what I hear, there's no need for those. Jo and Maddie were singing your praises at the staff meeting last night.'

'You have evening staff meetings?' Belle sounded more alarmed than she meant to.

'Not often – usually these things are informal over a cuppa as we work, but with Sabi leaving for a month or two, Maddie is struggling to cover all bases.'

Belle lowered her eyes to the array of cheeses in Ivan's glass-fronted fridge. 'Things are really difficult staff wise then?'

'It's not that long since The Potting Shed expanded to its present form, and Maddie and Sabi have strict policies on expenditure, so we are running on only a few staff. I think a student or two might be needed for weekends soon, but it's not my place to say.'

'Right.'

'Are you sure you're okay? Yesterday you hinted that you might not be taking the job here after all.'

'It's my younger son, Milo – he hasn't taken well to me getting a job.' Belle abruptly clamped her lips closed, before mumbling, 'I'm so sorry! I'm not sure why I told you that. My family issues aren't your problem.'

'Not at all. You're part of the team now and we look out for each other. Is there anything I can...'

Ivan's words trailed into thin air as Belle blurted, 'I'd better go. Jo will be waiting for me,' before her soft purple trainers all but jogged their way to the café's open doors.

'Ed!' Maddie's delight was clear as her boyfriend's face appeared on her mobile phone screen. 'This is a lovely surprise.'

'Hi, love. If you're too busy to chat, I'll call back.'

'As long as you don't mind me propping the phone up so I can keep weeding around the blueberries as we talk...'

'Not at all. So does you getting some gardening done mean it's less insane there today, and that Jem's smoothies are about to be made?'

'Yes, to both. Fancy helping with smoothie making this Saturday?'

'Can't wait. Love the Little Acorns Club.'

'The kids certainly love you.' Maddie winced as her thumb caught a sharp twig. Sucking it she asked, 'So what did I do to deserve seeing you at eleven o'clock in the morning?'

'I was meeting a client out of the office. I'm sneaking a coffee on the way back. Thought it would taste nicer if I spoke to you while I drank it.' He lowered his voice. 'It isn't a patch on Jo's.'

Examining Ed's surroundings more closely, Maddie could see that he was sitting in a stainless-steel-themed café. 'Not like you to bunk off?'

'My client meeting finished early. I thought I'd write up my notes here, before heading back.'

Maddie smiled. 'I'm glad you called. I miss you.'

'You do?'

Ed sounded so surprised that Maddie felt a jolt of disquiet. You didn't think I wasn't missing you – did you?'

'I guess not. Too much time on my own. I start to overthink a bit too much if I'm not careful.'

Maddie blew him a kiss. 'I thought overthinking was my specialist skill.'

'You don't have the monopoly.'

Putting down the handful of small weeds she'd gathered, Maddie gave Ed her full attention. 'You really aren't settling there, are you?'

12

Belle could feel the knowledge that she was going to let her new friends down weighing on her shoulders. A pressure made no easier by the fact she was enjoying her work. It might have been lacking in glamour, but as she listened to Jo's gentle instructions on how to enter a transaction into the till, she experienced a surge of joy at learning something new.

And Ivan likes you.

The idea made her pulse beat a little faster. *He has kind eyes.* She could tell he was a gentle man. *And a gentleman.* Belle stepped back from the till so Jo could show her how to issue a refund and refocused her attention on what he was doing.

'This isn't something you should have to do very often, so don't be afraid to ask for help if it comes up and you can't remember what to do.' Jo pressed a few buttons in quick succession.

'I'll be certain to ask.' Belle knew she was only half taking the information in. *What's the point if you aren't going to stay?*

'It's just a case of practice.' Jo glanced up at the wall clock. 'It's almost quarter past eleven; I ought to make sure there are enough pre-made sandwiches left, so we don't have to make them as we take orders over lunch.'

'I can do that.' Wanting to be on her own for a few minutes, Belle asked, 'Is it a case of simply counting what's left, or do I need to input the stock on a tablet thingy?'

Impressed, Jo smiled as he answered, 'Just see how many of each we have left – if there's less than four of anything, we'll make up more.'

'No problem.'

Sara found Maddie in the last polytunnel, sitting at the potting bench, her planning sheet for the Little Acorns Club was laid out in front of her.

'Maddie?'

'Oh, hello, Sara. Does Jo need me?'

'He needs one of us. Do you want me to go? You look busy.'

Maddie waved the blank piece of paper. 'You're very kind, but what I actually am is distracted and time-wasting. How about you?'

'I'm fine. Ivan is keeping an eye on both tills for a minute – would you rather come and man the shop while I serve coffee, or the other way round?'

Maddie gathered her paperwork together and banged it into shape. 'I'll do the till if that's okay. I'm miles behind with this lot, I can do it between customers.'

'That's not like you.'

'It isn't, is it.' The echo of Ed's confession ran through Maddie's head. *I hate it.* 'I've been thinking rather than doing.'

'Thinking needs doing too sometimes.' Sara pulled a face, knowing she'd also lost precious work minutes to overspeculation lately. 'I'll go and get my hands scrubbed, then I'll head to the café.'

'Much appreciated.' Maddie climbed off her stool.

'You okay?'

'Sure. Missing Sabi – organising was her area.'

'You're good at it too.'

'Thanks, Sara.' An image of Ed's mournfully apologetic expression flashed through her head. 'But that's not the same as enjoying it, is it?'

Ivan had lost count of how many times he'd told himself off for peering towards the café in the hope of glimpsing Belle as she passed by on the other side of the doors. The arrival of customers to his cheese counter merely punctuated his surveillance, rather than diverted him from it.

She's too young for you.

You haven't been interested in a woman in over twenty years.

Sheba would be jealous.

As his mind took him around in circles, he reminded himself that just because he found himself drawn to her, it didn't mean she would feel equally intrigued.

It's arrogant to even consider she might be interested.

She can't be older than thirty-two. She has at least one child... you have a nice quiet life. You don't need anyone – especially anyone with complications.

She doesn't wear a wedding ring. So does that mean...?

Ivan groaned and hopped off his chair, adjusted the white button-up coat he wore when he was serving cheese, and took off his hygiene hat. Moving away from the counter, he checked there were no customers heading his way, before walking towards Maddie.

I might be a million years too old for Belle, but perhaps I can at least help her?

'Maddie, do you have a minute?'

Tucking her legs up under her chin, Maddie wrapped her arms around her legs as she perched on a bench in the bluebell garden, listening to the calming silence coating her domain. Now that everyone had gone home the place had a special sort of quiet – a peace that normally helped her relax. Today, however, her head spun. The entire working day had disappeared in a blur of activity. She hadn't had time to eat, let alone think properly about Ed's confession that he wasn't enjoying being in Bristol or about Ivan's concerns over Belle.

Shuffling forwards from where she'd been sniffing the gravel, Florrie came and rested her head on the bench seat, her big brown eyes blinking up at her owner.

Stroking her dog's warm fur, Maddie turned towards her home – once a four-bedroom house, now a flat upstairs, and the garden centre's main shop downstairs. Off to her side ran six polytunnels, a greenhouse for herbs, and beyond those, the car park, where once Jo's orange coffee camper van had sat. Now, due to sheer hard work, her friends' support, a massive bank loan, and the loyalty of her regular customers, there was a café.

'It's all happened so fast. To think, we might have lost this place.'

Florrie gave a suitably sympathetic whimper.

'If we had, I wouldn't have you, my darling, would I?'

Clearly alarmed at this notion, Florrie jumped onto the

bench, knocking Maddie's knees to the ground, so she could flop herself down on her lap.

'Flo!' Maddie started to laugh. Laughter that unexpectedly turned to tears. 'Oh, Flo…' Hugging the collie tightly she sobbed into her neck. 'I have no idea why I'm crying – we might be short-staffed, but it's working.'

Staying obligingly still for once, even though her owner was making her fur damp, Florrie let out a whimper of solidarity, before yawning so widely that Maddie found herself joining in.

'They do say yawning is contagious.' Giving Florrie another hug, she gently pushed her dog to one side. 'I have to admit, I'm dog-tired – like you apparently!'

Wiping her eyes with the backs of her hands, Maddie blew out a steadying breath. 'Okay, so that's my moment's self-indulgence done. Let's think. Ed is not warming to his new job, Ivan is worried about Belle, and I don't have enough staff. So, what do I do?'

Florrie leapt off the bench and wandered towards the gate that led into the woods.

'That's your solution, is it? Another walk in the woods.' Levering herself off the bench, Maddie smiled as Florrie's tail wagged faster. 'Come on then, pooch – let's walk our problems away.'

Following Florrie around their usual woodland route, Maddie allowed her mind to consider the café's staffing situation.

By the time she'd been free enough to leave the counter and go to talk to Belle she had gone. 'I didn't even have the chance to thank her for coming in. She must think me very ungrateful.'

Florrie gave her mistress such an old-fashioned look, that Maddie couldn't help but laugh. 'Okay, maybe she doesn't, but if Ivan's suspicions are correct, and Belle is feeling conflicted between working for us and upsetting her child, I really must speak to her. If I have to readvertise her job, then the sooner I do it, the better.'

Slipping her hand into her pocket, Maddie's palm rested on her mobile phone. 'I should call her – shouldn't I, Florrie.'

Letting go of her phone again, Maddie kept walking. 'But she hasn't said anything, and she has helped so much. Jo can't say enough good things about her. Belle is a smart woman; she wouldn't just turn up and help if it was causing trouble at home.'

Deciding it would be better to talk to Belle in person, Maddie vowed to find time to speak to her the following day – assuming she came in at half past ten as promised. Having made that decision, Maddie turned her mind to the other problem. *What can I do to cheer up Ed?*

Maddie stared up at the sky. The clouds that had shrouded the sky all afternoon had cleared, leaving an open, mottled blue and grey canvas; a hinterland between day and night.

'Dark Skies!' Maddie opened her phone. 'Florrie, I need to speak to Ivan.'

13

*S*ara *would have told me if she'd found someone –*
wouldn't she?

Jo found Sara tending the parsnip plants.

As he entered the polytunnel, his arms were held out
straight before him, a huge bouquet of flowers resting across
both of them. He had what he hoped was a carefully neutral
expression on his face. 'These came for you.'

'Me? Hardly.'

'For *you*. A van from Big in Gardens just dropped them off.'

'From BIG!' Sara was horrified. 'From Maddie's main
competitor – from the people who…?'

'Almost conned her land from her. Yes.' Jo shoved the flowers
into her arms, indicating the small white envelope stuck to the
outside of their cellophane covering. It had *SARAH* written
across its front. 'Even aside from where they came from,
it's rather thoughtless to send flowers grown elsewhere to
someone in a garden centre.'

'They *can't* be for me.'

'No one else is called Sara here.'

You weren't going to sound put out – you were going to be
calm! Jo found his good intentions dissolving as pink infused
Sara's cheeks.

'Who are they from?'

'I don't know.' Even has she replied, Sara began to suspect

who might have sent them. *Tristan?* He would have seen it as an act of generosity, when in fact the nature of the gift couldn't have been more jarring. 'I've never been sent flowers before.'

'Well, now you have.' Turning to leave, Jo muttered, 'I need to open the café. It's almost ten.'

Increasingly alarmed by his offhand manner, Sara called out, 'Jo, it's just flowers, it doesn't mean…'

But Jo had gone. He hadn't looked back.

Sara glared at the gigantic bunch of flowers, largely made up of lilies. Tied with a red ribbon, they looked incongruous lying on the soil amongst the rows of vegetable sacks and fruit canes. Even before she read what Tristan had written on the inside of the gift card, Sara knew three things.

First: she had to get the flowers as far away from her as possible. *Assuming they are from Tristan, he wasn't to know that I'm allergic to the scent and touch of lilies.*

Second: this was more about the sender showing off his spending power than a wish to give pleasure to the recipient.

Third: that Jo knew she was allergic to lilies, but he'd still left her in a semi-enclosed space with them.

'Well, it can't be that he was jealous. Jo's just not like that, and anyway, why would he be…? But…' pulling on her gardening gloves, Sara tugged the envelope off the bouquet '… he wasn't just cross – his pride was hurt.'

Her heart thudded like a hammer in her chest as, moving into the open air, she undid the envelope. 'It must be from Tristan. Nobody else I know would send me lilies from BIG!'

It was.

A little something to say sorry for upsetting you. Tris x

Sara mumbled to herself, 'The first time someone gives me flowers and I can't touch them, Jo is put out, *and* they come from The Potting Shed's chief competition. How typical is that!'

Taking a deep breath, she went back inside, picked up the wrapped flowers and, holding them as far away from herself as possible, she tottered out of the tunnel, not entirely sure where she was going.

Deciding that the far polytunnel was the only logical place, she moved quickly – dumping them onto the potting bench before retreating fast. Only once she was outside did she notice a few early morning customers giving her odd looks.

I suppose I must have looked like someone dealing with an unexploded bomb.

Taking a few lungsful of non-lily-scented air, Sara was grateful to find that, despite a sharp pricking in her eyes, her encounter with her plant nemesis had been largely symptom-free.

'Tristan's not a stupid man – what's more he is business-savvy. If he'd stopped to think, he'd never have sent flowers from a rival business – so, that means he *didn't* stop to think.' Sara sighed as she confided in the nearest raspberry cane. 'He probably never does. Not like Jo. Jo always thinks things through. At least… he usually does.'

It was only when she was back in the tunnel with the vegetables, that Sara was hit with a new and contradictory feeling of indignation.

Jo still had no right to be offhand with me. I didn't ask *Tristan to send me flowers. And anyway, why shouldn't he?*

★

93

Although nervous about her forthcoming conversation with Belle – or to be more exact – how to start it without sounding intrusive – Maddie was feeling a lot more positive than she had the evening before. Thanks to her thinking time with Florrie and a chat with Ivan, she had been able to call Ed armed with a reason for him to come home more often.

Ivan had recently given up running Exmoor's Dark Skies constellation-gazing group – and Ed had agreed to take over. Normally the group met every other Wednesday from October until January – spending from ten o'clock at night until midnight lying on the moorland, staring up the wonder of the night sky. It was a calming, grounding, and peaceful experience that Ed had introduced her to soon after they'd first met.

Having checked with Ivan, Maddie had been delighted when he told her there was no reason why the group couldn't recommence in September rather than October – although that early on they were likely to see a lot less of the night sky.

Ed had seized on her suggestion.

'You are fantastic. There I was, longing for October to come round so I had a reason to come home mid-week, and the answer was obvious. Start Dark Skies a month early. From next week even!'

'Ed.' Maddie had spoken softly, her smile wide at his delight. 'You don't need a reason to come home midweek. You can just come anyway.'

'I know. I didn't mean...'

'It's okay, I knew what you meant. And I know you were worn out commuting every day, but this way, you just do one extra commute per fortnight. We'd get a bit of time together too. Something we might appreciate even more while Sabi's away.'

'Ah yes.' Ed's eyes had gleamed suggestively over the Zoom screen. 'Time without Jem in the house. Very precious.'

'Very.'

'And it's Friday tomorrow; I've already booked my train back.'

Enjoying the playful tone in Ed's voice, but not wanting to get distracted, Maddie had returned them to the point. 'So, will you contact everyone then? Dark Skies the Ed Tate way is coming!'

Now, having been up extra early to water all of the polytunnels, cash up, and run a hoover over the main shop before anyone else arrived, Maddie headed towards the last polytunnel, intending to catch her breath while Jo, Sara and Ivan ran the ship during the first, and usually quietest, hour of the day.

'I'm going to set the benches up ready for the Little Acorns group meeting on Saturday,' Maddie told the pile of trowels by the door of the polytunnel as she walked into the stuffy atmosphere, hooking back the plastic door cover, to let some air in. 'Then I'll try to catch Belle as she arrives – although goodness knows what I'll actually say to her and...' Maddie stopped talking. 'I can smell... lilies...'

Her eyes fell on a large bouquet of flowers. For a split second she felt a glow of pleasure, sure that Ed must have sent them. A moment later, she spotted the sticker attached to the cellophane and her eyes narrowed.

'Lilies from *BIG*.' Maddie flipped the bouquet over in search of an envelope, but the bunch of flowers appeared to be anonymous. 'Ed?'

A wave of disappointment hit Maddie, and she gave herself a shake. 'You shouldn't have assumed they were for you. Anyway, Ed knows I'm not keen on cut flowers. He'd buy me chocolates or take me out. And even if he did buy flowers he'd *never* order them from BIG.'

Maddie sat on a stool near the doorway. 'They could be for Sara or Belle, but not from someone who knows this place's history... unless someone has taken to sending Jo or Ivan flowers or... Jo...'

Maddie laid her notepad and pen down on the potting bench. 'Could they be *from* Jo for his mum? He's just left them here to pick up and take them to the care home later?'

She brushed away the notion. Even though they didn't grow flowers for bouquets at The Potting Shed, no way anyone who worked for Maddie would purchase lilies from BIG. 'My friends would rather buy flowers from a garage forecourt than BIG! They must have been delivered here in error, and someone has hidden them here out of the way. It *has* to be a mistake. What do you think, Dad?'

I think you should stop worrying about it and put them in some water.

Jo's conscience wouldn't leave him alone. He knew he shouldn't have been so short with Sara, yet he couldn't shift the feeling of betrayal that niggled at his brain.

She said she hadn't expected the flowers.

Picturing her reaction, Jo realised she'd been telling the truth, and guilt nudged away all other thoughts.

I've left her in an enclosed space with lilies.

Flicking on the milk steamer, letting the machine gurgle into a sharp burst of life, before he poured almost boiling milk into a metal jug, ready to make a hot chocolate for his latest customer. Appraising the small queue, Jo silently hoped that no one else would join it.

I need to get back to Sara, apologise for being offhand, and get those flowers as far away from her as possible.

A family of three came through the café doorway. As the mother lifted her young son up so he could choose a cake from the counter, Jo inwardly cursed. He couldn't just leave, and until Belle arrived, he couldn't take a five-minute break.

If Sara comes out in a rash or gets an asthma attack, it'll be my fault.

A feeling of panic overtook him as he took payment for the hot chocolate. As Jo took the next order, he apologised to his customer and fired off a quick text.

Maddie – could you help?

With a quick thank you, a promise to be as fast as possible, and saying he'd explain when he got back, Jo thrust his apron at Maddie as soon as she came in and dashed out of the café.

I shoved the flowers into her arms, knowing they could make her ill.

Jo found himself picturing Sara doubled over on the floor of the polytunnel, struggling for breath. His fast walk became a sprint as he wove between customers.

I jumped to conclusions. Those flowers could be from anyone – a friend, a grateful client – anyone. I would know if she was seeing someone because she tells me everything.

Jo came to an abrupt halt as he saw Sara tending a collection of fruit canes near the entrance to the tunnel.

She wasn't on her own.

A man with cropped blonde hair and a floppy fringe was standing close to her. The man he'd seen with Ed in the café. *Tristan*. He was standing with Sara – and they were deep in conversation.

Oh. I see. Turning on his heel, Jo stormed off. 'She doesn't tell me everything then.'

14

'**D**id you like them?'

'It was a kind thought.' Taking a step away from her visitor, Sara turned back to where she had been tweaking dead leaves from the fruit canes. 'What are you doing here on a Thursday?'

'Seeing you, of course.' Tristan leant against a bench that held pots of vegetable seedlings.

Determined to appear professional, Sara kept on working. 'You're on holiday in Devon. There are so many places to visit, why on earth would you want to come here?'

'I refer you to my previous answer.' His eyes twinkled. 'Normally, when I send a woman flowers, I get a warmer welcome afterwards.'

'Normally' implies he sends flowers to a lot of women.

'I'm *not* most women.' Sara didn't look at Tristan. His confidence unsettled her. Worse, it intrigued her – as did the fact that she didn't feel her usual shyness with him, but something between fascination and annoyance. 'Nor was I fishing for compliments.'

'I wasn't offering any. I simply wanted to apologise for my earlier behaviour, and to see if you had changed your mind about coming out with me. You're the most unusual woman I've ever met.'

'You know nothing about me.' Sara was surprised at the

determination in her voice. 'That's obvious if you think buying me overpriced flowers from a direct competitor might win me over.'

Tristan folded his arms, unexpectedly on the defensive. 'I *thought* I was doing something nice.'

'No, you were throwing money at a situation to either make me feel guilty about turning you down, or to bribe me into changing my mind.' Sara peered out of the polytunnel, making sure that there were no customers heading their way. 'And, while we're on the subject, you should know that I'm allergic to lilies.' Not daring to meet his eyes, she kept talking. 'I suggest you drive to the coast. Make the most of the late summer sunshine before it disappears.'

'I'm not keen on beaches – not unless it's the Caribbean of course.'

'Of course.' Sara felt offended on behalf of Devon's coastline.

'Obviously, if I'd known about your allergy, I'd never have chosen lilies. I would still have sent flowers though.' Tristan took a step further into the tunnel. 'But you're right, you aren't most women. I've never known any female not to be impressed by the idea of Caribbean beaches or posh flowers before.'

'Then you can't have met many women.'

He let out an elongated sigh. 'I've met loads. Just ask Ed! I'm even here with…'

Sara's head shot up. 'Are you telling me that you're here, on holiday, with a woman? And yet you sent *me* flowers and you are here – without her – chatting me up. What is *wrong* with you?'

'A great deal apparently. Gemma – my now *former* girlfriend – rattled off an incredibly long list of faults only yesterday.'

Sara knew her kind heart was in danger of doing an about-turn as she tried not to feel sorry for Tristan. He appeared bewildered at the accusations his ex had laid at his door. *Try to stay cross – he started chatting you up* before *Gemma broke up with him.*

'It seems I am "impossible to live with". Gemma's left me and taken a train back to London.'

Sara examined the raspberry cane before her. 'Maybe you should go back too – try and sort it out.'

'Nothing to sort.' Tristan brushed his fringe from his eyes. 'I've recently realised I've been chasing the wrong thing.'

'And the wrong thing is, what?'

'Looks over intelligence. An image rather than a person.'

Sucking in her bottom lip, Sara moved along to the next plant. 'That's something positive; realising how shallow your expectations were.'

'I don't suppose...' Tristan shook his head. 'No, it doesn't matter.'

'Suppose what?' Sara was surprised to see an expression of doubt on his face.

'You won't want to.'

'Oh, for heaven's sake, Tristan! Something else women do not like is men who play games! Just spit it out.'

'I wondered if you'd let me talk to you about it. About Gemma. About how I can stop making the same mistakes with women again and again.'

'Talk as a friend?' Sara lifted her eyes from her work. 'No strings and no more flowers from rival businesses?'

'Promise.'

'Okay.' A tingle of unease crept down Sara's spine as her instinctive kindness took over. 'But we aren't going *out* out.

I have too much to do. You can join me for lunch here if you don't mind waiting until one o'clock.'

'I was hoping for more of a dinner out and a bottle or two of wine, but if lunch is all that's on offer...'

'It is, yes.'

'Then, yes, that's great.' Tristan's demeanour instantly transformed. His smile was back in his eyes and, before Sara knew what was happening, she found herself engulfed in a giant hug. 'Thanks, Sara.'

'No problem – and by the way – there is no "h" on the end of my name.'

Maddie saw Belle slip into the café just as she pointed a customer in the direction of the shop's seed rack. 'If it's vegetable patch crops you're after, then September is the perfect time to plant broad beans. The seeds are over there. Pop them in now, and you'll get a decent early harvest next spring and summer. Otherwise, spinach, onions and garlic are good to plant now as well – they'll give you a good crop come late spring.'

'Broad beans and onions work for me.' The elderly gentleman happily headed towards the seeds and baskets of onion sets, as Maddie called after him.

'Just let me know if you need more help.'

Resigning herself to having missed the chance to talk to Belle before her on-the-job training started, Maddie thought perhaps it was just as well.

What on earth would I have said anyway? I'd have either been interfering or, worse, I'd make Belle think that Ivan had betrayed a confidence. I'll leave it. If she wants to back out of working here, it's down to her to tell me.

★

Apart from having to stop her inspection and tidying of the canes to direct a customer to where the trolleys were kept, Sara hadn't moved from the fruit polytunnel all morning.

However, rather than mentally planning the week ahead at Hawthorn Park as she normally would while tending the plants, Sara had swung first from guilt about having arranged to meet a man for lunch during the working day, then to an inexplicable unease at that man not being Jo, and finally to righteous indignation. *Why shouldn't I meet a potential new friend for lunch if I want to, male, female, or anything else? I don't need Jo's permission!*

Nonetheless, a sense of disloyalty hung over Sara as she decided to make sure she got to the café well before Tristan. That way she could ensure she was already sitting with her lunch, so that he would have to join her, rather than arrive *with* her.

That way, I won't be so obviously 'with' him.

Her plan was shattered at exactly ten to one, when a blonde head poked around the doorway to the polytunnel. 'Ready?'

'Almost.' Sara stifled a groan. 'I assumed I'd meet you in there. If you go ahead, I'll…'

'No way.' Tristan folded his arms. 'You are being taken to lunch. If I'm going to bend your ear about my troubles, then the least I can do is escort you to your toast and cake.'

What is it they say about the best laid plans?

Belle regarded the cappuccino she'd just made with mild

shock. The leaf pattern she'd created with the milk was perfect. 'I can't believe I did that.'

'You're a natural.' Jo carried the beverage to the customer awaiting her drink. 'It took me months of playing in my old coffee van to get that right, and you come along and do it in a day.'

'I'm not so sure. Could've been beginner's luck.' Belle wiped a cloth over the coffee machine's nozzle, cleaning it ready for the next customer, as Jo turned to see that Ivan was the next in line.

'Hello there. Grabbing a cuppa before the rush?'

'Absolutely.' Ivan waved his reusable cup. 'Americano please, and a slice of that delicious-looking carrot cake.'

Jo nodded. 'Can you deal with Ivan's order, Belle? I'll clear some tables.'

'Sure.' Belle was surprised. 'But wouldn't you rather I did that?'

'It's a simple black coffee, and you need to practise with the machine.' Jo smiled reassuringly. 'Don't worry, you've got this.'

Passing Belle his cup, Ivan lowered his voice. 'Forgive me asking, but are you okay, lass? I don't like the idea of you being torn between working here and your son's happiness.'

Trying to concentrate on what she was supposed to do when it came to making an Americano, and not on Ivan's kind enquiry, Belle placed an espresso cup under the coffee nozzle and left it squirting out strong black coffee while she held his cup under the boiling water dispenser. Filling it three-quarters full, she poured the contents of the espresso cup on top, before screwing on the lid to the travel mug. 'Here you go.'

'Perfect. Smells heavenly.'

'Carrot cake, wasn't it?'

'It was.' Ivan shuffled along the counter to the till. 'I hope you didn't mind me asking. I wasn't meaning to pry.'

Belle concentrated on balancing the cake between the tongs pinchers as she slid it deftly into a recyclable box. 'It's kind of you to ask.'

'So then, what is it that's bothering you?' he prompted, as he took his wallet from the inside pocket of his old green bodywarmer.

'I already love working here. But I love my son more. I need to talk to Maddie – but there's never a good moment. She's always helping someone, or I'm serving or...'

'I know what you mean.' Ivan lowered his voice further. 'You can tell me to butt out if you like, but if there is a message you'd like me to relay to Maddie, now is the moment. Elspeth has just arrived, so I'll be relieving Maddie in the shop shortly, so that she can have lunch, walk Florrie and Sheba and, if time allows, work on the books for an hour.'

'But I ought to be the one...'

Ivan gently held up his hand. 'Maybe, but you'll need to dash off after your shift, and there's only a million-to-one chance that Maddie will be free then.'

Belle pushed a hand through her hair, sending her ringlets bouncing across her shoulders. 'True. Okay, it's like this...'

15

Sara's whole body stiffened as Tristan placed a hand on the small of her back while they waited in the café queue. Not looking at Jo, she took a step away from Tristan, making a play of examining the food on offer. 'I can recommend the spicy parsnip soup. Not only is it made using our own veg, but it's created here, in the Forget-Me-Not.'

'Really, who by?'

'Jo of course.'

'The same chap who creates the coffee blends endorsed by Ditzy?'

'No need to sound so disbelieving. Jo's an excellent cook.' Sara knew guilt was making her sound much sharper than she intended. 'Sorry, you must think I'm all spikes.'

'My own little hedgehog.' Tristan winked.

'I'm not *your* own anything.'

'Message received.'

Sara gestured Tristan forwards to where Jo waited at the till. Her stomach was awash with anxious tension. 'Go on, it's your turn.'

'*Our* turn. I'm paying – what do you want?'

'I'll get mine. You get…'

'*I'm* paying.' Tristan's expression implied arguing was pointless. 'Now, was it soup or toast and cake?'

Meekly, Sara said, 'Soup please. And a latte.'

Tristan turned to Jo. 'Make that two soups, one of your fabulous coffees – a mocha – and a latte for the lady.'

'Certainly. *Sir*.'

Sara glanced sharply at Jo as he addressed Tristan, noting that his barely civil tone had also made Belle's eyebrows rise as she prepared two bowls of soup. Not knowing what to say, Sara went to find a table as far away from the counter as possible.

'Ivan was very nice about it – and I understand why Belle asked him to pass on the message – officially this time, what with me being so busy – but...' Maddie threw her hands into the air. 'I'm so sorry to throw this at you when you're still unpacking, but what do you think I should do, Sabi?'

'Nothing.' Sabi pulled a sympathetic face at her sister over the WhatsApp video connection. 'I know that sounds harsh, but Belle applied for the job, fully aware of what the hours were. What exactly did Ivan say?'

'That Belle's youngest son has a form of autism, which is kept in check by routine. He has reacted badly to the idea of her not being there to collect him from school and help him with his homework.'

'Right.' Sabi took a pile of immaculately folded blouses from her suitcase and laid them on the bed. 'So the decision is hers.' She pulled a face. 'It's shame none of the other candidates were good enough to replace her.'

'I wondered if I should offer to change her hours to fit the lad's routine.'

'Because you are a nice person – but how would that affect things at The Potting Shed? Would Jo manage if the hours were changed? We decided on ten until four because that's when we need help the most.'

Maddie couldn't argue. 'You're right, but I was thinking, we could say until three-thirty p.m. Easier for Belle and thirty minutes cheaper a day for us.'

Pursing her lips, Sabi picked up her phone and turned, giving Maddie a view of an amazing suite.

'Wow – that's an incredible room.'

Sabi smiled sheepishly. 'It is rather – this is the five-star accommodation. They really want to impress Henry.'

'No need to sound embarrassed – I'm pleased for you.'

'But I feel so guilty. I'm here and you're there dealing with things I ought to be helping with.'

Feeling equally bad for interrupting her sister's holiday with her problems, Maddie was about to apologise when Sabi spoke again.

'Let's be practical, when does school finish?'

'Three-fifteen.'

'Then, to *really* help Belle's situation, she would need a three o'clock finish, if not two-thirty.'

Maddie sighed 'Yeah, I know – but that's just not practical. I know she's more or less working those hours while she helps us out now, but when she leaves today, we'll still need her – if that makes sense. I'll see if I can talk to Jo about it. Maybe we can come up with a compromise.

'Belle is a lovely person, and I know she has already proved she's willing to put herself out for you by starting instantly to help over lunchtimes, and...'

'And you like her,' Maddie butted in.

'Much to my surprise, yes, I do, but if Belle has a problem, she should have come to you – not got Ivan to do it for her.'

'I think Ivan has a soft spot for her.'

Sabi sat on the edge of the bed in surprise. 'Ivan does? Wow. I always saw him as a one-girl man – and that girl is a black Lab called Sheba.'

The carrot cake had almost gone and, as Jo ran an eye over the counter, he saw they were getting low on teacakes and caramel slices.

During every one of the days that the Forget-Me-Not Café had been open, he'd experienced a surge of pleasure from watching the stock he supplied being happily devoured. Today, however, he was simply going through the motions. The end of the day couldn't come soon enough.

And then what? I go home with Sara and say what?

Lifting his gaze from where he was setting out a new batch of tray bakes, Jo watched Sara and Tristan. They were leaning towards each other, as if they were sharing confidences.

How has she got to know him so fast?

A feeling Jo didn't like stirred inside him. *Envy?*

Jo stopped moving and checked the queue. The worst of the lunchtime rush had passed, and there was only one old lady waiting, who he knew from previous experience would have tea and a slice of cake.

Why would I envy Tristan? He appears to be everything I dislike in a person.

'Belle, I need to nip to my van to fetch a sack of coffee. Will you be okay for ten minutes.'

'Sure.' Belle picked up an empty teapot. 'But don't be long – just in case!'

I envy him because he's spending time with Sara.

★

Jo mumbled angrily to himself as he stamped across the car park, 'I should be the one who sends her flowers.'

But I don't think like that – it has never occurred to me to send her flowers.

Jo knew he avoided talking about personal things – often not even realising they needed talking about in the first place; preferring that he and Sara got on with living, rather than discussing how they lived. But suddenly, Jo was angry with himself – angry that it had taken seeing her with someone Ed had said was untrustworthy to wake him up to the fact he'd been coasting.

I know I love her, but I can't give her – or anyone – a conventional relationship. She knows that! I thought we'd developed some sort of bond that went beyond friendship... We take long evening walks together, watch movies in front of the fire and share takeaways. That's like dating... isn't it?

Increasingly restless, Jo felt he had to act.

Who am I kidding? Everything Sara and I do is friend stuff. We live together, but in separate rooms because I'm not able to... and she didn't seem to be bothered about that side of things.

Kicking at a random piece of gravel, Jo let out a heavy sigh. *Maybe I got that wrong, or maybe she has changed her mind... maybe Tristan will change her mind for her?*

Jo mumbled to himself, 'I have to talk to Sara; to protect her from Tristan if nothing else – but how?'

Wishing he could talk to his mum, Jo fired off a text to Ed instead.

Your old uni mate's having lunch with Sara – should I be worried for her?

No sooner had he pressed send, than Jo felt disloyal to Sara. *I should have spoken to her, not Ed.*

Disguising his heavy grunt of annoyance with the noise of sliding open the side of his camper van, Jo hauled out a sack of coffee beans he wouldn't need until the weekend and dashed back to the café.

'I ought to go. I was only going to bring you up to date on Sabi's cruise, but it's so easy to keep chatting.' Maddie checked her watch before returning her attention to Ed on her phone screen. 'Belle gets a fifteen-minute break for a sit-down and a cuppa at two, and it's almost half-one already. I want to make sure Ivan and Elspeth are alright before I head to the café.'

'When does Jo get his break?'

'He doesn't seem to bother. He can have one, but he says he'd rather keep going. I suppose he's used to not stopping, having run a coffee van on his own for years.'

'Ah.'

Maddie's eyes narrowed. 'That was a loaded, "Ah". Are you about to go all legal on me, Ed?'

'Afraid so. Legally Jo has to have a break. Even if it is just two ten-minute stops spread across the day.'

'But if he's happy...'

'I know, love, but think about it – if there was an accident towards the end of the day, say on a Sunday, at the end of a busy week – and it was caused by Jo being tired... Say he spilt some boiling soup on a customer or scalded himself on the coffee machine. If it came out that he'd been working solidly without a break...'

'Okay, I get it.' Maddie flicked the end of her ponytail over her shoulder. 'I'll tell him, although how I'll cover his break too, I've no idea.'

'Sorry, love.'

'Not your fault, and I'd rather have advice than a lawsuit.'

'Talking of law, I ought to go and...' Ed picked up his phone to check the time '...oh, I've had a text from Jo.

'Really? From the café?'

'Yes – ah.'

'You're ahhing again.' Maddie immediately felt anxious.

Ed pushed a hand through his hair. 'Tristan is back.'

'Your former uni associate?'

'He's in the café having lunch with Sara.'

Maddie's eyebrows rose. 'Like a date lunch?'

'I expect that's what Tristan thinks it is. I can't speak for Sara.'

'The lilies!'

'Pardon?'

'I found a bouquet of flowers in the staff polytunnel. They'd come from BIG. I couldn't work out who would buy them. No one on the staff for sure, but...'

'That's vintage Tristan!' Ed scowled. 'I told him what you'd gone through to build this place up. How proud I was of you for overcoming BIG's underhanded attempts to take your land. He *knew* BIG was a rival and yet he *still* got flowers from them!'

Maddie frowned. 'We don't know for sure they were from him.'

'I'd bet on it. Jo's text is asking if he should be worried that Sara and Tris are having lunch together. My initial reaction is, yes.'

'You won't say that though, will you?'

'Wouldn't be helpful, would it.' Ed shrugged. 'But what should I say?'

'I've absolutely no idea. Where's Sabi when we need her?'

'Would she know the right thing to say?'

'I doubt it, but she'd say it anyway!'

16

The aroma of fresh baking filled Belle's kitchen as she hummed her way through the washing up. It hadn't taken her long to decide what flavour of cake to make as a thank you. She wanted something that had a British tradition, but with a hint of Jamaican fun.

Her first instinct had been to make a cake just for Ivan, to thank him for intervening with Maddie, but the thought of giving him a gift made her feel awkward – so a cake for everyone was the answer.

Keeping an eye on the clock over the kitchen door, to make sure she neither over nor under cooked the two pineapple upside-down cakes within the oven, Belle considered the shot of rum she'd added to the mix of the one for The Potting Shed. Perhaps it hadn't been such a wise move to add alcohol to a cake she assumed would be eaten during the working day? But it was too late now so she shoved the thought firmly aside.

I have a job and I love it.

Hearing footsteps thundering down the stairs, Belle stilled herself. Habit saw her mentally prepare herself. Following advice she'd received from a therapist she'd consulted after her son's initial autism diagnosis; she took three long slow breaths and, placing her palms flat on the old melamine kitchen table, she closed her eyes and counted backwards from ten to one. Her eyes flew open as her son arrived at the kitchen door.

'Hi, love, how's it going?'

Milo crashed down at the table, slamming his maths homework book out in front of him. 'Rubbish.'

'You need help, or just company while you work?'

'You don't help me anymore. You prefer your café.'

Belle counted to ten again. Forwards this time. 'Actually, I have good news about that. Do you deserve some good news do you think, Milo?'

Milo fiddled with the pencil he held. 'Maybe.'

Sitting next to her son, Belle spoke with the firm, kind tone she adopted whenever he was in danger of slipping into full-on angry mode. 'Milo, sweetheart, you can't stay cross with me forever for having to have a job. You're a clever boy – you know I need to work so we have a future.'

'Maybe.'

'Okay. So, can we do a deal?'

'A deal?'

Belle nodded. 'Yes, a deal – a compromise – like adults make all the time.'

'I'm only thirteen.'

'You're an intelligent boy who will be a man before you know it. Do we have a deal?'

'Okay.' Milo pointed towards the oven. 'Is there a cake for tea?'

'Yes. I have baked two, one for us and one as a present for my new friends at work.'

Milo stiffened. 'If you have new friends at the café, then you won't need me and...'

Having predicted his response, Belle carefully kept her expression neutral. 'Are you about to say that I can't have friends who aren't you and Niall?'

'Well...'

'Milo, I love you and your brother more than any other human beings on the whole planet, but I need friends too. Everyone needs friends.'

'I don't have...'

'You *do* have friends Milo, so please don't tell me you don't.'

'Sorry, Mum.'

'You have Darryl and Suzie and Tim – all in your class – all very nice and fun to be with – yes?'

'Yes. Okay.'

'Good. I don't want you feeling sorry for yourself because it's my turn to have new friends.'

Milo was quiet for a second, before he waved at the oven. 'What sort of cake have you made for me?' Seeing his mum's disapproving expression, he quickly said, 'I mean us.'

'Pineapple upside-down cake.'

'Ohhh... I love that.'

'I know you do. Why do you think I made it?'

''Cos, I like it lots.' Contrite, Milo glared down at his maths book. 'You said you had some good news.'

'Maddie and Jo at the café have agreed that I can finish work at three-fifteen rather than four o'clock. That means you'll still have to walk home with your brother, but that I'll be back in time to help with your homework each day.'

'Oh.'

'Is that all you can say?' Belle's smile faltered.

'Yeah.' Milo opened his maths book and tapped his pencil against a sum. 'I'm stuck on this one, can you help me?'

Sara had never known Jo so quiet. He wasn't a noisy person

by nature, and a companionable silence wasn't unusual, but this silence didn't seem in the least bit comfortable or companionable.

At least we travelled home separately, so we didn't have an awkward silence on the journey.

Jo had gone to see his mum before returning to Hawthorn Park while Sara had come straight home, made sure their guests had left the key with one of the groundsmen on departure as arranged, and had warmed some beef stew for dinner.

Now, two hours later, sitting either side of the kitchen table, she and Jo were pushing their food around their plates rather than eating it.

It was Jo who eventually broke the fraught silence. 'What did you do with the lilies?'

'I threw them – literally – onto the bench in the last polytunnel. I've told Maddie she can have them – if she can stand having plants from BIG in her flat – or to throw them away if she can't.'

'Throw them away?' Jo lowered his fork to his plate of stew.

'Aside from the fact I'm allergic to lilies, I don't like extravagant, meaningless gestures. Tristan was just showing off his money.'

A twinge of guilt nudged at Jo. *Did I assume too much? Perhaps Sara was just being polite by having lunch with Tristan.* Unable to leave the subject alone, he said, 'You must have got to know him a little bit by now.'

'We've spoken a few times. You've seen us – it isn't a secret.' Sara swallowed a forkful of dinner. 'Jo, hasn't it occurred to you that I might need some friends who aren't you or Ed or Maddie, Ivan, Elspeth and Sabi?'

'Of course it has. I've often thought you needed a few more people in your life. You don't get a chance to meet many people apart from the B & B guests, and they don't really count.'

'But?'

Jo went back to his dinner. 'There's no but. Everyone needs friends.'

Sara knew he was struggling not to ask more questions about her lunchtime conversation. 'But not friends like Tristan?'

Jo put his fork down again. 'I'll admit I'm uneasy about him. And before you say it, I know I have no right to tell you who you have lunch with, but I can't help wanting to protect you.'

'You think I need protecting?'

'From the likes of Tristan Harvey, yes. Not just you, women in general.'

Not wanting their conversation to dissolve into a row, Sara backtracked a fraction. 'The flowers were an apology. He had been rather old-school with some of his comments about women, which I didn't care for. It may surprise you to know that Tristan has a conscience under that flash exterior.'

'It does surprise me.'

'I think it surprised him.' Sara gave a humourless laugh. 'Jo, I had lunch with Tristan because he needed someone to talk to. I suspect he'd have rather spoken to Ed, but he wasn't there.'

Wondering why he wouldn't let the matter go, Jo asked, 'Someone to speak to about what?'

'I wouldn't normally say, as it's breaking a confidence, but as you're the person I trust the most in the whole world...'

'Am I?'

'You know you are.' Sara saw how sad Jo's eyes were. 'What's the matter? Is it your mum? How was she today?

I meant to ask as soon as you got back, but things have been a bit...'

'Frosty?'

'Ice age.' Sara gave him a weak smile.

'My fault. Too much imagination versus too little common sense. Take no notice of me.' Jo picked his knife and fork up again and cut through a gravy-soaked dumpling. 'Mum's no worse. The bruising's going down. I spoke to Michael and Carol, told them that Maddie is good to go whenever they're ready to sort a café visit.'

'Excellent.' Glad to be off the topic of Tristan, Sara took a sip of wine. 'Did they suggest a particular day of the week or time of day as being best for them?'

'Afternoons. About three – after they've had a post-lunchtime nap – but before they become too tired to cope with the trip.'

'Makes sense.'

'I assumed Maddie would want to do Mondays, but Michael seems to think that being there when the café is open, with other customers around, would be better. There'd be more going on and more atmosphere for the quieter ones to soak up.'

'That makes sense too.' Sara took a bite from a gravy-soaked dumpling, chewing for a while before she said, 'I bet your mum will love it.'

'That's if she's one of the guests.'

Sara was surprised. 'But surely...'

'I hope she will be, but I ought not to assume...' Jo sighed. 'I've been assuming without thinking a bit too much today.'

Sara got up and went around to his side of the kitchen table. 'Daft man. You and your overthinking.'

Hugging her tight, Jo smiled. 'I care so much for you, you know.'

'I know, and I you.' Sara let go of him and returned to her meal. 'But caring for me should include trusting me to pick my own friends. Okay?'

'Okay.' Jo lifted his glass of wine and reached it forward, chinking it against Sara's glass. 'You were going to tell me what Tristan wanted to talk about.'

'He is – or rather was – in Devon with his girlfriend. She dumped him. He needed to talk. I expect, now that he's offloaded, he'll go back to London.'

'Really?'

'Really.' Sara grinned. 'I can't say I blame her for going. He seemed to be more concerned about his father's disappointment than actually upset himself. Gemma – the now ex-girlfriend – had met with his parents' approval; something it is, apparently, very hard to do. Sounds like his dad is rather controlling. Almost impossible to please.'

'What did you say to him?'

'That he should be with someone because he genuinely likes her, not just to please his family. In a nice way, obviously.'

'Good for you.' Shovelling up a huge forkful of beef stew, Jo felt his appetite return.

'I feel a bit sorry for him to be honest.'

Through a mouthful of dinner, Jo gave Sara a rueful smile. 'I'm sorry about going all overprotective. Blame Ed, he told me about Tristan's reputation with women and I was worried for you. I should've known you would have more sense. Besides, you're not his type. I feel so much better now I know you won't be seeing him again.'

Sara stared up at the ceiling. Everything had been normal

for a split second; now she was angry all over again. Glad they had no one in the B & B that night, she slowly got to her feet. 'I didn't say I wouldn't be seeing him again. I said he was leaving for London soon. And as to me not being his type, he's asked me out *three times*. So what makes you think I'm not his type? Am I not pretty enough or blonde enough or something? You're making a lot of assumptions!'

Jo opened his mouth to deny this, but he didn't have the chance, because Sara had left the room.

17

Maddie never failed to be amazed by how enlivened she felt when in the company of the Little Acorns. A group of six under-elevens, they came every other Saturday, full of fun, ready to learn about gardening, the environment and – most of all – impatient to get their hands dirty.

Noel, with his impish nature, was, by silent agreement between Maddie, Ed and Jem, the acknowledged handful of the group – but even he was on his best behaviour today. No one wanted to mess up the chance to enjoy the culmination of several months' hard work.

'Do we really get to pick the spinach and the blueberries ready to make Jem's special smoothies today?' Kayleigh asked shyly.

'Absolutely.' Maddie gestured towards her partner. 'Ed has got the permission letters from your parents, so you can all have a go at picking our crops – but please remember – blueberry plants are prickly in places. When it is your turn to pick some blueberries, listen to what Jem says, and let her help you. If you'd rather not pick the berries Jem will do it for you. Okay?'

A chorus of 'Okay, Maddie' filled the polytunnel.

'Right then. Three of you will go with Ed to pick some spinach leaves and three will come with Jem and me to collect some blueberries. Then we will swap. You'll have a go at picking everything.'

'When do we get to do the smoothie drinking?' Noel thrust his arm into the air halfway through asking his question.

'After everything has been washed and checked to make sure that we only use the best leaves and berries – isn't that right, Jem?'

'Yep. Then we will use my special smoothie recipe to make a fabulous drink.' Jemima clutched three of the recipe cards she had designed to sell in the shop. 'As a treat, Jo has said we can use the blenders in the café. He's even brought in some special straws for you all to drink through.'

'Cool.' Noel did a little hand punch from his stool. 'I can't wait to get slurping.'

Sara was in desperate need of a coffee, but the number of people browsing The Potting Shed's shop, baskets on their arms, prevented her from moving far from the till. Deciding it was probably just as well, she felt her eyes stray towards the café's entrance.

Jo hadn't said anything at breakfast beyond announcing he would see her later. She regretted walking out on him the evening before, but she'd been so cross. Just when she thought he'd understood that Tristan was simply someone she'd speak to while he was in Devon, Jo had acted like she wasn't attractive enough to deserve his attention.

You know Jo didn't mean to insult you.

Sara tried to deflect her mind by checking on the number of paper bags beneath the counter, but her thoughts refused to quieten.

I am perfectly entitled to be annoyed. Sara gave a silent sigh, knowing she could only keep out of his way for so long.

It was easy-ish this morning, because Jo starts at The Potting Shed two hours before me on a Saturday, but what about this evening? I don't want us to be at odds at home.

Saturday evenings were traditionally spent making up the guest rooms before indulging in a takeaway and a movie in front of the living room fire. Sara suspected that was the sort of evening that Tristan would turn his nose up at.

Or would it? Maybe I'm misjudging him – perhaps he'd like a cosy night in. Maybe we're all misjudging him?

Sara smiled as she thought about how she and Jo always made work fun. They'd laugh and chat together while sorting towels, linen and replacing the mini toiletries in the ensuite bathrooms.

Ever since Jo had given up living in a small static caravan in Tiverton, and moved into one of her spare rooms, he'd been involved in starting up and running her small Airbnb business.

I don't want to do that alone.

Seeing a customer heading her way, a basket full of bulbs to hand, Sara pushed her thoughts to the back of her mind and held up a large paper bag, ready to be filled.

Tristan watched the scene before him in disbelief.

The polytunnel where he'd found Sara working two days before, echoed with triumphant and delighted giggles. Two sets of young children were busy harvesting various crops. By the doorway he could see that a woman of about thirty, her brown hair tied in a tatty ponytail, hands held out, was coaxing her charges towards a fruit cane. Beyond her, he could see Ed on his knees, as three more children knelt or crouched around him, tugging at some green plants.

Between the two groups, an older child was moving around, helping where she was needed, her arms full of leaves or pots of berries, depending on the moment.

Moving fast, Tristan stepped away before Ed spotted him and – the thought made him shudder – asked him to help.

Sara's stomach gave a low rumble, and she checked her watch. There was an hour until she could have a short lunch break. By that time, Maddie and the children would have already trooped through to the café to make up their smoothies.

Forgetting her annoyance at Jo for a moment, Sara smiled as she pictured him helping the six children turn their crops into smoothies. Jo was always at his best when Jem was there – despite her being twelve and him being thirty-one, they had a friendship many would be envious of. A friendship that had been first forged over a mutual appreciation for smoothie drinks and was like that of an older brother and younger sister.

A lump formed in Sara's throat. Her love for Jo tugged at her heart, followed by a pang of sadness for him that he'd never have children, even though she thought he'd make a great father.

I need to talk to him. We haven't spoken about 'us' for ages. Whatever that is. The sudden realisation that Jo was feeling insecure and was handling it badly made Sara sigh harder.

Goodness knows what Tristan would say if I told him Jo was asexual as well as trans…

'Penny for them.' Tristan appeared in front of the counter, almost making Sara jump out of her skin.

'Tristan!'

'Actually, by the look on your face they may well be worth nearer a fiver than a penny. How about I swap your thoughts for a coffee and some toast? My turn to be as good a friend to you as you were to me, when you listened to me offload.'

18

Belle had dithered back and forth about whether she'd give Maddie the cake that was sitting in the large cool bag under her coat peg. She knew it would be perfect to eat – having had almost forty-eight hours for the rum to seep into the sponge, infusing the pineapple and sugar-glazed topping.

Her boys had eaten, in a mere three sittings, the alcohol-free version she'd made for them, so Belle was confident it would be okay. But now she'd brought the cake in, she was shy about handing it over – especially as she wanted Ivan and Maddie to receive it together.

You just want Ivan to know you can cook.

The thought had played on Belle's mind, on and off, ever since she'd first decided to do something to thank him for speaking to Maddie on her behalf.

Why do you feel the need to impress him? He's got to be twenty years older than you – and even if he wasn't, you do not have the sort of life that would work with a partner in it.

Fear of Milo's potentially hostile reaction to a having stranger in their midst – especially one who might give his mother more attention than him – filled Belle with sadness.

She checked the wall clock. Sara would be in for her coffee soon, which meant that Ivan would be in half an hour after that. The thought produced a slight quickening of Belle's pulse.

Taking a firm hold of her cleaning cloth, she gave an internal tut. *You're a single parent with responsibilities. Get a grip and clean some tables.*

She was scrubbing a table which, in her introspection, she'd forgotten she'd already cleaned, when she saw Jo approaching her.

'Can you help me while we have a lull?'

'Sure.' Belle dropped the cloth, flexing her back as she straightened up.

'The Little Acorns will be here soon. I've got a couple of blenders ready for them to blitz their treasure, but obviously I don't want the kids in the kitchen – too dangerous. We'll cordon off a section of the café. Could you pop these reserved signs on the four corner tables, please?' Jo gestured to the back of the café. 'Those ones should be perfect as they're as out of the way as it gets, and as they're near the wall, there are two plug sockets handy for the blenders too.'

'No problem.' Belle beamed. 'The Little Acorns group sounds so much fun.'

'They seem to love it, and my goodness, they've been patient little souls.' Jo smiled. 'Jem came up with her Grow a Smoothie idea when The Potting Shed was in the earliest stages of expansion. The kids have been waiting since spring to taste the smoothies they've grown.'

'That is so cute.' Belle took the reserved signs from Jo.

'They'll need some sugar and some milk as well. Jem has pre-prepared everything. It's all in the cupboard by the fridge.'

'Great.' Belle swept a hand through her ringlets. 'Apart from the blenders, what else can I bring out?'

'Six – no, make that nine – tall glasses. Maddie, Ed and Jem will want to sample the goods too. And I've got the kids some stripy paper straws.'

'Ice, in case they want ice cubes?'

'Of course! Good thinking. There are several trays in the freezer.' Jo paused. 'Actually, it might be an idea to put the cubes into a few basins first, otherwise there might be shards of ice flying all over the place as they try to extract them from the trays.'

Belle laughed. 'I remember when my boys first discovered ice cubes, they loved popping them from the trays more than putting them in their drinks. Honestly, I feared an eye might be lost!'

'That settles it then.' Jo took a step towards the counter as he saw some customers coming into the café. 'As soon as I've got a minute I'll decant the ice cubes – if you could sort the tables now, then hopefully we won't have to do a mad scramble when the kids arrive.'

'Good plan. You best get on.'

'Thanks, Belle, you're a star.'

As she walked towards the far side of the café, Belle's anxiety calmed. *Of course I can give these people a thank you present, and it doesn't matter who I give it too. The Potting Shed understands the power of thank you.*

Tristan was having an unwanted masterclass in learning how to be patient. He was nowhere near as good at it as the Little Acorns.

Having expected to find Sara among the plants, he'd been surprised to see her working at the main till. Suspecting the chances of her dropping tools and joining him for coffee unlikely, he'd tried his luck anyway. Sara first reminded Tristan that she wasn't at liberty to stop work whenever she felt like it, then followed up with the gentle suggestion that, if she'd appeared in the middle of a court case and asked him to come for a drink, he wouldn't have been able to drop everything and leave. Which was true, of course, but comparing their careers was *obviously* unfair. There was just no comparison. *My job is far more important than hers!*

The hour he'd waited until her break had dragged by. He had never understood the appeal of gardens. His apartment, on the fifth floor of a private building, complete with a manned reception to keep casual visitors at bay, had a small communal garden for those inclined to sit in the open air. He'd only been in it once, and that had been when he was showing off his home to his then girlfriend.

'Tristan, if you want to talk to me, I'd get chatting if I were you.' Sara took a bite from her toast and marmalade. 'I only have thirty minutes.'

'What?!' Tristan lowered his mug of coffee to the table. 'I've waited all morning for you. Then it took time to queue up, get food and sit down – so we only have...'

'Approximately twenty minutes, and you're wasting them moaning. I *told* you that you didn't have to hang around.' Sara lowered her voice as she recalled some of what Jo had said. 'I'm not some bimbo keenly waiting to snap up your every word.'

Tristan's bright blue eyes dulled as he held up his hands. 'Mea culpa.'

Sara took another bite of toast. 'What did you want to see me for anyway? I assumed you'd be hotfooting it back to London.'

'I don't just dump my woes on someone and disappear. That would be unforgivably rude – especially as you haven't yet allowed me to thank you properly. Besides, I thought you were the one who needed to talk this time. I said I'd listen, and I meant it. Friendship is supposed to work both ways, after all.' Tristan appeared so offended by the implication that he'd taken her for granted that Sara instantly regretted her sharp tone.

'I know. Sorry. I'm fine though.' She smiled. 'Anyway, you've already bought me flowers and lunch. Consider your apology accepted.'

'Flowers that – unbeknown to me – you're allergic to and were from a rival business! I need to apologise all over again. And as I've accidentally annoyed you already today, it had better be something special.'

Sara could feel Jo's eyes on her as she mumbled, 'You don't have to.'

'I *do* have to.' Tristan leant back in his seat, crossed his arms, and scrutinised her face.

Immediately self-conscious, Sara found herself lifting her hands to cover her face. 'What are you staring at me like that for?'

'I wasn't staring, I was savouring the view. You're beautiful.'

'Oh.' Flustered, Sara focused on her lunch plate.

Picking up his coffee, Tristan changed the subject. 'So, when was the last time you went on a date?'

'What?'

'You know – that thing men and women do when they want to get to know each other better.'

'Or men and men or women and...'

'Yes, that too.' Tristan flapped Sara's response away.

'I last went on a date... Well, to be honest – I've never been on a date.'

Tristan stared harder. 'Why on earth not?'

'No one's ever asked me.'

'But you're...'

'I'm what?' Sara was feeling more uncomfortable by the moment.

'I was going to say lovely, intelligent, fun and pretty.'

'Fun?' She laughed. 'How on earth would you know if I'm fun?'

He gave her a lopsided grin. 'I was taking a punt.'

'Were you now.' Sara picked up her cup of coffee.

'Care to come out and prove to me you're fun?'

'Tristan, I...' Sara's eyes flicked to Jo, who looked caught out as she saw him watching her.

Having caught Sara and Jo's silent exchange, Tristan leant forward. 'Sara, he's your friend, not your keeper.'

Sara opened her mouth to protest, but Tristan was still talking.

'I was merely suggesting that you and I go out for a meal and a laugh before I go back to London. What do you say?'

'A non-date date – as friends?'

'Precisely.' Tristan chinked his cup of coffee against Sara's mug. 'A date without the pressures of me trying it on and you wondering how to turn down my advances.'

Sara couldn't help but laugh. 'That's nuts.'

Tristan's eyes flashed with promise as he leant forward. 'No, Sara, what's nuts, is that you're... how old are you?'

'Twenty-two.'

'What's nuts is that you are twenty-two years old and have never been on a date.'

'It's never bothered me. I'm not that sort of person. I'm quite happy with…'

'*Everyone* is that sort of person.' Tristan took Sara's free hand, holding it so gently that she was taken by surprise at the tenderness of the touch. 'Come with me. Let's dress up a bit, eat too much, drink too much, and have fun. Let me take one nice memory home from my disastrous trip to Devon. What do you say?'

Ivan realised, with a mixture of surprise and embarrassment, that he'd been clock-watching. He couldn't recall the last time he'd paid so much attention to the tick of his wristwatch's hands.

I've got to move past this. Belle's lovely – but she is young and full of life. I'm middle-aged and prone to arthritis. There is simply no way she'd…

The sight of Belle, a cake tin in her hands, walking with Sara, from the Forget-Me-Not, stopped Ivan's thoughts in their tracks. He could feel his smile getting out of control but was powerless to stop it.

'Time for the changing of the guard.' Sara picked up the spare hat Ivan kept for his helpers. 'Got a clean apron?'

'Under here.' Ivan bent down to retrieve a clean white coat. 'This'll be a bit big for you, lass. You'll have to roll the sleeves up, but it's clean and will satisfy those health and safety folk should they pop by for a pound of Stilton.'

Belle laughed. 'Love Stilton – in fact, I've yet to encounter a cheese I don't love. It's just so adaptable.'

'You're spot on there.' Ivan came out from behind his

cheese counter. 'Not many meals can't be enhanced with a spot of cheese.'

'My eldest, Niall, he's addicted to Cheddar. I've done him cheese sandwiches every day for his school lunch for more years than I care to remember. I did once suggest he have something else, but he gave me such a disapproving look that I've never suggested it since.'

'Obviously as intelligent as his mother.'

Ivan privately cursed his tongue. *Why did I say that? Now Belle's embarrassed, and Sara's amused.*

'Well, thanks.' Belle gave him a shy smile. 'I won't tell Niall though; it'll go to his head.'

Sara gave her a nudge. 'You had something to give Ivan.'

'Oh yes.' Belle looked down at the tin she'd temporarily forgotten she was holding. 'This is for you – for you *and* Maddie – and Jo – well… for *everyone* really, but I wanted to give it to you or Maddie. But Maddie is so busy with the kids…' Aware she was in danger of gabbling, Belle didn't seem to be able to stop talking. 'Anyway – it's a thank you. You've been so kind. If you hadn't spoken to Maddie for me, and if Maddie hadn't agreed to adjust my hours, and if Jo hadn't been okay with that…' Belle took a ragged breath. 'I'm just grateful I didn't have to give up this job. That's all. Here.'

Ivan accepted the tin as it was pushed into his arms.

'It's a cake. Obviously.' Her cheeks burning, Belle was relieved to hear the approach of six sets of wellies excitedly trying not to run through the shop in their haste to reach the café. 'Here come the Little Acorns. Must dash.'

As Belle disappeared, Sara turned to Ivan. 'I think she likes you.'

'Course she likes me. Everyone likes me. I'm nice.'

'You know what I mean!'

Ivan's cheeks warmed as he flicked open the till's lid. 'I ought to check how the receipt roll is doing.'

Sara grinned. 'The till rolls were all changed this morning.'

'So they were.' Ivan flushed further at his friend's knowing expression – but he smiled wider, nonetheless.

19

One by one, Jemima took the children into the café's washroom – once her grandad's downstairs bathroom – to clean their hands. Once they had spotless hands, she passed them to Maddie, who placed mini wipeable aprons over their heads. She, in turn, passed them to Ed, who did the aprons up.

As she watched from the safety of the other side of the counter, Belle nudged Jo. 'It's like a mini child-prep production line.'

'Isn't it.'

'You okay, Jo?' Belle frowned. 'Your bounce seems to have gone these last few days.'

'Tired – bit worried about my mum.'

'Of course.' Belle cursed her lack of thought. 'I should've kept my mouth shut.'

'Not at all.' Jo turned back to the till. 'Sorry, Belle. Lots on my mind.' He gestured to the cake tin, which was now open and sitting on the back counter of the café, away from the eyes of their customers. 'That really is an amazing cake. I knew you said you could bake during your interview, but lots of people can knock up a cake. You can *bake* bake.'

Belle's eyes flicked towards Ivan, who was currently tucking into a slice of her pineapple upside-down cake, alongside a coffee, on the other side of the café. He had his arm half round it, to disguise the fact he was eating something not on offer to the public.

'I've always loved baking. My Grannie Abebe was a passionate cook. Proper Jamaican food. Her toto cake was out of this world.'

'Toto cake?'

'Sure. It's really popular in Jamacia. Basically, it's your average sponge, but with grated coconut, allspice, nutmeg, ginger, and salt added in. Grannie Abebe threw in raisins and rum as well, to make it even more flavourful.' Belle laughed. 'I'm not sure there was any cake or dessert she didn't believe could be improved by a spoonful or two of rum.'

'Looking at the way Ivan is devouring your cake; I'd say he is in agreement with your gran.'

'Hope so, although he is such a nice man, he'd eat it to be polite, even if he didn't like it.'

'That's true.' Remembering what Sara had suggested about Ivan liking Belle, Jo began to wonder if the feeling were reciprocated. 'Ivan wouldn't be eating it with such an air of indulgence, nor would he be stealing appreciative glimpses at the cook when he thinks she isn't looking.'

'Oh.' Belle felt flustered. 'Well, that's nice then.'

Letting her off the hook, Jo gestured to the far tables. 'Looks like we are about to be deafened by blenders. I'll go and warn the two tables of customers near the door, if you could explain about the brief forthcoming racket to the folk in the middle.'

Nerves took hold of Jemima as she watched the children take it in turns to put leaves and berries into the blenders. Although she'd tried the recipes out herself to make sure they worked,

JENNY KANE

seeing the Little Acorns, their faces set in excitement, preparing their drinks sent her stomach into knots.

What if they don't like the taste?

'I wish Mum and Dad were here to see this,' Jemima said to Maddie as Ed helped Josie put a handful of blueberries into a blender.

'They'll be sad to have missed it.' Maddie gave her niece a hug. 'Take lots of pictures. We can send them some after work.'

Jemima pulled her mobile from her pocket, before calling over to Ed, 'That's full enough, or we'll have two mini smoothie volcanos.'

'Ohhh...' Noel lowered an over-generous handful of spinach leaves back into the bowl. 'That would be fun.'

'Fun, possibly.' Maddie gently eased him back from the blender. 'But a bit too messy for my liking. Now then, let's all sit down and let Jem pour in the magic ingredients.'

'Can't we do that?' Kayleigh asked as she watched Jemima pick up two bowls of sugar.

'Not this bit, but in a moment, you can take it in turns to pop in some ice cubes.'

Moments later, Mark was tentatively balancing two ice cubes on a tablespoon, before dropping them into the first blender, quickly followed by the other children – each depositing an ice cube into one or other of the blenders.

'Right, everyone...' Ed moved over to the plug switches on the wall. 'I want you to sit on your hands.'

Josie giggled as she pushed her hands under her bottom. 'Why?'

'Because Jem is about to put on the lids and start the blenders, and I think your parents would be cross if she blended your fingers too.'

'Ekkkk…' Josie squealed as the other children made disgusted faces – all apart from Noel, who seemed disappointed at the lack of gore risk.

'Are we good to go, Jem?' Maddie asked.

'Yup.' Jemima regarded the row of children. 'How about a countdown? Ready?'

'Ready!' they chorused.

'Okay then.' Maddie gave her niece a thumbs up. 'Five, four…'

'Three…' The Little Acorns joined in: 'Two… one… go!'

The deafening sound of both blenders drowned out all conversation in the café. Maddie glanced anxiously at the other customers and was relieved to see them all smiling in the direction of the youngsters, enjoying their excitement from afar.

A text flashed up on Jemima's phone only seconds after she'd sent it.

'It's from Mum. Look, Aunt Maddie.'

What wonderful smoothies! Love the children's happy faces.
So proud of you. Mum and Dad. Xx

Putting an arm around her niece, Maddie gave her a hug. 'I'm proud of you too. I think we can truly call your first smoothie session – from fledgling spinach and blueberry crop to drink – a resounding success.'

'I'm so relieved they all liked them. Not all kids will drink something so definitely pinky-purple.'

Maddie had to agree with Jem. 'I did wonder if Noel was

going to for one moment. He wasn't too impressed by the colour at first.'

'Probably didn't want to be the only one who wasn't brave enough to try it.' Jemima yawned. 'That was great fun, but I'm knackered now!'

Maddie gave her a final squeeze, before letting her go. 'Why don't you head into the flat while I help the others close up. The spare room is ready, and I bet Florrie would like the company. She's been on her own for two hours – which means she's either sulking, wrecking the place, or fast asleep.'

Sara had changed her mind about going out with Tristan so many times in the last three hours that she was beginning to feel dizzy. Now, as she cashed up the shop's till, the internal argument she'd been having with herself all afternoon began again.

It's just one date. It doesn't mean I'm going to run off with him! It's just dinner with a friend.

But he isn't really a friend – you hardly know him – and what you do know, you don't always like.

He makes me laugh sometimes and he knows how to have fun.

I have fun with Jo.

Making beds and watching movies we've seen before? I'd like to do something different – just once.

But what about Jo?

You don't have to do everything with Jo.

Jo doesn't trust Tristan.

But he ought to trust me to know what I'm doing. I'm just

trying to have some fun. Anyway, I'd like to find out what a date is like, and if Tristan is leaving soon anyway, then...

As if her phone knew she was having doubts, its screen flashed bright with the arrival of a message. 'Tristan.'

Sara hadn't been sure about giving him her number, but he'd said – not without reason – that if didn't have her number, he wouldn't be able to text her the details of where to meet.

Half hoping he'd messaged to say he was cancelling, taking the decision out of her hands, Sara read:

7.30 tonight. Exmouth – the South Beach Café. Where shall I pick you up from? T x

'Exmouth?' Sara mumbled as she closed up the till. 'I didn't tell him I lived near Exmouth. Did someone else tell him, or is it just a coincidence?'

Her eyes roamed back over the text. *The South Beach Café.* She'd heard a lot about it: how good the food was, how stunning the views across the bay were, but it was well out of her price range.

She swallowed. *No it isn't. You* could *afford it, you just haven't had any reason to go there, or anyone to go with, and you don't like spending your money on unnecessary things.*

Her father's voice came back to her. *You always need money in the bank in case the roof blows off.*

Sara may have been unsure of a lot of things, but she knew for certain that, if she did go, there was no way she'd allow Tristan to collect her. It would be hard enough explaining to Jo that she was seeing Tristan, without him picking her up in his expensive car.

Another text arrived.

Hope you aren't battling your conscience about whether you are allowed out to play or not. T x

'Of course I'm allowed!' The indignation that had simmered inside of Sara since Jo had implied she wasn't pretty enough for Tristan rose again. 'I can go out whenever I like. I just don't want to very often.'

Not sure if she was trying to convince herself or ease her own conscience, Sara fired off a reply.

Will see you outside restaurant at 7.25.

Then, taking a deep breath, she went to tell Jo she wouldn't be sharing a takeaway with him tonight.

20

Ivan pulled his van up to the bus stop. As soon as he saw Belle, her flowing purple skirt being blown around her ankles by the wind that had been building all afternoon, her hair, now out of the bandana, tumbling over her shoulders, he knew couldn't leave her there.

'Can I give you a lift somewhere?'

'Thanks, but I wouldn't want to take you out of your way.'

'We don't mind, do we, Sheba?' Ivan ruffled his Labrador's head, disconcerted to find himself wondering – again – what it would be like to stroke Bella's incredible mass of purple curls.

'Where are you going?' Belle peered along the road, unsure if she wanted the bus to miraculously appear ten minutes early, or not.

'Far side of Tiverton. Cove – do you know it?'

'Of course.' Belle's nod sent her hair bouncing around her shoulders. 'Cove's a nice little village. You live there?'

'Sure do.' Ivan smiled. 'You?'

'Tiverton.'

'Which bit?'

'Amory Park.'

'I know it.' Ivan gestured to the passenger seat that Sheba currently occupied. 'I'm more than happy to drop you back if you'd like a lift.'

'But it's out of your way.'

'By less than two minutes.' He turned to Sheba again. 'We wouldn't mind, would we, girl?'

'I'd be pinching her seat.'

Ivan pointed into the back of the van. 'Sheba, in the back, girl.'

Belle's eyebrows rose as the Labrador immediately jumped between the seats into the rear of the van, before turning to poke her head between the gap between the front seats. 'Wow, I wish my children were that obedient.'

Ivan laughed. 'You are not the first to say that.'

'I bet!' Belle opened the passenger door, her heart thumping in her chest. 'Well, if you're sure, thank you. It's a while until the next bus.'

'It's the least I can do after that incredible cake. I'd have gone back for a second slice, but I knew I'd have to drive home – and that rum…'

Belle chuckled. 'Potent?'

'That's the word.' Ivan, acutely aware he was staring at her dark eyes, switched his attention to the road. 'Have you ever wanted to cook professionally?'

Sliding into the seat, Belle hooked her flowing skirt in after her. 'Oh yes – not so much cooking – although I can cook – but baking. I find making cakes and biscuits very therapeutic.' She tapped her stomach. 'As you can tell.'

'Daft woman, you're gorgeous.' Conscious of the blush starting beneath his beard, he kept talking so she couldn't respond to his compliment. 'I love to cook – always have.'

'Always with cheese?' Surprised by how warm his comment had made her, Belle found herself relaxing into the seat, her hand automatically going out to fuss Sheba.

'More often than not.' Ivan's eyes flicked to the wing mirror.

'I'm planning cannelloni with a rich Somerset Cheddar and blue cheese sauce for this evening.'

'Not Mozzarella or Parmesan?'

'Too bland for me. I'm not keen on the stringy nature of Mozzarella to be honest.'

'Nor me.' Belle's nose crinkled. 'I tend not to cook much pasta. I can never get the seasoning quite right. It hadn't occurred to me to use a non-Italian cheese to give it a lift.'

Ivan chuckled. 'It does feel a bit disloyal, but I promise you, it's worth it.' He found himself adding, 'I'll have to cook it for you sometime.'

'That would be lovely. I could return the favour. Some traditional Jamaican cooking, just like my Grannie Abebe used to make. She loved teaching me to…' Belle's words trailed off. Feeling awkward, picturing Milo's reaction to having Ivan in their home, she changed the subject. 'I was talking too much wasn't I. My boys are always telling me off.'

'Not at all. I like it.' Ivan swallowed, cursing himself for acting too hastily and killing off the easy conversational atmosphere they'd been sharing. 'Tell me about Grannie Abebe – she sounds fabulous.'

'Oh, she was. I miss her terribly.' Belle stroked Sheba again, finding the dog's presence calming. 'She had a long life. Born in Kingston, she came over to the UK with my parents in the Sixties. Got a job in a restaurant in Bristol, before setting up her own little Jamaican café. Marvellous place it was.'

'Did you work there?'

Belle's smile faded. 'For a while, but my former husband didn't believe in women working, and so…'

Gripping the steering wheel tighter, Ivan resisted the urge to ask about her ex-husband. 'That was a shame. You'd probably have a chain of fabulous Jamaican restaurants by now.'

Belle dragged both of her hands through her mass of hair, pushing it back, so her face was free of curls. 'Maybe. I do sometimes wonder how life might have turned out different, but then, if I hadn't met Greg, then I wouldn't have my boys.'

'Everything happens for a reason.'

Watching out of the windscreen as they drove steadily along the link road from Uffculme to Tiverton, Belle asked, 'Do you really think so?'

'I do. My nan used to say that.'

'So did Grannie Abebe!' The unease that had passed through Belle disappeared as she remembered the big, round, smiling woman who had shaped her life so much. 'I was telling Jo about Grannie earlier. I can hear her now, standing over a bubbling pot of her stewing beef curry and saying, "Belle girl, don't you be worrying about the twists and turns of life. Everything happens for a reason, and there will always be stew in the pot."'

'Stew, rum and wisdom.' Ivan laughed. 'I think I'd have rather loved Grannie Abebe.'

'And she'd have loved you.' Watching the changing scenery through the passenger window, Belle added, 'She was a one-off. What about you? You said your nan used to say it too.'

'My nan and grandad – on my mum's side – they were as much parents as they were grandparents. My folks had full-on jobs, and so it was Nan who collected me from school, helped me when I was down, mopped up my first broken heart and all that stuff.'

Wanting to know just how often his heart had been broken, Belle asked instead, 'And did she cook?'

'Oh yes. Steamed puddings, you know, old-style comfort food with enough calories in one spoonful to keep a grown man going for a week.' He tapped his own belly. 'I carry the proof of her kitchen skills to this day.'

Belle fixed her eyes back on the road ahead as she laughed. 'Daft man, you're gorgeous.'

Ivan burst out laughing. 'Touché, lass. Touché.'

Turning left off the ring road that took them into the heart of Tiverton and the small estate of Amory Park, Ivan asked, 'Have the boys looked after themselves today?'

'Yes.' Belle's body instantly tensed. 'Niall said he'd watch Milo for me, and my neighbour, Mrs Bowen, she promised to be around on Saturdays in case of emergencies. It's not ideal but…'

'I'm sure they'll have been fine. The responsibility will be good for them. They'll have enjoyed a little freedom.'

'I hope so.' A cloud of concern crossed Belle's face. 'If they kept to the Saturday routine Milo is used to, it'll be okay – but if they didn't…'

'Routine is that important – even at the weekend?'

'Less so – but yes. Part of the weekend routine is that the routine is less strict – if you see what I mean. I'm hoping that me being out and arriving home after work will quickly become part of the routine as well.'

'I'm sure it will.' Ivan paused. 'Is Milo expecting you to get the bus back?'

'Yes.'

'So, will he be expecting you at an exact time?'

Belle sat bolt upright. 'I'm ten minutes early. I warned them I could be late because of the bus – but early might…'

'Throw him off?'

'Yes.'

Ivan turned the car into an estate of closely packed 1980s homes. 'How about we wait here until we see the bus come? As soon as it appears in the mirror, I'll drive you to the bus stop, then you can get out as if you've caught the bus.'

'You don't want to be hanging around with me for...'

'I do actually, Belle, if that's okay?'

'Jo?'

'Oh, hello, Ed.'

'What are you still doing here?' Ed pulled up a chair in the café and sat with his friend. 'I was about to lock up.'

'Lost track of time.' Placing his palms flat on the table, Jo went to push himself up, but Ed put out a hand and stopped him.

'I think you'd better stay here, or at least, come and have dinner with Maddie, Jem and me. I'm doing omelette and chips. Not quite the standard of cooking you are used to, but you'd be welcome nonetheless.'

Jo frowned. 'You knew Sara wouldn't be home for dinner then?'

'No. No I didn't.'

'Then why did you offer me food?'

'Because you're my friend. I suppose I assumed you'd call Sara and tell her you'd be eating with your mates.'

'Because everyone needs friends of their own.' Jo spoke so quietly, that Ed missed what he said.

'Jo?'

Standing up, Jo grimaced. 'Ignore me, Ed, I was feeling sorry for myself. Not a quality I'm proud of.'

'That's okay... we all do that sometimes. Any reason in particular?'

'Tristan.'

'Ah.' Ed groaned. 'Is he with Sara?'

'Yes. She gave me a lecture about being overprotective and about how she's quite capable of looking after herself. And it seems she feels sorry for him.'

Ed's eyebrows shot up. 'Sara feels sorry for Tristan? But he's a complete...'

'Apparently, she is aware of this. When I said I considered him a shifty bastard she said she was damned sure he was, but she wasn't a fool and was perfectly capable of putting him in his place if he overstepped the mark.'

Ed tilted his head to one side. 'You *do* believe she can take care of herself don't you?'

'Of course.' Jo spoke the words on autopilot.

'You don't sound convinced.'

Huffing out a sigh, Jo stood up. 'Normally, if it were anyone else, I'd say yes – totally. But this guy, he's different.'

'He *is* different. He's arrogant and can have a questionable attitude to women sometimes, but he probably means well. Maybe having Sara around might do him good.'

Jo looked hopeful. 'You think he's more genuine than he appears, then?'

'All I can know for sure is that Sara would never give anyone anything she doesn't want them to have. If she wants to be friends, it'll be that, and if she wants it to be more then it would be on equal terms. Don't worry, she's neither helpless nor brainless and she's not going to be pressured into anything.'

'Oh God!' Jo sat down again with a thump. 'I've been such an idiot!'

'How?'

Jo shook his head. 'No wonder she was cross with me! I just blundered on and on! Why couldn't I see that I was insulting her?' He grabbed his phone. 'I must call her.'

'Then come and have dinner with us. I know Maddie would like to talk over the dementia café and I need to pick your brains re Dark Skies. I've decided to start it up again from next week.'

'Thanks, Ed.' Jo took out his mobile. 'I'll call Sara and then lock up for you. I might even see if she'd like to come to Dark Skies with us.'

'Fabulous. I'll get the chips cooking.' Ed got up. 'Maddie and Jem should be back from walking Florrie anytime now, and believe me, they'll be starving.'

The ring of Sara's phone echoed in Jo's ear until it switched to voicemail. *Damn, she must be driving to wherever they're going.* He paused, before leaving a message.

'Just wanted to apologise for being a prat. Have a nice evening. See you later. Fancy a Dark Skies night with me, Ed and Maddie next week?'

Hoping she got the message soon, Jo headed to the light switches, and plunged the café into darkness.

21

Cut into the side of a cliff, the South Beach Café commanded views across the bay from an angle Sara had never seen before. Their table, open to the elements, but warmed by an overhanging heater and lit by hundreds of fairy lights, felt magical. Some would have called it romantic, but Sara suspected that Tristan saw it as seductive. *Jo wouldn't think of it as romantic – he'd simply say it was beautiful.* She found herself smiling as she recalled the answerphone message she'd listened to before getting out of her car.

'That's a smile to gladden a man's heart.'

'You're assuming it was aimed at you then.' Sara tutted as she picked up her menu, but her smile stayed in place.

Tristan's eyes glowed in the flickering light. 'Well, as there's no one else here with us…'

'Maybe I was smiling at the view.'

Deciding he didn't want to know if that was the case or not, Tristan asked, 'Are you warm enough?'

'Perfectly, thank you.' Sara gestured to the patio heater suspended above their table for two. 'It's amazing how much warmth they give out. I might suggest to Maddie that she gets a few. Could be good to open in the evenings more often.'

'The Potting Shed does evenings?'

'It's done one. When Davina Ditz came to do a talk in the spring. That's when she asked to endorse Jo's coffee. I can't tell you what a boost that has been to his...'

'Yes, I'm sure,' Tristan interrupted; the last thing he wanted to talk about was Jo. 'But surely you don't want to work more hours for Maddie by doing evenings more often?'

'I'm only part-time at The Potting Shed.'

'Really? You seem to work there nonstop.'

Sara laughed. 'That's because you don't arrive until after ten and you're always gone before four.'

'I'm on holiday!'

'And I'm not.' Sara, who had told herself on the drive over that the best way to handle Tristan would be like Maddie handled Florrie – firmly but without being overly discouraging – added, 'I'm not the only one who works for Maddie. She owns the business with her sister, Sabi – who is on holiday now. We are helped by Ed, as you know and often Henry. He's Sabi's husband, and their daughter Jemima joins in at the weekends sometimes. You might have seen her around yesterday helping with the kids' club.'

'Ahhh... I thought that was Maddie's daughter.'

'Her niece.'

'That makes more sense. I didn't think Ed was stupid enough to get tangled up with a woman with baggage.'

'Jem is *not* baggage.' Sara gripped her hands together, her voice taut. 'Come to that, no child, whatever their circumstances, is baggage.'

Tristan groaned. 'I think that must be a record.'

'A record?'

'Offending you within ten minutes of being with you.'

'Don't be silly, you'd offended me much quicker than

that.' Sara rolled her eyes. Tristan really did seem to live on a different ideological planet – or lack of ideology planet – than the rest of the world. 'What holiday stuff are you doing tomorrow, or are you off home?'

'You're obsessed with me going home.' Tristan opened his menu but kept his eyes on hers. 'Why would I leave when I'm in such good company here? You look great, by the way.'

'Oh, thank you.' Sara hadn't intended to spend more than five minutes deciding what to wear. She only had two outfits that didn't consist of various combinations of jeans and shirts or jumper, but nonetheless, she'd agonised between the two dresses she owned – wondering which would make the best impression on Tristan. It had been a new sensation for her to worry about her appearance – she wasn't yet sure if she liked that fact or not. 'I'm glad you like it.'

'I do.' His eyes travelled with open appreciation from her left off-the-shoulder sleeve, via the suggestive (but not too much so) view of her cleavage, to the right sleeve. 'If the food tastes as fabulous as you look, it'll be a great evening.'

Wondering if he was getting his chat-up lines directly from an outdated book, possibly entitled *How to Charm Any Woman*, Sara said, 'I'm not obsessed with you going home. I'm just surprised you haven't gone.'

'Why?'

'Because you're bored stiff.' Sara tried to ignore the fact that her heart was beating rather faster than usual under the heat of the stare Tristan was giving her.

'I'm not.'

'If you say so.' Sara broke eye contact, her pulse slowing as she scanned the menu. 'What will you have? There's so much to pick from.'

'It'll have to be seafood,' Tristan mused. 'Seems silly not to as we're here.'

'The crab salad sounds tempting,' Sara agreed. 'Nice and light. I wouldn't want you to feel the need to make comments about girls that have toast and cake on the same plate again.'

Tristan dropped his menu to the table. 'I'd never say...'

Sara's expression stopped his denial in its tracks.

'Okay – I *might* have said something like that. Sorry. I didn't know you'd heard me.'

'Are you only sorry because I heard you? If I hadn't overheard would a comment like that be okay?'

Tristan shifted awkwardly in his seat, glad that the two neighbouring tables were unoccupied so no one could hear him being caught out. 'Did you only come out tonight to tell me off?'

'Not only that – although that was part of it.'

Tristan's forehead creased, his surprise at her candour so apparent that Sara burst out laughing.

'Tristan, I'm here for two reasons. The first is because I've never been on a date, and I wondered what it would be like. The second, is because it occurred to me that if someone doesn't put you straight on how to treat women, you're either going to die alone after a string of disastrous relationships, or you'll be locked up on a sexual harassment charge, sitting in a cell bewildered at your situation.'

Unsure if he was offended, outraged, or terrified she was right, Tristan opened his mouth to protest, but Sara held up her hand and went on.

'I have a feeling that there might just be a nice man hiding underneath all that showing off. Why don't you let him have a turn at running your brain for a while? You never know, you might find a decent girl who'll love you for yourself, not your money or posh job and clothes. I mean, how can you live in the world we have now, and not see that women are your equals, not trophies to be won?'

Clearly flummoxed, Tristan took refuge in reopening his menu.

'I won't really have a salad.' Sara tapped the menu. 'I fancy the swordfish steak and sweet potato mash.'

'Sounds nice.' Tristan, wishing he hadn't driven so he could have a stiff whisky said, 'Let's keep it simple and make that two.'

'Good plan.' Sara rested back in her cushioned seat, wondering if she'd gone too far. 'Sorry if it felt like I was having a go at you, but I didn't want us to start on the wrong foot. Okay?'

'Okay.'

'Excellent.' Sara wiped the nervous perspiration that had formed on her palms onto her napkin. 'Then we can be friends.'

Only pausing for a split second before taking the hand she offered across the table, Tristan shook it. 'Friends. Friends who can share a half bottle of wine with their meal?'

'That sounds nice. But with a side order of a jug of water.'

'Deal.' He opened the wine menu and swiftly made a choice for them both, before remembering that Sara would probably want to pick her own drink. 'What would you like?'

'I don't know much about wine. Can you suggest anything?'

'I know a fair bit about wine actually – is that alright?'

Sara gave him a gentle smile. 'Of course it is alright. You know about wine, I don't – now if you'd high-handedly just ordered our drinks without asking me, that would *not* have been alright. But asking my opinion, even if I bow to your greater knowledge, that's okay.'

Feeling his patience being tested once again, Tristan concentrated on the wine list. 'Let's go with a Familia Martinez Bujanda Gran Reserva, 2011 – that's the best one they do in a half-bottle.'

Sara ran her finger down her copy of the wine list until she found it. 'Wow – that's not a cheap wine. I'm not sure…'

Tristan raised his hand. 'My treat. Remember.'

'Are you sure?'

'Positive.'

Having explained that Michael had suggested three o'clock in the afternoon as a good time for a potential care home visit, Jo said, 'What day of the week did you have in mind, Maddie?'

'I wondered about Wednesdays. Once a fortnight or once a month do you think?'

'I suspect fortnightly would work.'

Ed dipped a chip into a puddle of tomato ketchup. 'Should you suggest a trial run first? That wouldn't offend would it, Jo?'

'Not at all. In fact, Michael suggested that very thing. Just an ordinary café visit first, with a memory-style café next time.'

Jemima, who'd been cutting her ham and cheese omelette into strips, peered up from her food. 'What will you do at these special café meetings?'

'An excellent question.' Maddie took a sip of wine. 'It doesn't seem enough to simply ship them in, sit them down, and abandon them.'

'To some extent that would be fine – especially on their first visit, so no one is too overwhelmed. But if it goes okay, I wondered about small activities while they are here. We should talk to Elspeth.'

''Cos she's old?' Jemima asked.

Maddie couldn't help but laugh. 'No, love, because she used to be a care worker.'

'Whoops.' Jemima grinned.

Jo winked at her. 'Don't worry, I'm sure Elspeth would forgive you.'

'For now, then, let's set a date for – six guests?'

'Yes, that's four patients plus Carol and Michael.'

Maddie was surprised. 'I imagined six patients; they can bring more if they want to.'

'It's a question of them coping with six. One carer to two patients is the usual way. Jo speared another chip onto the prongs of his fork. 'You never know, if it works out okay, and our guests get used to us, a few more of them could come along, as we'll be on hand to help caring wise.'

'Maybe Elspeth would help too – if she was a care worker once,' Jemima suggested.

'She's already offered, bless her.' Maddie smiled at her niece as she turned to Jo. 'Do you want to suggest a week on Wednesday to Michael?'

'Why not this Wednesday?' Jemima asked.

'Because this coming Wednesday is the first Dark Skies of the season, and I don't want to be too worn out to enjoy it.'

Tristan didn't think he'd ever worked so hard over a meal. The conversation had veered from comfortable chat to fencing match and back again at periodic intervals. At least the food had been excellent.

'Did you like the wine?' Tristan tipped the last of his drink down his throat.

'Very much. You have excellent taste.'

'Thank you.' He held his glass up to the nearest lamp, showing how the residue of red liquid clung to the side of the glass. 'My father is something of a connoisseur. He taught me a lot about wine.' He sighed. 'It's about the only thing I do, appreciate wine that is, that he approves of.'

Noting the edge to Tristan's voice, Sara suspected he was speaking honestly for the first time that evening. 'Surely he approves of you being a barrister?'

'He'd approve far more if I worked at the High Court rather than for the Crown Court, taking care of criminal cases for the Crown Prosecution Service. I could have a position at the bloody Old Bailey, and it wouldn't be good enough.'

'But surely…'

Tristan lowered his gaze to the table. 'I know you'll want to see the best in my father, but it's hopeless.'

'You mentioned before that your father was demanding.' Sara almost reached out a hand to him, but thought better of it, as she said, 'It must be tough having unsupportive parents.'

He grunted. 'Mother would be supportive, but she's not allowed. Father's word is law – pun entirely intended.'

'Oh.'

'I bet you have mega supportive folk.' Tristan immediately apologised. 'That wasn't supposed to come out as bitter as it did.'

Feeling her throat go dry, Sara kept her focus firmly on the table. 'I'm sure they would have been. My parents are both dead.'

Tristan's hand flew to his mouth. 'I didn't... I'm sorry.'

'Thank you.' Sara took a sip of her wine. 'Do you want to talk about your father?'

'There's nothing to say beyond that I went into the law because he told me to. And at least he approves of my appreciation of wine.'

'That's something I suppose.' Sara met Tristan's eyes. 'Do I take it you'd rather have followed your passion for wine as a career than going into the law?'

'I'd have loved to.'

'There must be a way to convince your father it would be a good thing for you to follow your heart.'

'I knew you were a good person.' Tristan briefly laid his hand over hers before withdrawing it again. 'If there is a way, then I've yet to work out what it is.'

Saddened by the dull look in her companion's eyes and a little shocked to realise she'd not entirely disliked the touch of his hand, however brief it had been, Sara picked up her glass. 'What can you tell me about this then?'

Focusing on the wine, Tristan recovered his confident demeanour. 'It's a Rioja, obviously from Spain. It has been matured in oak barrels – that's what gives it the silky-smooth flow it has as it hits the back of the throat.' He gestured at her glass. 'Take another sip. Allow it to settle on the palate.'

Sara did as she was bid, letting the wine linger longer than usual in her mouth before it ran down her throat.

'Feel it?'

'Yes.' She could feel the memory of the rich liquid lingering in her throat.

His face eager, Tristan asked, 'And what *did* you taste?'

Sara felt self-conscious. 'I'm not sure. It was red wine. What else is there to say about it?'

'Go beyond that. Break it down. Could you taste fruit?'

Trying it again, Sara ran the liquid over her tongue, before swallowing and suggesting, 'Blackberries?'

'Almost – sharper. It's more like black cherry.'

Sara nodded. 'You're right… and there's another taste too – I'm not quite sure…' She laughed. 'I feel like one of those wine critics on the telly who goes on about how wine has a touch of tyre rubber about it.'

Tristan gave his first chuckle of the evening. 'Top tip, if someone suggests a wine has essence of rubber to it, don't buy it!'

'Point taken.' Sara relaxed against her seat back before leaping forwards again. 'Liquorice!'

'Yes!'

'Really? I got it right?'

Tristan glowed at her in delight. 'You did. Now for the tough one, what does its aroma put you in mind of?' Picking her glass up, he gently swirled the meagre contents before passing it back to her. 'Take a slow breath and close your eyes, then inhale over the glass.'

Doing as she was asked, Sara tried to concentrate. 'Am I right in thinking this will not be a foody scent?'

'You are.' Tristan sounded serious. 'Concentrate. You can do it.'

'Umm… I'm not so sure.' She sniffed again. 'I can detect the berries and the liquorice now I've thought about them.'

'Understandable. Now, take your time. Go beyond those

scents. Think about the smell you can feel on the back of your throat.'

'Feel a smell...' Sara focused on the dark behind her eyelids. 'Okay, I'll probably be making a total idiot of myself here but... it's not bicycle saddles, is it?'

'Yes!' Tristan clapped his hands in triumph. 'Well, sort of. Leather saddles. I was thinking of horse saddles – but hey, a saddle is a saddle, right?'

22

The car park at Haddon Hill was deserted but for a group of vehicles that, although familiar, neither Ed, Maddie nor Jo had seen since January, when they'd shared their last Wednesday night Dark Skies experience.

Greetings made, everyone agreed it was odd that Ivan wouldn't be joining them. Having been their group leader for years, he'd had to reluctantly step down from the role since his doctor had advised him against aggravating his arthritis in the cool, damp, night-time air.

As mutual hopes for the partial cloud cover to break further were shared, Ed checked that everyone had torches and suitable footwear. Meanwhile, Jo passed a bulky rucksack of recyclable cups to Sara, before taking two huge flasks of coffee from the back of his camper van. Satisfied that they were as ready as they could be, Ed raised his arm and pointed towards the wooden gate that separated the car park from the moors.

Maddie tipped her head back as she walked, her hand firmly in Ed's in case she stumbled on the uneven ground. Her breath caught in her throat as the clouds obligingly parted to reveal a canopy of stunning constellations.

'Never gets dull, does it.' Ed squeezed her palm in his.

'Breathtakingly beautiful.' Maddie slowed so that Sara could keep step with them. 'I'm so glad Jo persuaded you to come.'

'Me too. I've always meant to give it a go, but I'm not terribly good at being still. Dad could never hack it.'

Jo nudged Sara's shoulder with his elbow. 'I've brought some sticky tape to fasten you to the ground.'

Sara laughed. 'It'd better be strong.'

'Industrial strength.' Jo tucked his flasks more securely under each arm and turned to Maddie. 'I'd never have met Sara if her dad hadn't given Dark Skies a go. It was an attempt at relaxation.'

'A totally failed attempt.' Sara pictured her late father and his constant need to be on the go.

'But if he hadn't come along, he'd never have asked me to sell coffee at his open events.' Jo smiled. 'I have a lot to be grateful to your father for.'

Warmed by Jo's look of affection, Sara readjusted the straps of her rucksack. 'I think it's fair to say I'm very glad you came to Hawthorn Park.'

'Me too,' Maddie said. 'If Jo hadn't sold coffee for your dad, and then you, he might not have sold it for me!'

'Wasn't it Ivan and the Exmoor Drifters that brought Jo your way?' Sara asked.

'Partly. Sabi invited them to The Potting Shed, but there was a Dark Skies overlap, as Ed already knew of them because of this group, and had already asked Jo to consider joining us.' Maddie lifted the beam of her torch higher as they reached a steeper part of the moorland path. 'If Jo hadn't come, then The Potting Shed would never have been saved, and you and he wouldn't be sharing up at Hawthorn.'

Sara laughed. 'So it's all Dark Skies' fault then!'

Jo stuck his tongue out at her. 'Or your dad's fault for coming to Dark Skies in the first place?'

'Let's blame him – he won't mind.'

Sara's laughter sent a hit of relief through Jo. While they were no longer at odds with each other, neither had they been their usual relaxed selves around each other since her trip out with Tristan at the weekend.

At first, mindful of what Ed had told him, Jo had found himself double-checking every word he was going to say to her before he said it, as though he were walking on eggshells. In return, he suspected that Sara constantly considered how to frame her replies, rather than just speaking without the need to think first, as they normally would.

Having stayed up late for Sara on Saturday, after her evening with Tristan, Jo hadn't even waited for her to slip her shoes off before he'd dived in with a proper apology.

Sara, for her part, had accepted his apology. Then, taking him by the hand, she'd led Jo into the living room, curled up next to him on the sofa, as was their habit, and told him about every aspect of her South Beach Café experience.

Jo had particularly liked the bit where she'd described Tristan's expression while she'd laid out to him, in no uncertain terms, that he was in danger of ending up alone if he didn't start treating women as equals.

It was only later, in the quiet of his bedroom, that Jo found himself wondering what Tristan would make of his personal history. *If he is capable of being so dismissive of the women in his life, what would he make of anyone transgender?* The thought had made Jo shudder into his pillow.

*

'Okay, folks,' Ed called out across the group, 'this is the spot. The last of the evening light will fade fast now. As this is the first session of the series, and we aren't used to lying in the cold again yet, we'll go for thirty minutes instead of forty-five before we stop for some of Jo's fabulous coffee.'

This decision met with approval as Sara placed two thick travel rugs, side by side, over the moor's stubbly grass cover and Jo put down the refreshments.

'What do I do?' As their fellow constellation spotters lay down, Sara moved closer to Jo. 'I feel so small.'

'You are small.'

'Cheek!'

Putting a hand on her elbow, Jo guided her to the ground. 'Feeling small is normal. Promise.'

As everyone settled down, a dense hush covered the earth. Sara felt as though talking now would be wrong; that it would break some sort of magic spell. She felt quite overwhelmed by the broad, distant horizons surrounding them. Then she looked upwards, and the sheer size of the night sky made her feel almost dizzy.

'Whoa...'

'Amazing, isn't it,' Jo whispered.

'More than amazing.' Sara was surprised to find tears welling in her eyes.

'You can forget your celebrity TV shows, that's the real meaning of star-studded, right there.' Jo dug into his jacket pocket and produced a clean tissue. 'Here.'

'How did you know I'd need that?' Sara muttered as she dabbed at her eyes.

'Because it is impossible to see that panorama and not be moved, and because...' He paused, not sure if he ought to go on.

'Because what, Jo?' Sara rolled onto her side so she could see him as he viewed the nebulous sky.

'Because I know you.' He manoeuvred his beanie lower over his ears. 'I know I've already apologised, but I truly regret being such an idiot.'

'It was just a blip.' Sara looked back up at the sky. 'And when you see all of that up there, you can see just how insignificant our blips are.'

Not trusting himself to say the right thing, instead Jo raised an arm to the sky. 'You see that star, the one that seems brighter than all of the others?'

'Uh-huh.'

'That's the North Star. Whenever life gets too much, I search for that. It's always there. Sometimes it's shrouded in cloud – but it's always there.' Jo paused, before adding, 'You know I'm always going to be here, don't you? I'll always be right here.'

'Of all the stars we've seen during Dark Skies...' Maddie laid her head on Ed's shoulder as they lay, side by side, looking directly upwards '...I think the ones that make up Orion's belt are my favourites.'

'Can't argue with that.'

'They were the ones you pointed out to me the first time we came here.'

'So they were.' Ed exhaled slowly.

'You okay?'

'Very.' Ed gave Maddie a quick kiss under the cover of darkness. 'I'd forgotten how calming this was.'

'Me too. We both needed this.'

Watching as a wisp of cloud blew across the panorama, Ed murmured, 'I called Ronald today.'

Maddie lifted herself up onto one elbow, so she could see Ed's face in the gloomy light. 'He's okay, isn't he?'

'Retired,' Ed whispered. 'I called him to apologise for leaving so hastily, and…'

Realisation hit Maddie. 'You hoped he'd offer you your job back.'

'Yes.' Ed sucked in his bottom lip. 'I was too late. He decided to take my leaving as a sign to take the retirement he'd been contemplating on and off for ages.'

'Oh.'

'Lyle Solicitors are no more.'

Maddie felt a jolt of sadness as she whispered, 'I'm sorry you're unhappy at work.'

'I'm not sure I'm unhappy as such, it's just not what I thought it would be. Luckily, you make me very happy. I should have considered things more thoroughly before I took the Bristol job. I'd forgotten that many of the bigger law firms are all ambition and few scruples.' Ed addressed the sky. 'I just wanted to earn more money for us, for our future, so that one day I could be a good h…'

'Shush.' Maddie leant forward and kissed his forehead. 'I know, and it's appreciated. We're together, and that's all that matters. Come on, look up there – that view makes everything better.'

Sara was beginning to see why her father had struggled with stargazing. Even though they'd been very lucky that the clouds were wispy, giving them a largely uninterrupted view of a stunning sky, her mind couldn't settle. She'd been fine for the first ten minutes, but now she was restless.

Focusing her attention on the North Star, she wriggled, trying to get more comfortable, accidentally catching Jo's leg with her foot in the process. 'Sorry.'

'It's okay.' Jo rolled onto his side so they could talk without disturbing everyone else. 'You wishing you were at home with a glass of wine?'

'I'm not sure I'll ever be able to drink a glass of wine again without thinking of Tristan.'

Jo's newfound calm fled with that one sentence. He caught himself tensing and hoped Sara hadn't noticed. 'Oh?'

'You know I said he ordered expensive wine?'

'Yes.'

'Well, what I didn't get round to telling you, is that he knows quite a lot about it. I was sniffing the wine like that bloke who used to be on the telly repeats all the time – years back – wine chap… worked with a woman who was equally potty when it came to wine…'

'Oz Clarke.'

'That's him.'

'And Jilly Goolden.'

'Oh well done! I've been trying to think of the woman's name since Saturday night! Thanks, Jo.'

'No problem.' Jo could feel the thud of a headache begin in his forehead.

'When I see Tris again, I think I'll tell him he ought to give up his legal ladder-climbing and train to be a sommelier or something wine connected. I know it's what he wants. If it wasn't for his father…'

'See him again?' Jo could hear the strain in his voice as he interrupted. 'Hasn't he gone home yet?'

'Seems not. I had a text this afternoon – I got so busy I forgot to say. You mentioning wine reminded me.'

'Oh. Well, that's nice.'

'Jo?' Sara frowned as she whispered, 'You aren't going to go weird on me again, are you? It's just a meal at the Appleby Inn this coming Saturday.'

'No weirdness, promise.' Jo swallowed. 'I really am sorry about before.'

'I know, but honestly, there's no need to…'

Jo sighed. 'I know. It's just he's so… shiny.'

'Shiny?'

'You know, too good to be true.'

'Jo…'

'I know – and I promise, I *do* trust you to take care of yourself. One hundred per cent, but…' Jo abruptly raised himself to his elbows. 'Hang on, isn't the Appleby Inn near where he's staying?'

'What if it is?'

'Oh, Sara, why can't you see?' Sitting up properly, exasperation washed over Jo. 'He'll only have invited you to eat with him there because it's yards from where he's staying. I'd bet my life that he's already working on ways to get you spend the night with him.'

'*What?*'

'He'll view you as the rightful compensation he's owed after being humiliated by Gemma.'

'I beg your pardon!' Her voice no longer a whisper, Sara jumped to her feet. 'How *dare* you?!'

'Sara, I…' Aware of every set of eyes in the group on them, Jo felt embarrassment wash over him as he pleaded, 'I'm just looking out for you.'

'No you're not. You're trying to stop anyone else but you from being able to look out for me!'

Swinging round, desperate to get as far from everyone as possible, Sara stumbled, almost losing her footing in the dark. Feeling trapped and humiliated, sure that the silent watchers were no longer observing the skies, but her, Sara felt a hit of relief when Maddie, a torch in her palm, quietly whispered, 'Take my hand. I know the way. If we go slowly, we'll be okay.'

'But… what about Ed… the others. I…' Torn between anger and shame at ruining the first Dark Skies session in months, Sara whispered, 'I'm so sorry, Maddie.'

Jo hadn't yet spoken. The sound of Maddie and Sara's footsteps had long since faded away, and the bob of Maddie's torch had disappeared into the night. He was aware of the low hubbub of hushed conversations around him, as his fellow constellation spotters huddled together, their own torches alight while they sipped his coffee.

Jo suspected Ed had tried to speak to him, but all he could hear was his own confusion rattling around his head; a white noise drowning out everything else.

23

Munching her way through a piece of toast, Maddie read through the staff rota she'd sketched out on the back of an old envelope. Putting a big cross through the whole thing, she started again. Two minutes later she put down her pen and took solace in cuddling her dog.

'It's no good, Florrie; however I arrange each day, there is no way I can avoid Sara and Jo working together in the café all day. Thank goodness it's Saturday, and Ed is here to help.' Maddie closed her eyes. 'Dark Skies normally makes everyone feel chilled and ready to face the world head on; this time it left everyone feeling uncomfortable for days – like they'd witnessed a break-up and didn't know what to do about it.'

Florrie gave a sympathetic yap.

'I suppose you're right – it *was* a sort of break-up, but as Jo and Sara aren't really together, so…'

They're very together – just differently.

Maddie nodded to the fern in the windowsill. 'I wondered when you'd pipe up with a helpful thought.'

Perhaps they don't realise they are a couple.

'Maybe. I feel awkward every time I see either of them. Sara hardly said a word on the way back to the car on Wednesday night. Thinking about it, she hasn't said much since.'

You want to make things better, but you're afraid of saying the wrong thing and making it worse.

'That's what Ed says Jo did. He was trying to be supportive of Sara, even though he doesn't like Tristan – but then his fears for Tristan's intentions bypassed his brain, took over his mouth, and he cocked it right up. Jo ended up making Sara think he didn't trust her all over again.'

Florrie buried her head in her mistress's lap.

'Thanks for the cuddle, Flo.' Maddie scratched her pet behind the ears, 'But unless you can magic me a new member of staff to cover Belle and Jo's breaks every day…'

'I could do it today.' Ed popped his head around the door, a towel around his waist, his freshly showered hair damp. 'I worked with Jo on the van once or twice back in the day.'

'Really?' Maddie smiled. 'I hadn't realised you could operate a coffee machine.'

'Well…' Ed picked up the cafetiere of industrial-strength coffee Maddie had made '…I've never tried, but it can't be that hard.'

'It's not that easy either.' Maddie laughed. 'I appreciate the offer though.'

'How about you cover things in the café then, and I do the till?'

Taking up her coffee, Maddie took a big gulp of liquid. 'That would be great, thanks, Ed. Although it would mean that there'll be no members of staff outside for an hour. And you'll need to fetch Jem at lunchtime, and what about the rest of the week?'

'I could call Jem and ask her if she'd mind me fetching her at two rather than twelve.'

'No way. I promised Sabi I'd be there for her, and I will – we will.'

'Quite right.' Ed picked up a slice of toast. 'I rather like Jem being here – and she'll help too, even if she only keeps an eye on this monster.' He ruffled Florrie's fur as she came to say good morning. 'Is it tonight that Sara goes out with Tristan again?'

'Yes. I'll be glad when he's back in London.'

'Me too.' Rescuing some runaway butter with his fingertip, Ed shook his head. 'I can't see what Sara likes about his company so much that she'll see him even though she can see it upsets Jo.'

'It does seem out of character, but she's much younger than us. Ten years younger than Jo for a start – and her father died when she was very young, leaving her with nothing but responsibilities. Maybe she feels that this is her chance to have some fun. To be spoilt and cared for.'

Ed's eyebrows rose sharply. 'Jo cares for her.'

'I know, but he's not exactly forthcoming with nights out, is he? Jo is Jo. Sara knows that, but that doesn't mean she might not want wining and dining every so often.'

'Jo doesn't think romantically.'

'Sara isn't a hearts and flowers person either, but that doesn't mean she doesn't want to be taken out – to have fun – to do restaurants and movies and all that. Going out doesn't have to be romantic. But not ever going anywhere, ever, that's dull. And she's too young for a relationship that does nothing and goes nowhere.'

Ed wiped some crumbs from his lips. 'I think it's Jo you ought to be explaining that to, not me.'

Maddie grabbed Florrie's lead. 'If Jo needs that explaining to him, then he isn't going to be with Sara for much longer. That's if he *is* with her beyond friendship; we could have misunderstood the situation.'

'Of course they're together beyond friendship.'

'I've always thought so – but how do they see themselves?'

Ed pulled a face. 'Now isn't *that* the million-dollar question.'

'I think I'll see if Sara wants to have a chat. I know she didn't want to talk before, but the dust must have settled a bit now. Apart from Jo, she doesn't really have anyone to speak to, so if it's a question of talking to someone *about* Jo…' Hooking the lead onto her dog's collar, Maddie turned back to Ed. 'Putting our friends aside for a moment, we should discuss your job; there hasn't been much time to talk lately.'

'Honestly, love, it's not a problem. I'm a big boy – it'll be okay.'

'I don't like the idea of you being miserable.'

'Keep making me happy then.'

Maddie kissed Ed hard on the lips. 'Okay.'

Stepping back, Ivan admired the row of Cheddar truckles as they sat in his chiller cabinet. Deciding that there was room for an additional couple of Stilton wedges and a local Brie that was produced just six miles away, Ivan returned to the back of his cheese-selling area. Picking up his wares, he whistled quietly to himself as he rearranged them.

'You sound happy.'

Ivan looked up to see Belle heading in his direction. 'There's a reason for that.'

'You've found a rare cheese and you're anticipating sampling it on top of a pasta dish?'

'You guessed!' Ivan laughed. 'So, are you ready for your first official Saturday working here?'

'As I'll ever be.' Belle turned so she was facing the closed café doors. 'Although I preferred the atmosphere in there last week.'

'Jo's fallen out with Sara.'

'Maddie told me – thought I ought to know why things were a bit frosty.' Belle tugged a rainbow scrunchy off her wrist and wrapped it around her hair. 'I hope they've sorted themselves out overnight. While they're good at keeping things light in front of the customers, the air behind the counter is chilly, to say the least.'

'I called Ed, to see how his first Dark Skies meet as group leader had gone. I gather it was a bit of a disaster. Somehow an argument erupted between Jo and Sara, which resulted in Sara and Maddie leaving the moor and sitting in the car until the session was over, and Jo not saying a word to anyone for the remainder of what Ed had called, "an uncomfortable evening that even the galaxy couldn't make better".'

'It's such a shame.' Belle tugged at a stray ringlet. 'Maddie said that Sara didn't say anything about the situation apart from issue constant apologises for messing up the session while they waited in the car.'

Fastening his apron, Ivan said, 'They'll be okay.'

'I hope so.' Belle gestured towards the door. 'I should go in.'

'You want a lift home later?'

'Are you sure you...'

'Don't mind?' Ivan grinned. 'Definitely not. Anyway, Sheba told me I had to ask you. And I never let Sheba down.'

'Lots of customers.' Jemima peered out of the rear passenger window of Ed's car, Florrie at her side as they parked. 'Aunt Maddie must be busy.'

'It is a bit manic at the minute.'

Opening the door, Jemima grabbed hold of Florrie's lead as she got out of the car, hauling a bag of dirty washing after her. 'She doesn't have time to look after me too, does she? Nor do you.'

'Of course we do.'

Jemima fixed Ed with a stare that reminded him of her mother. 'I'm serious. Would it be better if I boarded full time until Mum and Dad are back?'

'Only if that's what you want to do.'

'Well, not really, but…'

'Then you shall continue to come. Your aunt and I like you being around. Anyway…' an image of Jo's unhappy face crossed Ed's mind '…we could do with your help. I don't suppose you'd have time between bouts of homework to help Jo and Belle clear tables and stack the dishwasher?'

'Payment in smoothies?'

'Goes without saying.'

Sara plucked three small weeds out from between the paving stones by the far polytunnel, before zipping open the plastic doorway and stepping inside. The enclosed warmth wrapped around her. Normally she enjoyed the sensation, likening it to a hug. Today, it felt oppressive.

The relief she'd experienced on clearing the air with Jo after her visit to the South Beach Café with Tristan might have been a lifetime ago rather than just a week.

How did this happen? One minute we were alright, then we went to Dark Skies and now…

Sara found herself scowling at the trays of netted bulbs Maddie had laid out for her to sort into bags for sale.

'We were fine, and then I told him about having one more meal with Tristan. Now Jo can hardly look at me!'

I've never been compensation for anyone. How dare Jo suggest that's how Tristan sees me? That all he's after is a leg over.

The tulip bulb in her hand remained silent, refusing to venture an opinion, as Sara was deafened by her own seething thoughts. *Jo claimed he trusted me, but he clearly doesn't. And I certainly don't need him to defend me from anyone!*

Suddenly needing air, she headed to the doorway and took some steadying breaths.

The stupid thing about it all is – I don't even know how I feel about Tristan anyway. I enjoyed our meal out – once he started talking about wine. But do I want more from him? From anyone?

His brief touch of my hand was nice – but that was it. It was just – nice. Nothing more – I don't think…

Increasingly confused by her own feelings, she stared out across the garden centre. Seconds later she found herself watching a few early customers making their way from the car park towards the shop. 'I bet they're heading in for a café breakfast.'

A stab of loss caught her unawares.

Jo will greet them with a smile and a warm welcome. All I'm getting is silence and sad eyes.

Sara picked some mud from her fingernails.

How can I fix this without backing down?

'I don't want to end up resentful about having to give up on my principles.' Sara told the nets of hyacinth bulbs awaiting her attention. 'But nor do I want my principles to ruin my life.'

Is it just principles though – or do I fancy Tristan just a little bit, despite his many faults?

The sound of approaching footsteps broke through Sara's unhelpful thoughts. Spinning around, she saw Maddie heading her way. 'Hello there, do you need me to be somewhere else?'

'Not yet. I can't promise I won't be dragging you away to cover breaks later though.'

Laying down the handful of bulbs she'd just scooped up, Sara gave her boss a searching look. 'You wanted to talk about Jo, didn't you?'

'More, give you the chance to talk to me if you wanted to.' Maddie picked up a tulip bulb and weighed it in her hands. 'But I'll go away if you like.'

Tugging off her gardening gloves, Sara blew out a puff of air as she leant against the bench. 'I'm sorry The Potting Shed's got caught in the middle of this.'

'Right now, I'm more worried about how you are.' Maddie took a high stool from beneath the bench and perched on its edge. 'And how unhappy Jo is, come to that.'

Sara turned a bulb through her fingers. 'I know the last thing Jo needs is for us to be at loggerheads, especially while he's so worried about Iris. I am too, but...' Sara threw her hands up in frustration.

'But?'

'I don't know. I was trying to figure it out before you came in.' Looking furtively around them, Sara muttered, 'Between you and me, I don't know how I feel about Tristan. I just know how society teaches us we *ought* to feel about someone who we choose to go on a date with.'

'And you don't feel those things?' Maddie tilted her head to one side.

'Not really.' Sara shrugged. 'I ought to at least want someone I date to kiss me – shouldn't I?'

Maddie put an arm around her friend's shoulder. 'It's usual to feel at least curious about what it would be like to kiss him– if not more.'

Sara nodded. 'Well, either I'm unusual or I don't fancy him.'

'Did you *want* to fancy Tristan?'

'Maybe. Jo isn't being Jo anymore and I… I don't want to be alone.' She shrugged shyly and closed her eyes. 'But I don't want to be with Jo just so I'm not lonely – that would be so unfair on him.'

'And on you.' Maddie tentatively asked, 'Do you think that's all it is with Jo then? Someone to live with so you aren't alone. I don't see you two like that – no one does.'

Sara shrugged. 'I don't know anything anymore. But all this has got me thinking.' She blew out a ragged breath as she confessed, 'I've realised I've never really had thoughts like that – fancying someone thoughts I mean. Apart from Jo when he first worked for my father – I thought I was physically attracted to him, but now I consider it, the whole idea seems, frankly, weird. Like I was trying too hard to feel what I thought I was supposed to feel.'

'And Tristan?'

'Physically, you mean?'

'Uh-huh.'

Sara shook her head. 'I only went out with Tristan because I wanted to see what dating was like. I'm not sure I liked it all that much.'

'Did you tell Jo that?'

Opening her eyes again, Sara groaned. 'Yes. But he was so upset I don't think he could hear me.'

'Maybe you should tell him again – and tell him what you've just told me.'

'I've tried telling Jo that Tristan and I aren't dating in the conventional sense.' Tears pricked at the corners of Sara's eyes. 'But he clearly doesn't believe me.' Pausing, Sara risked a glance at Maddie before adding, 'The thing is, I'm still not sure if it's just that I don't fancy Tristan, or if it's more general – that being attracted to someone physically isn't for me. I need to work that out for myself, and surely that will mean trying again with someone else. But if living with Jo means I'm going to have to avoid all male friends from here on in, in case he decides I'm going to run off with them, then...' turning back to her work Sara began to count bulbs into an open bag '...I can't live like that. I can't share my life with someone who doesn't trust me.'

'I'm so sorry.'

'Not your fault.'

'Even so.' Not sure what else to say, and knowing her intention to help hadn't got them anywhere, Maddie said, 'You don't have to answer this, but what is it you like about Tristan – on a friendship level, if you don't fancy him?'

Sara's laugh was short, and rather strangled. 'I've honestly no idea. Although, I know he's a lot nicer than he comes across.'

'Is being nice enough?'

Sara grimaced. 'Probably not; although I'd be lying if I said it wasn't pleasant – and rather flattering – to be seen with a good-looking man and being a bit spoilt.'

'Do you have fun with him?'

'Well – ish… we mostly disagree with each other – or I disagree with him.'

'That doesn't sound much fun.' Maddie's eyes widened in surprise. 'So, it really is the principle of the thing then?'

Sara wrinkled her nose. 'Does that make me rather selfish?'

'No, it makes you human.' Maddie got off her stool. 'But if you aren't having fun with Tristan, then maybe…'

'Maybe?'

'Maybe don't go to the Appleby Inn with him tonight.'

'And let Jo think it's because of what he said?' Sara tilted her chin upwards.

'I was thinking more that, if Tristan accepts you calling off a date with good grace, and simply suggests a new one, then you'll learn if he's truly your friend, or if he's using you as a way to pass the time while he's here.'

Sara sighed. 'You agree with Jo then, you think Tristan is using me?'

Not wanting to fall out with Sara too, Maddie picked her words with care. 'It's more that I have listened to Ed. He knows Tristan of old.'

'And doesn't think he's changed?'

'He suspects not, but,' Maddie added quickly, 'he hasn't spent much time with him of late, nor did he know until recently of the pressure his father put on him, so I admit he could be as wrong as you think Jo is.'

Dropping bulbs into the bags with more force than was necessary, Sara groaned. 'I hate this, Maddie. I *hate* it.'

'I know.' Giving her friend a hug, Maddie said, 'Take some time to think. I'll do my best to keep you off the café shift rota as much as I can, but…'

'We're short-staffed.' Sara gave Maddie a brave smile. 'Thanks for trying to help though.'

'I'm here anytime if you want to chat.'

'Thanks.' Sara sniffed. 'You won't tell anyone what I said about not wanting to kiss people and stuff, will you? That's something I think I always knew – deep down – but hadn't really admitted and I need...'

'Time to think it through?'

Sara nodded. 'Times like this, I miss Dad more than ever.'

'I totally understand that.' Passing her friend a tissue, Maddie headed to the doorway, 'However, the only thing I understand about your current situation is that you need to tell Jo what you just told me. I know you love Jo, and that Jo loves you. It's obvious.'

Ten minutes later, the potting bench was covered in rows of neatly labelled paper bags of bulbs. As she heaped them into their various baskets, ready to carry them into the shop, Sara replayed her conversation with Maddie through her head.

Why did it take talking to Maddie for me to realise how I feel?

Picking up her phone decisively, Sara tapped out a text before she could change her mind.

Hi Tristan. Can't do tonight. Not feeling well. Sara.

Then, with only a slight twinge of guilt at the lie, she picked up two of the baskets and headed to the shop.

24

Having filled Mrs Johnson's car boot with four ceramic pots and two bags of compost and being assured there was someone to help her unload at the other end, Ed wished The Potting Shed's most loyal customer a happy Sunday as she headed out of the car park. He was pushing the trolley back to the stand where they were kept, when he spotted Tristan's Porsche pull into the space Mrs Johnson's ageing Volvo had just vacated.

'Heavy lifting for Maddie's customers again?' Tristan shut his car door with a flourish.

'A few pots and some soil.' Ed, convinced Tristan was blissfully unaware of the problems he was causing two of his friends – and, by default, The Potting Shed in general, said, 'I take it you aren't here to buy anything.'

'I'll gladly buy you a coffee if you're allowed to take a break.'

Ed bristled. 'It isn't a case of being allowed or not. I choose to help.'

'Alright, mate. No need to be so touchy.'

'I wouldn't need to be touchy if you stopped to think before you spoke.'

Tristan pushed his fringe back from his face. 'You sounded like Sara then. She's always telling me off. God, all I did was offer to buy you coffee!'

Conscious that there was a possibility of them being overheard by customers, Ed spoke more softly. 'It's appreciated, but I'm working.'

'I'll go and see if Sara wants one then. See if she's feeling better.'

'Better?'

'She cancelled our date last night. Wasn't feeling well.'

Dismayed to hear Tristan talking as though Sara was now his girlfriend, and sure that she had been perfectly alright when he'd seen her yesterday, Ed said, 'I think it was just a headache.'

'Oh.' Not appreciating being dumped for a headache, Tristan rallied. 'As I said, I wanted to check she's okay.'

'Even though she always tells you off.' Ed's eyes narrowed. 'This "tell it like it is" attitude is a trait I've not seen in Sara before. Normally she's rather reserved.'

'Is she?'

'We each get treated like we deserve. Perhaps you should try acting like you don't need to be constantly put on the naughty step.'

'Alright, mate.' Tristan held up a hand in surrender. 'Come on, I was supposed to be on holiday with the woman I was going to spend my life with. Instead, I'm paying for a month in a cottage on my own.'

Relenting, Ed said, 'I know, and I'm sorry about that, but you must see that you're causing problems between Sara and Jo.'

'If Jo isn't man enough to...'

Ed sharply interrupted Tristan. 'You know nothing about Jo and clearly not as much about Sara as you think you do. I suggest you leave.'

'After I've seen Sara.'

'She's not in today.'

'Oh.'

Ed pushed his hands into his pockets. 'Please, Tris, just leave her and Jo in peace. He's a good bloke and doesn't deserve...'

'We all deserve what we get, don't we? Isn't that what you said? For goodness' sake, he isn't Sara's partner – he's just her friend! *I'm* the one who's seeing her,' Tristan snapped as he reopened his car's door. 'She'll be at home then?'

'I suppose so.'

'See you then, Ed.' Tristan jumped back in his Porsche and tore out of the car park, his tyres spraying gravel in their wake.

Maddie scrolled through her emails on her phone, while keeping an eye out for customers heading towards the till.

She was about to tap a quick text to Sabi to see how she was getting on, when a new message popped into her inbox. Seeing the words, HELP NEEDED: CASTLE LANE PRIMARY, Maddie opened the email at once.

Dear Miss Willand,

Please forgive me writing on a Sunday.

My name is Lia Matthews, I'm the reception teacher at Castle Lane (a primary school in Tiverton) This is something of a cry for help.

Tomorrow my class (twenty-eight five- and six-year-olds) were supposed to be having a visit from one of the National Trust gardeners from Knightshayes – however, due to an outbreak of a stomach bug, they're so low on staff that no one is free to come.

Then I recalled the email you sent about potential school visits to your garden centre. (I love the new café by the way – took my mum last week.)

Anyway – are you free to come and talk to my class about the importance of gardening tomorrow at 1.30 p.m. for about forty-five minutes?

Will totally understand if not,

Best wishes,

Lia Matthews (Miss)

PS: There is a small speaking fee.

Maddie's throat went dry as she reread the email. *Tomorrow!* Nerves prickled Maddie's neck, but so did a feeling of excitement as she realised she wanted to go.

We're closed tomorrow, so there's no staffing issue – plus it would be good practice if I have school visits here from October.

Picking up her phone, she was about to call Ed to ask his opinion, when she saw him coming in through the main doors. He looked worried.

'What's happened now?' Maddie's moment of optimism dissolved.

'Tristan was here. Left quickly when I said Sara wasn't in.'

'That's good isn't it – that he left I mean. The last thing we need is him and Jo in the same confined space.'

Maddie frowned as she recalled her last conversation with her friend. 'Sara sent me a text thanking me for the chat, and saying she'd taken my advice and called the date off to think things through.'

'Apparently she told Tristan she was ill.'

'Ah.' Maddie bit her bottom lip.

'He's gone to Hawthorn Park – at least, that's the impression I got.'

'Oh.' Maddie wasn't sure what else to say.

Ed tidied a pile of paper bags into shape. 'Jo isn't going to like the idea of Tristan being with Sara at their home.'

'But if Tristan and Sara are just friends, why shouldn't they meet up there? She really doesn't fancy him.' Maddie sighed, not wanting to betray Sara's confidence, but hating withholding information from Ed at the same time. 'But at the same time, she says he's a lot nicer than you or Jo give him credit for.'

'Sara's a good person, so she'll always think that other people are too.'

'You maintain that Tristan isn't?'

Ed dragged a hand through his hair. 'I can't say either way – not really. Back at university Tristan only had time for me because I was good at what I did. I never really knew him. I'm not sure he ever forgave me for getting better grades than he did.'

'Tristan wanted to be your friend in the hope that some of your intelligence would rub off on him?'

'Oh, he's intelligent – very much so – but I was better at applying my intelligence academically. When he turned up here he was astonished to find I wasn't working as a barrister. A waste he called it.'

'He's a high-flyer, and can't understand why you don't want to be?'

'Exactly. I like helping people because I enjoy making them feel better about whatever situation they are in. He likes helping people because it can be very profitable.'

An alarming idea struck Maddie. 'You don't think Sara believes she can save him from himself, do you?'

'No one can save Tristan from himself.'

Maddie sucked in her bottom lip. 'What if she *does* think she can help him be a better person? What if we're the ones who are wrong – and that all he needs is a chance to show he can be more than we're giving him credit for?'

'I'd like to think so.' Ed watched some customers leave the café, and head to the racks of seeds at the far end of the room. 'Every instinct in me says that Tristan is up to something. I just have no idea what that something is. Although, I do know he talks about Sara like she's his girlfriend.'

'Well, let's hope he goes back to London soon.' Maddie's eyes dropped to her phone, reminding her of why she wanted to talk to Ed in the first place. 'Can I talk to you about something else?'

'Sure.'

'I've had a request to talk at a primary school tomorrow. Do you think I should?'

Ed's smile reappeared. 'Absolutely. You're brilliant with the Little Acorns.'

'Thanks, Ed.' Maddie picked up her phone. 'Do you think you could do the counter while I nip into the café? I'll grab us a coffee each and answer the email while I'm queuing.'

'A plan with no flaws.'

Having fired off an email agreeing to visit the school tomorrow, Maddie was just wondering what she'd say to the children, when she reached the head of the café's queue. 'How's it going in here, Jo?'

'Very busy over lunch, but calmer now.' Jo waved a hand to Jemima, who was gathering used cups and plates onto a tray. 'Your niece is being a star helper as usual.'

'She's a good kid.' Maddie peered across the café. 'Belle on a break?'

'Yes, she's agreed to have three ten-minute mini breaks rather than one full half hour. Makes it much easier and she says she likes having the extra opportunities to put her feet up. She's just nipped out the back to phone and check on her boys.' Jo started to make a coffee. 'I assume you want caffeine.'

'And one for Ed please.'

'And Ivan?'

'Not this time, he'll be in for a break once I get to his stall. I'm going to cover it for half an hour.'

'This place is like musical chairs. Whichever till you're near when the music stops, is the one you work from.'

Maddie laughed. 'It's a shame Sara doesn't work on Sundays to help, but...' Her words trickled off. 'Sorry, Jo.'

'No need to apologise. In fact, I should apologise to you. I'm aware it's been a bit atmospheric here lately.'

Guilt stirred in Maddie's stomach, and she wished Ed hadn't told her that Tristan was on his way to Jo's home. 'It has a bit. Maybe you should take Sara out and talk to her properly.'

'A date you mean?' Jo looked even more uncomfortable.

'Not a date, just two people going out for fun.'

Returning his attention to the coffee machine, Jo swapped Maddie's cup for Ed's and set the jet of caffeine going. 'That's what Sara says she's doing with Tristan.'

Not wanting to interfere, but at the same time, wanting to help, Maddie coaxed, 'Then why don't you do it too? You know, take her out, have fun.'

'We do go out, walking and stuff.'

'Then try something different. Take her out for dinner. A change of scene might make it easier to talk. Let's face it, here you're both at work and even at home you're at work now it's a B & B.'

Jo added some milk to Ed's drink. 'Luckily, Hawthorn hasn't got many bookings just now. It makes me feel a bit less guilty about not being there to help at breakfast time.'

Maddie's whole body went cold. 'Not being there?'

Keeping his gaze averted from his employer, Jo muttered, 'I didn't go back after work yesterday. Couldn't face watching her getting ready to go out with Tristan. I stayed in the van at Mum's care home. Sara doesn't want me involved in her new social life and Mum needed me, so...'

'What? I had no idea, I...' Maddie stopped talking, not knowing what else she could say.

25

'I don't know where I am with Sara. Let's face it.' A shadow passed over Jo's pale face. 'It's not like we could be a proper couple – not like everyone else is.'

'Sod everyone else!'

Jo's eyes widened at Maddie's firm tone. 'But...'

'There are no buts. You two are you two, and it works.'

'Worked. Past tense.' Jo grimaced. 'I don't blame Sara. It was inevitable she'd want a traditional relationship.'

Maddie swallowed as she remembered her conversation with Sara. 'Tristan won't be around for long.'

'You misunderstand me. Much as I dislike him, it isn't Tristan as such. But...' Jo cradled his drink. 'He's got me thinking about what he, or any other bloke, can offer Sara. Everything that I can't. I don't mean money – she's got heaps of that anyway. It's the whole having a relationship that leads to being a couple – a family maybe...' Drawing in a heavy breath, Jo went on, 'If it isn't him, it'll be someone else. It's made me see just how much I... Well, let's just say I can't stay around and watch that, but nor do I want to stand in the way of Sara having the life she wants. I want her to be happy.'

'Oh, Jo.' Maddie shook her head. 'I wish Sara had been around to hear you say that.'

'What good would that have done?'

'It would show her that you've left the manor because you love her, not because you don't.'

'Oh.'

Maddie raised a sorrowful smile. 'It doesn't matter how you're wired; you blokes are all differently hopeless.'

'True.'

'Don't you see – it isn't that you don't love her, just that it's translated differently.'

'I guess.'

'You guess correctly.' Maddie exhaled. 'And I'll let you into a secret.'

'Which is?'

'We women are hopeless too.' Maddie spoke faster, mindful of the chance of customers needing her at any moment. 'Why not ask Sara out tonight?'

'Tonight?'

'Yeah. It's Monday tomorrow, so neither of you are working here. You could make it a late one. Have a meal, go for a walk, *talk* to each other. Draw a line under all of this. Tell her how you feel.'

'I suppose I could.'

'At least try, Jo. Not just for you and Sara, but for all of us. It's awful seeing you both like this.'

Jo nodded. 'You're right. I must do something – even if it's only to clear the air so we can work together. I'll think about what to say.'

'Don't think for too long.' Maddie found herself visualising Tristan racing his way towards Hawthorn Park. 'And by the way, Jo, Sara *didn't* go out with Tristan last night. She cancelled on him.'

★

Jemima closed her physics textbook with relief. Her least favourite subject by miles, she always felt a moment of triumph when she managed to complete her homework without having to ask her dad for help.

Not that he could help today. Jemima wondered where her parents were. Somewhere in the Caribbean was all she knew for sure. While they had contacted her every day to say hello, the texts were always brief and generally commented on poor mobile and Wi-Fi connections.

Looking across the café, where she was sitting with her laptop, school bag, and the remnants of a smoothie and a bacon sandwich, Jemima's eyes landed on Jo. It was the second time she'd seen concern cross his eyes, only to then witness him shake it away whenever a customer approached.

The previous day Jo had been quiet, but she'd put that down to the fact it was extremely busy, and his worries for his mum after her fall. Now she wasn't so sure that was all that was on his mind.

Waiting until there was a lull in trade, Jemima tucked her schoolwork into her bag and took her chance.

'Jo, do you have thirty seconds?'

'For you, always.' Washing his hands, Jo came out from behind the counter. 'Stuck on your homework?'

'No, it's all done.' Jemima tilted her head back as she regarded her friend. 'Weird seeing you without your hat on all the time.'

Bursting out into laughter, Jo was suddenly aware that he hadn't laughed in days. 'A tatty grey beanie isn't exactly on the health and safety executives' hygiene wear list.'

'True.' Jemima threw her arms wide open and wrapped them around her friend. 'I thought you might want one of these.'

After a split second of surprise, Jo returned the hug. 'How did you know I needed a hug?'

'Call it a hunch.'

'Got a few things on my mind.'

'You want to talk about it?'

'Suddenly I don't need to. The power of one of your hugs has worked its magic.' He reviewed the queue, which Belle was handling easily. 'Could you be a star and clear those three tables? I need to nip out and send a text.'

Would you like to go out to dinner with me tonight? I'd like to explain why I'm such a fool. Jo x

Sara's brow furrowed as she read the text.

He didn't come back last night. There's work needs doing here – and I'm having to do it alone.

Staring at the mobile, half wanting to say yes to his offer, but at the same time furious with him for leaving her in the lurch, Sara sighed. *Is there any point? What could Jo say that he hadn't said before?*

Closing the back door to her home behind her, Sara walked from the house towards the entrance to the bluebell woods, trying to frame her response as she went. Over the past few days she'd become less and less certain of where she was with Jo. His only explanation for not returning to Hawthorn last night had been a short text saying he'd decided to stay close to the care home for a while.

He must think I'm stupid.

Perching on a bench near her front door, Sara was still torn between accepting or declining Jo's invitation when the crunch of tyres over gravel made her look up. Despite herself, she felt a hit of disappointment when it wasn't a bright orange camper van she saw appearing in her driveway, but a sleek black Porsche.

Sara's eyes narrowed. She'd deliberately not told Tristan where she lived. *How the hell has he found me here?*

Elspeth flicked her long grey plait over her shoulder as she strode forward, her walking stick clicking confidently across the laminated floor towards Ivan's cheese counter. 'Maddie called. Asked if I'd nip in and discuss the dementia idea sometime, so I've hotfooted it over.'

Ivan grinned. 'Hotfooted it?'

'Grabbed a taxi.' Elspeth swapped her stick into her other hand as she came to a stop. 'Maddie sounded so exhausted that I thought I'd come and see if you needed some cheese-selling relief, so someone else could take a break.'

'Elspeth, you are a wonderful woman.' Ivan took off his white hat and passed a spare one to his friend. 'I've not had the chance to see how much of your *Bee Lucky* range has sold this week. You may need top up stock.'

'I'll check later.' She moved closer and gave him a conspiratorial smile. 'A little bird tells me you've taken a liking to Belle.'

'Which little bird might that be?'

'The littlest – Jemima.'

'How did she...? I mean, she's got it all wrong. Belle and I get on well, that's all.'

'Is it indeed? Then why is your beard doing such a poor job of hiding your blushing cheeks?'

Peeling off his apron, Ivan gave in. There was no hiding things from Elspeth's practised eye. 'Belle is twenty years younger than me. To ask more than friendship of her would be utterly ridiculous.'

'Or it could be the making of you. Of you both.'

Ivan's eyebrows rose so high, they were smothered by his fringe. 'You don't think I'm crazy?'

'At seeing a chance to be happy, whether with a new friend or someone who might be more than that? Why is that crazy?'

Ivan remembered how Belle's forehead always creased with concern when she spoke about her children. 'It's not that straightforward.'

'It never is.' Elspeth plonked the hygiene hat over her grey hair, then trapped her plait within the confines of the apron coat. 'Why not just relax and see what happens?'

Slipping her phone into her pocket, Sara crossed her arms. 'How did you find me?'

By way of response, Tristan wiggled his mobile in front of him.

'Are you telling me that you typed my name into the search engine, and it gave you a map that brought you straight here?'

'Sort off. I put Hawthorn Park in, and it led me straight here.'

Returning to the bench, Sara sat down. 'I've never mentioned Hawthorn to you.'

'Ed said you were here.'

'Ed would never...'

Tristan threw his hands up in a 'who knows' gesture. 'I bet he assumed I knew where you lived. It's a bit weird that you've never told me.'

Sara's annoyance melted in the face of his wounded-puppy expression, and her words came out as a sigh. 'You really don't have any idea do you.'

'How do you mean?'

'I've told you nothing about my life because you haven't asked me about it. Surely it hasn't escaped your notice that every conversation we've had revolved entirely around you? Every time you do phrase an enquiry about me, you immediately answer it with some related information from your own life. It's no wonder you never keep a girlfriend if you aren't interested in them as people.'

Tristan opened his mouth to protest, but Sara was still backing up her argument.

'Last night, despite me saying I wasn't well, you phoned. A call to check I was okay, that would have been fine – but no, it was to put pressure on me to change my mind. And during that call you asked me if I'd gone to university, but before I could reply, you gave me a blow-by-blow account of how you had to study law to please your father, the attending of said degree, and how you managed to secure excellent articles and are now a barrister of the most sought-after nature.'

'You appeared interested.'

'I was. I was also wondering when it would be my turn to speak.'

'I asked about your job.'

'No, you asked me how often Ed helps at The Potting Shed and if I thought he'd worked out that he was wasting his life. My answer was ignored as you carried on talking. It was that conversation – or your half of it – that led to you telling me about how you became a barrister – occasionally punctuated by your repeated surprise that Ed isn't one.'

'But...' Tristan felt out of his depth, and he didn't like it. 'But... I have a Porsche.'

'What the hell has that got to do with anything?' Sara burst out laughing. 'I have a manor house. Which one of us would win at Top Trumps, do you think?'

26

Despite having told himself he would not check his phone again, Jo checked it anyway.

There was nothing from Sara.

At first, he had reasoned away the lack of response: she was out for a walk and her signal was down, a frequent occurrence in the grounds at Hawthorn Park. But as closing time at The Potting Shed came and went, and she still hadn't replied, the wave of positivity he'd been clinging to – that it wasn't too late to mend things with Sara – faded away.

You'd think she'd reply, even if it was just to say no.

Not sure what to do or where to go, Jo sat behind the wheel of his camper van, at the exit to the garden centre's car park. 'If I go right, I could drive up to see Mum. If I go left, I could go home... well, to Sara's place.'

The idea of Hawthorn no longer being home brought tears to his eyes.

'This needs sorting.'

Jo clicked on the left-hand indicator and eased the van into the flow of traffic heading towards the coast.

Sara tried not to laugh as Tristan collapsed onto a bench in her father's memorial garden. His complexion was a much darker red than she was sure he'd like, and although he was obviously attempting to disguise how out of breath he was, she could see his rib cage moving in and out as his lungs coped with the shock of taking physical exercise in the open air rather than the gym.

'I warned you it was quite a trek, and you said – and I quote – "No bother, I do an hour's cardio every day".'

Wiping a hand over his forehead, Tristan growled, 'I hadn't realised your estate was so extensive.'

Unease crept over Sara as they stood in the formal garden she'd planted in her father's memory. 'Just how extensive did you think it was then?'

'What?' Tristan shrugged. 'It was just a turn of phrase.'

'Right.' Sara changed the subject. 'I could do with a cuppa. Would you like one before you leave?'

'Leave?'

'Yes, you know, that thing you do once you have visited someone and it's time to go.'

'I haven't even told you what I'm doing here yet.'

'So, tell me.'

'I wanted to give you one of these.' Tristan produced two tickets for an evening at a local hotel, which was hosting *An evening of fine food accompanied by a string quartet*. 'It's on Wednesday night. I'd like to take you before I go back to London on Friday.'

'You are finally going back then?'

Tristan flashed a smile at her as he tucked the tickets back into his jacket's inside pocket. 'Trying to get rid of me?'

'Yes.' Sara checked her watch. 'I have work to do. New guests arrive tomorrow, and I'm behind with getting the bedrooms ready.' *Because Jo hasn't been here and it's not the same on my own.* Suddenly she remembered Jo's text. Sara extracted her phone from her pocket.

'Do you mind if I send a text. I've a message waiting and… rats, no signal. I'll do it in the house. We've heaps of Wi-Fi boosters in there now we're open for business.'

'We?'

'Me and Jo.' *Or maybe it's just me now…*

'You okay? You've gone pale.' Tristan stepped closer, placing a gentle hand on Sara's shoulder. 'If he's let you down, I could help you.'

'Jo's visiting his mother. She's sick.' Confusion as to why she was covering for Jo when she was so cross with him for not being there mingled with guilt. *Iris really is ill. Perhaps Jo does want to be nearer her for a while? Am I reading too much into this?*

'Sara?' Taking courage from the fact she hadn't shaken his hand off her shoulder, Tristan reached down and took her hands in his. 'Are you okay?'

'What? Yes, of course. Sorry.'

'So, how about I help out?' Tristan winked playfully. 'Just throw me an apron and I can skivvy with the best of them.'

Despite the tug at her heart, Sara found herself laughing as she picture Tristan attempting to help in a domestic situation. 'I can't imagine you wrestling a duvet cover into place.'

His eyes flashed at her in a last-ditch attempt at turning on the charm. 'Oh, you'd be amazed what I can do while wrestling a duvet.'

Jo cursed the M5. He cursed every holidaymaker who had

chosen that moment to head to Cornwall and was, like him, stuck at a standstill near junction 29. For reasons unknown, all three lanes of the main route to the far reaches of the south-west of England were blocked.

Jo couldn't help wondering if life was trying to tell him something.

Perhaps I should just let her go.

'I admit it, I'm impressed.'

Tristan's ability to make a bed with perfect hospital corners had surprised Sara.

'Benefits of a public-school education.'

'You had to make your own beds?'

'The housemaster was terrifying. It was best to do more than you strictly had to if you didn't want your life made an utter misery.'

Adjusting her preconceptions about Tristan's easy life a fraction, Sara smoothed a hand across the newly laid duvet. 'Sounds horrid.'

'He was, but he taught me a lot about surviving. I doubt I'd have risen so high in my profession if I hadn't learnt from his ruthlessness.'

Not entirely sure that was a good thing, Sara placed at set of towels at the foot of the bed. 'Come on, one more room to do.'

'Your room?'

Sara laughed. 'Of course not! No – our next guests are two couples travelling together, so two rooms.'

'Fair enough, but I really would like to see everything, so when we've finished, any chance of the grand tour?'

'Okay.' Sara's smile faded as she pushed open the bedroom door.

Maybe I should say my next guests, not our next guests now? As soon as Tristan's gone I'll call Jo – whatever the outcome, we need to talk.

The radio's traffic report did little to ease Jo's frustration. He'd been stationary for half an hour, and there was little sign of movement. All the travel reporter had been able to confirm was that a caravan had toppled over, making passage south impossible.

'I only need to get to the next junction.' Jo had long since switched off his engine, got out of the driver's seat and opened the back of his van to retrieve his ever-present flask of coffee.

He almost checked his phone but stopped himself.

If she'd replied, I'd have heard the notification. Sara clearly doesn't want to go out tonight.

He poured a cup full of his most popular coffee blend into a cup.

Not with me anyway.

Tristan admired each and every room Sara showed him.

Finally they passed through a stunningly period yet practical kitchen, before reaching a lounge, complete with two comfortable leather sofas and a fireplace, already endowed with a roaring fire. He knew, without doubt, that Sara was sitting on a gold mine.

Making himself comfortable on the sofa nearest the fire,

Tristan patted the seat next to him. 'Come and tell me all about your life plan.'

Sara threw a log onto the fire, sending sparks of orange flickering up the chimney. 'Run this place as an Airbnb and work part-time for Maddie.'

'That's all very well for the short term, but that's hardly a life plan. This house could do so much more for you. It would make a cracking hotel.'

Sara sat on the sofa opposite Tristan. 'Jo and I talked about the hotel option, but Airbnb works for us just now. It gives us the chance to learn a few of the ups and downs of having guests in the house.' Talking quickly to drown out the voice at the back of her head that was shouting, *Are these still joint decisions, or just my decisions now?* Sara added, 'It's also more flexible. If we want weekends or certain weeks off, we can work bookings around them. Can't do that with a hotel.'

Brushing aside the mention of Jo, Tristan said, 'But you wouldn't have to worry about that. You're the owner. You could hire a manager and staff, then sit back and watch the profits rise.'

Standing back up, Sara gave her visitor a critical stare. 'I need that coffee. Would you like a drink?'

Tristan didn't hear her, he was too busy visualising a squad of neatly uniformed staff, discreetly moving around the place, helping guests as needed, while disappearing just as discreetly when they weren't required.

'Evening meals would work well in your dining room. There's just enough bedrooms for this to have a boutique feel – exclusive rather than large. That means we can charge considerably more than you would for a larger establishment.

Of course, work would have to be done to add en suites to those rooms that don't have them, but the returns we'd get from guest profits would cover the outlay very quickly.'

We? 'Tristan...'

He missed Sara's warning tone.

'As Hawthorn is rather remote, we'd need a wide-ranging evening meal menu – but if we secured a good chef... What a great opportunity that would be for someone after their first Michelin star. I might know just the chap. He's got the deftest touch when it comes to menu construction. Always manages to get the balance right.

'You'd have overall say over everything of course, although you'd need to dress rather better. And...'

'And Jo?' Sara asked the question quietly, but with enough edge to cut through Tristan's overenthusiastic plans. 'Where does he fit into this "we" you keep mentioning?'

'If he sticks around – which, let's face it is unlikely – then maybe he'd find a role in the grounds. Seems the outdoor type. We'd need a reliable gardener, and if Jo's worked with Maddie, I'd put money on him knowing one end of a spade from the other and...'

If he sticks around? Nausea swam in Sara's stomach as Tristan's words sent the reality of losing her friend home.

'Alright, that's quite enough. I'd like you to leave now.'

Tristan's brow furrowed in confusion. 'Did I say something... Oh I see! I didn't mean to imply there was anything wrong with how you dress. You're a very attractive woman...' He stood up and took a meaningful step towards Sara. '*Very* attractive.'

'Tristan, I don't give a stuff about your opinions on my dress sense. This is *my* home.' She had no idea how she kept her voice level as she battled through her disbelief to process Tristan's plans for her home. 'It was my father's before me. While I appreciate that you see potential in this place, I'd rather you didn't tell me what I ought to do with it. And the implication that you'd be part of those plans... it's ridiculous! We hardly know each other.'

He held his hands out to her. 'I didn't mean to interfere. I got carried away. I can see so much potential here. I can't abide wasted talent. I told you how I feel about Ed not being a...'

'Several times.' Sara took a step back. 'And as I've said to you before, Ed has a life he is happy with. That's enough for him.'

'But do *you* have a life that you feel happy with, Sara?' Tristan adopted a sympathetic tone, 'I don't think so. You could be and do so much more.' He looked at his watch. 'You say Jo works here too, but where is he? He should have been here to do the beds with you. The Potting Shed closed ages ago, so where is he?'

Sara opened her mouth to argue, to repeat that he was probably seeing his mother or helping Maddie, but Tristan had already changed the subject.

'The potential here is leaping from the walls.'

'Potential to make money, or potential to live a happy life?' Sara interrupted pointedly.

Tristan laughed. 'Same thing isn't it.'

'I'd like you to go. Now.'

Jo tapped his steering wheel as the queue of traffic before him finally began to crawl forwards. They might only be moving at a snail's pace, but movement was movement, and Jo had a feeling he had to get to Sara. Quickly. Before it was too late.

Sara had spun around on the soles of her socks and marched back towards the kitchen before Tristan's brain had caught up with events.

Tristan raced to keep up with her. 'What did I say this time?'

'Seriously? You come in, spend less than an hour helping me, and assume that gives you the right to tell me what to do with my home! Not just that, but that I should accept you as a part of that future.'

'It's common sense. Using both of our skill sets. Your people skills, my business and legal flair and...'

Slipping on a pair of old shoes, Sara stormed through the back door, feeling the need to be outside. Her home felt too small for her, Tristan, and his ego.

'Common sense? I hardly know you and you certainly don't know me.'

'I do! You have a great smile...' Tristan found himself jogging to keep up with her as she skirted the side of the house, making her way to where his Porsche was parked '...and a fabulous laugh and you're fun. You are patient and kind and you've taught me so much about what I should and shouldn't do with women and...'

'Clearly not enough!'

'I thought I was helping.'

'Helping? You consigned my best friend to being a gardener – not that that's a bad job, but it isn't *his* job. *And* you told me that running an Airbnb is a waste of time.'

'I said no such thing.'

'The implication was clear.'

Silence fell between them as Sara reached the Porsche.

Tristan sighed. 'I am trying to change you know. You really have helped me.'

'Please go now.'

'I'd like to learn more about you and...' He waved the tickets toward Sara. 'What about these? Are you coming?'

Jo's heart sank as he saw the Porsche parked as the top of the drive. He didn't know it was Tristan's car, but then who else would it belong to?

Too late to turn around, he kept driving. As he got closer, he could see Sara and Tristan talking by the car.

'You can't seriously be asking me out again after that?'

'Please, Sara! You're good for me. My last night before I leave. Come on?'

'You have more last nights than Cher!'

'I promise I won't bother you before then. Just one more trip out. Meet me in Exeter on Wednesday. Please.'

'I don't think so.' Sara turned as she heard the sound of tyres coming up the drive. 'Jo!'

Seeing the orange camper van approaching Tristan lunged forward. 'Time I was off then.' He'd wrapped Sara in a bear hug and, before she realised what was happening, Tristan's lips were pressing hard against hers.

Panic flared inside Sara as a sense of suffocation took hold. In that moment she knew for certain. This was *not* what she wanted, not from him, or anyone. Fortunately, no sooner had the scent of his aftershave hit her, than Tristan had let go again – it was all over in seconds.

Then he was in his car and driving away. A shocked Sara was almost sure he'd waved at Jo as he whizzed by.

27

All Maddie could think about as she drove home from the local primary was how much she wished Ed would be there when she got home, so she could share her joy at how much fun she'd had with them.

Knowing that three-thirty in the afternoon was far too early to call him, she imagined Ed's proud face when she told him that she'd invited the school to The Potting Shed to see her plants growing, and to have a go at planting things themselves.

Heading to the flat-cum-shop, knowing that Florrie would be desperate for a walk by now, Maddie was surprised to spot Jo's camper van in the car park. Assuming he'd called by to drop off stocks off coffee, she diverted towards the café, calling out, 'Hey, Jo,' so that she didn't make him jump as she crossed the hushed shop.

'In here! Behind the counter.'

She found Jo on his hands and knees, a bucket of soapy water at his side, a rolled-up cloth in his hands. His clothes were spattered with water.

'Whatever are you doing?'

'Knocked over a carton of milk.' Jo rocked back on his haunches. 'It went everywhere.'

Maddie dropped her handbag onto a nearby table. 'Shove over, I'll grab another cloth.'

'No, really.' Jo spoke fast, wanting neither her help nor company. 'It's almost sorted. My own fault. I was trying a new latte flavour out – I got clumsy.'

Taking in the drawn lines around his face, Maddie asked, 'Have you slept?'

'Not a great deal.' Jo threw his cloth into the bucket and squeezed it back out; milky residue mingled with the suds.

Suspecting she knew the answer to her next question, Maddie asked it anyway. 'Did you go out with Sara last night?'

'No.' Jo stood up, his trousers, damp from where he'd been kneeling in the spilt milk, stuck to his legs. 'Actually, I was going to come and see you once you were back, I wondered if you'd mind me living in the car park for a bit.'

'Things are that bad?'

'I should never have given up my caravan to move into Hawthorn, but at the time it seemed so…'

'Perfect?'

'Yeah.'

Not sure what to say, Maddie gave Jo an awkward half-hug.

'I didn't get a reply to my text asking Sara out, so I went to the house. Thought we should sort ourselves out, but I needn't have bothered. I arrived in time to see Tristan kissing her, just prior to him zipping off in that posh car of his.'

'You're kidding!'

'It was all very clandestine – like I wasn't supposed to see. But then, he even gave me a friendly wave as he left – as if he was just a mate saying hi. Bastard.' Jo picked up the bucket and poured the dirty water down the sink. 'I stayed in the care home car park last night, but I can't make a habit of that, so I wondered…'

'Course you can stay!' Maddie pointed upwards. 'You can

have my spare room in the flat during the week – we only need it for Jem at the weekends.'

'Thanks, but I'd rather keep to myself, if that's okay.'

'Whatever you think best.' Knowing that Jo was, by nature, a very private person, Maddie hesitated before saying, 'You didn't actually speak to Sara then?'

'No point.' Jo's eyes reflected his resigned sadness. 'A picture says a thousand words and all that.'

'But what if you're wrong? What if…'

Jo cut through his friend's words. 'I've gone through all that, Maddie. Believe me. As I said before, if Sara needs more than I can give her, then I'm not going to stand in her way. I'll tell her so soon, but I need a little time… you know.'

Confused, knowing that – unless she'd been lying to her – kissing Tristan had not been on Sara's agenda, Maddie took a deep breath before asking a question that was screaming for an answer. 'Will you be okay working together?'

'I hope so.' Jo wrung out his cloth before dropping it into the bin. 'To be honest, now she's with Tristan, I doubt Sara will stay. He doesn't come across as the sort of chap who has a working partner.'

'I honestly don't think he's "with" Sara. Are you absolutely sure…'

'I know what I saw.'

'Okay. You can stay in the car park as long as you need to. Here.' Maddie passed him a key from her pocket. 'This will give you access to the public loos. You're welcome to use my bathroom in the day and evening, but I doubt you'd want to run the Florrie gauntlet in the middle of the night.'

'Thanks, Maddie.' Jo gave the floor a final wipe and stood

up again. 'This needs to be left to dry. Would you like me to walk Florrie? I could do with the exercise.'

'And some canine wisdom?'

'It can't hurt.'

'Then, yes please, I've a fair bit to catch up with here.'

'How was it at school?' Jo ran his hands under the tap, scrubbing over the milk residue.

'Fabulous. The kids were great. I've invited them to come here next week.' Maddie's smile returned as she recalled the happy faces looking up at her from the classroom's tiny chairs. 'With a potential school trip here once a month on a Monday, and the dementia café on a Wednesday, I feel we are doing something community-positive alongside selling things.'

'From what I've heard of him, your dad would have approved of that.'

'He would.' Maddie hooked her bag back onto her shoulder. 'Family and community were more important to him than even his plants – and that's saying something.'

Having been reassured by Hawthorn's latest guests that they were more than happy with their accommodation, and that they'd find her if they wanted anything, Sara stuffed her feet into her walking shoes and headed into the grounds.

Even though Tristan had lent a hand in the bedrooms, without Jo to help her get ready for their four guests, Sara had been too busy to think. During the scrubbing of the bathrooms and the hoovering of the carpets, she'd forced herself to remain focused on the tasks in hand and not let her mind wander.

'I never dreamt the skills I developed to force me to get

on with life after Dad died would be so useful.' She kicked through a spattering of leaves, an early sign that autumn was just around the corner.

Heading into the heart of the woods, taking the path she'd intended to walk the day before, when Tristan had turned up so unexpectedly, Sara buried her hands into her coat pockets and strode forwards, her pace keeping up with her rapidly unfurling thoughts.

I ought to have replied straight away to Jo's text about going out. I shouldn't have left it, but – the sense of confused frustration and anger that seemed to go hand in hand with thoughts of Jo and their friendship these days took hold – *he left me to cope here with no warning at all.*

Stepping over a fallen branch, Sara made a mental note to tell her grounds manager about it tomorrow.

Jo must have seen Tristan kiss me, or he'd be replying to my texts now.

The sound of a crow cawing made her look upwards into the boughs of the trees above.

We've been here before – me texting Jo, Jo ignoring my texts – basically he's run away. Again. Just like he did when that horrid Hazel came to The Potting Shed in the spring and tried to punish him for breaking her heart years ago.

Leaning back against the trunk of an oak tree, Sara closed her eyes and let the sound of the breeze cutting through the trees wrap around her. The rustle of the leaves above, however, failed to work their usual soothing magic, and she was soon remembering the invitation that Tristan had left with her.

I'm not changing my mind. Even if things were right with Jo, I wouldn't be going – not after Tristan reordered my entire business as if it were his own. He discounted Jo as if he were nothing!

Guilt gnawed at her. *This is all my fault.*

The memory of Tristan's kiss made her shiver. *I thought kisses were supposed to be nice – but that...* She gulped. *If Tristan stealing a kiss without asking makes me feel nauseous, that tells me all I need to know.*

Checking her phone, Sara was relieved to see a signal. *I'll try one more time, then that's it.* Her stomach knotted as she reminded herself: *This is not about Tristan – this is a matter of principle – I should be allowed to choose my own friends without Jo's say-so.*

I did NOT kiss Tristan. He kissed me. I did NOT like it. He leaves for London on Thursday. Where are you? Are you still part of our Airbnb business?

A second later her phone burst into life. She grabbed it, hoping it was Jo, only to see Maddie's name flashing on her screen.

'Sara, please don't think I'm interfering, but I really need to talk to you about Jo.'

Florrie nudged at Jo's legs as if urging him to hurry up.

'You're telling me I've kept you out too long, I take it.' Jo ruffled the collie's head. 'Come on then, let's weave back through the wood.'

As they turned round, Jo's stomach growled, reminding him how long it had been since he'd been able to face food. 'I think we both need some dinner, Flo.'

He'd only taken two steps towards The Potting Shed when his phone vibrated in his pocket. Standing still as he read the text from Sara, Jo's heart thudded in his chest as he ignored Florrie's pointed yap.

'An unwanted kiss.' He crouched down, pulling Florrie in for a cuddle she didn't want but stoically withstood. 'Do we believe that, Flo?'

A wag of the dog's tail chimed with Jo's thoughts. 'Yes, I think we do. No matter what my paranoia may have told me, Maddie's right – Tristan Harvey really isn't Sara's type, but...' He paused, his eyes running over his phone screen again. 'Sara hasn't asked if I'm okay, she hasn't said sorry – she just asks where I am and if I'm still part of Hawthorn Park.'

Florrie let out an impatient yap.

'You think that serves me right?'

Jo was tempted not to reply to the text but knew that they'd both been childish enough. With a heavy heart he said, 'Time to do the right thing, Florrie. The best thing for Sara.'

I'm staying in the camper in The Potting Shed car park. I expect I'll see you tomorrow. Of course I don't mind you having friends, but sooner or later one of them won't just be a friend. You'll not want me around then. Best I let you go now. It'll only get harder if I don't. I'm sorry about leaving you with so much work. Truly I am.

A lump formed in Jo's throat as he added:

I think we should give each other some space for a while. xx

Knowing he could have written much more, but that an

essay in text form was never a good idea, his finger hovered over the send button.

'You know, Florrie, I've a feeling I love Sara more than I thought I could ever love anyone.'

It was another thirty seconds before Jo sent the text, by which time his appetite had completely deserted him.

28

Stood by a table in the shop, Belle picked up one of Jemima's 'Grow Your Own Smoothie' recipe cards and tapped it against her hand. They had inspired an idea the previous evening, and she'd been desperate to talk to Ivan about it ever since.

Glancing towards the cheese counter, she saw Ivan was in full conversational flow with two customers, each happily sampling tiny cubes of cheeses off the ends of cocktail sticks. Belle had no doubts that he liked her, just as she had no doubts she liked him – but no, she was sure it would be impossible for them to be more than friends.

She shrugged off the despondency that always assailed her when she worked through all the reasons why it was best for them to just be good friends and nothing more. First, Milo. Second, the fragile nature of her heart after having her feelings so casually abused by her ex. Three, the twenty-year age difference. Then there were the issues that came with dating someone you worked with, should things go wrong. You only had to look at Jo and Sara. The way they moved gingerly around each other during the half an hour they had to work together each day was enough to tell Belle that it wasn't worth it. She had a job she loved with good people. *I'm not going to gamble my heart and risk losing one and breaking the other.*

Putting the recipe card back in its rack, Belle checked the

time. There were three minutes of her break remaining. Taking her chance, she moved across the shop as Ivan's customers left, each clutching a paper bag of whichever cheeses had appealed to them the most.

Belle's pulse beat a little faster as Ivan saw her approach. His smile, always broad, seemed to grow a little wider for her. *I'm probably imagining it.*

'Sales going well then?' She pointed in the direction of the retreating customers.

'Can't grumble, although I must admit...' Ivan tapped his counter '...I could do with things picking up a bit.'

'You're okay though?' Belle was surprised by the panic she felt at the prospect of Ivan being unable to keep his corner of The Potting Shed going.

'I am, but costs are rising all the time. I make less here than I did when I was on the road with a different customer base every week.'

'You're still part of the Exmoor Drifters though, aren't you?'

'Their manager, no less.' Ivan gave a quick doff of his hat. 'But running the admin side of things, taking the bookings and such, only brings in a fraction of what I made on the stall.'

'An idea to improve sales would be welcome then?'

Ivan's eyebrow rose. 'Are you cooking something up, lass?'

'Quite literally perhaps. I've had an idea but...' Belle checked her watch '...I don't have time to explain it all to you now. I can't be late back to work, especially as we have the first dementia café this afternoon.'

Ivan pulled a sympathetic face. 'How's Jo?'

'Quiet.'

'Poor guy. And poor Sara too come to that. She's not herself. Not seen her smile this week, which is not normal at all.'

Belle freed her scrunchy from her hair, letting her curls bounce around her shoulders for a second, before scooping them back up and tying them into a neater knot. 'Jo's fine with the customers – you'd never know he was heartsore – but as soon as the people have gone…'

'The mask comes off?'

'Yeah.' Belle turned to face the café. 'Must go. I'll tell you my idea next time.'

'How about tonight?' Ivan had spoken the words before he realised, he was going to. 'I said I'd make you my cannelloni with Cheddar and Stilton sometime – why not today?'

Belle hesitated. *Because I can't just do things when I want to do them.* 'I'd love to – really, but I can't today.'

'Oh, okay.'

'Friday?'

Ivan's face lit up again. 'You have a deal. I'll text you.'

'You don't have my number.'

Ivan picked a business card up off his counter. 'Mine's on here, along with my address. Drop me a text, then I'll get your number.'

'Will do.'

Belle had only taken one step away when Ivan called after her, 'Or maybe call me after work instead? Always nice to talk.'

Ed's number flashed up on Maddie's phone screen as she crossed from the herb greenhouse to the shop.

'Hey, you. This is a nice surprise.'

'Just wanted to wish you luck for your first Forget-Me-Not dementia café.'

Maddie ducked into the currently empty vegetable tunnel, so she could talk to Ed in private. 'Thanks, I'm a bit nervous, but Jo's confident it'll be straightforward and that the carers will be in the driving seat this time round.'

'Will you run the café's counter while Jo's with his mum? I assume Iris is one of the guests.'

'She is. Jo wasn't sure if she would be, as she's not been quite as compos mentis since her fall, but she'll be there.'

'Good.' Ed took a sip of coffee and then asked, 'And Jo and Sara?'

'Fragile. They're doing a good job of keeping things light, but they're avoiding each other on the whole. Jo's still camping in our car park.' Maddie sighed. 'I've tried talking to Sara, but she doesn't want to discuss it.'

'I could kill Tristan.'

Maddie suddenly stood up straight. 'Of course. Why don't *you* talk to him? Maybe if Tristan understood what he's done...'

'I don't have his number. Anyway, he'll know exactly what he's done.'

'You think so?'

'Yes... unless...' Ed's sense of fair play kicked in '...unless this time he really does like her. Sara I mean.'

Maddie groaned. 'Sara doesn't want Tristan – at all. She maintains this is all about Jo's inability to let her be friends with other men. But I didn't think Jo *did* jealousy.'

'He doesn't – normally – but he can be rather overprotective. Add to that his stubborn belief that Sara will eventually abandon him in favour of a conventional relationship, so he might as well let her go now, and you have a no-win situation.'

Maddie rubbed her temples with her spare hand. 'They need their heads knocking together.'

'True – but who's going to do it?' Ed grimaced. 'Must go. I've got a meeting in five.'

'Hope it goes well.'

'Thanks, but it'll be utterly pointless as ever.' He winked. 'Roll on Friday night.'

Belle had already cleaned and reserved five tables, removing several of the chairs so that there was plenty of room for wheelchairs or Zimmer frames.

'Have you explained to the other customers what's happening?' Belle ventured as Jo opened a box containing a red velvet sponge cake.

'No. It's just a new set of guests, after all.'

'Fair enough.' Belle passed Jo a large cake plate. 'That looks delicious.'

'Red velvet is Mum's favourite cake.'

'Maybe eating it will trigger some nice memories.'

'Thanks, Belle, that's a nice idea.' Jo smiled. 'As soon as Maddie and Elspeth get here, I'll go and wait for the home's people carrier and help Michael and Carol escort everyone in.'

'I'm looking forward to meeting your mum.'

Jo exhaled slowly. 'She's not really... Mum's great, but she isn't always herself. She could say anything.'

'You're worried she'll offend people?'

'Not so much offend, as not make much sense.'

Realising how nervous Jo was about this forthcoming visit, Belle said, 'It's going to be fine. This is a good thing you and Maddie have arranged. And the other customers will understand if things are a little less ordered in here than usual. There but for the grace of God et cetera...'

Jo nodded. 'I thought you were a Buddhist?'

'I am.' Belle grinned. 'Doesn't stop me using old clichés though.'

Relief flooded through Maddie as the quiet that had descended on her café, broken only occasionally by the sound of stilted small talk, was abruptly infused with laughter. The sound, utterly free and joyous, was coming from a rather wizened old man in a wheelchair, who had said something Maddie hadn't been able to hear from the other side of the counter, but which had clearly tickled him.

Seconds later Iris was laughing too, as were the carers and another man whose name Maddie hadn't caught. Only the fourth member of the little group remained quiet, her anxious eyes darting around the café. Maddie had the feeling that she'd have fled the scene if she'd been able.

Grateful to see that Elspeth had also noted the lady's discomfort and was now attempting to engage her in conversation, Maddie moved closer to her waitress. 'Belle, do you think you could hold the fort here? I want to check how it's going.'

'No problem. It's picked up now that bloke, Billy I think he's called, has them laughing.'

'Even so, I'd like to make sure everyone is comfortable.' Maddie took off her apron. 'My business, my responsibility.'

★

'Jo, how's it going?'

Moving closer to Maddie, Jo gathered up empty mugs and plates as he spoke, his voice low. 'Mostly good. Cynthia is a bit uncomfortable, but Carol and Michael assure me that is a standard situation. They hoped a change of scene might help, but...'

'She does seem a bit uncomfortable, even with Elspeth trying to engage her in conversation. Has she eaten or drunk anything?'

'Nothing.'

'I'm not sure I'm happy about her being here if it's making her feel worse rather than improving her day.'

'I'll talk to Michael.'

'Jo!' Iris's voice suddenly rang out. 'Is that Sara?'

Maddie and Jo turned as one, and Jo hurried to his mum's side. 'No, Mum, it's Maddie. The lady who owns this café, you remember?'

'Do I?'

Jo winced at his clumsiness at saying *remember*. 'Sara is working in the greenhouse.'

Maddie sat down next to Iris. 'Hello, Mrs Dunn, pleased to meet you.'

'Hello, Sara love.'

Maddie opened her mouth to speak, but Jo leant closer and said, 'It's Maddie, Mum, not Sara.'

A brief flicker of uncertainty crossed Iris's face, but then it was forgotten, as she carried on talking. 'This is lovely. I always liked going out for tea.' Iris's volume rose to just short of a shout. 'You had a tea set didn't you, Jo. Had little flowers on it. Tiny little cups they were.'

'I did. We drank orange squash out of the teapot.' Jo's pulse quickened, dreading what his mother might say next.

'Regular dollies' tea parties we had.'

Standing up abruptly, Jo turned to Michael. 'Do you think we should call it a day now, Michael? I think Cynthia's had enough.'

29

Belle could feel the heat in her cheeks as she poured out a bowl of cornflakes for Milo. She knew it shouldn't be so difficult to say what she wanted to say, and yet each time she mentally framed how to tell him she had a date, images of his negative reaction loomed large in her head, making her want to give up on the whole idea.

'You two got everything you need for today?'

Milo stirred a spoon through his breakfast. 'You asked us that already.'

'So I did.'

Niall raised one eye away from his phone screen. 'You okay, Mum?'

'Totally, sweetheart.' She gave her eldest child a wide smile. 'It's just, well… My new job it's…'

'Keeping you away from the house too much.' Milo stirred his cornflakes as he interrupted his mother.

'No, it isn't.' Niall gave his brother a sharp glare. 'We're fine, Mum. What were you going to say about your new job?'

'It doesn't matter.' Belle boxed up her children's packed lunches. 'You guys eat up. Can't be late for school this early in the term.'

Tugging on her gardening gloves, Sara ran to the vegetable

tunnel, where she was supposed to have started work ten minutes ago.

'I hate being late,' she told the plants as she stepped into the trapped warm air. 'But my current guests are so demanding. Boy, do they like to talk! Without Jo...'

She stopped. It was no good thinking like that. Jo might have been good at fielding the conversations of their guests while she cracked on with the breakfast, or cooking for her while she chatted, but he'd gone now. *He abandoned our business – and me – just like that.*

Sara felt her mind spiralling in ever-decreasing circles as she tried to reason things out all over again.

Tristan wants more from me – but I don't want him.
Jo didn't believe me, and so he left. And that's that.
I hate this.

Grabbing a broom from its place beneath the bench furthest from the entrance, Sara swept the path that ran around the tunnel in an oval loop, helpless to stop her mind revisiting the same old ground.

Tears gathered in her eyes, and she swept faster, the bristles of the brush scratching the paving slab pathway. *Tristan wasn't even a real friend!*

The text arrived on Belle's phone as she was emptying the dishwasher.

Thinking ahead to tomorrow night. Do you like pesto?

For a split second Belle smiled, then reality hit as she reread Ivan's message.

I have to cancel. I can't go.

She pulled a stack of plates from the dishwasher's rack.

But I want to go. She took a deep breath. *I'll tell Milo tonight. It'll only be a for a few hours anyway.*

Sliding her phone from her pocket, Belle texted fast, before she could change her mind.

I love pesto – thank you.

Two minutes later, Ivan replied.

Elspeth is coming to run my counter later. Do you want to take a quick walk at break time?

Belle checked the time. Her break was in two hours' time. She could share her idea with Ivan then, just in case she didn't get to dinner with him, pesto or not.

Love to – but only if it's not raining. Forgot my coat.

Ivan's reply of, You can share my umbrella, sent a wavelet of happiness through Belle of the sort she hadn't experienced in years.

Sara stifled a yawn as Maddie came into the polytunnel. 'Morning, how was the dementia café yesterday?'

'I'm not absolutely sure.' Maddie bent to pick up a leaf that had blown in onto the path after her.

'How do you mean?'

'Jo's mum was convinced I was you and couldn't be persuaded otherwise.'

'Oh.' Guilt hit Sara, as the thought that she ought to have been there for Jo – or at least his mum – resurfaced, just as it had at frequent intervals during a largely sleepless night.

'She started telling me – and everyone nearby, such is the volume of her voice – about a tea set and dollies Jo had as a child.'

'Ah.'

'Yes. Jo called a halt after that.'

'I did wonder if he'd be nervous about what Iris might say.'

'He admitted as much to me before the first café.'

'It's not that he minds people knowing about his past, but it sort of, I don't know, jars him. He doesn't like being thought of as the person he was – but never truly was either – if you see what I mean. Consequently, he is far more comfortable if the matter is never raised.'

'Makes sense. Jo was not his normal calm self during the visit. Mind you...' Maddie paused '...he hasn't been himself for days.'

'I know... but...'

Maddie held up her hand. 'I wasn't about to blame you – or Jo for that matter – but whatever principles are at play here, it would be good if you two sorted them out. This has gone on long enough. It's like you're stuck in a time loop.'

'I know.' Sara lowered her voice as some customers passed the tunnel's entrance. 'I don't understand how we got to this point.'

'Did you tell Jo what you told me about not fancying Tristan – or anyone for that matter?'

'We never got that far.'

'Maybe try again? You know where I am if you want to talk.'

'Thanks, Maddie.' Sara plucked a dead leaf from the nearest plant. 'So, the dementia café – Jo ended it suddenly.'

Maddie frowned. 'He did. I think that maybe stopping the session when he did might have been the right thing to do anyway, his personal worries notwithstanding. One of the guests, Cynthia, was clearly out of her comfort zone.'

'In what way?'

'She appeared anxious and kept herself withdrawn. Elspeth didn't seem concerned. Said it was not at all unusual in dementia patients, and that if Cynthia kept coming, she'd soon relax and engage. Jo is going to talk to Michael later about whether he thought it was a beneficial trip or not – for all of them, not just Cynthia.'

Tucking a short strand of hair behind her ear, Sara said, 'Jo might not want Iris to come again. Just in case she says more than he would like.'

'I know.' Making sure she wasn't overheard by two customers who'd just entered the polytunnel, Maddie whispered, 'And you – how are you, Sara? I'm not asking about you and Jo again, I'm just checking that you're coping at Hawthorn on your own?'

'I'm used to coping alone.'

'I know.' Maddie sighed. 'I'm sorry.'

'You haven't done anything to be sorry for.'

'Even so, as I said, if you need to talk, or if you can think of anything I can do that will speed up the fairy godmother coming to sort you and Jo out, then let me know.'

Sara laughed. 'Thank you, but I'm not sure Jo believes in happy ever afters.'

'It always feels odd taking a walk, even a short one, without Sheba at my side, but she's happy with Elspeth today.' Ivan opened the wooden gate so Belle could leave the bluebell garden and step into the wood behind The Potting Shed.

'I can imagine. How long have you two been together?'

'Twelve years.' Ivan paused for a second. 'I dread the day when...'

'She's fit and healthy. No need to dread in advance what's not arrived yet.'

Flicking his eyes to the side, he found himself instantly reassured by Belle's certainty. 'Buddhist thinking?'

Belle laughed. 'As I say, I try – sometimes it's not so easy.'

'You want to talk about it?'

'I'd rather talk about the idea I've had.' She checked her wristwatch, before unhooking the scrunchy from her hair and shaking it loose around her shoulders. 'We only have fifteen minutes until duty calls.'

'Tell me all, I...' Ivan abruptly stopped walking. 'Oh hell, I didn't think.'

'Pardon?'

'We're walking. I sit down most of the day, and so I need to walk when I can – keep the arthritis on its toes – but you've been on your feet all day. Should we be heading for the nearest bench?'

Belle shook her head, sending her purple curls bouncing around her shoulders. 'Honestly, it's fine. There's a difference between being able to stretch the legs properly like this and the short shuffles we do around the café. Anyway...' she gestured around her '...we should make the most of the weather before autumn fully claims the earth for winter.'

Ivan, tried not to stare to hard at Belle's curls as they leapt with every step she took. 'That is a lovely way of thinking about the seasons.'

'My Grannie Abebe again.'

'A wise woman, as I suspected.'

'Oh, she was.' Belle buried her hands in her skirt pockets. 'So, I had this idea – it might not be any good, but you did say you could do with some extra income.'

Charmed by her uncertainty, Ivan said, 'Go on. I'm intrigued.'

'I wouldn't want you to think I was interfering.'

'It hadn't crossed my mind.'

'Well, you know Jemima made those smoothie recipes?'

'Yes.'

'How about you make some recipe cards too? Cheese-based meals – pastries, savouries, and main courses. It was your alternative cheese cannelloni that gave me the idea.'

'A meal I hope we'll enjoy together tomorrow.'

'Yes.' Feeling herself flushed with heat, Belle sped up her pace, so she was ahead of Ivan. 'What do you think?'

'I think it's brilliant.' Ivan ran a hand over his stubbled chin. 'We'd have to cost it. Maddie sells Jem's cards for a pound apiece. I suspect they can sell them so cheaply because they designed and printed them themselves. I don't have the skills or the equipment to do that. Do you?'

'Not really.' Belle paused. 'My boys could do the designing, and we have a printer. I'd have to investigate its quality though.'

Ivan nodded. 'Shall we try anyway, and then rethink after we've got a few templates together? If it looks as if it won't be cost-effective we can just chalk it up to experience.'

'Good plan. We'd have to test each recipe first to make sure it worked. And we'd need a photograph of each completed dish on the cards to show what it's supposed to look like.'

Ivan agreed. 'I could have a recipe as a featured dish each week and put the associated cheese on a discount to encourage sales.'

'Or you could keep the cheese price the same, but deduct the cost of the card from the price when a customer buys both the cheese and the recipe?'

'That's an even better idea.' Ivan hadn't noticed that he'd linked his arm through Belle's until after he'd done it. 'But it will depend on what we decide people will be prepared to pay for each recipe.'

Briefly squeezing his arm with her free palm, Belle said nothing, letting the moment of closeness go unremarked as they kept walking.

After a second of silence, Ivan found himself relaxing at her side, feeling the presence of the robust woman radiating through him, producing a contentment he hadn't felt in decades. 'I'd have to consult Maddie of course – make sure she's happy with us doing them.'

'And the recipes would need to be your own originals. That way we'd avoid copyright issues.'

'That's not a problem. I've been cobbling together my own recipes for years; I've just never written them down.' Ivan fought the temptation to stroke the hair that occasionally floated across his shoulder. 'We could start with tomorrow night's meal, if you don't mind me scribbling ideas down as we eat.'

JENNY KANE

'Sounds like a good idea.' Belle waved an arm towards the gate back to the garden centre. 'We're almost back.'

'Shame.'

'Yes.' Belle wondered how to extract her arm without seeming rude or giving the impression she'd let him link with her out of obligation.

'Linking arms,' Ivan said breaking the tension, 'it feels odd doesn't it – good odd – but still odd.'

Belle laughed. 'I'm glad you said that. Although, I'm not sure odd is the right word – more... I don't know... it feels, sort of...'

'Right?'

'Yes.' Her words faltered as she shyly added, 'It does feel right, but...'

'But I'm twenty years older than you – twenty-one years to be exact. I'm fifty-six, and you're thirty-five.' Ivan's efforts to keep his words light failed. 'If that's a problem – well, of course it's a problem... I just meant...'

Belle waved her free hand while stepping one pace closer, enforcing the link of their arms. 'Your age is not a problem. Really. The problem is...'

Ivan whispered as their eyes met, 'Is?'

'My family... it's complicated.'

'Life is complicated. It doesn't mean you have to face it on your own.'

Belle said nothing as she unhooked her arm from his, before holding out both of her hands for him to take instead.

'Belle.' Ivan moved closer. He found himself inhaling the scent of shea butter from her hair. 'I...'

The shrill ring of Belle's mobile made her jump back as though she were a teenager caught in a compromising

234

situation. 'I'm so sorry.' She blanched as she opened her phone. 'It's probably Jo saying they are busy and need me back early or… Oh.'

'Belle?' Ivan reached out a hand as he saw concern flash across her face.

'It's the school.' A sinking feeling took hold of Belle's stomach. 'I'll have to take it.'

30

It was only now she was home that Belle allowed herself think. Until then she'd been operating on automatic. All that had mattered was getting to her son, finding out what had happened, and bringing him home.

Belle knew she'd been foolish to turn down Ivan's offer of a lift, rather than get a bus from work into Tiverton, but she'd needed to be alone to think how to approach the school-based confrontation to come. She had a routine to cope with her son's situation, and she needed it as much as Milo needed his.

Closing her eyes as she sat at the kitchen table, Belle let the quiet of the house invade her restless mind. She could no longer hear Milo, who'd been pacing his room like a trapped bear for the last half an hour, moving around. If his usual pattern was repeating itself, he'd have lain down and fallen fast asleep.

It's been so long since this happened. I thought we were winning.

Belle let a long, ragged sigh escape from her lips. Not only did she have Milo to worry about, but also whether she'd hurt Ivan's feelings in her haste to get to Jo and explain she had to leave.

Jo had been lovely about it, but she knew she couldn't leave him in the lurch like that again. *What if Elspeth hadn't been*

*around to take over from Ivan, so he could run the main till,
while Maddie stepped in for me?*

The fact that the school's head teacher had been so
apologetic hadn't helped. Her hands were tied by school rules;
she'd had no choice but to suspend Milo for two school days.
Normally, allowances would be made, but as he'd destroyed the
artwork he'd been working on and reduced a classmate to
tears, they'd had to be strict.

Tears trickled from the corners of her eyes, but Belle brushed
them away. If Milo saw her upset, that wouldn't help one jot.
She had feared the new job would be a potential trigger, and
now, indirectly, her fears had been realised.

Belle cursed her carelessness.

Ever since her father had died, she'd taken to wearing his
overcoat. It was a huge old hefty garment, with plenty of
pockets and had the ability to make a person feel safe, just by
having it wrapped around them. Even though it was far too
big for him, Milo quite often borrowed it. Belle had always
rather liked that he wanted to remain close to his grandfather,
even though he had only been nine when he died.

But today the wearing of his coat had sparked trouble.

Mrs Nettle, the art teacher, had spoken softly when she'd
joined Belle and Milo in the head's office. She'd explained that
Milo had been getting on well. A creation of a large collage of
his home, which he'd been working on over the last three
classes, had almost been complete. Then he'd announced he
was cold, and asked if he could wear his coat. Having been
apprised that Milo was expected to have a few difficulties
in settling into his new school year, Mrs Nettle had agreed.
A move that caused no problems at all at first. In fact, he'd
seemed more relaxed than before, snug in the oversized

garment, working carefully so as not to get any of the paint he'd been using on the coat.

It had been a few minutes later when he'd put his hand in the coat pocket and discovered a piece of card. Mrs Nettle had handed the card over to Belle – it was Ivan's business card.

Belle opened her eyes, twisting some curls through her fingers.

If I hadn't left Ivan's card in that coat pocket... if Milo hadn't borrowed it... if I hadn't been foolish enough to think that I could have a relationship...

Grannie Abebe's suddenly voice cut through her mind. *No good mithering over ifs, girl.*

'I know, Grannie, but...' Belle swallowed '...I don't know what to do.'

Of course you do, so get on and do it.

'Maddie might not want me back after I messed her about today.'

She might not, but if you don't talk to her, you won't know, will you?

'Always so blunt.'

Not blunt. Practical.

Belle smiled through her gloom as she remembered the determined old lady who'd tackled life with one hand stirring a wooden spoon through some concoction or other, while the other would be held out in practical friendship to anyone who needed it.

Pushing her palms flat on the table, Belle heaved herself upright and headed to the kitchen cupboards.

'Well, Grannie, if all else fails, there's always baking.'

Always.

Belle placed a large mixing bowl on the kitchen counter.

'The thing is, Grannie, Milo's fractured logic decided that I had Ivan's card because he was my boss. He got it into his head that Ivan's the one responsible for making me work and not being around so much. When I explained to him – again – that I work for Maddie and Sabi, and that Ivan is just a friend and colleague, he didn't believe me.'

Continuing to mumble under her breath, Belle weighed six ounces of caster sugar onto her scales. 'Turns out, Grannie, that Milo had seen me getting out of Ivan's car at the bus stop. He didn't like that. Thinking back, I guess this has been brewing for a few days, but I hoped his surliness was just him adjusting to me getting a job.' A large dollop of butter joined the sugar in the bowl. 'He didn't know who the man in the car was – but once he found the business card...'

And the artwork and his fellow pupil?

'The teacher didn't see what happened. All that Milo will say is that he doesn't like me working and it has ruined our home – hence attacking his picture of our house I suppose. The other pupil tried to stop him, but Milo screamed at him to butt out in language the teacher couldn't let pass unpunished.'

I suggest a teaspoon of extra sugar in that cake.

Belle gave a weak chuckle. 'Good idea, Grannie.'

And the man who gives you lifts? Ivan?

'Won't be giving me lifts anymore.'

Maddie closed the dishwasher and switched on the eco cycle option as Jo finished sanitising the serving counter. 'I know you've been busy, but did you get a chance to call the care home?'

'I did.' Jo untied his apron and dropped it into the laundry bag by the back door. 'Michael was very positive about the café session. Apparently, Cynthia was full of it once she got back to the home. Told anyone who'd listen what fun it was. Not uncommon behaviour for her apparently. She often withdraws into herself while watching the world around her, then claims to have been the belle of the ball afterwards.'

'That's a relief. I was worried we'd emotionally scarred her.'

'Not at all.'

'So,' Maddie asked, 'do we do it again, or was that our one and only shot at a dementia café?'

'They would like to do it again.'

'And you?'

'Me?'

'Could you face doing it again?'

'I think so, but we need to have a focus. Have something for them to do rather than just consume coffee and cake.'

Maddie opened the till to sort out the takings. 'I was thinking about that. It might be a mad idea but, how about inviting the Little Acorns to have tea with them?'

Jo's face lit up. 'That is a great idea.'

'It would depend on what the children's parents say, and it would need to be more of an after-school thing. They could do colouring in together and stuff.'

'Sounds good. Perhaps the kids could plant them something too. Provide a gift that could grow on their bedroom windowsills.'

'That is an even better idea.' Maddie paused as she counted out a handful of ten-pence pieces. 'I'm going to plant hyacinth bulbs with the school children coming here on Monday; I could do the same thing with the Little Acorns on Saturday and ask how many of them could come on Wednesday afternoon.'

'Maybe plants that are already visible would be better. Some of Mum's friends might forget there are bulbs in the soil, and think they have an empty pot on their windowsill.'

Maddie bagged up her coins. 'Perhaps they could create some mini gardens in a pot instead.'

Jo ran a critical eye over the clean café. 'Thanks, Maddie. Mum would like that.'

'How is Iris?'

'Physically better. Still mentally drifting obviously.'

'I'm sorry she thought I was Sara.'

'Not your fault.' Jo stacked some chairs onto the tables. 'You're female and my friend – that's like being the same person to Mum sometimes.'

Maddie kept her eyes on the contents of the till as she said, 'Sara felt bad about it. I suspect she feels guilty that she wasn't there for your mum – and you for that matter.'

'Then she should have come, shouldn't she.'

Maddie had only just kicked off her walking boots, and undone Florrie's lead, when her mobile rang. Sabi's name flicked across the screen.

'Hey, Sabs, how's it going and where are you?'

'A day at sea today – it's rather lovely I must admit.' She raised a glass to the screen.

'You've taken to drinking before lunch?' Maddie teased.

'Doesn't count if it's Bucks Fizz. Anyway...' she put down her glass and focused on the screen '...are you coping with keeping the accounts up to date? Oh, and did you order new trowels? There were only three left in stock, and the compost order needs checking too, and...'

Maddie broke in, 'Sabi, you're on holiday. You don't need to worry about all that.'

'I know I left a list of things to do – but you're so busy and...'

Wondering where her sister had left this list, Maddie smiled. 'Everything is in hand – don't worry.'

'And you don't find having Jemima too much?'

'She's a wonderful helper when she's here, so no, I don't. Now, go and find Henry and have a nice time!'

'Promise you're okay, Mads?'

'Promise!'

Maddie's phone had only been silent for a moment, when Jemima's name flashed across the screen. Two minutes later, half sitting, half lying on her sofa, her dog on her lap, Maddie was discovering she was to have a weekend without her niece.

'And you're sure you're, okay, Jem?'

'Absolutely. Don't worry, Aunt Maddie. I'm staying at school this weekend because I want to help with the autumn craft fair, not because I feel bad about Ed having to ferry me to and from school.'

'Then I hope it goes well.' Maddie smiled. 'The Little Acorns will miss you.'

'I'll miss them. Tell Noel I said he should behave!'

'Will do.'

'I'd better go. It's hockey practice in a bit, and Miss Hawkins gets a bit sharp if you're late.'

Maddie laughed. 'Sounds like games mistresses everywhere.'

'That's what Mum says.'

'We were not blessed with the kindest PE teachers at our

school.' Sad that she wouldn't be seeing her niece that weekend, Maddie said, 'Now off you go, or you'll be in trouble.'

Realising, as she hung up the call, that she'd been so busy she hadn't even aired Jemima's bedroom since the previous weekend, Maddie gave Florrie a hug. 'I'll miss her, but perhaps it's as well she's not coming.'

A short bark from the collie underlined her mistress's sentiments.

'Now then, Flo, what do I do first – hunt down Sabi's list, call Belle, to find out if I will have a full complement of staff tomorrow, or call Ed to tell him that we have a weekend to ourselves?'

31

'All I know for sure is that I never want another day like yesterday.' Maddie rested her head against Ed's shoulder as they lay back against the bed head, clutching mugs of coffee as they fortified themselves against the arrival of the working day.

'You survived it though. Despite being busy and having no Belle.'

'Only because you helped me with the end-of-day stuff when you arrived in the evening, because Elspeth gave up her precious beauty-product-making time and came for a few hours and Ivan agreed to close his cheese counter at three, so he could do the till while I helped Jo. If Sabi were here it would have been different, but she's not.' Maddie sighed. 'I hated having to call Belle and tell her we need her today, no matter what.'

'We might manage. I'm here, and Sara's here from eleven.'

Maddie shook her head. 'If Belle doesn't come, then Sara will have to cover the café all afternoon. Sara and Jo had to do an hour in the café together yesterday. It was as if an ice age had descended. If they'd argue it might help, but they stoically say nothing to each other, letting things simmer.'

Ed grimaced. 'I honestly don't know what to suggest about those two. Is Tristan still turning up at all hours?'

'Not seen him for a while actually, but I've been so busy, I may simply not have noticed.'

'Maybe he's gone home.' Ed took a sip of his drink. 'The last thing we need is him turning up today, especially with the Little Acorns in.'

'Sara has agreed to help with that.' Maddie bit her bottom lip. 'I'll need you to help too, but also to keep an eye on the garden centre in general. Make sure no one needs help and isn't getting it.'

'No problem. I love working here, you know that.' Ed finished his drink and threw back the duvet.

'And you hate working *there*.' Maddie pulled a face. 'How's it been this week? You haven't said much about your work over the last few days.'

'Same old. I'm getting used to it.'

'That's not the same as enjoying it.' Joining Ed in getting ready for the day, Maddie said, 'How about searching for a new job near here – maybe in Tiverton, Wellington or Taunton?'

Ed blew his girlfriend a kiss across the bed. 'Actually, I've been doing just that. There's nothing at the moment. But I'll keep trying.'

Maddie dropped the pair of socks she was about to put on and leapt across the bed in a manner that would have made Florrie proud and hugged Ed tight. 'I'd love you to be here all the time.'

Looking into her eyes, Ed nodded. 'Me too.'

'I know you only took the Bristol job for us – for this place. I can't tell you how much I love you for that, but I'd rather we lived on toast and fish fingers for the rest of our lives than you be unhappy every day.'

Ed laughed. 'You already live off toast, and I did notice a twenty-four-pack of fish fingers in the freezer...'

'Oh shush!' Maddie pushed him back on the bed with a giggle.

'I wondered about asking Jo if he'd like to come out for a drink with us later.'

'Good idea, but why don't just you two go? He might open up if you're on your own.' Maddie passed Ed two slices of toast and marmalade as she moved around the little kitchen.

'Maybe, but you and I hardly have any quality time together as it is.'

'We just had some very good quality time.'

Ed grinned. 'Trouble with that sort of quality time, is that it always leaves me wanting more.'

'That's what a girl likes to hear.' Taking a canvas bag from a drawer, Maddie dropped a packet of biscuits into it to share with the Little Acorns. 'How about I give you and Jo a head start and then join you for food?'

'Perfect solution.'

A hopeful yap from under the table reminded them that they weren't alone. 'Okay, Florrie, you can come too, but only if you promise not to beg passers-by for chips.'

Ivan's hand automatically went to Sheba's head. He patted her fur for reassurance as he brought her and Florrie to heel. They'd just crossed The Potting Shed's car park, after finishing their usual pre-opening Saturday morning walk, when, turning to see whose footfall he could hear coming through the gates, Ivan saw Belle before she saw him. She looked flustered and, if he was any judge, hadn't slept much.

She wasn't alone.

Milo?

A tall slim teenager followed Belle at a slight distance, his mass of black curls hiding his forehead, adding to the tense, nervous air he projected, as if he was stuck between fight and flight.

Not sure if he should approach them or not, Ivan felt as if his feet were stuck to the ground. Although he'd messaged Belle several times the previous day, he'd only received a single response.

I'm fine. Hands full. Back soon – sadly I won't be able to see you for dinner. B.

It annoyed Ivan how often he'd read that text, focusing his attention on the word "sadly" in the hope that there was a chance of her agreeing to reschedule their dinner date.

The memory of their walk and their almost kiss had lit a spark within him, a pilot light burning in his chest... one he now feared would blow out before he'd had a chance to kindle it into life.

Hoping he sounded relaxed, Ivan smiled. 'Good morning, Belle, and this must be...'

'Milo.' She kept her gaze on the building before them. 'Have you seen Maddie? I need to talk to her.'

Ivan reached down to Florrie, who, on hearing her mistress's name, had leapt to her feet; her movement causing Milo to take a further step backwards.

'It's alright. This is Florrie – she won't hurt you. I'm Ivan by the way, pleased to meet you.'

'How would you know if she'd hurt me or not?' Milo scuffed his trainer toes against the gravel.

Acutely embarrassed, Belle turned to her son. 'Milo, please!'

'Well, this is his fault, isn't it?' He stabbed an accusing finger in Ivan's direction. 'And that Maddie's! If they…'

'No.' Belle spoke with such soft calm, despite her obvious awkwardness, that Ivan's heart melted for her. 'You know there is no fault here, Milo. You *know* that. We've been here before haven't we, and we will work through it just like we always do.' Keeping her expression neutral, she went on, 'As I've explained, it was Ivan's business card you found.' Belle gave Ivan a pleading look. 'I suspect you were just about to go and settle Florrie and Sheba into the flat before work, weren't you?'

'Yes… Yes, that's right, I was.' Ivan unhooked Sheba's lead and pointed to the back entrance to the garden centre's main building.

'She knows the way on her own?' Milo's expression changed in an instant as Sheba trotted off as requested and his attention diverted to Florrie. 'But not this one?'

'Florrie's much younger. She'd follow Sheba alright, but I can't be sure she wouldn't get distracted along the way. In a place like this, where often there are a great many people, I don't want her getting into bad habits, so for now she stays on a lead.' Ivan turned to follow his dog. 'I expect I'll see you both later.'

Having decided her idea to produce mini gardens as gifts for the members of Charlton Lodge was far too ambitious – not to mention costly in terms of raw materials – Maddie hastily filled a tray with small wicker baskets from the main shop and carried it towards the furthest polytunnel. Placing one basket in each of the potting-up spaces on the bench the children sat at, Maddie headed back to the body of the garden centre.

'All I need now, are a dozen red, pink, and purple cyclamens. What do you think, Dad? Brightly coloured flowers for the residents to enjoy and low maintenance on the watering and feeding for the staff?'

Sounds good to me.

Laying out six dustpans and brushes, so that the children could clean up any soil they spilt while putting their flower gifts together, she turned her attention to the second half of their activity afternoon.

'We're going to talk about how plants change in the autumn, Dad.'

You going to have them collecting fallen leaves?

Maddie clapped her hands together as her father prompted her subconscious.

'That is an excellent idea. I was going to ask them to draw some autumn scenes but getting them to do something practical sounds much more fun. I can feel a trip into the woods coming on!'

Maddie was halfway between the tunnel and The Potting Shed's main shop ready to collect her cyclamens, when she spotted Belle heading into the shop. A teenage boy was trailing at her heels.

Surely she hasn't bought her son to work?

Maddie stopped moving for a second, ashamed of her instant dismay, knowing that Belle wouldn't have had her son in tow unless it was essential. Fixing a positive expression on her face, Maddie followed her into the shop. 'Hi, Belle, all okay?'

'Yes. Well... sort of.' Belle was immediately apologetic. 'The thing is...'

'You have your son with you.' Maddie gave them both a warm smile. 'Hello, Milo.'

Belle shot a sideways glance at an unresponsive Milo. 'I didn't want to let you down, but I couldn't leave him either. It wouldn't be fair on Niall and...' Belle's words dissolved into little more than a whisper '...but I can go home if you'd prefer. I don't want to be a burden. I love my job but...'

'Family first.' Maddie inclined her head in understanding. 'Belle, you're excellent at your job, and I haven't forgotten how you put yourself out for us when you first worked here, but, while I have no problem with Milo sitting at a table in the café all day, won't he be bored stiff?'

'He has a load of homework to do and his phone to play on.' Belle bit her lip as she turned to her son. 'Don't you, love?'

Taking Milo's quiet grunt as confirmation, Maddie checked the time. 'Okay. We only have twenty minutes until opening, so I'm afraid I'll have to leave you to get settled, Milo, as I must crack on. Jo's already in there.' She turned to Belle. 'I have the Little Acorns this afternoon, so I can't help out in the café once they are here, but if you need me before then, just text, okay?'

32

Although he'd practically begged to take her out the last time she'd seen him, Sara hadn't heard anything from Tristan since his unexpected appearance at Hawthorn Park.

Sara reasoned the situation out as she drove towards The Potting Shed for her eleven o'clock Saturday start. *Let's face it, although Tristan's occasionally crossed my mind over the past few days – he hasn't been on my mind, not really. I don't miss him – I miss him paying me attention.* Slowing down to negotiate the junction that took her onto the M5, and on towards The Potting Shed, her thoughts went where she didn't want them to go.

It's Jo who's on my mind. It's him I miss.

Bored stiff, Tristan lounged against the outside of the herb greenhouse, his arms crossed as he watched Sara from a distance. She was moving from the fruit and veg tunnel to the main shop, a customer at her side. His expression lightened as he spotted another familiar face. Moving forward, Tristan called out, 'Ed mate, got time for a coffee?'

Managing not to roll his eyes, Ed said, 'Sorry, the Little Acorns club begins in half an hour. I'll be helping with that.'

Tristan wrinkled his nose. 'I don't know how you stand it.'

'You've made that plain.' Ed kept an eye on the shop door. 'I assume you're waiting for Sara to come out?'

'You assume correctly.'

Only just hanging on to his temper, Ed said, 'Tristan, she's working.'

'I've come to let her know I'm heading back to London soon.'

'You keep saying that, but you don't leave.'

Tristan tapped the side of his nose. 'I've been a bit busy over the last few days.'

Ed's eyes narrowed suspiciously. 'You're on holiday – aren't you?'

'I *am* on holiday; I just became aware of a possible business opportunity and have been doing some research into it. Laying the groundwork you might say.' He stood upright, moving his back off the glass wall. 'I didn't want Sara to think I'd forgotten her.'

'Tris, please just go back your cottage. If Sara wanted to see you, she'd have called. Does she even know you're here?'

'Not yet. I'll go as soon as I've spoken to her.' Tristan adopted a conciliatory tone. 'But as she's busy, I'll fetch her a coffee and bring it out to her.'

Knowing that Jo wouldn't be thrilled to see Tristan, even if he was only collecting some takeout, Ed thought fast. 'The café is heaving. If it'll speed up your leaving, I'll fetch two takeouts – one for you and one for Sara. I can queue-jump to some extent. But please, once you have given her a drink, leave her to get on. Yes?'

'Deal. Cappuccino for me, thanks, Ed.'

★

Belle passed two full takeout cups to Ed while watching Milo, who was sitting at the furthest point of the café, his headphones on, his legs kicking back and forth under the table. His homework remained untouched in front of him.

'Thanks, Belle. Which one is the cappuccino?'

'Cappuccino?' Belle frowned. 'You don't drink that, do you? I did you a tea.'

'It isn't for me. Cappuccino and a latte.'

'Sorry, Ed. I'm all over the place. I'll do another one.' Belle lowered her voice as she busied herself with the cappuccino, her eyes moving from her task to where Jo was refilling the sandwich fridge. 'Please don't tell anyone. I've already smashed a plate this morning. I'm not normally so clumsy, but…'

'It's okay. Forget it.'

Belle's eyes darted back to her son as she worked.

'Can I take Milo a drink over for you?'

'That's very kind, Ed, but he's had plenty already.'

Passing back through the shop, Ed saw Sara bidding goodbye to the customer she'd been helping and slowed his pace to intercept her.

'These are for you. Well, this one is.' Ed raised the cup containing the latte. 'This is for Tristan.'

Sara's eyebrows rose. 'He's here?'

'And determined to talk to you, despite my explaining how busy things are. He wanted to get you a coffee, but I thought avoiding contact with Jo would be sensible.'

Taking the two cups, Sara's eyes dulled. 'Thank you.' She paused. 'I didn't mean to make Jo unhappy, it's just that…'

'Maddie said – principles.'

'Sounds silly said like that.'

Ed made no comment. 'I'm going to ask Jo out for a drink tonight. Maddie's going to join us for some food too. Why not come along?'

'Oh, I don't know. Things are so awkward.'

'Come anyway. Eight o'clock at The Cider Press. Please.'

Ivan hadn't seen or heard sight nor sound of Belle since he'd left her in the car park, on her search for Maddie. Although he knew she was working in the café, and that Milo would be with her, Ivan couldn't shake the feeling that her current predicament was his fault. Even the conversations with his customers, that he usually enjoyed so much, couldn't lift his mood.

I should have taken her unease about Milo's reactions to change more seriously.

His unhelpful musings were interrupted by the ring of his mobile. For a split second he hoped it was Belle, but then he saw Elspeth's number flashing on the screen. Five minutes later, he was placing his 'back soon' sign on the cheese counter and heading towards Maddie, as she worked her way through a short queue at the main till.

Having passed Tristan his drink, Sara kept walking towards the furthest polytunnel. She was determined to keep enough space between them, so she could dart out of the way if he attempted to kiss her again.

Chasing after her, Tristan spoke fast. 'I know you think you need to punish me for assuming a bit too much with your business, but you don't need to work extra hard to prove a point. For goodness' sake, take a break and have your drink with me.'

'You arrogant…' Sara stopped in her tracks. 'I won't thank you for the coffee, because Ed got it, and I doubt you even paid for them.' Having made sure they weren't being overheard, Sara asked, 'Why are you here? We didn't part on the best terms last time. And, just in case it didn't register with you – I do *not* appreciate being kissed in such a manner and…'

'What manner? You're a very attractive woman, and I'm an…'

'Oh my God!' Sara hissed under her breath. 'You were about to justify it by saying you are an attractive man, weren't you! Well, to lots of women you might be – but I'm not a fool, Tristan. I know it was a fake kiss delivered entirely to annoy Jo. *Please* just go back to London.'

Leaving Tristan where he stood, Sara didn't look back as she wondered where the realisation that his kiss had been fake had come from – and why she hadn't worked that out before.

'So…' Maddie was flushed after running across the garden centre. 'Change of plan. Ivan has just heard from Elspeth. She's called in sick. Nothing serious, but she isn't up to running the cheese stall while he covers the shop.'

'Poor Elspeth,' said Sara with a sympathetic grimace. 'Should I man the shop, so Ivan can stick to the cheese counter? Would you two would be okay without my help?'

'It's a case of there being someone to also keep an eye on the outside customers and make sure no one is waiting for advice.' Maddie sighed. 'I had hoped you'd help me pot up with the kids, Sara, while Ed watched the customers, and then you swapped. Ed could help me walk the Acorns through the woods, while you kept an eye on things here.'

Ed could hear the approach of children and parents outside. 'Whatever we do, we need to decide quickly.'

'I hate depriving Ivan of sales, but I can't see any other way.' Maddie groaned. 'It's so last minute.'

'Elspeth must be feeling bad to have pulled out.' Sara frowned.

'I know. I hope she's okay.' Maddie waved as she saw Noel's face peep around the polytunnel's door. 'In you come!'

'We just need one more pair of hands – or eyes, don't we.' Sara looked at Ed, who immediately frowned as he guessed what she was suggesting.

'But he'd be useless. He'd never get his hands dirty.'

'Who wouldn't?' Maddie asked as she readied herself to greet their guests.

'Tristan's here.'

'What?' Maddie shook her head. 'Jo would hate it.'

Sara sucked in her bottom lip. 'Yes, I know he would. I wouldn't enjoy it much either to be honest. I was just trying to help.'

'And it's appreciated.' Maddie gestured to Kayleigh and Sam to hang up their coats as they came in. 'But I'd rather manage as we are and lose sales, than risk making the situation with you and Jo any worse.'

★

Belle walked so fast across the shop floor that she was just short of jogging as she held out a cup of tea and a toasted sandwich.

'I'm guessing you're starving.' She laid the offering next to the till.

Ivan reached out for the sandwich. 'Famished. Thank you.'

'How is it in there?' He waved his free hand towards the café.

'Nuts.'

'Best get on then.'

'Yes.' Belle gulped. 'I'm sorry about cancelling dinner. I really did want to come.'

'And I really wanted you to come, but you have commitments and I respect them.'

'Thank you.' Belle turned to go, but Ivan called her back.

'Is he okay in there?'

'Bored.' Belle shrugged. 'I keep expecting him to tip over into resentment – which wouldn't be good.'

'Would Milo like to help me, do you think?' Ivan hadn't known he'd make the offer, but as soon as the words were spoken, he knew he meant them.

An hour passed before Milo put his hand around the café door and stared across to the main till. Ivan only spotted him because he happened to look in that direction as a customer left him.

Feeling nervous, Ivan beckoned the lad over. Telling himself that Milo must be more anxious than he was, he tapped the seat next to him.

'Come on, Milo. Your mum tells me you're a bit bored,

and I know being with an old bloke like me isn't exactly exciting, but if you want something to do, then you could help me.'

Eyeing Ivan with open suspicion, Milo's attention turned to the till. 'Can I use that?'

'I don't see why not. Here.' Ivan subtly gestured in the direction of a young family walking towards them. 'You watch while I serve these people. Then you can press the keys on the till for the next customer, okay?'

As she listened to her younger son's heavy footsteps running up the stairs and the slam of his bedroom door, Belle wasn't sure if she was about to laugh or cry. Already in possession of a cup of peppermint tea that Niall had pushed into her hands the moment her coat was off, she replayed the conversation she'd had with Milo on the way home. In fact, it hadn't so much been a conversation, as a nonstop, rather breathless commentary on everything he'd done while helping Ivan.

'Ivan let me use the till. It was dead easy. Ivan did the money at first, but he soon saw I was quicker at change than him, so he let me do it. He *trusted* me to do it. I like that. He did the talking to people – I didn't want to do that. We were like a team – he talked, I tilled, and he did the packing of stuff into bags or boxes. I did the money, Mum... I was allowed to count out the cash *and* use the card machine and...'

Exhaustion washed over Belle as she took a sip of her drink. Trying to keep up with Milo's shifting moods had always been a challenge, but this was different. This affected life beyond their home and school.

She recalled her only question to her son, shoehorned into his monologue account of the last few hours at The Potting Shed. 'You liked Ivan then?'

'Not really, but I liked playing with the till.'

33

The Cider Press hummed with low-level conversation and the crackle of a fire in the hearth. Background music was just audible via the few speakers dotted, at unobtrusive intervals, around the stone walls, as Jo and Ed settled into their first pint of Exmoor Ale of the evening.

'What did the Little Acorns' parents say about joining the dementia café on Wednesday?' Jo placed his glass on the nearest beer mat.

'Two out of six are coming.' Ed raised his pint to his lips. 'The others either have after-school clubs or have parents with work commitments who can't fit the extra trip in.'

'That's not bad.' Jo took a sip of beer.

'I get the impression that Noel, in particular, is looking forward to giving out their gifts.'

'That sounds like Noel. At least we can be certain he won't go shy with the older folk.'

'That's for sure.' Ed took another drink as he recalled the six-year-old's eager planting of his cyclamen basket. 'Kayleigh is coming too, and she's not as shy as she was.'

'I'm very grateful to Maddie for this. Mum has always loved kids. She's never said it, but knowing she'd never have grandchildren must have been a disappointment for her.'

'As long as you're happy, she's happy.' Ed put his glass down, wondering if this was a good time to bring up the subject of Sara. 'Anyway, you could adopt one day.'

'Maybe.' Jo put down his ale. 'Mum was a great mum – not all parents would be so accepting of a child who wants to change gender.'

'I know it's none of my business, Jo, but this thing with Sara – you do know it's a matter of principle, don't you? It's nothing *at all* to do with her not wanting you in her life.'

'I rather assumed that's why you asked me for a pint. To tell me off about Sara.'

'I'm not telling you off. Not at all.' Ed's heart sank. The last thing he wanted was to fall out with his friend. 'I just wondered if you knew, that's all.'

'Knew that she thinks I'm trying to control her? Yes, I know that.' Jo's posture changed from being a semi-relaxed slouch to sitting bolt upright in his chair. 'I don't mean to. It's just that I don't trust Tristan – I mean, would you?'

Already wishing he'd left the subject alone, Ed said, 'If he was my lawyer, I'd trust him. He's well known for getting the verdict he wants – not because he can manipulate a jury's decision with his rhetoric, but because he's good at picking the right cases to defend or prosecute.'

'But as a potential boyfriend?'

'I would advise women to keep at least one full bargepole's length between themselves and him.'

'I wish you'd tell Sara that.'

'There's no need to.' Ed was beginning to wish he'd insisted on Maddie joining them for the whole evening. 'That's the point, you see – she doesn't see Tristan as a boyfriend. He'd like her to, but she's not budging. He's just someone she knows. One I think, if I'm reading things correctly, she does not take any crap from.'

Jo's eyebrows rose.

'Tristan has a habit of making her hackles rise. Only today she sent him packing when...'

Jo leant forward. 'Today? He was at The Potting Shed?'

Ed gave an internal groan; he hadn't meant to let Jo know that Tristan had been around. 'He turned up to see Sara. When she wouldn't stop work to speak to him, he tried to insist, but she sent him off with a flea in his ear.'

'She did?' A flicker of hope crossed Jo's face.

'I didn't tell you because I didn't want to add to your burdens. He was there and then he was gone.'

'He hasn't been around as much – at least, I haven't seen him.'

'Tristan told me, when I went to see what he wanted, that he'd been busy working on a future business idea.'

Picking his drink back up, Jo said, 'Why can't he just bugger off back to London and leave us in peace?'

'He's going back soon. At least, that's the impression I got.'

'I'll drink to that.' Jo took a draught of beer. 'Let's talk about something else. I'm sick to death of thinking about that man.'

Ivan had almost phoned Belle so many times that his indecision as to whether to leave her alone or not was driving him mad.

His cannelloni dinner hadn't tasted anything like as good as usual, but he knew his heart hadn't been in it when he cooked it.

'Come on, Sheba.' Ivan grabbed the dog lead off a hook on the kitchen wall. 'Let's walk this off.'

★

Maddie hooked a chip off the plate in front of Ed even before she'd sat down, ushering Florrie under the table with promises of snacks later if she was a good girl.

'Sorry I'm late.' She took hold of the bottle of lager Ed had already brought her. 'I was about to leave when Ivan called. He popped in to see Elspeth while walking Sheba. She has a bad head cold. Nothing serious, but it's left her feeling heavy and tired, so she's taken to her bed for the time being.'

'Sensible.' Jo picked up a slice of pizza. 'But not great for The Potting Shed.'

Maddie agreed. 'I gave Sabi a quick call to see if she had any idea about when she'd be back. She was a bit vague, but she thinks there's about two weeks of her trip still to go.'

Ed pushed one of the four sharing plates he'd ordered towards his girlfriend. 'Here, eat some of these chicken wings. You must be famished.'

'Thanks.' Maddie picked one up, along with a serviette to cope with the sticky coating on the chicken. 'Today has just dissolved. Lunch didn't happen.'

'Lunch very much happened in the café. We were nonstop from eleven-thirty until one-thirty. I'm so glad Belle came.'

'I didn't get the chance to ask her about Milo before they left. How did he get on in the café? It was a long day to just sit.'

'Didn't you hear?' Jo was surprised. 'Ivan took him under his wing. Got him helping at the till. Did a fabulous job apparently.'

'Really?' Not sure how she felt about letting a potentially disruptive thirteen-year-old loose among her customers, Maddie just said, 'I didn't see him or Belle before they left. Sara took over the till from Ivan when it was time for him to go, so I could tidy up after the Acorns and check the plant stock before opening tomorrow.'

'Ivan did the talking and Milo did the till.' Jo smiled. 'Ivan told me he checked every transaction afterwards, and not only was Milo accurate with his change each time, but he was also so quick that the throughput increased dramatically, and customers didn't have to queue so long. You know how people are – if they think they'll have a long wait, sometimes they just give up, so that's lost sales. Milo stopped that happening.'

'That's wonderful.' Maddie took a bite of chicken. 'I'll text Belle in a minute to ask her to thank Milo.'

'She'd like that. The poor woman was on tenterhooks all day, worrying if he'd cause a scene.' Jo peeled a piece of ham off his pizza slice and popped it into his mouth. 'You know, she has another son, Niall. He's older. I wonder if he'd like a weekend job?'

'That's a great idea.' Ed turned to Maddie. 'Someone young to do the carrying of compost, watering the plants and so on? Might be handy.'

'It would – but what about Milo?' Maddie asked. 'I get the impression that his brother keeps an eye on him at home. If one comes here, they'd both have to come, and although Milo was obviously on good form today, what about the days when he isn't? I have to put the business first on this.'

'Of course you do.' Jo selected a new piece of pizza.

'It's a shame though. It could have been a short-term solution.' Ed nodded. 'You're right though. It's not like Jem helping out. She may technically be too young to work here, but it's partly her business.'

Maddie played her fork between her fingers. 'I might talk to Belle on Tuesday anyway. If Niall wants to work here once he's sixteen, and there's someone to care for Milo – then I'd be more than willing to give him a go.'

'Good idea. They could both work for you now, as long as it was out of school hours, but insurance wise, you'd be better waiting until they're sixteen if you wanted them to be on the books.' Ed picked up his mobile.

'Expecting a call?' Maddie asked.

'No, just checking the time. It's become something of a habit at work.' His eyes flitted to the door, but no one came through it. 'Can't believe it's quarter past eight already.'

Sara tried to ignore that she was sitting on the sofa with a takeaway and a movie without Jo for the second weekend on the trot. She had almost taken up Ed's invitation for a trip to the pub, but there were new guests due tomorrow evening, and as she'd promised Maddie she'd work an extra shift tomorrow, the bedding needed changing and rooms cleaning tonight.

Yawning at the rather feeble film that was failing to make her laugh, Sara could feel all the personal progress she had made since the loss of her father melting away.

His death had hit her hard. Not just because she was so young, but because, having already lost her mother, it had been just her. There was no other family to run the estate, and she'd gone from being her father's carer to the manager of Hawthorn Park at the tender age of twenty-one. It hadn't been until Jo had re-entered her life, after a period of separation, that Sara had slowly got herself together enough to reopen

the park to the public during the bluebell session and now –
thanks to his encouragement and help – she had a growing
Airbnb business as well as her part-time job among friends at
the garden centre.

'I miss you, Jo.' Picking up her mobile, Sara stared at the
screen. She knew it wouldn't take much to tap out a text, to ask
to see him. To talk about everything. To try and clear the air.

'But it ought to be him that apologises to me.'

Hearing herself getting on her high horse again, Sara spoke
sternly. 'Stop it, woman.' She looked around her. The house
was so empty, so quiet. 'You can speak your mind to Tristan –
so why not to Jo?'

Because with Jo it matters...

Sara was in the process of putting her phone down again
when a text flashed up on her screen.

> Apologies for offending you AGAIN. Forget the recital.
> How about I take you out for the day on Thursday? Bit of
> shopping, lunch, dinner before I say goodbye. T x

Sara shut her eyes for a moment. Tristan seemed to have an
unerring ability to do things at moments that were the most
inconvenient for her muddled thought processes. She sighed
before replying:

> I work on Thursdays. It was nice to meet you. Safe trip back
> to London. S

Seconds later Tristan replied:

> Go on – we'll have fun. I've grown fond of you telling me off.

Anyway, I have something very important I want to talk to you about. T x

Typing a quick reply, Sara asked:

What something?

Come on Thursday and you'll find out. T x

Yawning again, Sara typed fast.

I don't think so. Goodnight. S

Resting her head on the back of the sofa, Sara wondered what on earth Tristan had come up with now. If it was more about running a boutique hotel, she didn't want to know.

Closing her eyes, she realised that there was no way Maddie could spare her on Thursday anyway, so even if she'd wanted to go, she couldn't.

34

As Maddie ushered three primary school children towards three small watering cans, Sara placed her hands gently over those of a five-year-old. Easing a hyacinth bulb into a pot with Sara's help, the little girl giggled nervously as she covered it with earth.

'There you go, Sasha, your very own plant.'

Brushing the soil from her palms, the little girl beamed as Sara passed her a pen. 'If you write your name on one of those labels over there…' she pointed to a roll of white stickers on a nearby table '…then you can pop it on the pot, and your plant won't get mixed up with everyone else's.'

'Thank you.'

As Sasha bounded off to join her classmates, Sara returned to the bench to help her next charge. 'Hello there, I'm Sara. Do you need some help with your bulb?'

The boy held up his bulb. 'Which way does it go?'

'Like this.' Sara picked a bulb off a nearby tray and held it out in front of her, so that the roots faced downwards.

As the boy pushed the hyacinth into the earth he'd heaped into his flowerpot, Sara became conscious of being watched.

'Jo?' Sara's insides contracted as she saw his drawn face. 'Have you come in on your day off to help too?'

'Only briefly.' Jo turned from Sara and addressed the little boy. 'Nicely planted. You could fetch your name sticker now.'

'Cool.'

As the lad rushed off, Sara said, 'You must have been watching a while to know the drill.'

Not confirming that he'd been quietly observing Sara for almost fifteen minutes, Jo said, 'I wondered if you, Maddie, and Mrs...'

'Miss Matthews.'

'Right, Miss Matthews, would like a cup of something while the kids have their orange juice.' He pointed to a row of refreshments on the far side of the tunnel. 'Then I'll go to see Mum.'

'Thanks, Jo, that's very kind.'

'I try.'

'You're always kind.' Swallowing hard, Sara gestured towards Maddie. 'Better ask the boss, just in case health and safety won't allow hot drinks around the children.'

'Of course.' Jo took his grey beanie from his jacket pocket and placed it on his head.

Knowing that he only fiddled with his beanie when he was anxious, Sara mumbled, 'I should get on.'

'Sure.' As Jo watched the children tackling their potting task he asked, 'Do you want a hot chocolate if Maddie says yes to drinks?'

'Please.' Sara could see a little girl at the end of the bench putting so much soil into her pot that there was no chance a bulb would ever fit in as well. 'I really must get on.'

'Of course. That's a bulb-related emergency right there.'

Sara hurried back to her work, not sure if she'd heard

Jo say, 'You'll make it better though, you always do.' Or if she'd imagined it.

Pulling his camper van into the care home car park, Jo was surprised to be instantly hailed by Michael.

'I saw you arrive from my office window.'

Jo patted the bright orange bonnet affectionately. 'She's tricky to miss. Everything alright?'

'Very much so. Iris and Billy are still full of their trip to the Forget-Me-Not. Billy has been telling anyone who'll listen that it was a breakout, Colditz style, but with good tea.'

Jo laughed. 'No wonder Mum gets on with him so well. She has always had a puckish sense of fun.'

'That does not surprise me at all.' Michael grinned. 'And, although you were worried about Cynthia, she's been fine. Her daughter was delighted to be told all about it on her visit yesterday, albeit hearing a rather different version of events to the one you and I might remember. She's keen to go back.'

'I was going to come and talk to you about that. Two or three of the children from the Little Acorns will be there too – as we suggested when we last spoke.'

'That's great.' Michael walked towards the home with Jo. 'However, it wasn't the next café meeting that brought me out to meet you. It was your coffee.'

'My coffee?'

'You're endorsed by Davina Ditz, the famous gardener, aren't you.'

'Miraculously, yes. Why do you ask?'

'My brother is in the trade – owns a small chain of coffee shops on the coast – Bideford, Bude, Barnstaple.'

'All the B's?'

'He just needs Babbacombe and Broughton for the set.' Michael smiled. 'The thing is, his regular supplier has become unreliable, and he's hunting for either a new supplier or an additional, alternative blend of coffee – or maybe both. I promised I'd ask if you sold your blends elsewhere, or if you keep them exclusive to The Potting Shed?'

'The B & B near Exmoor where I work uses it too.' Surprised by the unexpected enquiry, Jo tugged his beanie from his head, trying not to think about the fact he wasn't working at Hawthorn Park anymore. 'I've never thought about selling to other places.'

'Can I tell my brother, Pete, that you'll consider allowing him to sell your blend?'

'Sure.' Jo crossed his arms. 'I would have to make sure I could produce the quantity he'd need, so I can't promise anything beyond giving it some thought at this stage.'

'You do the blending yourself?' This time it was Michael who was surprised.

'With my friend... Sara.' Jo felt his shoulders sag as he struggled to keep his voice level. 'I'd need to talk to her first. I use her kitchen to work from.'

'Of course.' Michael produced a business card from his wallet. 'These are Pete's contact details. Have a think and give him a shout.'

'I will. Thanks.' Wondering how he was going to bring up the subject up with Sara, Jo slipped the card into his mobile phone case. 'Best go and see Mum.'

Ivan had been in two minds about whether he should ask Belle if she'd like to go for a walk with him, Sheba and Florrie, on her day off. In the end, he'd got cross with his own indecision and sent her a message anyway.

Her instantly positive reply had seen him grabbing both dogs' leads and climbing into the van before his reply, Be there soon, had finished sending.

Twenty minutes later, Belle was climbing into his van, her dark purple dungarees tucked into a pair of bright pink wellington boots, her vast amounts of hair crammed into a blue bandana.

'I'm glad you could come.'

'I almost couldn't,' Belle admitted. 'Milo was supposed to be suspended until tomorrow, but the school relented. He's gone in but is working alone with a teaching assistant.'

'That's good.'

Belle nodded. 'It is. They've offered us a one-to-one TA in the past, but I was always reluctant. I so badly want him to be able to cope in all social situations, I thought he shouldn't have too many people to use as a crutch. I wonder, perhaps, if I hadn't...'

'Now, lass, that's no good, is it. You've done what you think is right for your lad. No one can do more than that.'

'Thanks, Ivan.' Belle reached into the back of the van to greet Sheba, who'd been patently waiting to say hello, and Florrie, who'd been rather less patient. 'Hello, girls.'

'A walk along the canal okay with you?'

'Lovely.' Belle buckled up her seatbelt. 'How come you have Florrie too?'

'I offered to have her from last night until tomorrow morning. Give Maddie a chance to do the school trip and prep for the new week, without this impatient hound begging for attention every five minutes!'

Belle laughed as Ivan switched the engine on and headed towards Tiverton's Old Road car park, and the path towards the Grand Western Canal. 'I've been meaning to message you all weekend, but I didn't quite know how to start. Silly really, because "thank you" would say it all.'

'It was fun having Milo helping me.' He paused. 'I'm assuming that's what you're thanking me for?'

'And for being so nice about me letting you down.' She glanced across at his grey stubbled face. 'I really did want to come over for dinner.'

Ivan struggled to keep his eyes on the road rather than on Belle. 'I'm glad. Maybe we'll make that dinner eventually.'

'I hope so.'

A group of mallards quacked across the canal in what appeared to be angry conversation. The water, the colour of pea soup – complete with leaf croutons – rippled every now and then, suggesting the presence of fish just below the opaque surface.

Sheba, her lead tucked over Ivan's shoulder, wandered along the towpath, keeping a neat pace with the humans. Florrie, her lead firmly on her collar, was taking great delight in investigating every new clump of weed, grass or hedgerow that lined the canal's edge.

'I've not been along here since I used to bring the boys in their pushchairs. We'd come and feed the ducks.'

'A pastime that unites mothers everywhere.'

Belle laughed. 'Sure does.' Conscious of the fact they'd

linked arms the last time they'd walked together; she wasn't quite sure where to put her hands. Glad that she'd worn something with pockets, Belle delved her palms into the dyed linen.

A few seconds passed before Ivan said, 'I had another idea. Taking your recipe card idea, a step further.'

'Go on.'

'Why should we stick to cheese-based products? The Potting Shed sells all sorts of veg and fruit; we could do recipes featuring all of it.' Ivan gave Sheba a pat as they slowed to wait for Florrie to sniff out a patch of nettles. 'What do you think?'

Taking a moment to think, Belle turned so she was facing her friend. 'It's a great idea. Although, it'll mean we'd have to spend a lot of time together to sort it all out.'

'We would, wouldn't we.'

'We would.' Belle slipped her palm into Ivan's free hand. 'Lots.'

35

Steering the camper van into the driveway to Hawthorn Park, Jo slowed to a crawl as he drove towards the house. His hands tapped anxiously against the steering wheel as he got closer to his home. *Former home?*

As he wondered whether he'd be welcome or not, an image of Sara helping the children with Maddie that morning returned to his mind. She'd looked content and comfortable. *A natural mum.*

During his visit to the care home, in an attempt to sow the seeds for her visit to The Potting Shed in two days' time, Jo had told his mum about watching Sara and Maddie working with the school children. She'd been – or had at least appeared to be – interested in hearing all about the planting of the hyacinth bulbs. As she'd tired, however, Jo found himself talking as much to himself as to Iris, musing over the chance to sell on his coffee blends and how he'd fallen out with Sara. He hadn't mentioned Tristan, but his mother had obviously been more attentive than he'd realised, for she'd suddenly looked right at him and said, 'It'll be another man then, will it?'

'Sort of.'

'Then apologise.'

'But I have. Lots.'

Raising a weary hand up, she'd given him a sleepy smile.

'Apologise again anyway. Believe me, you'll have done something wrong, even if you can't work out what it is.'

He hadn't stayed at the care home for long after that. She'd closed her eyes and slipped into sleep; her short, hippo-type grunts a sure sign that Iris would slumber for a while.

'Honestly, Mum,' Jo returned to the present as the house came into sight, 'just when I think I've lost you to the grip of a muddled mind, you say something that shows you're capable of being as sharp as a tack.'

Bringing the van to a halt in its usual space, Jo noted a people carrier parked in the guests' parking space. The realisation that he hadn't known there was a booking for that week made Jo feel worse than ever.

Exhaling slowly, he headed to the back door, hesitating as he got there. It didn't feel right to just walk in, even though he had a key. Knocking, he wondered what the chances of Sara hearing him were if she wasn't in the kitchen.

The faint sound of footsteps crossing the stone-flagged kitchen floor made Jo's pulse race a little faster.

As the wooden door was drawn back, Jo's breath caught in this throat. He had no idea how to say what needed saying, but it was too late to plan. Sara was right in front of him, her eyes fixed on his.

Normally, at that time of the evening, Jo would be sitting next to Sara on the sofa, either with a TV drama, or sorting out lists of things to do over a glass of wine or mug of hot chocolate. Tonight, however, they were perched either side of the large kitchen table, the mugs of tea in front of them made from perfunctory habit rather than because they were thirsty.

So far, they'd said very little. Jo had asked if the current guests were nice, and Sara had told him one was vegan and had forgotten to tell her before arrival. In return, Jo had reported that his mum was looking better, told her about the dementia café, and how his mum had muddled Sara up with Maddie before talking about when he'd had dolls and tea sets as a child.

Sara nodded. 'Maddie told me about it. Don't worry, loads of kids have tea sets when they are young, whether male or female.'

Jo was unconvinced. 'And dolls?'

'Action Man is a doll.'

He puffed out a short laugh. 'I suppose so.'

'Loads of the boys at my primary school played with dolls. And I played with cars come to that.'

'Point taken.' Silence descended back cross the table for a few painful seconds, before Jo said, 'I don't know where to start.' He hugged his mug to his chest. 'Apart from saying I'm sorry again, obviously.'

Sara kept her attention on her own mug, a jauntily patterned piece of china that seemed at odds with the awkwardly subdued mood. 'Thank you, but… do you know what you're apologising for?'

'A great many things, but mainly for making assumptions and coming across like I think you need me to tell you what to do or who to see.'

'Thank you.' Sara quietly coaxed, 'Go on.'

'I know you need friends, and I don't expect you to have friends that are always my friends too.'

'But?'

'I don't trust Tristan.'

Sara lifted her mug to her lips and blew across the top in an attempt to cool the contents quicker. 'But can't you at least trust *me* to handle things myself?'

Jo paused, wanting to explain himself properly. 'I believed I was being protective at first, but then I got thinking – overthinking. I tried to say before, but I messed it up.'

'You think I'm going to get fed up with you and want more than you can give. That I'll eventually desire a conventional boyfriend – without allowing for the fact that my future is my decision.'

'Well, I...'

'Jo. I have loved you for a very long time – for who you are. You know that – just as I know the limits of the relationship you can give me. Why is it okay for you to believe that I accept that of you, but you won't believe it of me?'

'But... Tristan he...'

'He gave me the chance to see what a date was like. I told him upfront that's all I wanted. I had fun – but only with the restaurant part. I had no urge to walk along with him, hand in hand, or cuddle him, and I certainly didn't want to do anything more. His kiss was a shock and most unwanted.'

Unable to speak for a few moments, Jo had a vision of Sara helping with the school children. 'You're young and feelings can change. There might be someone out there who will cause you to crave a straightforward relationship eventually. Plus... you'd be such a good mum.'

Surprised by Jo's response, not to mention his earnestness, Sara hastily put her mug down, almost slopping its contents over the table in the process. 'And you can't be a dad, is that it?'

Jo stared at his hands, not trusting himself to speak as emotion blocked his throat.

Getting up, Sara moved to the opposite side of the table. Laying one hand over his, she reached out with the other and gently eased his chin around, so Jo was looking at her.

'Yes, I'm younger than you, and I can't promise nothing will ever change – nobody can do that – but I can tell you again that I have no intention of looking for anyone else. No one can promise more than that.' She took a deep breath before addressing the other issue. 'As for a family – we have years and years to work out the family thing. There are children who need adopting, there are children to foster, there are options for surrogacy and all sorts of things but...' Sara laid a finger over his lips, stopping Jo from speaking for a second '...as you pointed out, I'm only twenty-two. It's too soon to worry about something as big as having a family. Isn't it enough for us just to be *us*?'

'Us as in friends, or us as in – well, *us*. A couple.' Jo talked faster. 'We've never really stated it – not properly – not out loud and...'

'*Both*. We are friends and – unconventional though it might be – we *are* a couple. Partners. Girlfriend and boyfriend, if you want to use the terms – just in our own way.'

'Before your father died you wanted a conventional relationship.' Jo stared at their interlocked hands. 'I needed to be sure that wasn't still the case. I wanted to give you a chance to be sure, as well.'

Sara kept a firm hold of his palm. 'And I appreciated your caution, your consideration, and how much you wanted to be sure I was happy. I still appreciate it. But I've changed, Jo, and after losing so much so young, I can't think of a better life than the one we have. In a way Tristan coming along has done us a favour – he's shown me how lucky I am with the life I have with you, here. Tell me honestly, did I give you any reason to believe I was unhappy with our life?'

'I guess not.' Shaking his head, Jo sighed.

'I'm still cross with you for being so high-handed.'

'But Tristan's an...'

'Arse?' Sara agreed. 'Yes, but I suspect under all that brashness there is a very insecure person.'

Not wanting their conversation to dissolve into a row, Jo bit back the desire to tell her he suspected she was wrong. Instead, he said, 'You always were a far nicer person than me.'

Sara picked up her mug. 'It isn't that. It's a question of giving everyone the same benefit of the doubt that I'd like to be given if someone was unsure about me.'

Jo smiled. 'Ed told me that you aren't putting up with Tristan's lazy sexism.'

'I'm not.' Sara grinned. 'Perhaps that's what I'm for? Maybe fate sent him my way to free him from the Victorian attitudes he's picked up from his father.'

'I hope you're right.'

'Even if I'm not, he'll be gone on Friday anyway.'

'I'll not pretend I'm sorry about that.'

Sara took back her hand and wrapped both palms around her mug. 'There was *no* relationship between me and Tristan – but, Jo, it *has* been nice having someone else to talk to. I love your company and that of our friends, but there is always room in life for more people.'

'Of course.'

'I've enjoyed having other things to talk about – learning about another person's life. Even if the conversations tended to dissolve into fencing matches.'

'University would have been so good for you.' He risked a glance in her direction. 'You could go. Get a degree.'

'We talked about that in the spring too, remember? I decided to stay here and run the park and the B & B – one day I may change my mind, but right now this is enough. And I thought *we* were enough.'

As Jo's eyes met hers, Sara went on, 'You do see that I've been cross with you because I shouldn't be made to feel guilty for spending time with a passing acquaintance.'

'I know. I was just trying to look out for you – even if I did mess it right up.'

Seeing Jo's earnest expression beseeching her to forgive him, Sara was tempted to listen to the voice at the back of her head telling her to forget everything that had happened. *Wipe the slate clean – move on, just the two of you as if nothing has happened.*

'I really am sorry.' Jo shuffled in his seat, filling the sudden silence.

'I know, and I'm sorry too. While you've been away, I've seen that however much I do want to run this place, I can't do it alone. I had to cancel a booking today. Two sets of friends were coming the day after tomorrow, and I just couldn't manage it all. The cleaning, cooking, shopping for food and so on. Not with The Potting Shed as well. It's too much.'

Jo went cold. 'You had to cancel, because of...'

'What did you expect? I'm doing my best, but it's only me here. You didn't even warn me you were going.'

'I thought... I couldn't stand the idea of watching you going on a date with...'

'A date I didn't go on.'

'I know – at least, I found out after the event.' Jo sighed.

'If I'd thought for even a second that I was taking business from Hawthorn Park, then…'

Sara placed her palms flat on the table. 'Either way it's done now. I just hope they don't put up a bad review on TripAdvisor after such a last-minute cancellation.'

Understanding precisely how bad a poor review for a new business like Sara's could be for its future, Jo pulled off his beanie, twisting the fabric in his hands. 'I don't know what to say.'

'What's done is done.' Sara paused, before forcing herself to say, 'Let's talk about something else. We can have a proper catch-up. It feels like months since we talked. You got any news I've missed?'

'Not really – oh.' Jo stopped dead. 'Actually, yes, I have.'

'Well tell me then!'

'Someone wants to sell my coffee blend.'

Jo had begun to relax as he told her all about the request for his coffee blend, his mum and Billy and how he'd feared for Noel's fingers, even though he'd sat on his hands during the smoothie making. It came as a shock when Sara suddenly returned them to their original conversation.

'Well, it looks like we can still have a civilised conversation.' Sara felt her heart beat faster in her chest, not yet ready to admit how much she'd enjoyed chatting to Jo. 'I feel bad about The Potting Shed. The way we've been behaving – it isn't fair on the others at work.'

'I know what you mean.'

'How about we promise to leave our home problems outside of work?'

Jo nodded. 'I'd like that.'

Not quite ready to forgive him for his high-handed manner and presumption, Sara stood up. She knew that if she didn't ask Jo to leave now, her resolve to hold on to her principles would dissolve and she'd ask him to move back in. 'I have lots to do. Maybe you should get back to The Potting Shed before the last of the light goes?'

'What? Oh yes, of course.' With a sinking heart, Jo tugged his beanie back into place, his hopes of Sara offering him his old room back in tatters. 'Absolutely. I'll see you tomorrow then.'

36

'I think that's brilliant!' Maddie paused as she and Ivan refilled the baskets of fresh vegetables they kept by the till. 'An entire set of recipe cards! Are you sure you and Belle have time?'

'It won't be an instant thing, but it'll help all of us in time. We've no plans beyond producing each one on a small scale, printing them locally, and selling them around the place. If you're okay with it, Belle's Niall will design and print them. We just didn't want to get ahead of ourselves if you weren't keen on the idea.'

'I *love* the idea.'

'That's great. Thanks.' Ivan grinned. 'Niall is keen – apparently it could count as coursework for his GCSE design and technology course at school. He's been struggling to come up with a project – so this could be it.'

'That's fabulous.' Maddie gestured to the rack of smoothie recipes. 'Jem's cards are selling well, so the more the merrier.'

'We thought they'd appeal to folk who wanted a few individual ideas, rather than having to buy a book just to get the one recipe they wanted.'

Maddie smiled at the gleam in Ivan's eyes. 'So, when are you going to invite Belle to your place so you can sample the first meal, ready to adapt it for a card?'

Ignoring the knowing expression on his friend's face, Ivan said, 'I'll see if we can get a plan of campaign together later. Best she has a few days to let things settle with Milo. Anyway, it's dementia café day, isn't it?'

'It is.' Maddie placed the last parsnip into the basket and folded the sack, trying to keep dust spray to a minimum. 'I'm hoping they'll like the gifts the children have made them.'

'They'll love them.' Laying a handful of carrots into place, Ivan asked, 'Heard from Sabi?'

'Most days I get a text. I suspect she's feeling guilty about disappearing so fast. I had a couple of photos through via WhatsApp this morning.' Maddie couldn't help sounding wistful. 'They're in the Maldives – it looks stunning.'

'Beautiful place I believe, although I've never been.'

'Nor me.' Maddie retrieved the till key from her pocket. 'Tropical seas and someone else cooking my meals are going to remain a distant dream for a bit.'

Ivan tilted his head to one side. 'When was the last time you had a holiday?'

'In the spring with Ed.'

'Maddie, that was one night in a hotel less than ten miles away, and you were so busy, you didn't even stay for breakfast. I meant an actual break away.'

'Oh, well – let me see... Long before Dad died. About six years ago I guess.'

Ivan patted her shoulder. 'Then it's high time you had another one.'

Turning towards the till, Maddie laughed. 'And just who'll run this place while I'm gone?'

*

'Hey, Belle.' Sara waved across the café as she helped Jo carry in a stack of boxed cakes.

'Sara!' Belle's hand flew to her mouth as she realised how surprised she'd sounded, not just to see Sara, but to see her in a companionable situation with Jo.

Laughing, Sara turned to Jo. 'See, told you everyone would be relieved we've stopped being stupid.'

'Sorry, Belle,' Jo apologised to his colleague. 'Normal service will resume immediately.'

'That's wonderful.' Belle hooked a stray purple curl up into her scrunchy and, not feeling she could pry by asking if they were back together or just being friendly, got down to business. 'The fridge is already sorted, and I've cleaned the tabletops, so I'm yours to command.'

Jo laughed. 'It's like having my own genie from the lamp. Belle, you are wonderful.'

'She sure is.' Ivan came through the café's door. 'Can I borrow Belle before we open? We have Potting Shed plans to discuss.'

'How intriguing!' Sara turned to Jo, who shrugged.

Belle beamed. 'Did Maddie say yes then, Ivan?'

'Sure did.'

'Say yes to what?' Jo asked.

'I'll tell you in a bit.' Belle took an A5 pad from her apron pocket. 'Come on, Ivan, let's go and play with your cheese.'

Jo's eyebrows rose as he grabbed an apron. 'Now there's a chat-up line I've not heard before!'

'It has to be local produce that forms the heart of the first few cards, don't you think?'

'Absolutely, lass.' Ivan gestured to his counter. 'And if we start with cheese, there are many varieties, each with their own tang and taste and strength. Then a few for the traditional but different cheeses – Somerset Brie, Stilton, smoked and so on.'

'But which recipe?'

'Beyond the cannelloni, I was thinking Welsh rarebit – it's easy enough for adults or supervised children to try.'

'Brilliant.' Belle jotted the idea in her notepad. 'I wondered about omelettes and lasagne as well. Simple dishes that can be lifted with the addition of really good quality cheese.'

'Perfect.' Ivan lifted two different truckles of Cheddar from his counter. 'These two would be ideal for both rarebit and omelette – they are full of flavour, but not too overpowering. They're also not too pricey, so a household budget wouldn't be overstretched.'

'And for the lasagne?'

'This one.' Ivan reached in to select a black-wax-covered truckle. 'Somerset born – hails from near Glastonbury. Plenty of poke, with a slight nutty edge that brings out the flavour of the tomato-based sauce in the meal.'

Belle smiled. 'You've really thought about this, haven't you.'

He nodded. 'That isn't all I've been thinking about.'

A warmth filled Belle as she replied, 'Nor me.'

Looking over his shoulder, making sure Maddie was fully engaged in cashing up the till, Ivan quickly placed a hand on Belle's. 'It was a lovely walk on Monday.'

'It was. Next Monday work for you too?'

'Very much so. Fancy Exmoor this time?'

'That would be wonderful, but are you sure you'll be okay walking across the uneven ground?'

Touched that Belle had asked, Ivan said, 'If it rains, we'll have to rethink it, but if it's dry, I'll be fine. We could hit Haddon Hill. I miss going up there for Dark Skies.'

'I'm sure you do.' Belle slid her hand free. 'I'd best get on.'

'Me too.' Picking up his hat, Ivan plonked it on his head with a wink. 'No rest for the wicked.'

'Oh yes, and do you have a wicked side?'

'You'll see!'

'Ohhh... promises, promises.' Belle tucked her notepad back into her apron pocket. 'Would you like to come back with me after work to discuss the recipes some more? I'm staying later today because it's dementia café day. I'd offer you dinner too, but maybe we should see how Milo reacts to you simply visiting first – if that's okay?'

'It is perfectly okay. I'd love to come back with you.'

'Milo likes you. Well, he likes how you let him use the till.'

'That's as good a place to start as any.'

'Mrs Johnson, you're an angel!'

The old lady laughed, as Maddie slipped six packets of cress seeds into a paper bag. 'I swear your regular purchases keep us going.

'Daft lass!' Passing a few coins over the counter, Mrs Johnson laughed. 'I was an angel once. In a school play.'

'I bet you were wonderful.'

'Not really, but I recall laughing a lot.'

'That I can believe,' a male voice called from just beyond the till.

'Ed! What are you doing here?' Automatically checking her watch, and finding it was only eleven in the morning, Maddie was torn between delight and worry that something bad had happened in Bristol. 'Dark Skies isn't for hours yet.'

'Just fancied seeing you, so I booked a few days' holiday.'

Mrs Johnson leant forward and patted Maddie's hand. 'I've said it before, and I will say it again – that lad of yours is a keeper. Don't let him go!'

'I've no intention of letting him go.'

'That's nice to know.' Ed smiled at their customer. 'Can I carry anything out to your car, or fetch you a trolley, Mrs Johnson?'

'No thanks, my dear. Just the cress today. I'm off to the café. Meeting my friend Daphne. Jo'll probably hide when he sees us coming. Daphne's a lovely lass, but rather challenging drink wise.' The old lady became conspiratorial. 'I can't even pronounce the coffee she has. And oat milk! I mean, whoever milked an oat? The world's gone mad.'

As she shuffled off towards the café, Ed joined Maddie behind the counter. 'Me being here a nice surprise?'

'The best!'

'Good, because I've booked us a restaurant table for dinner before Dark Skies.'

'You have?' Maddie gave him a hug. 'It's been ages since we went out.'

'Way too long.' Ed rubbed his hands together eagerly. 'For now, however, what would you like me to do first?'

It wasn't until the text arrived that Sara realised she'd forgotten about Tristan.

That should tell me all I need to know.

She read the message.

Have you asked Maddie for tomorrow off?

Rolling her eyes, she typed:

I told you I'm not coming. Safe trip home.

Turning back to where she was sweeping out the herb greenhouse, Sara was startled when her phone began to ring. 'Oh, for goodness' sake.' Glad no one was in the greenhouse with her, she answered quickly. 'Tristan, I'm at work and I said no.'

'I know you did, and I don't want to hassle you, but...'

Surprised by his vaguely panicked tone, Sara interrupted, 'Are you alright?'

'Of course – well, ish. The thing is – I know it was wrong of me, but I sort of promised you'd be there, and without you...'

'What promise?' Sara rested back against a plant-filled shelf as the relief she felt at being back on speaking terms with Jo was replaced with unease.

'I know I shouldn't have, but I sort of assumed you'd come tomorrow, so I booked for two, and now...' Tristan began to speak faster '...well, they'll only let me attend if I can prove I have a business that will benefit from the workshop. So...'

'Whoa!' Heat pricked the back of Sara's neck as she left the greenhouse, jogging towards the privacy of the far polytunnel. 'What workshop? What promise?'

'The day out was just a ruse – I was going to surprise you. You were to be my guest on a sommelier workshop in Exeter. It's rather exclusive and terribly hard to get onto.'

'I told you that you're gifted with wine, but what's it got to do with me?'

'Ah, well, that's the thing, you see. The workshop is aimed at people who run hotels, or wish to run hotels, and so...'

'My home!' Sara hissed out the words. 'How could you? I told I wasn't interested in...'

'Yes, yes, and I'm sorry, but this could be my way out of law. I know I should have been honest with you, but when the chance came, I grabbed it. Anyway, it was your idea!'

Sara couldn't believe what she was hearing. 'My idea?'

'Yes! You were the one who said there must be a way that I could follow my passion for wine and convince my father I had a worthwhile path of my own to follow.'

'Well, I...'

Tristan suddenly sounded contrite. 'I regret that my mild exaggerations of the truth involved you personally.'

'Mild exaggerations! More like massive fibs!' Sara paused, her eyes narrowing, ... 'Hang on, involved *me*, not just my home?'

'I *might* have told my father you're my girlfriend, and we were going to run your hotel together.'

'You did *what*?'

'Come on, Sara, I didn't think you'd mind. I had to – Father knows the man running the course. You don't know what it's like having a bully as a father. Nothing I do is ever good enough. If I can do this workshop, I'll be able to show the right people that my knowledge of wine is more than a passing fancy; prove to my father that it's not just a passing fad. Escape from the bar and, if I can impress the right people, I can get my foot in the door of...'

Sara had stopped listening. 'I can't believe you'd use me like this!'

'I tried to explain! It's my father – you don't understand.'

'Of course I don't, I don't have a father anymore, do I! And mine would never, *never* have behaved like that!'

37

Jo had carried on buttering bread the entire time a furious Sara had spoken. 'Now that you've calmed down and you're no long ready to murder Tristan for his assumptions, what will you do?'

Surprised that Jo hadn't instantly told her to block Tristan from her phone, Sara said, 'I wasn't going to do anything. He's pushed his luck too far this time. More fool me for cutting him so much slack before!'

Jo paused mid-buttering. 'You're far from a fool. I'm a solitary creature, but you aren't. Being solitary was forced upon you. Now, thanks to this place, you are finding your social wings again. This time you were unlucky with who you were social with, that's all. I still think going to uni or meeting people some other way – evening classes or something – would be good for you.' He almost added, *good for us even* – but stopped himself just in time. It was bad enough that Tristan was making presumptions about Sara and their future, without him making the same mistake.

Sara released a lungful of air she hadn't realised she'd been holding in. 'I was nervous about telling you about Tristan's call, in case it set us back again.'

'I'm glad you told me. I know we aren't well – mended – but just talking feels so much nicer.' Jo placed three slices of baked ham between two pieces of granary bread. 'Do you think Tristan would be a good sommelier?'

'I do, actually. On the few occasions we were together, when we talked about wine, it was the only time he was truly comfortable with himself. There was front, no pretending, just a guy with a passion.'

'Is that what made you say he was a nicer guy than he appeared to be?'

'Yes.' Sara paused. 'His father is controlling – that's why he does the job he does – and why he has such an unfortunate manner a lot of the time. I ought to have explained better, but I was so...'

'That doesn't matter anymore.' Jo wrapped a set of sandwiches in a paper bag. 'I think you should ask Maddie if you can take Thursday off.'

Sara put down the block of cheese she'd been about to pass Jo's way. 'Who are you, and what have you done with Jo Dunn?'

'I mean it. If Tristan was doing something he liked and got free from the expectations of his father, who you say is at the root of a lot of his crappy behaviour, then might he become a nicer person? A better person? Perhaps you can help him do that.'

'I'll consider it.' Sara shrugged. 'In all honesty, it's probably a nonstarter whatever I decide. Maddie won't be able to spare me tomorrow anyway.'

'No problem, Take the day off. You've earned it. In fact, your timing could not have been better.'

'Really?' Sara wasn't sure if she was pleased or not.

'Ed's here! He arrived not ten minutes ago. He's taken a few days off and is willing to help here. He can do your job tomorrow.'

A wave of guilt hit Sara. 'But, Maddie, if I'm here tomorrow too, you'd have less on your shoulders. You might even have time to do some paperwork and stuff or spend time with Ed.'

'True, but you have a business to run as well. I'm sure you need the time to sort that out, don't you?'

'Well – yes. Although, I had been invited into Exeter by a friend, so…'

'Even better!' Maddie tapped a pile of paper bags into order on the till's counter. 'You deserve some fun.'

'So do you.'

'I'm going out for dinner with Ed tonight before Dark Skies.'

'That's great.'

'I'm so excited. We haven't been on a date in months.' Maddie found herself beaming. 'Anyway, you take tomorrow off. Enjoy yourself!'

I'm not so sure about that.

'Oh, and while I think about it, I have a favour to ask. I don't suppose you'd have Florrie at Hawthorn tonight? No worries if not. I don't want to upset your guests or anything, but Ivan is going to Belle's and as Ed is taking me out…'

'Absolutely. No problem at all. I'd be delighted to Florrie-sit.'

'I?' Maddie paused. 'I thought you and Jo were okay again?'

Sara bit her bottom lip, 'We're getting on okay. But things aren't what they were – I haven't asked him to move back in.'

Disappointed for Jo, Maddie gently asked, 'Will you, do you think?'

'I honestly don't know.'

With Jo's word that he'd be supportive, and a promise he wouldn't come 'the heavy friend' about the situation at the last minute, Sara sent a message.

> I'll come – but if asked outright. I won't lie about you being part of my business.

The reply was almost instant.

> Wonderful! All I need is you and Hawthorn Park to give me an in.

Apprehension trickled down Sara's spine.

> I don't have to do the workshop too, do I?

> I've paid for you, but if you'd rather, I'll explain you're a sleeping partner. Once the workshop begins, you can claim a headache and leave if you want.

'Claim a headache?' Sara typed a fast reply, her former lie rising in her mind.

> I'll go in with you, explain wine is your interest, but I can't leave if you've paid for me. That would be rude and wasteful.

> Let's worry about that on the day. I will see you at 9 a.m. for brunch at the bistro by the cathedral. We can talk the course through first.

Wondering what on earth she was letting herself in for, Sara typed:

9.30 a.m. at the earliest. I have guests who plan to leave at 8.30 a.m.

Tristan's response was instant.

9.30 a.m. it is.

After typing a swift See you tomorrow, Sara slipped her mobile into her pocket, and went to report to Jo.

'The care home people carrier is here!' Sara zipped into the main shop, calling over to Maddie at the till, before dashing into the café to alert her friends.

'Any sign of Noel and Kayleigh?' Jo left the counter, ready to help Michael and Carol with their visitors.

'Not so far.'

'That's good. I know Maddie asked them not to come until the older folk had had time to settle, but that doesn't mean that's what'll happen.'

Sara laughed. 'You mean Noel might be overenthusiastic?'

'The thought had crossed my mind.' Jo checked his watch. 'School has only just finished, so he'll be at least half an hour yet.'

'I'm going to keep an eye on things outside while Ed runs the till, but if you get busy, call me, and I'll come and help Belle.'

'Excellent. Thanks.'

Jo moved a couple of surplus chairs out of the way. 'It's a real shame Elspeth isn't well enough to come.'

'She'll be better soon.' Sara began to help with the chairs. 'Strong as an ox, but best she rests while she can. Let's go and greet our guests, I'd like to say hi to your mum before I crack on.'

Having patiently watched Kayleigh deliver her carefully planted basket to Cynthia, Noel proudly carried his cyclamens towards Iris. Walking behind him, Maddie smiled as he thrust the recently planted flowers out towards Jo's mum.

'We made this for you. Hope you like it.'

Crouched next to his mum, Jo helped guide her arm as she reached out for the basket. 'For me?'

'Yeah. We made them in Little Acorns.'

'Like oak trees?' Iris frowned, a worried confusion in her eyes.

'Yes, Mum, like oak trees. Noel and his friend are in a gardening group here. It is called Little Acorns.'

'That's nice, Joanna dear.'

Jo flinched. A cold sweat abruptly prickled across his back. *Did Maddie hear her?*

A panicked Jo was furtively looking about for a reaction from the people sitting around him, when Noel piped up, 'I bet you have a sister or a friend or someone called Joanna don't you, Jo. My nan gets my name mixed up with my cousins *all* the time. I was Harry yesterday. At Christmas she called me June! In December too!'

Unable to prevent the nervous chuckle that erupted from his throat, Jo offered Noel a seat next to Iris. 'My nan used to get muddled all the time too. It doesn't matter though, does it. We love them anyway.'

Noel nodded sagely. 'My nan is great. She buys me toffees.'

Wondering if Noel's grandparent wasn't just lovely, but very clever in giving her grandson a sweet that had the potential to slow down his verbal flow, Jo said, 'My mum is fonder of cake than sweets, aren't you, Mum?'

'Red velvet cake is my absolute favourite.' Iris shuffled in her seat, before muttering, 'That's right, isn't it, Jo? That was the one I liked – wasn't it?'

Seeing his mum was in danger of becoming insecure, Jo spoke gently. 'It's been your favourite for a long time. Would you like some now?'

'Yes please.'

'I'll get it.' Maddie jumped up. 'Does anyone else want anything?'

'Another tea?' Billy called from his wheelchair. 'Lovely cups of tea always taste even lovelier when they are served by a pretty girl.'

Michael and Carol exchanged glances, but Maddie held up her hand. 'It's okay, I take all the compliments I can get. Would you two like anything else?'

'I'm good thanks.' Michael gestured to a full latte glass. 'Carol?'

'Not for me, either. Cynthia and I are still going strong with this pot of tea.' She smiled at her companion. 'More cake for you, love?'

Cynthia shook her head sharply, but then made the tiniest nod Maddie had ever seen.

Carol smiled. 'Another piece of cake here as well then please, Maddie.'

As Maddie made her way to Belle at the counter, Jo looked at Billy; he was cradling the cyclamen plant Kayleigh had given him earlier. 'Would you like me to keep that safe for you until you go home?'

'Thanks, my boy.' Billy passed over the basket. 'Goodness knows where I'll put it. My farmhouse is so full you know. Edna has pot plants in every windowsill.'

'You live on a farm?!' Noel's eyes widened. 'I like farms. We had a school trip to a farm. Cows are huge!'

Iris nodded vigorously. 'Do you remember when we had a holiday on a farm, Jo? About eight you were. Those cows in that field... you remember?'

Relief shot through Jo as Iris once more related to him properly. 'I do! I was terrified. They were so much bigger than me. They started chasing after us when we crossed their field. It was like the cows were herding us!'

'Scary!' Kayleigh looked up from where she'd been sucking orange juice through a straw.

'It was.' Iris clapped. 'We ran to the gate! Didn't we run, Jo.'

'Like the clappers, Mum.'

'Dropped our picnic.' Iris gave a raucous laugh. 'You got cows on your farm, Billy?'

'Just hens, lots of hens.'

As Maddie came back with a slice of cake and some tea, Noel whispered, 'Does Billy really have a farm?'

'No, not anymore. He did once though.'

Noel tapped his nose, making Maddie suspect someone had told him that's what wise people did, as he said, 'It'll be that dementer thingy muddling him.'

'Afraid so.'

'At least it's nice thinking you've got a farm, even if you haven't.'

Maddie smiled proudly at the little boy. 'Yes, Noel, it's a lovely thing to think.'

The singalong to 'Old Macdonald had a Farm' was as unexpected as it was fun; made livelier by the other guests in the café joining in – animal noises and all. As the children and their parents left in a flurry of hugs and waves to Iris, Billy and Cynthia, a lump formed in Jo's throat.

The thing I dreaded happening happened – Mum called me by my dead name – and no one batted an eyelid.

Jo knew that Noel would never understand how grateful he was to him for just ploughing on with his muddled-names theory.

Four o'clock, and the end of the café, had arrived at speed. Billy and Cynthia were already waiting in the people carrier for the trip back to Charlton Lodge. Maddie was clearing the tables, while Belle chatted to their regular customers as she turned the café's open sign to closed.

Helping his mum on with her coat, Jo said, 'Ready to head back to the car, Mum?'

'Sit a moment.' Iris patted the seat next to her.

Doing as he was told, a strange sensation flooded Jo. For a moment he felt he was with his real mum, not the dementia-addled woman who inhabited her body most of the time. 'Are you okay?'

'Yes, son.' She reached out and took his hand. Then, as if she was seeing him properly for the first time in years, Iris said,

'I can't remember if I told you – so I'm telling you now. I'm so proud of you, and I know without a shadow of a doubt that your father would have been proud too, had he lived to see you grow into the marvellous man you are today.'

'Mum, I...'

'No. No more to say.' Iris reached out for her walking stick. 'It's time to go.'

38

Having made sure her guests had enough tea, coffee, biscuits, and hot chocolate to see them through the evening, Sara climbed down the stairs of Hawthorn Park.

Rain hammered against the window as she put her head around the door to her private living quarters. *I'd be asking Jo if he wanted a cup of coffee about now.*

She paused in the doorway, watching the flames dance in the fireplace. Florrie was curled up, fast asleep, on the mat before the hearth. 'Are you okay, girl?' Kneeling down to stroke Maddie's dog, Sara sighed. 'Jo and I got on well today. Maybe I was harsh not asking him to come back.'

Florrie murmured non-committally in her sleep, making Sara smile. 'Oh very helpful – not.'

I still don't feel if he trusts me anymore – not in the ways that matter.

Florrie suddenly looked up from her resting place and, shuffling around, rested her head on Sara's lap.

'What's that, Florrie – you think all ways of trust matter?' Sara blew out a sigh that was so heavy it made the flames waver. 'I was just thinking the same thing. I always suspected you were a mind reader.'

Jo weighed his mobile phone in his palm as he perched on

the slim bed that took up the majority of his camper van. He needed to talk to someone – *I need to talk to Sara.*

Lying back, his long slim body hanging off the end of the bed, Jo checked his watch. 'If I was at Hawthorn Park, we'd be sitting in front of the fire, the guests having been settled – probably with a movie on the telly and the fire raging.'

He closed his eyes. 'What can I do to fix us?'

'Sod it.' Sara leant forward from the sofa, swiped up her mobile, and pressed Jo's number, mumbling, 'We got on well today, Florrie; it isn't so weird that I should call. I want to check on his mum after the café visit. That's all.'

Jo jumped as the mobile he was about to use to text Sara burst into life in his hand. His pulse leapt as he saw her number on the screen.

'I was just going to text. Everything okay?'

'Yes.' He could hear Sara swallow before she added, 'Florrie is spark out on the rug and the guests are settled. I was wondering how your mum got on today.'

Suddenly Jo found himself blurting out, 'She called me Joanna today.'

'Oh, Jo! I'm so sorry. You should have said before.'

'We were busy and, if I'm honest, I needed to process it.' Jo rested back against his bed. 'I was so worried she'd do that, and now she has, I'm not sure what I was worried about.'

'Did anyone overhear her?'

'I suspect Maddie did, but she didn't say anything.' Jo

grimaced. 'Noel heard and immediately pounced on her mistake, comparing it to similar name-calling errors his Nan makes.'

'Was that good, or not?'

'Good I think. It made the slip normal.'

'It *is* normal – even if your mum didn't have dementia, it wouldn't be that odd for her to occasionally say daughter instead or son, her instead of him. She's only human, and you were Joanna for a long time.'

'Mum has always been brilliant at pronouns and such. I can only recall a few slip-ups, even early on, when it was a new concept.' He listened as the wind and rain lashed the side of the van. 'I'm so lucky.'

'What is it, Jo?' Sara's voice became coaxing as she asked, 'What's bothering you beyond Iris's slip-up?'

'Beyond missing you and wishing I hadn't messed us up?'

Sara whispered, 'Yes, Jo – beyond that.'

'Mum told me how proud she was of me – and how proud Dad would have been.'

'But that's lovely.'

'It was. Really lovely.'

'So why the sad voice?'

'It reminded me of the woman Mum was before. It was as if, just for a few minutes, she was Iris Dunn; a woman of endless energy with a wicked laugh. A hardworking, kind human being with time for everyone. Not dotty, frail Iris, the old lady with dementia.'

Ed raised his glass of lemonade and chinked it against Maddie's wine glass. 'Cheers!'

'Likewise.' Maddie took a sip of the perfectly chilled Pinot. 'It's a shame it's raining so much that Dark Skies has had to be cancelled, but on the other hand, we do get to relax over dinner, rather than clock-watch.'

'I had wondered about cancelling anyway, so I could have you all to myself for longer, but as it would have been only the second of the season, I didn't think I should.'

'Meanwhile, the good old English weather had other plans.' Maddie turned to the window. The old stone bridge she could see outside, which had taken people, animals and vehicles over the River Exe for hundreds of years, was only visible through a fog of steamed-up glass and raindrops. 'No heron spotting for us this time.'

Ed smiled at the memory of their first dinner date, taken in that very pub almost a year ago. 'I can't believe it's been so long.'

'It's gone in a flash.' Maddie reached out a hand and held Ed's palm across the table. 'Thank you for bringing me here tonight. It's such a treat to get off site for a while.'

'My total pleasure.' Sitting back as the waitress arrived and deposited two plates of rare steak and chunky chips on the table, Ed added, 'It's been the best time of my life.'

Maddie flushed with pleasure. 'Mine too – even with all the hassle with BIG and the dramas over the conversion of the house into a garden centre shop and flat – it's been an incredible adventure. I've loved being able to share it all with you.'

'Likewise.' Ed cut into his steak, approving of the perfectly cooked meat. 'And now, Sara and Jo are settled again – and Ivan appears to have found someone to share things with.'

Maddie chewed thoughtfully. 'I'm so pleased for him and Belle. I hope they're having a nice evening.'

'Janga soup is a Jamaican soup consisting of janga – that's Jamaican for freshwater crayfish – and various vegetables. Grannie Abebe used pumpkin, carrots, onions and sweet potatoes, usually seasoned with garlic, thyme, scotch bonnet peppers and pimento.'

'That sounds amazing. Although – maybe we should put the scotch bonnet peppers as optional – they're so hot, they're not for everyone.'

'Good point.' Belle nodded. 'We could suggest green chili as an alternative.'

Ivan scribbled the name of the soup down on their ideas list. 'That's one for the non-cheese recipe cards – actually, it would be a wonderful autumnal dish. Maybe we should get Niall on that recipe first. Use it as an experimental card to give to Maddie to see if the cards actually sell. Pumpkin season is almost upon us.'

'So it is.' Belle nodded. 'The years seems to fly by. I work by school terms, and no sooner does one start, than it's ending and I'm thinking ahead to what the boys will be needing next term.'

'Your boys are very lucky to have such a caring mum.'

'You're very kind.' Touched by Ivan's compliment, Belle glanced anxiously towards the closed kitchen door. 'I ought to check on Milo really.'

'Don't let me stop you.' Ivan nodded at the carriage clock, sat next to a large floral jug, on a haphazardly stacked dresser to one side of the kitchen. 'It's almost six-thirty. I ought to be going. I bet your boys will be getting hungry.'

'I hadn't realised the time.' Belle abruptly stood up. 'Dinner is always at seven. If it's late, then...'

'Milo?'

'Routine, you see. It is so important. He might be fine if it's late, but... I never like risking it. Especially when so much else new is going on.' She looked around her kitchen as if she was surprised to find the meal she'd planned wasn't already cooking on the hob.

Noting the panic in her voice, Ivan rested a hand on her arm. 'So, what were you going to cook tonight?'

'Chinese chicken stir-fry with noodles.'

'A nice quick meal. I'll clear up our notes; you chop the chicken. Then, if you show me where to find the noodles, I'll boil some water and get everything ready, before leaving you in peace to eat with your family.'

'I can't ask you to help and not stay to eat!' Belle was already on her feet, taking the chicken from the fridge as Ivan knocked their paperwork into a neat pile.

'Of course you can. I need to get back and Sheba has been very patient.'

Even more flustered, Belle said, 'Poor Sheba! I can't believe I forgot about her. I was so engrossed and...'

'Having a nice time, I hope?'

'Very much.' Belle picked up her meat knife and placed it over the first chicken breast. 'But I shouldn't have been. I am a mum with responsibilities and...'

The door to the kitchen flew open, and a mobile phone shot

across the room, hitting the large floral jug that sat on the edge of the dresser, smashing it to smithereens.

'No!' Tears sprang to Belle's eyes as she ran for the fallen shards as Milo, red with anger, stepped around the door, glowering at the damage his missile had caused.

Ivan froze. All his instincts told him to rush to Belle's side, but the glare in Milo's eyes stopped him.

Finally finding her voice, Belle's words came out in a shocked hush: 'Milo, how could you?'

The sound of footsteps thundering down the stairs immediately preceded the arrival of Niall. 'What the hell was that noise? I heard a smash.'

Belle straightened up and held out two of the larger fragments of the broken jug.

'Grannie Abebe's favourite jug!' Niall ran to his mum's side. 'What happened?'

Despite opening and closing his mouth, no words emerged from Milo's mouth as he looked from his mum's face to her hands, to the remains of her jug on the tiled floor, and on to his phone, its screen, remarkably, intact.

Unable to stand his inaction any longer, Ivan crouched down to the fallen jug. 'The pieces are big, there might be a way to save it – if we can find…'

Milo yelled across the room at Ivan. 'It's your fault! Not mine!'

Every single muscle in Belle's body felt as if it might snap as she picked up the fallen phone and put it in her pocket. 'Milo, Ivan has just been helping me with…'

'People like that only employ people like us because they want to tick a box!'

The accusation came out like a bullet. Belle saw Ivan flinch, incomprehension on his face, as Milo carried on, turning to his brother, his claims completely out of sync with events. 'I bet that Willand woman had no black people on the payroll, so when Mum turned up, she thought she'd better grab her quick.'

Niall was shaking his head, as Ivan turned sharply and held Milo's gaze with his own. His words, while not loud, were to the point. 'Listen, Milo – even if you ignore everything else I ever say, believe this – neither Maddie nor her sister have *ever* cared about ticking boxes! They don't care if a person is black, white or sky-blue-pink. They *are* interested in three things when it comes to the people who work for them. One: whether you a good human being who can get on with other people. Two: that you have green fingers or can cook. Three: that you will work hard, even if you're having a bad day and simply want to go home and put your feet up.'

Milo lowered his eyes and shuffled awkwardly to his usual seat at the kitchen table.

Softening his tone, Ivan added, 'Milo, Maddie is one of life's good people. She hasn't had it easy. You might see her as owning a growing business and land, but what she actually owns is a huge bank loan and a hell of a lot of responsibility.'

'But Mum is *always* there! I never...'

'I know you don't like this, but you know your mum's only working so she can provide for you.' Ivan gave a heavy sigh. 'And now I've come along and knocked you even further off your axis haven't I? I'm sorry, Milo.'

Milo's face creased in confusion. '*You're* sorry?'

'Of course. Being thirteen stinks, even when your ordered

world isn't being changed around you.' Ivan spoke carefully, remembering what Belle had told him about her son. 'You like things to be ordered, don't you – for things to stay the same?'

'Uh-huh.' Milo swallowed. 'I... I get unsettled. Mum says I get flustered.'

Ivan smiled. 'Great word that, flustered.' He stood up. 'I get flustered sometimes – but not as much as I used to. Would you like to know my secret?'

Milo's lips stayed firmly locked together, but he nodded anyway.

'Sheba. My dog. I know you've met her before, but would you like to say hello to her properly?'

'Is she here?'

'Outside, in your garden. She needs a walk. Shall we go and have a walk while your mum makes your dinner?'

'I... I don't do walks until the weekend.'

'I bet you don't normally throw things across the room and break your mum's special things either.'

Milo hung his head. 'No, I don't.'

Belle bit her lips together. 'I thought you liked Ivan, Milo. You liked the till.'

'I wasn't cross with Ivan.'

'Wherever did you get the idea that Maddie only wanted me because I was black?'

'There was something on Twitter just now about employers getting into trouble for not being inclusive and...'

Privately cursing social media, Belle said, 'And you put two and two together and made five.'

Milo's forehead furrowed. 'No, Mum, two and two can only ever make four.'

'Oh, Milo.' Belle ruffled her son's hair. 'What am I going to do with you?'

'You could give me my phone back.'

'I don't think so, Milo. I'm not sure you deserve it for a while, do you?'

39

'Milo isn't even allowed on Twitter. Mum doesn't like either of us using social media 'cos of the ideas it puts into Milo's head. His friends must have been talking about it at school again. He is easily pressured into doing things.' Niall sighed as he carefully passed Ivan a bag. 'I think I found all the pieces that Mum had chucked in the bin.'

'Thank you.' Transferring the load to the floor of the passenger seat, Ivan peered inside at the collection of pottery shards. 'I may not be able to save it, but if I can, I will. Don't tell your mum in case I can't. I don't want to get her hopes up.'

Niall glanced over his shoulder towards the house, where he'd left his mum and Milo cooking their dinner. 'You could stay. We could talk about the recipe cards. I've designed some. My teacher is dead keen on the idea.'

'There's nothing I'd like more, Niall, and I'm looking forward to seeing your cards, but...'

Niall interrupted, his voice earnest. 'I think Mum would like it if you stayed.'

'As I said, I'd like it too, but Milo needs time. Right now, he'll be feeling awful about the jug and jumping to conclusions.'

'He always feels bad after he has a moment, but it doesn't stop him having them. He'll probably feel worse about not having his phone for a while than about what he did.' Rubbing the toe of one trainer with the heel of the other, Niall asked, 'Did he say sorry while you were with Sheba?'

'In his own way.'

'You mean no.'

Ivan smiled. 'He said sorry to Sheba for keeping her waiting for her walk. That's a start.'

'I'm stuffed!' Maddie laid down her dessert spoon, having thoroughly licked it clean.

'I'm not at all surprised. I imagine you'll be slipping into a carb-coma any minute.' Ed laughed as Maddie rested back against her seat, her hands on her belly. 'Sponge chocolate and caramel biscuit ice-cream, plus caramel sauce...'

Sticking her tongue out at him, Maddie said, 'You're just jealous because your apple pie and clotted cream was so much smaller than my pudding.'

'True!' Ed grinned. 'Your body is probably in shock. A whole meal without any known bread product involved.'

'It was delicious, but you have to go a long way to beat my cheese on toast.'

'That is true.' Ed refilled Maddie's wine glass. 'Especially when you go mad and add a dash of Worcester sauce.'

'Are you teasing me, Edward Tate?'

'Yes. Coffee?'

'I honestly don't think I could. I'm not sure I'll get through this wine to be honest.'

'That's a very defeatist attitude.'

'Perhaps, but...' Maddie looked out into the dark '...we'd better go back soon. The evenings are closing in, and the weather's so bad. I have a few jobs to do around the tunnels before bed too.'

'No, you don't.'

'I do. I didn't get to water or…'

'Before you say it, Sara watered and swept the tunnels while you were with the Forget-Me-Not guests, and I helped her finish off the bits she'd didn't have time for while you were cashing up.'

'Really?'

'Yep.' Ed pushed Maddie's wine glass closer to her. 'And although there is bound to be other stuff to do, it can wait.'

'I need to do the books. Sabi will kill me when she gets home. I've been a bit slapdash with my ordering and a bit random when it comes to writing things down.'

'Don't worry, I have custody of her accounting tablet for the non-café bits, so we can get it all up to date tomorrow.' Ed drained the last of his alcohol-free lager. 'Any word on when she and Henry are coming back?'

'Not so far. They are in the Maldives. Sabi sent me some beautiful photos.'

Ed tilted his head to one side. 'Do I detect a touch of wistfulness?'

'Not at all.'

'Maddie?'

'Well, maybe a bit, but please don't think that's because I'm unhappy here. Tonight has been wonderful.'

'And it's not over yet.'

'I really can't face coffee, Ed.'

'Nor me. I'll grab the bill, then we'll get going.'

Maddie sighed. 'Probably best. It has been nice to escape

work for a while though. The trouble with living over the shop is that you're never quite off duty.'

'I said nothing about going home.'

'But?'

'Head to the car. You'll find an overnight bag plus your wellies, waterproof trousers and jacket in the boot.'

Maddie jumped to her feet and ran around the table to hug her boyfriend, oblivious to the curious glances of their fellow diners. 'Puddle splashing?'

'Well, we've got the weather for it!'

'Belle?' Ivan cradled his landline phone's receiver next to his ear. 'Everything okay there now?'

'I just wanted to apologise.'

'You have nothing to apologise for.'

'Feels like I do.' Belle paused. 'Milo just told Niall and me what you said to him when you were with Sheba. About how being a grown-up means doing things for other people before yourself and thinking ahead and so on.'

'Uh-huh.' Ivan studied the salvaged pieces of jug, knowing, now that he'd heard her voice, how much he wanted to mend it for her, even though he wasn't yet sure how. 'I hope I didn't overstep the mark.'

'Not at all. You even used Grannie Abebe as an example and got him to tell you about her.'

'I thought talking about her, and how much you loved her, might help him see how much breaking the jug hurt you.'

'He loved her too – both boys did. And Papa Harri.'

'Your grandfather?'

'Yes. Quiet. A real sweetheart.' Belle gave a soft chuckle. 'Couldn't often get a word in if I'm honest.'

'Milo told me about the cooking lessons his gran gave him.'

'He's a good cook when he decides he wants to do it. Actually, he's good at everything when he's in the mood. He's clever.'

'Doesn't surprise me at all.' Ivan swallowed. 'Look at his mum.'

'I don't know about that.'

'Well, I do. Now, tell me, have you eaten?'

'Yes, dinner's all done; Milo's accepted he won't be getting his phone back until I decide he's earned the right to have it, and is now watching TV; and Niall's on his computer. Did you find food?'

'I picked up fish and chips on the way home, and very nice it was too.' Ivan chuckled. 'Not quite the same as Janga soup mind!'

Belle laughed, her voice beginning to relax down the line. 'You know, according to Grannie Abebe, that particular soup is an aphrodisiac, which gives long endurance to men.'

'Is that right? Tell me more...'

'Are you sure the owners of the pub won't mind?' Maddie felt self-conscious as they splashed their way to the deserted pub garden.

'I asked to make sure. They said they're happy if we're happy, but asked us to keep away from the river's edge.'

'I'm not surprised.' Maddie admired the rushing water, some three metres from where they stood. The rain, falling heavier now, bounced off the moving torrent. 'I bet the other diners think we're mad.'

'I doubt they'll even notice. I could hardly see out of the window when we were eating, due to the heating steaming up the windows, plus the raindrops – and now the night is drawing in.'

The raindrops were cool against Maddie's face. 'We wouldn't have seen a thing if we'd gone up to Exmoor tonight.'

'Nor would we have been able to do this.' Ed bent his knees and leapt, landing in a fast-filling puddle, spraying water everywhere.

Laughing as her thirty-four-year-old boyfriend splashed from puddle to puddle, Maddie took a leap of her own. 'There really is no better balm to life's worries than puddle hopping in the rain.'

Twenty minutes later, their waterproof clothing soaking, their wellies smeared with mud, Ed and Maddie headed to the car, giggling with the silliness of their moment of complete abandon.

Sinking into the passenger seat, taking off her wet outer layers, and flinging them into the footwell in the back of the car, Maddie said, 'The problem with so much fun is that I never want it to be over.'

'I hear you.' Ed tugged off his jacket, sending droplets of puddle water up his jumper sleeve. 'Bugger, I was trying to be so careful not to do that – and I did it anyway.'

'Never mind, it'll dry.' Maddie fastened her seatbelt. 'Ed?'

'Uh-huh.' He grabbed some tissues and wiped around his wet wrist.

'I didn't want to ask earlier, but how's Bristol? I mean, did you really fancy a few days' holiday, or did you badly need out for a while?'

'Ah.' Ed dropped his wet jacket into the back of the car and swivelled around so he was looking directly at Maddie. 'I haven't resigned or anything.'

'But?'

'You know I said that everyone at work is a bit driven?'

'Yes.'

'Well, that's the thing you see. They're all nice and everything, but the fact is, I simply don't fit.'

'Oh, Ed.'

'Don't get me wrong, I'm not being deliberately excluded, but I'm struggling to find common ground with anyone. There's no camaraderie because our aims in life are so different.'

'Whereas you fit right in at The Potting Shed.'

'I do. At least, I feel as if I do.'

'You do.'

'I know we tried living together with me commuting every day, and I got tired and grumpy, but would you mind if we gave it another go? Hopefully it wouldn't be for long, as I'd look for a job based locally at the same time.'

'And we could have our nice evenings back.' Maddie was delighted.

'Short evenings until I leave Bristol, but yes.' Ed reached out and took her palms. 'And I could get to talk to someone I love, in person, every day. I know we didn't live together long, but I desperately miss waking up with you.'

'I miss you too. Zoom and WhatsApp are not the same.' Maddie leant forward, kissing Ed gently on the lips. 'Actually, I've an even better idea, how about you jack in your job, live with me, and work at The Potting Shed full-time until you find work, rather than work in Bristol while you're looking?'

'Are you serious?' Ed felt a grin starting that he couldn't control.

'One hundred and ten per cent! You're miserable at work, so if you can cope with little or no wages in return for hard work for a while, plus Sabi's occasional bouts of snobbery, and lots of toast...'

'Damn right I can!' Ed gave Maddie another kiss before leaping out of the car, back into the pouring rain, and opening her car door. 'I'll resign tomorrow!'

'That's fantastic, but what are you doing? Get back in the car – you'll be drenched through.'

'No point, we aren't going home.'

'What do you mean?'

'I've booked us a room here for the night. Come on!'

40

'How are you feeling about meeting Tristan today?' Jo spooned some cereal into his mouth as he watched Sara moving around her kitchen via his phone screen.

'A bit weird, to be honest.' Sara slid some plates into the Aga's warming oven. 'It was one thing spending time with him on my terms, but this feels different.'

'You do enjoy his company though?'

'Mostly, although with hindsight, I wonder if that's because he's the first person I've ever felt able to stand up for myself with, without having to rev up to the confrontation first and without going through hours of anxiety afterwards.' She paused. 'I think maybe... well, I really did love my dad, but...'

As Sara's words petered off, Jo coaxed, another spoon of cornflakes halfway to his mouth, 'But?'

'But Dad instilled so many things in me – things for me to be cautious about.'

'In trying to care for you – by making sure you'd be okay after he was gone – he took some of your confidence away. Is that what you mean?'

'I think so.' Sara sighed. 'But there's something about Tristan that makes me reassert myself.'

'Probably because his level of offence is positively medieval, and you can't believe it.'

Sara shot Jo a fond look as she prepared some bread for

the guests' bacon sandwich breakfasts. 'There *is* something unbelievable about him. It's like being in a badly rehearsed play with me as his prompt, coaxing out the correct lines when he's talking to female characters.'

'Hopefully today will be a turning point. If his father's expectations are behind his Neanderthal attitude, as you suspect, then this could be the first step on Tristan's own path. If he wasn't following in his parent's footsteps all the time, he might put in more effort to be a decent human being.'

'Thanks, Jo. It's so much easier knowing you understand my need to try and help him.'

'I was being paranoid before.' Jo put his spoon in the bowl and moved nearer the phone. 'You'll never know how much I wish I hadn't been.' A little voice at the back of his head told Jo to stop talking, but his lips kept moving anyway. 'You know, Tristan is exactly the sort of man I imagine was the type your father used to warn you about. The sort he was always worried would love your inheritance and not you. That's why...'

Sara suddenly looked away from the screen. 'Got to go, Jo. Guests.'

Jo felt his insides go cold as the screen abruptly went blank. *Why did I have to say that about her dad?!*

As he slowly got up from the end of the bed, Jo frowned. *Sara's kitchen floor echoes when you walk on it. I heard no guests approaching...*

Sara pulled at the woollen knee-length navy blue dress. It was the only dress she owned that Tristan hadn't seen before. From the moment she'd left her car in the Phoenixhay car park, she'd been wishing she'd worn tights underneath, rather than just her long boots and socks. It wasn't that she was cold as she waited in the cathedral square, but as she stood outside the designated bistro, the three inches of visible flesh on each leg made her feel vulnerable and wanting to be as covered up as soon as humanly possible.

Flicking her bobbed hair behind her ears, cursing her eternal need to be early, Sara was debating whether to nip into the branch of Waterstones next door to the bistro, when she saw Tristan approaching from the across the quad. He was extremely smart, in a suit, complete with waistcoat. As soon as she saw him – or rather, his look of disapproval – she knew her dress option was wrong. It might only have been a fleeting frown, but it told her all she needed to know.

'This is the place. They'll kit you out.'

Sara eyed the bay windowed boutique suspiciously. 'Are you sure they won't take one look at me and do a *Pretty Woman*?'

'Pardon?'

Sara's eyebrows could not have shot higher. 'You know, *Pretty Woman*, the film with Julia Roberts and Richard Gere. The rich guy takes the... Oh never mind. Just watch the movie; you might learn something.'

'If you say so.' Tristan wrinkled his nose. 'I've made you an appointment so...'

Sara's hand had been halfway to the shop's door, but now she dropped it. 'Appointment?' Her next sentence came out in a hush of disbelief. 'You knew I'd wear the wrong clothes?'

'Well, I...'

'Why not just tell me what I should have worn?'

Tristan mumbled as if embarrassed, 'The truth is, I wanted to treat you. You've been more than kind *and* have put up with my occasionally crass behaviour. I knew you wouldn't let me see you again in a date capacity; this was my last chance to say thanks.'

'Oh.'

'Is that a good "oh" or a "go to hell" oh?'

'It's a surprised "oh".' Sara accepted defeat. 'Okay, I'll let you Eliza Doolittle me this once – but I should warn you, I'm not wearing anything I feel wrong in, nor am I letting you break the bank. It's not as if the people at the workshop need to be impressed by me, is it.'

Removing the protective layer of clingfilm from the leftover red velvet cake, Jo smiled at the memory of yesterday's dementia café. Of all the things he'd expected in his new job, he'd never foreseen a rousing chorus of his favourite childhood nursery rhyme.

Maybe that's what sent Mum into saying how proud Dad would be of me – he used to sing that to me when I was a little kid.

As he plated up the remains of his mother's cake of choice ready to sell, he tried to picture his father. Each year it got more difficult. A tall man, slim like he was, Jo remembered his scent most of all. He'd had no time for the 'modern fad' of scented deodorant for men, instead sticking to the liberal use of Imperial Leather soap when he'd washed, creating a clean masculine aroma that had lingered all day.

Miss you, Dad. Mum does too. I'm beginning to wonder if...

The door to the café opening pulled Jo from his thoughts. Belle came in, her mass of purple hair bouncing around her shoulders as she rushed across the room in a flurry of apologies.

'The bus was late! I'm so sorry, Jo.'

Jo waved the problem away. 'I hadn't noticed, and anyway, you're only ten minutes behind. A late bus isn't your fault.'

'I'll do ten minutes extra later obviously.'

'There's no need for that.'

Taking her apron off the hook, Belle replaced it with her coat and went to scrub her hands in the sink. 'That's very kind.'

Jo's forehead furrowed, as he noticed how tired Belle looked 'You okay? You seem flustered.'

'Milo was a bit of a handful last night. I'm not great if I haven't had my full eight hours.'

Sensing there was more to Belle's unusual lack of bounce than a broken night, Jo said, 'If you need some time out to rest at any point today, just say; otherwise, let's get this place ready to roll.'

'Actually, Jo...' Belle glanced towards the door she'd just come through. 'Would you mind if I very quickly spoke to Ivan. It's work-related – a recipe card idea we had for The Potting Shed.'

Jo paused in the act of pouring coffee beans into the grinder. 'Sure. Go for it. I'm on top of things here.'

Watching his right-hand woman zip out of the café at a speed just short of a jog, Jo couldn't help but smile at the thought of her budding romance with Ivan; a smile that wavered as he wondered what Sara was doing at that very moment.

★

Ivan positioned his weighing scales carefully, as he decided what size wedges to cut a truckle of Somerset Smoked Cheddar into. Opting for six large and two small pieces, he lifted the cheese in his gloved hands, and put it in place.

'That looks rather therapeutic.' Belle gestured to the wire cutter as she approached her friend.

'Morning, lass.' Ivan swept the wire across the cheese in a smooth firm motion, slicing a triangle of Cheddar away from the main body of the truckle. 'It's a satisfying job.'

'With very sharp wire!'

'Unbelievably sharp.' Leaving his task, Ivan noted the tiredness in Belle's eyes. 'Bad night?'

'It shows, huh.'

'A bit.' Ivan tilted his head to one side. 'But I bet if you gave the world that dazzling smile of yours, all signs of fatigue would disappear.'

Belle laughed. 'You sweet talker you.'

'First time I've ever been called that!' Ivan repositioned the cheese wire over the truckle. 'How's Milo this morning?'

'Quiet.' Belle pushed her hair back over her shoulders. 'He knows he got things wrong.'

'Everything seems black and white to him until someone points out all the shades of grey, right?'

'That's it – then the confusion comes in. Then he gets angry with himself for making the mistake.'

'I'm so sorry about your jug.'

Belle sighed. 'It was just an object.'

'No, it wasn't.' Ivan wished he could come around the counter and hug her. 'Do you want a lift home tonight?'

'Won't that mean you finishing early?'

'I hardly sell after three o'clock. I'm thinking of asking

Maddie if I can finish at three-fifteen, the same as you. Then I can do my Exmoor Drifters' admin from four until six o'clock each day, rather than in the evenings.'

'If Maddie says yes, then a lift would be great, but no worries if not. The bus will be just fine.' Belle checked her wristwatch. 'Are you sure though – closing an hour earlier, I mean. If you need the money…' Her words petered out. 'Sorry, not my business.'

'Not at all. I'll open longer again at Christmas – all assuming Maddie and Sabi go for me adjusting my hours.'

'I'm sure they will. And who knows, the recipe cards might bring in more trade for you. Niall is excited about creating them for us.' Suddenly feeling self-conscious, Belle said, 'I wanted to apologise again for Milo.'

Removing his gloves, hat and apron, Ivan came out from behind the counter. 'Come here, lass.'

Engulfed in his arms, Belle found herself caught between three conflicting feelings: total peace, a sense of safety and the need to cry as if her heart was broken.

41

It came as a shock to Sara to realise that she was having a good time. Unlike the character in *Pretty Woman*, the lady running the boutique, who introduced herself as Louisa, had a contagious smile and easy manner. She also had no trouble believing that Sara was there under some level of sufferance.

'I've met plenty of men like Mr Harvey, don't you worry.' Louisa unhooked a silk blouse from a rack of clothing, all of which magically fitted Sara as if each item had been designed specifically for her.

'Even in this day and age?' Sara submitted to having the blouse slipped over her arms.

'Oh yes.' Louisa stood back to assess the effect of the blouse, whipping it back off Sara's body before picking another blouse, only fractionally different, and passing it to Sara. 'There's still a small core of men who haven't noticed that it isn't 1970 anymore.'

'The ones with money I guess?'

'More like, the ones who think they are worth more as human beings than they actually are.' Without waiting for a response, Louisa regarded the latest ecru silk blouse to adorn Sara's body. 'That's the one! Now, trousers or a skirt?'

'Trousers? Really?'

'The relief in your voice!'

'It never occurred to me Tristan would permit trousers!'

Louisa narrowed her eyes as she critically observed Sara's legs. 'His instructions were to make you look like an executive, with femininity. If he can't be bothered to be more specific, then he'll get what he gets.'

Ruffling the fur under Florrie's ears, Maddie whispered, 'Can you keep a secret?'

Her puppy yapped obediently, making Maddie burst out laughing.

'You can?' Hooking Florrie's lead back on her collar as they reached the gate to The Potting Shed after a brief walk, Maddie looked out across her domain. 'I wish Sabi was here. She might drive me mad sometimes, but I miss talking to her.'

Florrie nudged at her mistress's knees.

'I know I can talk to you, darling Flo, but it's not quite the same.' Maddie smiled. 'I've made a decision – I think – but maybe I shouldn't...'

The collie nudged Maddie harder.

'Yes, I know, it isn't a decision if I only *think* I've made it.' Checking the time, Maddie felt a twinge of guilt at not rushing back to work. 'Maybe I'll just see if Sabi has a signal.'

Sitting on the nearest bench, Maddie pressed in her sister's number.

With her sister's reassurances ringing in her ears, Maddie crossed through the shop, arriving at her partner's side. 'Have you contacted your boss yet?'

'Not yet.' Ed looked up from the laptop he'd been

tapping into between serving customers. 'I've written several resignation emails and then deleted them. I can't seem to get the wording right.'

'How much notice will you have to work off?' Maddie picked the hand sanitiser off the desk and sprayed her hands liberally.

'A month.' Ed shifted over, so Maddie could sit on the stool next to him. 'Each time I start it, I wonder if I'm doing the right thing.'

'You've changed your mind about working here while you search for another job?'

'Not for a second.' Ed put a reassuring arm around Maddie's shoulders. 'It's just, how would a local solicitor's office feel about taking on someone who tried it with the city boys, and gave it up to work in a garden centre – even if that garden centre was close to said applicant's heart?'

'I hadn't thought of that.' Maddie looked around them. The shop was already dotted with customers, even though it was early in the day, and she knew that, by lunchtime, they'd be too busy to chat. 'Then maybe don't get another job after all.'

'Just work here?'

'Why not? Apart from the lack of wages and long hours obviously.'

Flinging his arms around her, Ed gave her a quick kiss. 'Why not indeed! I have savings and well, this empire is going to grow and grow. Plus, you need new staff. Who better than someone who doesn't expect payment beyond cuddles and toast?'

Maddie shook her head as she smiled. 'Minimum wage will happen. It's got to go through the books – Sabi is very strict about things like that. I just asked her about it.'

'You called Sabi?'

'I did. I was sure it was the right thing to do, but it's a shared business so...'

'Absolutely. Then minimum wage it is.' Ed saw a young woman with a packet of seeds in her hand approaching the till. 'Would you serve while I fire off this email? Suddenly I know exactly what to say.'

Sara tucked into her eggs Benedict with an appetite she'd been trying to ignore since she'd donned the first of many blouses at Louisa's boutique.

'Peckish?' Tristan sipped at his espresso.

'Starving. It's no joke cooking breakfast for other people, but not having time to eat yourself. Anyway, I assumed we'd be eating at half-nine, and it's almost eleven-thirty.'

'The wait was worth it. You look lovely.'

'As opposed to looking like a bag lady?'

'I didn't say that.' Tristan put down his tiny cup. 'I told you, I wanted to treat you.'

'And you did.' Sara couldn't deny how good she felt in her new silk top, close-cut black trousers, neat cerise jacket, and kitten heels. 'But I'm yet to be convinced it was a thank you gift, rather than you paying for a way not to be embarrassed at being seen with me.'

'I assure you...'

'Either way...' Sara dabbed at her lips with a serviette '...the clothes are beautiful. Thank you. So, what time is the workshop and what do you want me to do and say when we get there?'

'Six o'clock.'

'Six!' Sara couldn't believe it. 'I could have gone to work, and still helped you!' She gestured to her new outfit. 'And if you think there's any chance of me staying clean until six, then you're in for a shock. I always seem to attract dirt. I don't think I have a single shirt without a stain on it.'

'Keep your hair on.' Tristan gave a furtive look around the room, noting the curious expressions on their fellow diners' faces. 'We'll go shopping.'

'What for?'

'Whatever you want. And I've booked us afternoon tea.'

Sara's mouth opened but she couldn't find the words.

'You do like shopping, don't you?'

'Not really.'

Tristan was stunned. 'But you said you had fun with Louisa.'

'She was a lot of fun, but that's not real is it. That was once-in-a-lifetime stuff for pockets far deeper than mine.'

'But…' Tristan stuttered for a second, before exclaiming, 'you have a manor house, Sara. Surely you can afford some of the good things in life?'

He just wants your money. Sara could hear her dad's voice as echoing Jo's warning words as he ate his breakfast. 'A home like mine, not to mention the land it's on, eats money. Anyway, I like living simply.'

'A laudable ideology, but surely you splash out occasionally?'

'It's never crossed my mind.'

'Then it's high time it did. Come on.' Tristan dropped a pile of ten-pound notes on the table and stood up. 'You're going to help me later, so let me help you relax and spend some of your hard-earned cash on yourself.'

Reaching for her coat, Sara felt a shiver run down her spine as her dad's voice nudged the back of her mind for a second time.

Remember what I told you, my darling; there are men out there who can't see you other than for the estate you own...

'Have you heard back?'

Maddie found her partner in the old potting shed shop, among the sacks of compost.

Ed opened his mobile and flicked to his emails. 'Nothing yet.'

Stepping back out of the shed, Maddie kept her eye on the main door to the garden centre's shop. 'I'd better go back. I left Ivan watching his till and mine. I was driving myself mad wondering if you'd had a response to your resignation.'

Ed stole a quick kiss. 'I'll come and tell you as soon as I hear.'

'I'd like to tell everyone you're joining the team, but maybe we'll keep it to ourselves until it's official.'

'Good idea.' Following her towards the shop, Ed said, 'Sabi was really okay with this?'

'Totally. By the sound of it, by the time she's finished her cruise, she'll have so many prospective interior design clients, she'll probably be begging you to take over her accounting role too.'

'Talking of which,' Ed surveyed the garden centre, 'as things are quiet here for a minute, should I head into the house and update the books?'

'Oh, would you?'

'Might as well start as we mean to go on.'

'In that case, you'll find a heap of printed-out receipts on the kitchen table – they're under the fern.'

'The fern you talk to when I'm not here?' Ed grinned.

'That's the one.' Maddie chuckled. 'Don't let it give you any backchat.'

Workshop isn't until six! Thought I should let you know in case you texted to ask how things went later. Sara

A jolt of disquiet tripped through Jo as he read Sara's message. *Why hog her for the whole day? What are you up to, Tristan?*

No problem.

Jo only just managed to stop himself from adding: *Let me know if you need me to invent an emergency to rescue you.*

'Admit it...' Tristan placed the handfuls of paper bags from designer outlets under their hotel table '...you've had a great time.'

'Maybe.'

'Maybe?'

'Alright, it was fun.' She picked up a bag and gave it a hug. 'I can't wait to wear this jumper. I don't think I've ever owned anything so soft.'

'I'm glad you like it.'

'You didn't need to buy it for me.' Sara, who'd resolutely refused to purchase anything she didn't need, had found herself being gifted a jumper and three dresses, all of which were far too good to wear at home or work. 'Buying me to clothes for the workshop is one thing, but I'm uncomfortable about you treating me for the sake of it.'

'Relax. I like buying things for other people.'

'Well, I'm buying afternoon tea. No arguments.' Sara almost blanched when she saw the prices on the menu but was determined to foot the bill anyway.

'As if I'd be foolish enough to argue with you!' Tristan laughed. 'Actually, I'm grateful you were willing to play shops. I'm a bit nervous about what the rest of the day may hold. You've helped taken my mind off things.'

'You haven't said much about the wine taster's workshop.'

Tristan diverted his attention to the menu. 'Traditional cream tea and sandwiches with tea?'

'Oh what, umm... yes please. Or maybe coffee if that's possible?'

'This is the best hotel in Exeter – of course it's possible.'

His sharp reply made Sara feel as if she should immediately apologise. 'Sorry, I didn't think – I'm not used to...' She stopped talking as the waiter arrived to take their order.

Sitting back, Sara lifted her mobile off the table, when a sharp tut from the waiter was followed by him informing her that there was a strict no phone policy within the restaurant.

Feeling told off for the second time in as many minutes, even though all she'd been about to do was make sure her phone's sound was off, Sara slipped it into her handbag, hot with embarrassment.

Tristan reached a hand across the table and briefly clutched her wrist. 'I should've told you about their policy with mobiles. I suppose you were going to message Jo.'

Not caring for his tone, rather than explain she was only going to put her phone away, she said, 'Jo likes to know I'm alright.'

'Business partners aren't usually so possessive.'

'He's my partner *and* my business partner.' *Well, he was...*

Tristan laughed. 'Don't be silly, Sara. No way is he your partner. Friend, yes, but more than that – no.' He picked up one of the dress bags. 'I bet he doesn't even know what size you are.'

'What's that got to do with anything?'

'Everything! Sometimes your unworldliness is so cute.' Tristan dismissed her indignation with a smirk. 'When you showed me around your home, you even pointed out his room. You don't even share a bed!'

'Our sleeping arrangements are nothing to do with you!'

'You're a gorgeous young woman – why on earth would he want a separate room?'

Wishing she hadn't risen to the bait and talked about Jo, Sara spoke through lightly gritted teeth: 'I'm here to help you get through a wine workshop. Let's talk about that instead.'

Jo's phone vibrated in his trouser pocket. Up to his eyes in cappuccino orders, he carried on helping Belle work through a steady queue of customers. Only once the final young mum and her toddler were served with drinks and cake, did he check his phone.

'Jo?' Belle saw her boss reach out for the counter as the blood ran from his face. 'What is it?'

'Mum's care home. I need to call them back.'

Hurrying to the back of the kitchen, Jo pressed in the numbers as if on autopilot. An instinctive certainty swept over him.

You've gone, haven't you, Mum.

42

Jo didn't hear Belle at first. It was only when she placed her hands on his shoulders and gently eased him around to face her, that he realised he wasn't alone in the kitchen's far corner.

'What is it, Jo? You're as white as a sheet.'

'Mum.' He'd intended to say more, to explain he had to leave, but no more words would come.

'Oh, Jo, you poor soul.' Immediately guessing the situation, Belle steered him towards one of the two chairs they kept behind the counter and sat him down. 'You stay there for a minute; I'll fetch Maddie.'

'Thanks, but I have to go.'

'I know you do, but you also need to get there in one piece. Let things sink in as much as they can while I sort things this end.'

Jo jumped up. 'Oh God, the café! I can't just…'

'Yes, you can.' Belle lowered Jo gently back onto the seat. 'I'm going to make you a coffee. You've had a shock and it's going to be a long few days for you. Would you like me to call Sara?'

'I'll do it.' Jo fumbled his mobile back out of his pocket.

'There's two customers waiting. I'll serve them, then I'll get reinforcements. Okay?'

'Okay.' Gripping his phone, Jo felt as if he was tumbling down a rabbit hole. Nothing seemed real.

After pressing in Sara's number, he wasn't that surprised when no one answered. He hung up and began to text.

Sara. It's Mum – she's...

His finger hovered over his phone's keypad. He didn't want to type the next word.

The display of finger sandwiches, mini cakes and scones, artfully arranged on a three-tier cake stand, was temptingly delicious. Sara, however, had little inclination to eat.

'Can you say that again please?'

'I said, it's high time you had someone to show you how a woman of your standing should be treated.'

'My standing?' Sara's words were barely above a hush.

'Oh, come on, you might fool everyone else, but you don't fool me with that act.' Tristan's confident expression sent shivers of disquiet through Sara, the cakes in front of her turning more leaden in appearance with each passing second.

'Act?'

'You were in your element in the boutiques we visited today. To the manor born.'

'What?'

'I've been busy over the last few days. I looked you up, Sara Northcott.' Tristan took a slim cucumber sandwich from the display and weighed it in his palm. 'You must be worth a fortune, and yet you scurry around in scruffy clothes and do a part-time job at a down-at-heel garden centre.'

'Looked me up?' Sara turned icy cold, despite the overheated restaurant. She wanted to pull her jacket closer around her, but at the same time, she wanted to take it off and put her old woollen dress back on. Or better still, her jeans and a jumper.

'Sure, your business is listed as a house of interest on the Internet and your mother is in *Who's Who*. For God's sake, woman, you're an heiress!'

'You've been spying on me.'

Tristan scoffed as he took a mouthful of sandwich. 'Hardly – all the information is in the public domain. Anyway, I've been to your house.'

'And I didn't deny it was mine.' Sara stood up.

'Where are you going? Our tea has only just arrived.'

'I'm going to the washroom – anyway, my appetite has gone.'

'If you're worried about the calories, then don't be. What I have planned for the evening will work them off in no time.'

Sara's brain began to work overtime. 'I told you, I'll come into the workshop, but I'm not actually going to take part. Anyway, it'll just be standing around sampling wine won't it. Calories will be going on, not off.'

Tristan calmly poured himself a cup of tea. 'The workshop's been cancelled.'

'What?' Sara's insides clenched. 'When did that happen?'

'While you were in the boutique.'

'The boutique? When I was with Louisa? *Before* we'd had brunch?'

Tristan added some milk to his bone-china teacup. 'There's no need to say it like that. We've had a good day, haven't we?'

'But…' Sara was so stunned the words wouldn't come out.

'But nothing. You needed a day off. A proper one. I'm sorry I had to withhold information to make you relax, but…'

'Hang on…' As she sat back down with a thump, Sara's

throat dried as she interrupted Tristan's confident flow. 'Just now you said, "planned for the evening." If the workshop is off, just what *did* you plan for this evening?' A sheen of perspiration coated Sara's palms. *Jo was right – he's been right all along.* 'The wine workshop, where was it going to be held exactly?'

'I said it's cancelled.'

'That wasn't my question.' A creeping suspicion that she'd been well and truly played came over Sara.

'Here. In the conference suite.'

Sara stood up again, suddenly desperate for some space. 'If you'll excuse me, I need the bathroom.'

Maddie took over in the café as Belle brought Ivan up to date on events.

'Poor Jo, he adored his mum.' Ivan ran a hand through his beard. 'How's he holding up?'

'Too soon to say. He's in shock. I won't let him drive to the care home until he's had a coffee.'

'Maybe Ed should drive him?'

'That's not a bad idea. We'll manage for a bit. I wondered about suggesting shutting the café, but Maddie needs the trade, bereavement or not.'

'Will you cope okay in there?'

'Sure, but I won't be having that lift home at three.' Belle wrapped one of her curls around a finger. 'I need to call the boys. I'm glad I gave Milo his phone back this morning. Just this once he will have to put up with his routine being disturbed, fallout or no fallout.'

'How about I fetch them and bring them here after school?'

'Well, Niall would come, but…' Belle felt a surge of affection for the man before her. 'I'll call them – if you wouldn't mind fetching them once they've got home… I know the café will be closed by then, but Jo stays until at least five setting things up for the next day. I'd like to do that for him.'

'Do you know what to do?'

'I'll work it out.'

Ivan nodded. 'Right then, you contact Niall and Milo, explain the situation, and we'll go from there. If Milo won't come, I'll wait with the boys at your place until you call me to fetch you back.'

'You can't keep going up and down the link road, just to ferry me about!'

'Yes, I can.' Ivan's tone brooked no argument. 'Now, give Jo my best, and I'll see if Ed's free to drive him into Wellington.'

Splashing her face with cold water, Sara stared into the washroom's mirror.

I thought I was helping him. She closed her eyes against her naïve reflection.

I'll go back to the table, collect my things, leave, and block Tristan's number from my phone the second I'm in the car.

'I'm going to drive you to Charlton Lodge.' Ed knelt before Jo. 'Iris wouldn't want you driving in a state of shock.'

'But The Potting Shed…'

'Will cope.'

Sara watched Tristan from the doorway that separated the main restaurant and the washrooms. He was sipping his tea with the air of a man who owned the place – or thought he ought to.

Returning to their table, she studiously avoided eye contact with everyone else in the room. Her heartbeat thudded in her chest.

I've stood up to him before without even thinking about it – why does it feel different this time?

As she approached, Sara saw Tristan looking inside one of her shopping bags. It contained a dress he'd brought her: green, with a long hemline and a split in the thigh. She'd felt beautiful in it. Now the memory of trying it on made her feel cheap.

I should have listened to Jo.

Thinking of Jo, she wondered how she'd tell him about her day. *Things are better between us – but not right. I do wish that…*

'You took your time.' Breaking through her thoughts, Tristan poured some coffee, from a large silver pot, into Sara's cup.

She said nothing as she focused on the collection of bags under the table. Together they'd spent more money in a few short hours than she'd make in a month at the Airbnb.

What a waste.

Feeling a pang of loss for the jumper she'd genuinely fallen in love with, Sara picked up her coat and handbag. 'There was no wine workshop here today. They've never held such an event on the premises.'

A cloud descend over Tristan's expression. 'You checked up on me.'

'As you did on me.' Sara's shoulders threatened to shake, but she firmly pushed them back.

'I assume you found Hawthorn Park on the Internet and researched me from there?'

'I said I did. It's public knowledge.'

'So Ed didn't tell you where I lived as you claimed.' Sara shook her head. 'I didn't think he would, not without asking me first.'

Tristan glanced around him. 'Could you lower your voice. It's…'

Taking no notice of him, Sara carried on. 'I agreed to come today to help you follow your true passion. I thought I was helping you to escape the shadow of your father – to live the life you wanted, rather than the one he foisted upon you. But all you wanted was to get your leg over my body and your hands on my business. Every part of you is fake.'

'How dare…'

'Don't bother.' Sara put on her coat. 'I've given you more benefit of the doubt than anyone I've ever met, because I hoped there was some good in you. I even felt sorry for you! I believed you deserved a chance. But it turns out you're just someone with an eye for the main chance – in this case, my home. All that talk about turning it into a boutique hotel – that wasn't just a sudden idea – it was your main intention.'

A flash of emotion in Tristan's eyes betrayed him.

'Ah, I'm right.' Sara's anger combined with a shot of sadness for the incredibly clever yet utterly stupid man before her. 'What did you think would happen next? That I would hand over my house keys after a night of passion and say, go for it, let me know when my home is totally overrun with strangers, and hey, let's set a date for a society wedding?'

Through gritted teeth, Tristan growled, 'I think you should sit down. You're drawing attention to yourself.'

'No, I'm drawing attention to *you*.' Sara perched on the edge of her seat, ready to run as soon as she'd said her piece. 'I spoke to the lady on reception. Not only did she tell me that there's no workshop, but that a room has been booked in your name. For tonight.'

'She had no business…'

'Perhaps not, but in her defence, I played you at your own game, Tristan. I told her I was your partner, and so when I asked if Mr Harvey's room was available yet, she was happy to help.'

Suddenly uncomfortable, Tristan muttered, 'I'm staying here tonight. That's all. A treat before I go home.'

'I hope you enjoy it. And the champagne, I'm informed, is already chilling for you.' Sara gestured to the shopping bags as she stood up. 'Feel free to see if you can find someone who'll fit into those clothes.'

'But I spent a fortune on you!' Tristan was no longer calm. 'Staying with me is the least you can do!'

'I *beg* your pardon?'

'I've spent all day trying to make you into a better version of yourself! Showing you what you could become. It was fun! You owe me one night at least!'

Sara could see a waiter hurrying, in as discreet a manner as possible, in their direction, presumably on a mission to evict her from the premises. Quickly, she growled, 'I came here today because I thought I could help you follow your own dreams; to escape your father and become happier – even if it meant fibbing about your connection with my home to get you on the wine course. A course that never existed! Now you have the gall to say *you* were trying to improve *me*! Well, if you think sex with you would improve anything then you need to take a long hard look at yourself. And, for your information, sex isn't something I'm interested in anyway! If you'd bothered to get to know me properly, rather than simply working out how much income my inheritance might bring, you'd have made less of a fool of yourself.'

His jaw dropped as the waiter arrived at their side.

'Sir, madam, if I could just ask you to…'

'I apologise.' Sara gave the waiter a tight smile. 'I was just about to leave, anyway.'

Ed turned to Jo as they pulled into Charlton Lodge car park. 'Would you like me to come in, or wait here?'

'You might as well go back. I could be a while.'

'Are you sure?'

'Positive.' Jo unclicked his seatbelt and opened the door. 'It's a strange thing, but I think Mum knew.'

'Knew she was going to die?'

'Just yesterday she was saying how proud she was of me – and she seemed, I'm not sure, peaceful at the same time. When the call came from Michael, I wasn't surprised. It was as if she'd already warned me.'

43

Jo hadn't moved for almost an hour. His back was slouched against the wipe-down armchair as he stared at the empty bed. Stripped of both sheets and mattress, its metal sprung frame resembled a skeleton.

A sudden heavy patter of rain blowing against the picture window drew Jo out of his stupor. It was already dark; the bad weather was drawing in the night with a speed that reminded him autumn had most definitely arrived.

Once he'd said goodbye to his mum, the undertaker had taken Iris away. Michael and Carol had been very kind – telling him he didn't have to rush things; that he could come back whenever he was ready to sort out what happened next, but Jo didn't want to leave – not yet.

Surveying his mother's few possessions, he spotted the basket of cyclamens Noel had presented her with only twenty-four hours before.

'I'm going to miss you so much, Mum.' Wiping the back of his hand over the tears that had long since dried to his cheeks, Jo blew out a puff of air. 'When I was a child, you told me to always think of others first, no matter what the situation, no matter how hard the choices.' Throwing a suitcase that had been living under the bed since Iris had arrived at Charlton Lodge onto the bedframe, Jo opened the wardrobe, ready to pack up his mother's meagre collection of clothing.

'There's no escaping the fact that this care home has a waiting list, and your room is going to be needed by another poor soul battling to remember who they were. So...' he took another ragged breath '...I'd better get on with it.'

Easing a blouse from a hanger, Jo folded it neatly into the case. As he worked, glad to be busy, he found himself treating her garments with more reverence than she ever had.

No one gets into heaven for precise folding, Jo.

He could hear her now – her words covering for the fact that she'd never been able to make anything neat in her life. Even folding a towel into a square had been beyond her, a fact he knew had secretly frustrated her, long before dementia had hit.

Turning to a chest of drawers, he scooped out a mess of beige tights and bed socks, only to stop dead. His gaze rested on two old exercise books hidden at the very bottom of the drawer.

'I'm glad you're here, Sara.' Michael looked up from his desk. 'The last couple of times I've gone in to offer coffee, Jo's not even noticed I was there.'

Sara wrinkled her nose as she tugged at her unfamiliar clothing. 'I was in Exeter, in a place that insisted on having mobiles off. I didn't see the message until I was sitting in the car in the car park out of the rain. Then I hit the rush hour traffic on the motorway. I was beginning to think I'd never get here.'

'He'll be pleased to see you.'

Not wanting to share her flickering doubts on the subject of her and Jo, but knowing she wanted to be there for him, Sara sighed. 'I hope so. I didn't even stop to answer his message. He's probably thinking I don't care.'

'I'm sure that's not the case. He'll just be grateful you got here as soon as humanly possible. To be honest, I suspect he's in that non-thinking period of bereavement shock where time has no meaning.' Michael gave her a bracing smile. 'I'll give you twenty minutes, then I'll bring some drinks.'

'Thank you.' Taking a deep breath, Sara headed along the corridor that led to Iris's room and pushed open the door. 'Jo?'

There was no movement from Jo as she closed the door quietly behind her. Sara could see him, sitting in his mother's armchair, an old exercise book on his lap, another open in his hands. His eyes were completely focused on its contents.

Sitting next to him, Sara said nothing as she placed a palm on his leg.

'My school exercise books – well, two of them.' Jo kept his eyes on his studiously neat teenage handwriting. 'I had no idea Mum kept them.'

A knot of emotion formed in Sara's throat. 'You were her son. She loved you so much; it's not surprising she kept a few of your school memories.'

Inclining his head, Jo said nothing as his fingers traced over the script as though he was trying to capture something of the writer.

'Jo?'

'I… I haven't seen her writing in years.'

Sara's forehead creased in confusion. 'Your mum's writing? Oh, I see.'

With shaking hands, he closed the book and showed Sara its cover. She read: *Joanna Dunn. History. Year 1.*

'Oh, Jo.' Reaching out, Sara wrapped her arms around him.

Sniffing hard, he mumbled, 'Michael and Carol have been wonderful. They've helped so much. I didn't even know there was funeral cover in place. Everything is already paid for.'

Accepting his change of subject for the moment Sara stroked his hair. 'Amazing woman, your mum.'

'I'd wondered if I'd have to sell my van to give her a good send-off, but as ever, Mum thought of everything. She would never talk about her funeral.'

'But she'd dealt with it anyway.'

'Yes.'

'Very Iris.'

'Pre-dementia, Iris, anyway.' Jo reopened the exercise book. 'I've been trying to remember her – Joanna – but all I can recall is being out of kilter with the world. Of being stuck on the wrong axis.'

'And now your world axis is right.'

'Thanks to you.' Jo gripped her hand.

Sara wiped a tear away with her free hand. 'It wasn't thanks to me. It was thanks to your bravery and your mum's unwavering support.'

Quiet for a moment, Jo squeezed Sara's hand. 'We'd been out for a walk – Mum and I – when I first told her I was supposed to be male. It wasn't long after we'd lost Dad. A month maybe.' Jo's voice cracked, and he began to sob. Then he held on to Sara as if his life depended on it, his eyes screwed shut, as his shoulders shook with grief.

Michael had been and gone with his promised cups of coffee, but Jo had barely noticed. The tears, now stopped, blotched his pale face. Extracting herself gently from his side, Sara passed Jo a cup.

'Here, have a drink. It's only lukewarm, and it won't be anything like as good as your coffee, but it'll help.'

Knocking the contents of his mug down in one, Jo wiped his lips with the back of his hand. 'Sorry I cried all over you.'

Sara, her own eyes sore from tears, said, 'You needed to let that out, anyway I'd have been jealous if you'd cried on someone else's shoulder.'

Jo was jolted by the sudden remembrance that it wasn't just his mum he was grieving for, but the loss of his closeness with Sara. 'You would?'

'Course I would.'

After closing his eyes for a second, Jo opened them again. 'You know, when I told Mum, about me not being me back then – on that walk – I think that was the last time I cried like that.'

'Relief at unburdening yourself I expect.'

'And relief that Mum didn't look at me in disgust and tell me to sling my hook.'

'Iris would never have done that.'

'Some parents do. The stories I've heard – it would break your heart. I was so lucky, Sara. So lucky with my mum.'

'What did she say once you'd told her?'

Moving his chair closer to Sara's, Jo put his hand over hers. 'She took my hands, looked me straight in the eye and told me she'd suspected for years, but trusted that I would be ready to tell her in my own time.' He smiled as fresh tears glossed his eyes. 'I remember how fast she spoke, as if she was reciting a speech, one she'd been ready to give for ages. She used the correct pronoun from that moment on – with a few mistakes here and there of course – habit and all that. Mum said everything would be okay, and that whatever happened, she'd always be there.' Jo's eyes flicked to the empty bed. 'And now she's not.'

Sara rested her head on his shoulder. 'She was an old lady, who'd had a good life. It's a cliché I know, but better to go like this – peacefully in her sleep – before another horrid illness gave her pain, or her dementia robbed her of the rest of her mind.'

'I know.' Jo smiled through his grief. 'I made Mum one promise on the day I told her I was a boy. I promised that I wouldn't steal her daughter's past. She was scared of being deprived of all the good times she'd had being Joanna's mum.'

'That can't have been easy, when all you wanted was to move away from your dead name.'

His expression became rueful. 'Never once did she make me keep that promise. The time before I became Jo remained unspoken. Mum even swapped all the photos of my younger self that she had around the house for either headshots, so there were no dresses visible, or for current shots. Only now that it's too late to thank her, can I see how strong she was back then. How I – unintentionally – had given her a second bereavement not long after her husband had gone.'

'Oh, Jo.' Sara took him back into her arms, as a second wave of tears overtook the first.

44

The early morning mist laid droplets of damp air across Maddie's hair as she hurried towards Ivan's van as it pulled into the car park. She was already talking as Belle opened the passenger door.

'I'm so grateful to you, Belle. And to your boys. They were fabulous yesterday.'

'They loved it. So much so, that they're coming back after school today. Milo has specifically asked if he can sweep out the café again tonight. I hope that's okay?' Belle reached out a hand to greet Florrie.

'More than okay.' Maddie mentally ticked that job off her to-do list.

'I won't pretend I wasn't nervous about Milo having a moment while he was here after school yesterday, especially as the need for his help was rather sprung upon him.'

Hearing the anxiety she had for her son in Belle's voice, Maddie reassured her. 'He's a dab hand with a broom, not to mention the till. As soon as he's old enough, Milo's got a Saturday job here if he wants one. And if Niall ever feels like joining the team, he's welcome the moment he's sixteen.'

'You mean it?' Belle's eyes widened. 'He's sixteen next month, actually.'

'Then, if he wants it, he can have a Saturday job. This is a family business, so let's keep things within our families.'

Maddie spoke as Sheba emerged from the van and she and Florrie began their daily sniffing ritual. 'Ivan and Milo seem to have struck up a rapport.'

Watching Ivan unloading cheese truckles from the refrigerator section of his van, Belle lowered her voice. 'Ivan had a private word with Milo the other night – Milo went a bit off the rails – jumped to some incorrect conclusions – and ended up smashing a jug that had belonged to my grannie. I was really upset... Anyway, since Ivan spoke to him Milo's been trying extra hard. I've no idea how long it'll last, but I'm making the most of it, while it does.'

Suspecting that Milo was enjoying the company of an older man who, judging by the interaction she'd witnessed between them the day before, treated him as an equal, Maddie moved their conversation on. 'I'm ever so grateful for you coming in early today, Belle.'

'Least I can do. Any word from Jo?'

'Sara called last night. He's as okay as possible. Luckily, they have no guests at Hawthorn Park until a week tomorrow, so they've a little time to draw breath at home. Jo intends to come in this afternoon, but we'll see how it goes. It'll depend on whether he slept last night, and how much there is to do arranging the funeral.'

Emerging from the back of his van, his arms laden, Ivan said, 'I can understand Jo wanting to work, but with Ed here, and Milo and Niall on standby to help clear up tonight, then we can manage if he can't face it.'

'That's what I told Sara.' Maddie bit her lip, knowing it'd be tight manpower wise, but not impossible. 'She's going to come in this afternoon as usual but wants to help Jo with paperwork and stuff at the care home this morning.'

'There's always a lot of that.' Ivan nodded. 'I called Elspeth last night, to let her know what had happened and to see how she was. She was telling me about when she organised her parents' funeral. Red tape and a half apparently.'

'It's never fun.' Belle took a few of the cheeses off the pile balanced in Ivan's arms.

'On the plus side, Elspeth is much better, and on standby to come and run my counter if needed.'

'That's great. Thanks, Ivan.' Maddie eased Florrie back from trying to explore inside Ivan's van. 'If Jo wants to come in, simply to keep himself going, then obviously he's welcome. I know I needed to keep as busy as possible when Dad went.'

Belle agreed. 'I was the same when Grannie Abebe died; she was like a mother to me.'

Crouching down, Maddie hugged her dog to her side. 'So much grief unites us in this place, Florrie.'

'Better than grieving alone.' Belle smiled. 'Come on, Ivan, let's get to it.'

'You got it, lass.' Ivan gestured with his head towards the van. 'If you wouldn't mind shutting the door, I'll set up the counter and then walk the dogs before kick-off.'

'This coming Monday?' Ivan sat next to Belle, wincing slightly as his knee clicked. Stretching the offending leg out after a busy day of sales. 'That's incredibly quick. Will all the official paperwork and so on be sorted by then?'

'Jo seems to think so.' Addressing her small pool of staff as they gathered for a post-work catch-up around a table in the café, Maddie elaborated, 'Michael and Carol are old hands at this, as you'd expect in their line of work, and they've been helping Jo and Sara sort things out. There's no family to consider but Jo, and the crematorium had a spare slot, so they're moving fast.'

'No point in dragging out the pain.' Belle ruffled out her tangle of curls. 'When Grannie died it took weeks to get everything sorted. The wait for the funeral was worse than the funeral itself.'

Maddie agreed. 'It's one of the reasons neither Jo nor Sara made it to The Potting Shed today – they've been all systems go on planning. It seems Iris was quite specific in her requirements.'

Ed passed a tray of coffee-filled mugs across the table. 'How do you mean?'

'She left strict instructions for a low-key, short funeral, with just friends. No hymns or – in her words – "anything dreary". She wanted a wake instead, with laughter and cake – red velvet cake to be precise.' Maddie waved a hand around her. 'I've told Jo he can use the Forget-Me-Not or even the bluebell garden if it's a dry day. Obviously, we're closed on a Monday, so the timing from our side is perfect.'

'I love the idea of a party-style send-off, but…' Belle looked around her '…it's Friday today, and we've been really busy. I'm almost out of the most popular cakes and I've not had a chance to order more or check to see what Jo has pre-ordered to arrive tomorrow. Saturday and Sunday will be busier still – then it's Monday. Are we going to be ready in time? And how about the guests? Even if everyone who comes along is local, will they come at such short notice? How many people are we catering for?'

Maddie held her hot chocolate to her chest. 'I've been thinking exactly the same since Jo called. I don't want to let him down, or Iris come to that.'

'You couldn't say no though, love. Anyway, I'm sure Jo and Sara will have had the same thoughts and be working on it.' Ed frowned as he got up. 'Give me a minute. I need to make a quick call.'

As Ed darted outside, Niall and Milo appeared through the back door to the kitchen. Milo's eyes shifted nervously over the small group until his eyes rested on Ivan. 'We've walked the dogs. They're curled up in the back of your van.'

'Thank you, Milo.' Ivan took his van keys from the teenager. 'And you, Niall. Hope that Florrie wasn't too much of a troublemaker?'

Maddie laughed. 'I notice you didn't ask if Sheba caused trouble.'

'Ah, but my Sheba is not a walking firework.'

Milo gave a shy smile, as he and Niall sat with the adults. 'They were both good. It was fun.'

Grateful for the dog-walking service, Maddie asked, 'Can I get you boys a drink while we wait for Ed to get back?'

'I'm okay thanks.' Niall smiled.

'How about you, Milo?' Maddie could see the younger boy looking hopefully towards the chiller cabinet. 'A thank you for letting us keep hold of your mum during your family time. I'm ever so grateful.'

'Oh.' Milo's surprise echoed around the room. 'You are?'

'Yes, we take family very seriously at The Potting Shed.' She gave him what she hoped was a sincere smile. 'So, can I get you that drink?'

Milo's eyes flicked to his mum, who gave an affirming dip of her head. 'Could I have a smoothie, please?'

Maddie moved to the fridge. 'Orange and mango or spinach and kiwi?'

'Spinach and kiwi. It's my favourite.'

'That's Jem's favourite too.'

'Who's Jem?'

'My niece. She'll be here tomorrow. If you want to come and help, then you can meet her.'

Before Milo could reply, Ed returned. His face was flushed. A wave of worry hit Maddie. 'What's happened?'

Ed sat back down and grabbed his cup of tea. 'I took Monday off work. No way am I missing Iris's funeral. Jo's going to need his friends.'

Ivan's eyes narrowed. 'Your expression suggests that your employer did not take kindly to the request for compassionate leave, even though it's just an extra day added to your current leave.'

'They did not.'

Maddie reached out to take Ed's hand. 'But surely...'

'They used words like *convenient* and *suspicious* in light of my recent – ill-advised in their opinion – decision.'

'Oh hell.' Maddie squeezed his hand tighter. 'But you *have* to be here. Jo will need you, Ed. I will need you come to that.'

Ivan and Belle exchanged glances, before Ivan asked, 'What ill-advised decision?'

'Every time I think I can't feel more exhausted, I prove myself wrong.' Maddie sat on the bench in the bluebell garden and rested her head on Ed's shoulder.

'I'm beginning to know what you mean.' Stroking a hand through her long brown hair, Ed glimpsed up at the sky. 'It's a beautiful night. I bet the stars are clear up on Exmoor.'

'If I had the energy, I'd say let's go, but I'm afraid I don't.'

'Nor me.' Ed looked down at Maddie's dog, who was curled up under a nearby picnic table. 'Even Florrie is spark out.'

'I don't know what Milo and Niall did when they took her for a walk, but it's worn her out.'

'We should employ them as inhouse dog walkers.'

'That's not a bad idea.' Maddie exhaled slowly. 'What are you going to do about work?'

'I'm not going in until Tuesday. They can be as difficult as they like, but I can prove we have a funeral to go to if I must.'

'They aren't going to make your last month working there very comfortable, are they?'

'Most people will be fine, but my boss is not impressed. It's been made very clear that the dedication to helping others I claimed to have is proving somewhat lacking.'

Maddie was incensed on her partner's behalf. 'If they stopped to get to know you for five minutes, then they'd realise that's totally untrue. It's *because* you like helping people that you're leaving!'

'They see it as me coming in, using up resources, and then leaving.' Ed watched some leaves fall from the nearest tree. 'I can see their point of view, but their reaction to me needing one extra day off has killed any sympathy I had for them.'

Looking around the bluebell garden, currently devoid of its namesake but holding the promise of a carpet of blooms come late spring, Ed changed the subject. 'It's a shame it's been too wet and misty to hold the dementia café outside. Come the summer, I can picture Billy and friends out here.'

'I'd be very happy to have them again, but if Jo would rather we didn't host them again...'

Ed surveyed the view, which stretched beyond the garden centre, into the wood, and a large field, full of wild grasses, owned by the neighbouring farm. 'I'm sure he wouldn't want to stop the others from coming, but maybe we should give it a few weeks.'

'Let's see how Monday goes. Michael is bringing Billy and Cynthia from the home to the wake. Otherwise, it will just be all of us and a few of Iris's former neighbours – more Jo's friends than Iris's.'

'Only because she hadn't many friends left, poor soul.'

Maddie closed her eyes. 'It's a horrid thing to contemplate – outliving all the people who loved you.'

'It is.' Ed held her tighter. 'I had a thought, about this garden.'

'Go on.'

'Something to encourage more wildlife and, perhaps to act as a memorial to your father and Iris.'

Maddie sat up straight, immediately making Florrie sit up and come to her side. 'Sara has a memorial garden to her father. I had wondered about that here, but I don't know – Dad was such a practical person. He wouldn't want something just for the sake of having it.'

'How about a pond – a pond that the Little Acorns could help fill with fish and tadpoles, as well as the appropriate plants. And a pond that can be surrounded by irises, and provide a focus for people coming to sit here, with takeout drinks from the café?'

Maddie threw her arms around Ed. 'That's brilliant! We could even have a fountain.'

'I bet you'd love it, wouldn't you, Florrie.' Ed smiled at the collie. 'Although keeping you out of the water might prove challenging.'

'Oh heck – maybe we shouldn't.'

'Or maybe we should, and just make sure Florrie's never here on her own.'

Maddie chuckled. 'Or we could just accept that, once in a while, we'll have a very soggy doggy traipsing all over the flat.'

45

'I can't stop long, Ivan. Jo's in, but there's still heaps to do. I just wanted to show you this.' Belle passed a prototype recipe card across the counter. 'Niall did this for me last night. I didn't tell you in the van as the boys were with us, and Niall's a bit self-conscious about it. Thinks it's not good enough.'

Ivan took the card.

Belle pulled anxiously on a curl. 'What do you think?'

'It's fabulous.' Ivan's eyes lit up. 'Perfect. All we need is a photo of the finished product to add on. And making the first recipe red velvet cake is a really kind gesture.'

'We ought to bake one first – just to be sure we have the recipe correct.'

'And once we're tested the cake, we could ask Niall to make up a few cards to give out on Monday.' Ivan scanned through the ingredients. 'Do you think he could do it? This mock-up is great. If he's producing stuff of this standard, his GCSE coursework mark will be sky-high.'

'I'm sure he could. He and Milo seem to have been born being able to do anything technical – unlike me, who struggles with rebooting the router when the Wi-Fi plays up.'

'You and me both.' Ivan smiled. 'Right, if we want this ready before the wake, then it'll mean testing the recipe tonight. Do you think Milo will go for that? Either you coming to me or me coming to you? I think we should bake it together – don't you?'

'It would certainly be more fun.' Belle grinned. 'But that aside, yes, I do. Quality control is needed for a start. Plus, I'm a hopeless photographer, and we'd need a photo for the card.'

'Maybe we should get one of your boys to do the picture too – and to help with the testing.' Ivan became thoughtful. 'Having said that, Milo's had a lot of my company this week – and he's got to put up with me today, once his homework is done anyway. I don't want to push our luck.'

'He and Niall are already hitting their maths tasks in the corner of the café. If you'd told me that the prospect of a day's hard work here and a chance to walk two dogs was the incentive my children needed to get their homework done, I'd never have believed you.'

'More likely the prospect of being paid.'

'Paid?' Belle's eyebrows rose in surprise.

'Maddie told them they'd be seeing some envelopes containing pocket money by the end of tomorrow.'

An embarrassed heat infused Belle. 'She doesn't need to do that.'

'Maddie values her workers. It'll be good for Milo to feel valued...' Ivan faltered '...I didn't mean to imply that you didn't value him. I just meant...'

'I know what you meant.' Belle placed a hand on Ivan's shoulder. 'I've not been at The Potting Shed long, and sometimes the kindness I'm shown here is a bit overwhelming – especially after Greg...' Belle broke off as she checked her watch. 'I really must get on.'

Reaching out, Ivan took hold of her arm, his gentle palm

resting on her dark green sleeve. 'It's none of my business, and you can tell me to butt out, but you've previously implied that your husband wasn't as kind as he might've been.'

'He wasn't.' Belle pursed her lips, the calming atmosphere of The Potting Shed lending her strength. 'I'm not ready to tell you about him yet – but I will one day, if… if that's alright.'

'Whenever you're ready.'

Slipping her hand into his, Belle found herself muttering words she had never imagined she'd ever say again. They tumbled from her lips, surprising her as much as they delighted Ivan. 'I think I'm falling for you. Is that alright to say? Because if it isn't I need to know – I *need* you to tell me now – before I fall further. I couldn't bear to work here if…'

Glad that Maddie and Ed were nowhere to be seen, Ivan wrapped his arms around Belle's waist and pulled her close. 'I fell in love with you the second I saw your purple curls and your killer smile. Does that answer your question, lass?'

Resting her forehead on his chest, Belle let out a ragged sigh of relief and joy. 'Oh yes, that answers my question.'

Jemima ran from Ed's car. Weaving her way through the late lunchtime customers, she made a beeline for the café.

As she reached the door to the Forget-Me-Not, she paused, searching for Jo among the bustle of people queuing for their turn at the till. Spotting Belle, she then saw Sara moving around the tables, stacking used cups and plates onto trays.

Assuming her friend must be in the kitchen, she darted past Sara, hunting down her friend. She'd expected to find him in his usual industrious state, buttering bread at high speed, or stirring the soup pot. Instead, Jo sat on a stool in the corner by the back door. He was staring into space, a pen in one hand and a notepad in the other. She faltered, unsure that he'd want to see her.

'Jo?'

He looked up, as if surprised to find himself in the café's kitchen. 'Jem.'

Suddenly Jemima had no idea what to say.

Seconds later, she realised she didn't have to say anything, as Jo hugged her so tightly, that she was left in do doubt that he was pleased to see her.

'Jem's going to count the sandwiches and restock the cold drinks before she gets on with her homework.' Revitalised by the arrival of his young friend, Jo examined the remaining three slices of cake on display in the counter. 'I'll open a new chocolate cake, but otherwise, as it's already half-two, I think we'll say, when it's gone it's gone.'

Sara took off her apron. 'Good idea. Belle has the counter under control, so if you're okay for a bit, I'll go and water the tunnels and make sure there's nothing else Maddie needs doing before I head home.'

Jo rested a hand on Sara's shoulder. 'Are you sure you're okay with doing all the phoning round? I feel it ought to be me who invites people to the funeral, but...'

'Time is tight, and it's okay. I have the list of people, starting with Iris's former next-door neighbours. Once we know who's coming, then we'll know how much cake to buy.'

Belle passed a cappuccino to a customer as she called out, 'Don't be worrying about cake. Ivan and I are on that.'

'Are you sure, Belle?' Jo gripped his notepad of things to do.

'Sure. I've been making red velvet cake for years. Much nicer than buying it in. Which other cakes would you like?'

'Do you mean it, Belle?' Sara was relieved at not having to find the cakes on top of everything else.

'Consider it our contribution to the funeral.'

Despite the circumstances, Jo found himself smiling. '*Our?* As in, Ivan and you?'

Belle tugged at a random curl. 'He's coming round to help me cook later, that's all.'

'Just to help you cook?' Jo's eyes twinkled as a fresh grin spread across his face.

Sara nudged his arm. 'Take no notice of him, Belle. I think it's lovely. And Iris would approve of home-made cake. Thank you.'

'Are you Milo?'

'Yeah.'

'I'm Jemima – or Jem if you prefer. Maddie's my aunt. I was about to get a smoothie to help me get through my homework. Do you want one?'

'Oh.' Milo flicked his eyes anxiously towards his mum. 'Well… is that okay?'

'Sure. I'll sort the list of drinks later and we can pay when the queue has gone.'

'Right.' Milo kept his eyes firmly on his textbook. 'Why are you being nice to me?'

''Cos Ed said you were nice. You've been helping Maddie and Ivan.' Getting up, Jemima took two smoothies from the fridge, waved them in Belle's direction, so she knew they were taking stock to pay for later, and sat back down again. 'I don't suppose you're any good at physics?'

'I am.'

'Thank goodness. How about I swap you a smoothie for some help with my homework?'

Belle didn't know Maddie's niece as well as she'd have liked, but that hadn't stopped her from wanting to give the twelve-year-old a massive hug all afternoon.

'The only reason I didn't,' Belle said to Ivan as she turned on her oven as they prepared to bake red velvet cake after work, 'is that it would have disturbed her and Milo. Even with the friends he's had since primary school, I've never seen him so engaged with someone his own age before.'

'Jem's one of the best. Kind heart, open mind. Jo adores her like a little sister.' Ivan checked out of the window to see if the boys were in sight yet. 'Niall and Milo with be soaking if they don't bring Sheba back soon – that sky is looking increasingly threatening.'

Belle waved a hand towards the mobile on the table. 'Feel free to text Niall and tell him to cut the walk short.'

Ivan smiled. 'That's trust is that – letting me use your mobile phone.'

'You've let my sons look after Sheba – rather more precious than a phone.'

'They've built up a rapport with her.' Ivan tapped a quick message into the phone, warning the boys of the impending rain. 'Anyway, I suspect she's looking after them, rather than the other way around.'

Scrubbing her hands under the kitchen tap, Belle laughed. 'You may be right. So then, fancy being cook's runner?'

'I'm yours to command.'

Belle pointed to the larder. 'In that case, best fetch me some self-raising flour and sugar from the cupboard.'

Ivan had only been in the cupboard for a second, when he called out. 'Sorry, lass, I can't see them.'

Putting on an apron as she went to explain the layout of her culinary domain, Belle found herself wrapped in a clinch.

'Okay, I lied.' Ivan held her close. 'Not something I make a habit of.'

'This time, you are completely forgiven.' Belle muttered as her lips met his.

Jo kicked off his shoes and headed to the kitchen.

Sara's kitchen now – not our kitchen. Jo felt a renewed sense of loss as he carried the large cardboard box he held in his arms towards the table. It contained the last of Iris's possession to be removed from her bedroom at Charlton Lodge.

Swallowing back the reminder that he was a visitor at Hawthorn now, Jo took a deep breath as he looked at Sara. 'I'm not sure I can face these.' Jo regarded the box warily. 'I have no idea how old some of these photos will be.'

Pulling the box of albums towards her, Sara pointed towards the door. 'I think you should go and have a long hot shower, put on something cosy, and join me by the fire when you're done. I'll do this.'

'But… But I don't live here anymore.'

Sara felt a lump form in her throat. 'You're my friend and I'm more than happy for you to use the shower.'

'Okay. Thanks.' Jo stayed where he was, his eyes firmly on the box as Sara went to open it. 'You'll see...'

'I can cope with whatever I see, but right now, you can't. You are living your present and your future, not your past.'

'Thank you.' Jo eyed the box suspiciously. 'I will search through them one day, but not yet.'

'Totally understandable.' Sara lifted the lid off the box. 'We just want one photo of Iris for the order of service – yes?'

'Please. Maybe one of her and Dad.'

'Would a baby photo of you and your mum be allowed?'

Jo's heart thumped faster. 'If it's just me all wrapped up, you know – new-born or something.'

'Understood.' Sara peered into the box. 'Now, go and have that shower. You look done in.'

'But there's so much to do!'

'Ivan and Belle are baking, and Maddie and Ed are making sure that The Potting Shed looks its best. Michael and Carol are on the case with visitors from Charlton Lodge, and I've invited everyone on the list you gave me – and all but one person is coming. So that's approximately twelve guests. All you need to do is think of what to say.'

Jo's already pale face blanched to the colour of tapioca. 'Say?'

'There's got to be a eulogy, Jo.'

'Oh hell... I suppose there does.'

'You don't have to be the one who reads it though.'

Jo closed his eyes. 'I do, you know. I owe Mum that much – and so much more.'

'Milo...' Ivan opened the back of his van to let Sheba in '...I know you've helped a lot lately, but I wondered, if you'd mind helping me with one other little thing.'

'What's that?' The teenager looked at Ivan with an air of caution, but without the suspicion he'd previously conveyed on him.

'It's for your mum...'

OCTOBER

46

Florrie bounded through the wood, stopping every now and then to investigate a particularly interesting pile of fallen leaves. Following her dog, Maddie linked her arm through Ed's. 'I think this is my favourite part of the day. Cool, but not freezing. Crisp and fresh, yet slightly ethereal.'

'I know what you mean.' Ed glanced up through the canopy of part-naked branches. 'Misty mornings not murky mornings.'

'Beautiful colours too.' Maddie pulled her scarf tighter around her neck, laughing as Florrie dived into a particularly satisfying heap of crisp bronze leaves and sent them spraying around them.

'I've missed this.' Ed kissed Maddie's cheek as they wove along the wood's narrow pathways. 'The quiet moments before the chaos of the day. Walking through Bristol's streets from my room to the office isn't quite so atmospheric.'

'I'm sure.'

'The company's rather lacking too.'

'Huh?'

'Are you with me, Maddie? Worried about the wake?'

'What? Um – no. I was thinking about something else.' Maddie stepped over a particularly gnarled set of tree roots. 'Obviously, I want it to be everything Iris wanted, but Belle and Ivan have played a blinder. I forgot to say, Ivan called while you were in the shower.'

'Crikey, that was six o'clock. Early start for him these days. Like old times when he went out with the farmer's market.'

'That's exactly what he said. I think he's adjusted to beginning work at half-nine rather better than he thought he would.' Picking a ball from her pocket, Maddie threw it for Florrie. 'Off she goes. What are the chances of her bringing back the ball rather than an interesting twig?'

'Fifty-fifty.'

'She delivered a pebble instead of the ball yesterday.'

'Strange pooch.' Ed spoke affectionately as Florrie returned, the ball in her jaws. 'Seems the tennis ball is in favour today.'

'Good girl, Flo.' Maddie threw the ball again.

'So, what did Ivan want?'

'Ivan?'

'You were saying Ivan called while I was showering.'

'Oh yes…' Maddie shook her head. 'My head is like a sieve this morning. To say that he and Belle baked late into the evening. They have enough cake and tray bakes to feed us for a week.'

'That's great.' Ed graciously received a branch from Florrie. 'Where's the ball, girl? Go on, go find it!' Wiping his bark-dampened hand on his coat, he added, 'And Milo didn't mind Ivan being in his home? That's a good sign.'

Maddie smiled. 'You've noticed he and Belle are operating like a couple as well then.'

'Hard not to.' Ed watched Florrie nosing her way along the ground ahead of them. 'Let's hope it works out.'

'You think it might not?' Maddie bit her bottom lip.

'No idea. There's a bit of an age gap, and Belle's family isn't without challenges, not to mention that Ivan has been a bachelor for a very long time.'

'Too much adjusting on either side for a proper relationship then?'

Ed turned to Maddie in surprise. 'You sounded positively defeated then. Are you sure you're okay?'

'I was just thinking how well suited Jo and Sara are – and well, I know they're talking now, but they aren't right yet. It made me think… I guess I like everyone to be happy.'

'Nothing wrong with that.' Ed let go of Maddie's hand as they navigated a slim section of the woodland pathway. 'Either way, I'm glad that Jo didn't have to order in last-minute cakes through the company – makes the accounts awkward – and it'll be so much nicer to have home-made stuff.'

'I've told Jo he can use the coffee and tea though.' Maddie's frown deepened. 'I hadn't considered the situation in terms of accounts and stock. This is why I need Sabi!'

'Don't worry, I'll get Belle to check the stock prior to the event, and again afterwards. We can account it as a private event.'

'But I'm not charging for the use of the venue.'

'A loss leader to see if such events are worth your while?'

'And I'm not charging for the coffee or tea either?'

Hearing the edge of panic creeping into Maddie's voice, Ed gave her a quizzical look. 'It'll be fine. The café's making money. The Potting Shed is working. You don't need to worry quite so much about money until you're paying more staff wages.'

'Take no notice of me. I've got used to worrying!' Taking the rediscovered ball from Florrie, Maddie slipped it into her pocket as the collie had been distracted by a fresh fall of leaves scattering to the ground from above.

Ed retook Maddie's hand. 'Today will be sad, but positive.

From what I know of Jo's mum, she wouldn't want anyone to wallow in grief, and...' Ed was interrupted by the buzz of his phone announcing an email. 'At last.'

Maddie hardly dare ask, as she said, 'From Bristol?'

'Yup. Hang on.' Ed scanned the email.

Maddie wrapped her arms around herself as she waited to hear Ed's news.

'My boss wants to see me at nine tomorrow morning. It doesn't say anything else.'

'Ahh.' Maddie blow out a long breath. 'Does that mean you need to go back to Bristol tonight?'

'Better had. Can't risk a train delay in the morning.' Ed grimaced. 'I also need to give my landlord notice on the bedsit. Might as well do that tomorrow.'

'Makes sense.'

'I think they might try to persuade me to change my mind about leaving – my boss, not my landlord, obviously.'

'You won't though – will you?'

'I just told you I'm going to give notice on the bedsit.'

'Oh yes – so you did.'

'Whatever it is, stop worrying.' Ed kissed the top of her head. 'Staying here with you is the best decision I've made in years. I wish I could give them a reason that they'll understand for my leaving though. Saying I don't like how money-focused they are isn't going to do me any favours if I want a reference in the future.'

Maddie swallowed and, slipping her hand down into Ed's, she gently pulled him to a halt. 'Actually, ummm... I've been thinking about that.'

'Thinking about my references?'

'No, the future.'

Ed regarded his girlfriend's flushed complexion. 'Is that what you're fretting about it?'

'Not worried as such...' Maddie spoke quickly '...although seeing Ivan and Belle together and wondering how they'll make it work – if they decide to of course – and then Jo and Sara had problems...'

'We've just agreed that they're all fine.'

'Yeah – I know, but it made me think.' Maddie peered up at Ed through her tatty fringe. 'Sorry I'm being a bit...'

'Flaky? Look, love, I know you've got a lot on, but The Potting Shed is doing well, and...'

Shaking her head fast, she cut across Ed. 'It's not The Potting Shed's future I was thinking of, but ours. I miss you so much when you're not around – and with you being unhappy at work on top of seeing our friends having issues – well... that's why I'm a bit nervous.'

'Nervous? Why would you be...'

Ed's words came to an abrupt halt, as Maddie dropped to one knee. 'Ed Tate, will you marry me?'

Shock stole Ed's ability to reply for a second, then, gripping hold of Maddie's hands, he lowered himself to his knees. He could feel the damp ground seeping through his jeans as he reached out and ran a single finger across her pale face.

'Will you?' Maddie breathed the words, her whole body held along with her breath.

'Yes. No question. Totally yes. Very much yes!'

'I don't think I'll ever get the stains out of either of these pairs of jeans.' Maddie's eyes shone with pleasure as she held up their dog-walking trousers.

Ed laughed. 'They were ruined in a good cause.'

'The best.' Maddie threw the offending garments to the bedroom door, ready to put them in the washing machine later. 'I've never done that outside before.'

'Nor me.' Ed chuckled. 'Not sure Florrie is going to forgive us for a while for ignoring her for so long.'

Maddie laughed. 'She didn't even notice! That heap of fallen twigs kept her fully focused.'

'Good!' Ed grinned. 'So, how does it feeling being a fiancée rather than a girlfriend?'

'Really rather wonderful. You?'

'Fantastic!' Ed peeled off his jumper. 'It'll feel even better when I've had a shower though. Fancy scrubbing my back?'

Maddie waved her mobile towards Ed as he put on a clean shirt. 'I've had an email from Jem's school; we can collect her at two.'

Ed brushed at the sleeves of his suit. 'I'll leave about one then. I'm glad they're letting her come. She didn't know Iris, but Jo will be glad to have her there.'

'So will I.' Maddie stared at her partner across the room.

'What is it?'

'I can't believe you said yes.'

Laying his suit on the bed, Ed leapt forward, grabbed Maddie around the waist and picked her up, so that they were face to face. 'You didn't think I'd say no to being your husband?'

'I hoped not.' Maddie giggled. 'And you're sure you're not cross that I asked you before you asked me?'

'Of course not! Saves me a job.' Ed winked.

'Cheek! Asking to spend the rest of your life with me would have been a chore, would it?' Maddie chuckled as she was lowered back to the floor.

'It is work, work, work around here!' Ed chuckled as he patted the side of her bed, and Maddie sat down. 'I trust you believe me when I say I intended to ask you.'

'Of course, but...?'

'Why didn't I?'

'Well, yeah.'

'I only hadn't got round to it because of all this job stuff – being in Bristol, living apart, having a sort of half-relationship in the week...'

'But not for much longer.' Maddie put a palm on Ed's knee. 'I'm so pleased you'll be here with me.'

'Me too, soon to be Mrs Tate – if you want – you could stay as a Willand or...' Ed leant in for another kiss, but Maddie placed a finger over his lips.

'Willand-Tate sound okay?'

'Perfect.' Knocking Maddie's hand away, Ed brushed his lips against hers, only to have Maddie move away.

'With extreme reluctance I am going to have to stop you there.'

'Spoilsport.' Ed gave a mock sigh. 'But you're right – there are things to do.'

Maddie's smile faltered. 'Maybe I shouldn't have asked you today of all days, but it felt right and...'

Copying his fiancée's earlier action, Ed put a finger to her lips. 'I'm very glad you did, and I think Iris would approve. Something positive and forward-thinking happening on the day when we celebrate her life.'

'I hope so. I wouldn't want to offend Jo though – so maybe...'

'Tell everyone another time – not today?'

'Might be for the best. We don't want to appear insensitive. But it is a shame.'

Ed squeezed her hand. 'I'm bursting to shout it from the rooftops.'

'Perhaps we should wait until Sabi and Henry are home?'

Ed forced himself to stand before he weakened and threw Maddie back onto the bed. 'Depends how long it is before they get home. The last time I spoke to Sabs, she mentioned that stops in Spain and Italy were scheduled before they headed back to Southampton. I'm not sure I can keep quiet for that long about being this happy!'

47

Jo set the sheet of paper on the counter. He'd stared at it so long that the typescript blurred, each word bleeding into the next.

'It's a good eulogy. Heartfelt.' Sara paused in the act of wiping down a set of chairs. 'No one will mind if you read it from the paper.'

'It doesn't feel right.'

Drying her hands on a towel tucked into her apron pocket, Sara came to Jo's side. 'Nothing's going to feel right for a while. I have plenty of days when I don't feel right, and Dad's been gone a while now. I'm sure Maddie and Sabi would tell you the same if they were here.'

'You're probably right.'

Sara picked up the paper. 'And this really is lovely. You had me in tears before you headed back to your van last night.'

'Exactly!' Jo stabbed a finger in the eulogy's direction. 'Mum wanted laughter and fun; she didn't want loads of crying and wailing.'

'There's no way you're going to avoid tears all day. I'm confident there won't be any wailing though. And don't forget, you can have happy tears. Shared joy for Iris's life is allowed, and that might lead to tears.'

'I suppose so.' Jo pointed to the two small speakers he'd

brought into work with him. 'I hope the music is right. I've gone for Mum's favourites… it's a bit of an eclectic mix.'

'Iris was an eclectic person.'

'True enough.' Laughing, Jo couldn't argue.

'Come on, stop worrying about the words. If you end up going off at a tangent and not saying what you've written, I'm the only person who'll know and I won't tell a soul.'

Jo sighed. 'Maybe I should have waited longer – it's all happened so fast. Mum's not been gone a week yet. You don't think she'd think I'm in a rush to get rid of her, do you?'

'No, I suspect your mum would have said there was no point in waiting when you can crack on. And what's more, she would love how everyone has come together to help get her wake sorted so quickly.'

'Everyone's been so kind.' Jo steadied himself against the counter. 'It's going to be strange not going up to the care home anymore.'

'I know.' Sara went to slip an arm through his but stopped herself. 'Do you need a bit of time to yourself?'

'I'm okay.' Jo swallowed. 'I'm so grateful to Michael and Carol. They made Mum's life so much better than it might have been.'

'Well, you can tell them that later. And Billy!'

'I think Mum was sweet on Billy.'

'Really? Good for her.' Sara nodded towards the coffee machine. 'How about I make us a drink and we have a break. There's not much more we can do until we go to the crematorium apart from changing our clothes.'

'Good idea. I'm at the point of inventing jobs just to keep going.' Jo slumped onto a recently cleaned chair. 'Sara?'

'Yes?'

'What happened in Exeter with Tristan?'

'Ahh.' Sara placed two cups by the coffee machine. 'I wondered if you'd ask – I would have said, but it didn't seem important, not with your mum and everything.'

'It's very important – it's blocking us being us, but... well, as you say, with Mum... and then whenever I thought about it, I was too scared to ask. We might not be as we were, but we're friends, and I desperately don't want to lose that again.'

'Nor do I.'

'So...' Jo took a deep breath. 'Did you end up having to do the workshop?'

'There was no workshop.'

'What?' Jo's eyes narrowed.

Gathering her thoughts while the coffee machine's nozzle noisily shot hot water into the mugs, Sara said, 'You were right about Tristan all along.'

'Oh. I'm sorry.'

'Are you?' Sara passed Jo his coffee.

'Yes, you believed you were helping someone, and...'

'They were just taking advantage – well, trying to.' She sighed. 'I feel such a fool.'

Jo lowered his mug to the table. 'I think I'd better hear this story from the beginning.'

Belle got as far as the café's doors, but then quietly backed away.

'Are you okay, lass?' asked Ivan, his arms similarly laden with cake tins.

'I think Jo and Sara are having a heart-to-heart.' She rested her tins on the till's counter. 'I think we should give them a minute or two.'

'In that case...' Ivan put down his own tins and took hold of Belle's hands. 'I have something for you, from Milo.'

'From Milo?'

Seeing her forehead pucker Ivan added, 'It's a good thing.'

'Okay...'

'You take a seat; I'll be one minute.'

Belle watched as Ivan walked as quickly as his knees would allow, back out towards the car park. His old wax jacket was crumpled at the back from where he'd been sitting in the van, his greying hair needed a cut and his jeans had seen better days. 'He's cosily crumpled.' A broad smile crossed her face. 'And he gets on with my boys.'

Wondering what he had from Milo, Belle glanced towards the café. She could faintly hear that a conversation was still going on, but not what was being said. She had no time to speculate however, for Ivan was back, a carrier bag cradled in both arms.

'This is from Milo. With Niall's help he's... well, you'll see.' Passing the bag to a bemused Belle, he stepped back. 'Careful now, it's fragile.'

Peering into the top of the bag, Belle hesitated, before reaching in and extracting something covered in a thick wrap of old newspaper. Her breath caught in her throat. 'Is this...?'

'Open it and find out.'

Gently removing the layers of protection, Belle found herself holding Grannie Abebe's jug in her hands. 'But...' Her words dissolved as a finger traced the lines of carefully applied epoxy glue that had reformed her favourite jug. 'Milo did this?'

'With help.'

'You.' The disbelief in Belle's voice cracked as her throat, hoarse with the effort of not crying. 'You did this for me... showed Milo and Niall how to... Grannie's jug...'

Putting the battered – but now whole – jug reverently on the till counter, Belle threw her arms around Ivan and burst into tears.

'Hey... it was supposed to make you happy.'

'It has!' Belle sniffed hard against his shoulder.

'I suggested Milo give it to you later, but he wanted you to have it before the funeral. It was supposed to cheer you up.'

'Every time I think I've worked out my son...' Belle struggled to rein in her emotions '...he takes me by surprise.'

'He's a good lad at heart.'

'He likes you. Do you have any idea how rare that makes you?'

Running a hand through Belle's hair, Ivan held her closer. 'I'm not sure about rare, but my gran was always telling me I was unique.' He chuckled. 'I'm not sure it was always meant as a compliment.'

Ed checked the time. 'I'll have to leave in half an hour to pick up Jem. Do you want to go and tell Jo and Sara there's an hour until you guys have to go so they can come and change?'

'Yeah, yeah... in a minute.'

'Are you alright?'

Maddie brushed down her black dress. 'I haven't worn this since Dad died.'

'Oh, love, I wasn't thinking.' Ed put his arm around Maddie. 'Are you okay? I could go and fetch Jo and Sara if you need a minute.'

'I'll be okay, but a minute would be appreciated. Oh, and here...' Maddie scooped up a set of keys from the bedside table. 'Can you give these to Belle or Ivan? They'll need to lock the gates behind us when we leave.'

'Sure. I'll check they've all they need to get the finishing touches in place.' Ed got as far as the door before calling back, 'By the way, I've checked the train times – the six o'clock train claims to be running tomorrow from Tiverton Parkway to Bristol Temple Meads.'

'You've booked a ticket? Maddie's face burst into a smile. 'You're staying tonight after all?'

'Too right! We got engaged today, remember!'

48

Belle propped the pile of 'Iris's Red Velvet Cake' recipe cards by the coffee machine. Each one held the recipe, a photograph of the cake, and the words: 'In memory of Iris Dunn, much-loved Mum,' written in script on the back.

'I think they're perfect. Niall has surpassed himself. I could never produce anything so professional-looking.' Ivan rested a hand on Belle's shoulder.

'His graphic design teacher let him use the school's printer and laminator as it's part of his project. I'm not sure we'll be that lucky when it comes to producing the others.'

'Either way, Jo'll be touched. A kind tribute, without being sickly.'

'I only met Iris twice, and not when she was at her best obviously, but she didn't strike me as someone who'd have time for anything twee or sugar sweet.'

'That's the impression Jo always gave.' Getting back to work, Ivan placed a huge Victoria sponge cake onto a plate and began to cut it into slices. 'Just the tablecloths to put on, and I think we're done until everyone arrives.'

Unhooking her apron, checking to make sure her bright purple dress had remained clean while she was setting up, Belle put her hands on her hips and surveyed the space critically. 'Just the music to put on.'

'Let's do that now.' Ivan picked up the memory stick Jo had

left with them. 'It's one of those things we'll forget at the last minute if we leave it.'

'I hope the funeral's gone alright.' Belle checked the time. 'It'll be over by now. Maybe just a bit of standing around afterwards making small talk.'

'I can't see that happening this time. Iris said no flowers, so there'll be no arrangements to wait for, and everyone is coming back here anyway.' Ivan fiddled with the USB stick and the docking station. 'I hate these things. What's wrong with a CD player!'

'Come here! I'll do it.' Belle took the stick from Ivan's fingers and turned it round. 'You had it back to front, you numpty.'

'Oh, what it is to be young!'

Even though Ivan had laughed as he spoke, a cool shiver ran up Belle's spine.

Seeing the devastated expression on her face, Ivan realised his blunder and spoke fast. 'I didn't mean... I was embarrassed at having the thing the wrong way round and...' Stopping talking, he levelled his gaze on Belle. 'I do *not* think you are too young for me. I hope you don't think I'm too old for you. But if our undeniable age gap is going to be more a problem then we...'

'I don't think it is. I mean, it feels right. Doesn't it?' Belle stepped closer, her wide clear eyes fixing on Ivan's.

'To me it does.' Ivan ran a hand over his beard, stumbling over what to say, and wondering how one casual sentence could kill the mood so quickly. 'I suppose there's bound to be some issues.'

Belle shook her head, sending her hair coiling across her back. 'Bound to be, but what couple doesn't have issues?' Sucking in her bottom lip, Belle pushed the USB stick firmly into position and clicked play. 'So, we get to know each other a little better, and we see if it feels right tomorrow and the next day and the next.'

As Louis Armstrong's 'Wonderful World' burst from the speakers, Ivan ran a hand through her hair. 'You are a wise woman, Belle Shepherd.'

'Even for a young 'un?'

'Especially for a young'un.' He held out his arms. 'Shall we dance?'

Jemima slipped a palm around Jo's hand, while Sara took his right arm, and they headed towards the crematorium's car park.

Grateful for his friends' presence, Jo felt the momentum that had been keeping him going over the past couple of days begin to wane. Suddenly, he didn't want to go back to The Potting Shed and be with other people. He wanted to jump in his orange camper van with Sara, and head on to Exmoor. He wanted to lie down next to her and talk and talk until the world was right again as they stared at the sky until nightfall.

'Jo?' Jemima felt her friend's footsteps slowing. 'Do you need to sit down? You've gone a bit pasty.'

Looking at Jemima as if he was surprised to see her, Jo frowned. 'Sorry?'

Sara guided them towards a low stone wall that ran around the edge of the crematorium's car park. 'I think you should perch here for a minute.'

Allowing himself to be sat on the granite stone, Jo let out a heavy gust of breath as he took a folded order of service from his pocket and looked into the face of his mum. She was forty years younger and shining with happiness as she stood next to his dad. 'Mum's really gone, hasn't she?'

Tears sprang to Jemima's eyes. She'd seen Jo, hurt, angry, sad and confused before – but now he appeared utterly lost, and she had no idea what to do or say. All she could think about was her own mum, and more than anything else, she wished she was there, rather than hundreds of miles away.

'She has.' Sara crouched down in front of Jo. 'You can be very proud of the fact that, despite time being so short, you have done all your mum asked of you today.'

'It was such a quiet funeral – hardly anyone was...'

Jemima swallowed back a lump of emotion as she said, 'Jo, you know that if your mum hadn't outlived her friends the place would have been packed out.'

'Jem's right.' Sara nodded. 'Iris knew the situation. She asked for a short funeral and a fun-style wake precisely because she knew there weren't many left to mourn her.'

'I suppose...' Jo's attention was diverted by a burst of laughter from the left.

Sara couldn't help but smile as she saw Michael wheeling Billy down the ramp from the crematorium to the car park. The old man had his arms in the air, and was screaming with pleasure, as if he was zooming along a roller coaster.

Jemima looked over at the ramp. 'Is that Billy then?'

'The one and only.' Sara took hold of Jo's hand, the rush of warmth it gave her taking her by surprise. 'That's the attitude Iris wanted today.'

'It is, isn't it.' Slipping off the wall, Jo stared down at his hand as it interlocked with Sara's, and he found a smile nudging his frown away. 'Mum always had a lot of fun in her. When I was little, she was the one who wanted to go to Alton Towers and the like. I'd be keeping her company – although if any of her friends asked, she'd claim she was only going 'cos I was desperate to go on the rides.'

'I think I'd have liked your mum.' Jemima watched as Billy was helped into the home's people carrier. 'Do you think we should go? Ed and Maddie'll be almost back at The Potting Shed by now.'

'Jem's right.' Sara took her keys from her pocket. 'We ought to get there before the guests.'

'We should.' Suddenly stopping, Jo dropped Sara's hand. 'Actually, you two get into the car. I'll only be a minute.'

The main room of the crematorium was empty but for Iris's coffin, sitting, as per her instruction, untouched by the crematorium staff until every single guest had left the car park.

I'm not having anyone I know watching me smoking up the sky! How dismal would that be?

'Hi, Mum.' Placing both of his palms on the walnut casket, Jo closed his eyes. 'Before you go, I… I wanted to say thank you.'

'Well, that is something I didn't think I'd see today.' Maddie couldn't stop chuckling as she watched Jemima and Billy doing a part-jive part-rumba, with her niece steering the old man's wheelchair in time to 'Rock Around the Clock'.

Ed held out his hands to Maddie. 'Never been to a funeral with dancing, but Iris left instructions so…'

'Who are we to argue?' Maddie allowed Ed to lead her onto the patch of space they'd cleared in the middle of the café. 'I feel it's important you should know, I can't dance.'

'That makes two of us!' Ed drew her in close. 'We'll need lessons before our first dance.'

Maddie drew back with an alarmed squeak. 'Oh hell, I hadn't thought of that.'

Jo looked across at his friends. 'You two okay?'

Immediately feeling guilty for enjoying herself, Maddie said, 'I stepped on Ed's foot. I'm no dancer.'

Jo pointed at Jemima and Billy. 'Well keep away from those two. That's a real toe hazard right there!'

Belle, a tray of cake slices in her hands, came to join them. 'I can't help thinking Iris would've been in her element!'

'She would.' Jo nodded at the happy faces around them. 'Thank you so much for sorting this, Maddie – and this cake, Belle – it tastes unbelievable.'

'Least I could do.' Belle gestured to the gathering of guests sitting around the edges of the café, all in bright colours as per Iris's instructions, all happily chatting between dances. Even Cynthia, sitting close to a solicitous Carol, appeared as if she'd relaxed into her surroundings. 'Any of you want some cake before I do the rounds?'

'I couldn't eat another thing.' Ed tapped his stomach.

Maddie's eyebrows rose. 'Are you telling me a food has been invented that actually fills those hollow legs?'

'Miracles do happen!' Ed laughed. 'Anyone want a drink?'

Jo smiled. 'I'm okay for now, but if you'll excuse me for a moment, I'd like a bit of fresh air before I read Mum's eulogy.'

'Sure, you carry on.' Ed gathered up some empty cups and carried them to the counter as Jo turned to Sara.

'Come with me?'

*

The early October air was unseasonably warm as Jo and Sara sat on the steps that led into the herb greenhouse.

Breaking the silence, Jo turned so that he could see Sara's face. 'I have a confession.'

'You do?'

Taking a deep breath, Jo blurted out, 'I lied. I didn't not ask about Exeter and Tristan because you didn't mention it or because of Mum. I didn't ask because I was afraid.'

'Afraid?'

'Of Tristan being nice after all.' Jo paused, before explaining, 'You see, if you'd become friends with him, then he'd have been part of our lives and I was afraid of going backwards – of being judged by someone who I'd want to be nice to, to please you.'

The warmth she'd felt when she'd held Jo's hand returned as Sara said, 'You assumed that, because of the antiquated way he spoke about women, Tristan would be judgemental towards you.'

'Not such a leap.'

'Sadly not.' Sara sighed. 'I don't think he knew.'

'Makes no difference. If he'd been part of our lives, Tristan would've found out.' Jo raked a hand through his hair. 'I'm not ashamed of who I am, but it took me so long to find a group of people with whom I felt totally comfortable.'

'You were afraid of losing it?'

'Tristan would have changed the dynamic – not killed it – but changed it. I was selfish. You should have whichever friends you like.'

'Jo, we've discussed this – you were right; Tristan was...'

'He was. But he might not have been.' Jo grimaced. 'I have another confession.

'Go on.'

'I wasn't just being overprotective. I was angry with myself. I think that's why I was an idiot and stewed for so long.'

Sara's eyes narrowed. 'Angry with yourself, not me?'

'I wanted to be the one who took you on your first date, but I lacked the courage and well... we... As I don't...'

'Stop right there.' Sara laid a finger over Jo's lips. 'Let's go out for a curry tomorrow night. Yes?'

'Yes.'

'And the subject of Tristan Harvey is one hundred per cent done. Closed. No hauling over the coals, Jo. Tristan is gone and we've both learnt a lesson or two. Subject closed, deal?'

'Deal.'

Letting the gentle breeze wrap around them, Sara laid her head on Jo's shoulder. 'I wondered about doing that degree after all.'

Jo sat up straight. 'That's a brilliant idea.'

'You think so?'

Feeling his pulse quicken, not sure he wanted to ask the question, Jo asked anyway. 'Where did you fancy going?'

'Sara gave him a playful push, 'Open University! We have a business to run, and I have a part-time job as well.'

'You aren't leaving to study?'

'Leave you, just when I've got you trained to make the perfect guest breakfast – are you insane?'

A smile lit up Jo's eyes. 'If I'm back on breakfast duty, does that mean...?'

'I'd like you to come home – will you?'

'Like a shot!' Jo shuffled closer to Sara.

'I'm not going anywhere without you, Jo.' Sara kissed his cheek. 'You're my North Star, remember.'

49

Jem slipped her mobile phone onto the table before her. Her parents' sixth senses had clearly been working overtime, for in the last ten minutes she'd received a volley of text messages apologising for the lack of contact due to dodgy Wi-Fi over the past twenty-four hours, and saying that they'd be home soon and how much they missed her.

'You okay?' Jo pulled out a seat next to his young friend.

'Better now.' She tapped her phone. 'I needed to hear from Mum. And Dad obviously, but...'

'It's okay. I get it.' Jo waved the piece of paper in his hand. 'I could do with mine right now. Thank you for coming today. I know you didn't know Mum but I'm glad school let you out.'

'I wanted to be here.'

'Thanks, Jem.' Jo waved the eulogy. 'Goodness knows what Mum would make of this.'

'Sara said it was good.'

'Sara is biased.' Jo blew out a puff of air.

'Does that mean you two have stopped being silly now?'

'Yes, we've stopped being silly. It didn't feel silly at the time though. It felt like I'd had my right arm lopped off.' Jo held the piece of paper out before him. 'It's weird giving the eulogy at the wake and not the funeral anyway.'

'It's what your mum wanted.'

'It was.'

'Why don't you do it now? Once you've read the eulogy you can relax. Everyone needs a break from dancing, and Belle's cake is so good that we have all eaten too much, so the older folk might nod off any minute.'

'I was going to read it just before everyone went home.'

'Just do it, Jo...' Jemima titled her head toward Billy '...before my dance partner falls asleep and is robbed of the chance to heckle.'

'You're right.' Getting up before he could change his mind, Jo turned back to Jemima. 'You wouldn't, um, stay close maybe?'

Too touched to speak, Jemima nodded and stood with her friend.

Ed lowered the volume of the music as their final guest left the café, Ivan following them out, ready to let them through the locked garden centre gates.

'That really was an excellent eulogy, Jo.'

'After all my rehearsals, I hardly stuck to the words I prepared.'

'Doesn't matter.' Ed took a tray from the counter and filled it with used cake plates. 'You spoke from the heart. Iris would have been so proud.'

'I hope so.' Seeing his friends dotted around the café, each busily tidying up after his mum's care home friends and old neighbours, Jo smiled. 'Thanks for today, Ed.'

'No need to thank me. It's Maddie and you who run this empire – although...' Ed lowered his voice '...I'm joining the team.'

'What?'

'I'm going to give up the job in Bristol and work here.' Ed's face lit up as he shared his news. 'I would have talked it over with you normally, but you've had your hands full lately.'

'That's fantastic!' A few of the knots of tension in Jo's shoulders eased. 'We so badly need more staff, and you love this place almost as much as Maddie does. Not to mention, it'll be great to have my best mate handy.'

Only just resisting the temptation to tell him about their other news, Ed grinned. 'Thanks, Jo. Just one month at Bristol left. Going there was such a bad move. But the grass felt greener at the time.'

'But if you hadn't taken the gamble, you wouldn't be coming to work here, would you.'

'Suppose not.' Ed realised he hadn't thought of it that way. 'Me and Maddie, you and Sara, and now Ivan and Belle... I can't help thinking that both Maddie's dad and your mum would heartily approve of the family feeling here.'

'I know Mum would.' Jo gestured towards the door. 'I want to thank Michael and Carol before they go. I'll see you in a minute.'

Hoping he hadn't left it too late, Jo jogged out to the car park just in time to see Carol climbing into the people carrier next to Cynthia as Michael slammed the back doors shut, keeping Billy's wheelchair firmly in place.

'Michael!' Jo called out in case the care worker hadn't heard him approach. 'I wanted to thank you once more before you went.'

'No worries, I was about to head back to find you.' Michael zipped up his coat as the evening sunshine dipped behind a cloud. 'I'll miss your mum.'

'Thanks.' Jo, suddenly solemn, said, 'I wondered, could you

tell your brother, the answer is yes. I'll be in touch with him about the coffee. I would have contacted him before but…'

'I told him about your mum, don't worry. I'll let him know to expect a call.' Michael gave Jo a friendly pat on the back. 'It was a smashing do. Iris would have loved it.'

'Thanks. I hope so.'

'Except for one thing.'

'Really?' Jo's face fell. 'Did I forget something she asked for?'

'Not at all. But that's what I was about to come and find you for. She wanted you to have these.'

Opening the passenger side of the vehicle, Michael passed Jo a box. 'Careful, it's heavy.'

'What's inside?'

'Iris's last wake wish. You'll see.'

Jo frowned. 'But I followed all of the instructions she left.'

'And so did I.' Michael waved as he climbed into the van. 'Take care, Jo.'

Jemima's yawn was so wide it made Maddie laugh. 'You need fresh air young lady.'

'I swear school isn't as tiring as clearing up a café!'

'I bet it isn't.' Maddie nodded towards the door. 'We've almost finished. How about you take yourself a smoothie, go and fetch Florrie and Sheba from the flat, and meet us in the bluebell garden in five minutes?'

As Jemima grabbed her aunt's flat keys and a spinach and kiwi concoction from the fridge, Belle came to Maddie's side. 'I'll need to come in a bit earlier than usual tomorrow to empty the dishwasher, but otherwise we've done all we can do today.'

'Awesome.' Sara beamed. 'A fantastic afternoon. Iris would have loved your recipe cards.'

'Hope so, sweetheart.' Belle smiled back just as Jo came in. 'What on earth have you got there?'

'Michael had it. Apparently, this contains Mum's last request for the day.'

'What is it?' Sara came to Jo's side as he rested the heavy cardboard box on the nearest table.

'I've no idea. But knowing Mum, it could be anything!'

'Here.' Ivan passed Jo some scissors from the utensils pot. 'Only one way to find out.'

Snipping his way through some tightly sealed sticky tape, Jo opened the lid, half afraid of what his mother might have done. Thirty seconds later he was shaking his head in disbelief as he discovered two giant magnums of champagne. 'Now this really is pre-dementia Mum!'

Sara's clap of approval stopped abruptly as she spotted an envelope in the packaging. 'Jo, there's a letter.'

His hands shook as he split the envelope open. 'Oh…'

'Jo?' Sara stepped a little closer.

'I'm okay. Listen…

'*Hello son, I've no idea how dusty these bottles or this note will be by the time you get them – very, I hope! I'm giving this box to Michael now, while I'm still on the planet fifty per cent of the time.*

'*Now, if you've been a good lad – which I'm sure you have, you'll have done this all very fast – with no hanging around being maudlin. A nice quick service and a wake with a bit of a dance.*

'*If Michael has done as he was told, everyone should have gone now except for you and your family…*'

Jo broke off, his gaze falling to Sara as he whispered, 'I couldn't give her a family. I...'

'But Jo.' Sara moved closer. 'Look around you.'

Taking in his friends' encouraging expressions, Jo gulped, taking a second to gather himself before returning to his mother's messy handwriting.

'...*your family, so now is the perfect time to find some glasses, open these monsters and raise a glass to your old mum. I've had a good life and you've looked after me so well – but it's your turn to live now.*

'*Really live, son!*

'*Love always, Mum x*'

As Jo laid down the letter, Sara took hold of his hand. 'I think we should do exactly what Iris wanted.'

'Now?'

'Now.' Sara turned to Ed. 'Could you fetch some glasses?'

'Certainly.'

'Let's take everything into the garden. Jem's out there already with the dogs.' Maddie was already making her way to the glasses cupboard with Ed, when Sara called across the room.

'Belle, don't switch on the dishwasher – there's going to be lots more to go in at any moment!'

'To Iris!'

Raising their glasses, the friends stood together in the bluebell garden, drinking a toast to Jo's mum.

'I know it's an odd thing to say...' Jemima sat next to Jo on the nearest picnic table '...but today's been fun.'

'It has, hasn't it.' Jo sipped his champagne. 'And so very Mum.'

'I'll never forget seeing you wheelchair dancing with Billy, Jem!' Maddie poured a top-up of champagne into Jo's glass. 'I wonder what your mum and dad will say when you tell them?'

'Dad will think it was great; Mum will ask if my toes got run over.' Jemima laughed. 'But it was fun! He's so silly.'

'Billy is the perfect example of how to grow old disgracefully, but with style.' Jo looked over at Sara. 'I think I'd like to visit him once in a while.'

'Good idea.' Ed pointed to the centre of the garden. 'Talking of ideas, Maddie and I had one about this place, didn't we, love.'

'We did. We thought it would be nice to add something more to this garden – something I can use when teaching the Little Acorns. A pond, maybe with a fountain. Some fish perhaps?'

'That sounds gorgeous.' Belle smiled and Ivan came to her side.

'We want to grow irises around it, in memory of your mum.' Maddie turned to Jo. 'What do you think?'

'I think Mum would have liked that. She loved being outdoors. Thank you, it's a lovely idea – and great for The Potting Shed too. I can just imagine Noel and the gang getting soaking wet helping to fill it!'

'So can I!' Belle laughed. 'Well, I'm afraid I need to get home. The boys have been very patient lately, but I never like to push my luck. It's been a good day.'

'It has.' Jo shook Ivan's hand. 'Thank to you too, Ivan. I'm assuming you're running Belle home?'

'I might just offer my services.'

Jo met his friend's eyes. 'Good to see you happy.'

Ivan dipped his head in acknowledgement, not quite sure what to say.

'Actually…' Ed caught Maddie's eye, as she gave him a silent nod of the head '…before you go, we have an announcement. We weren't going to say yet, but if you don't mind Jo – it isn't about your mum, but we do have champagne, so…'

'Oh wow!' Sara leapt to her feet. 'Really?'

Maddie burst out laughing. 'We haven't said it yet!'

'I'm right though, aren't I?'

'Maybe!'

As Florrie nudged at Maddie's legs, Ed refilled everyone's glasses. 'As Sara, and probably the rest of you, have already guessed, I would like to officially announce that the amazing, kind, beautiful and madly overworked Maddie Willand and I are engaged!'

'About time too!' A familiar voice called out across the bluebell garden.

'Sabi!' Maddie let go of Ed's hand and rushed towards her sister. 'You're back!'

'Mum!' Jemima joined her aunt in throwing her arms around the unexpected arrival. 'I've missed you so much. And Dad. Where's Dad?'

'I'm here, sweetheart.' Appearing from around the polytunnel, Henry raised his bag-filled hands. 'Looks like we arrived with the duty-free just in time!'

Maddie beamed. 'I'm so pleased to see you both, but when we spoke I got the impression you'd be gone a little while longer yet?'

'We got off the ship in Italy and flew home, rather than heading on to Spain. I felt bad for abandoning you for so long, and we were missing this one.' Sabi kissed the top of her daughter's head.

'Missed you too, Mum.'

Sabi stood back from her sister and hugged Jemima firmly to her side. Maddie was surprised to feel tears prick at her eyes as her sister and niece held on to each other.

'Did you have a good time?'

'Amazing, but we'll tell you about that later.'

Stepping forward, Jo slapped Ed heartily on the back in congratulations as he went to help Henry with his bags. 'Would that be wine and more champagne?'

'It would.' Henry's eyes widened as he saw the bottle on a nearby picnic table. 'Wow; good stuff. Compared to that, what we've brought is mere plonk! Where on earth did you get…?'

'My mum. It was her parting gift.'

'What a wonderful gesture. We were so sorry to hear about Iris, Jo.' Henry glanced anxiously at his wife. 'We haven't just crashed into a wake, have we?'

As Ivan, Belle and Sara came to Jo's side, he smiled. 'We were just raising a glass to Mum now that her wake is over. And, you know what, I think she would have totally loved that we were celebrating an engagement too.'

'Absolutely! Something to look forward to, as well as a good life to look back on.' Sara slipped her hand into Jo's. 'Very sensible and forward-thinking was Iris.'

Jo nodded towards the opened champagne bottles. 'So, why don't we make this an impromptu engagement party. Mum would approve of that. Alright, Maddie? Ed?'

'If you're sure, mate.' Ed nodded.

'One hundred per cent sure.' Jo beamed at Sara. 'Ivan, Belle, would you mind helping us get some cake from the kitchen while we grab some more glasses?'

As their friends dashed towards the kitchen, Sabi turned to

her sister, a wide smile across her suntanned face. 'So, when's the wedding, where's it to be, and can I do the décor?'

Maddie burst out laughing as she slipped her arm around Ed's waist. 'No idea, not a clue, and yes of course you can!'

Letting go of her mum, Jemima knelt to fuss Florrie. 'Well, we don't care when the wedding is, do we, girl, just as long as both you and I can be bridesmaids!'

About the Author

JENNY KANE is the bestselling author of many romantic fiction series. These include the Mill Grange series, Abi's Cornwall series, and the Another Cup series. She has had bestsellers in the Amazon Romance, Contemporary Fiction and Women's Fiction charts and multiple other bestsellers. If you enjoy Jenny's writing, then why not follow her author page for updates on all of her new releases!

Acknowledgements

To all the lovely folk who work at The Old Well in Willand, Devon – especially the café girls! These wonderful people were as much an inspiration behind the writing of The Potting Shed stories, as the garden centre itself.

Special thanks must go to the team at Aria (Head of Zeus), especially Martina, for being so enthusiastic about The Potting Shed series.

Finally, to my agent Kiran, of Keane Kataria: thank you for your constant help, valued input, and kind guidance.